'Reload, damn ... ... ... ... ... ... ... ...re still twenty fee... ... ... ... ... ... ... lf staring right d... ... ... ... ... ... ...n, which had bee... ... ... ... ... ... ...e man grasp the twine that would set it off and started to duck just as the *Hebe* slewed round to slam into the French ship. The crack of wood and breaking ropes from aloft, as the yards and rigging became tangled, was audible even over the din of battle. The long cannon, now just a few feet away, went off with a deafening roar, a streak of orange fire extending like a searing finger to engulf him. The sound was deafening and the fire struck his coat, burning his cheek and filling his nose with the acrid smell of spent powder and scorched cloth.

Tom Connery lives in the centuries-old port of Deal in Kent with his wife, also a novelist, and two children. Born in 1944 he has had more jobs than birthdays but is now a full-time writer.

*By the same author*
Honour Redeemed

# A SHRED
# OF HONOUR

---

## Tom Connery

ORION

An Orion Paperback
First published in Great Britain by Orion in 1996
This paperback edition published in 1997 by
Orion Books Ltd,
Orion House, 5 Upper St Martin's Lane,
London WC2H 9EA

A CIP catalogue record for this book is
available from the British Library

ISBN 0 75280 849 4

Typeset by RefineCatch Limited, Bungay, Suffolk
Printed and bound in Great Britain by Clays Ltd, St Ives plc

*To the Valour Boys*

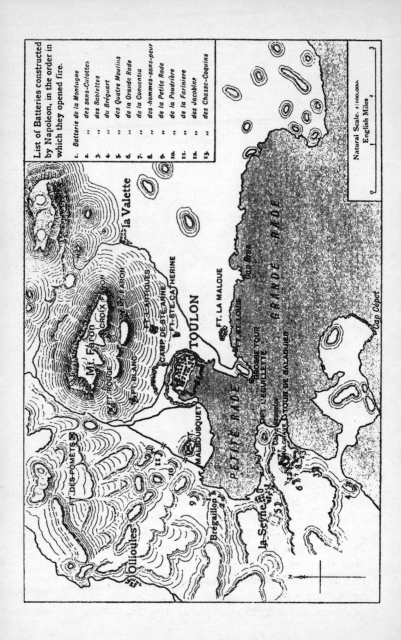

List of Batteries constructed by Napoleon, in the order in which they opened fire.

1. Batterie de la Montagne
2.   ,,   des sans-Culottes
3.   ,,   des Sablettes
4.   ,,   du Bréguart
5.   ,,   des Quatre Moulins
6.   ,,   de la Grande Rade
7.   ,,   de la Convention
8.   ,,   des -hommes-sans-peur
9.   ,,   de la Petite Rade
10.  ,,   de la Poudrière
11.  ,,   de la Farinière
12.  ,,   des Jacobins
13.  ,,   des Chasse-Coquins

Natural Scale. 1:100,000.

English Miles

# Chapter one

It was bad luck for Lieutenant George Tenby Markham that the first shot fired in the engagement took Captain Frobisher in the throat. Firing at that range, on a Mediterranean swell, the Frenchman had been very lucky. The heavy calibre musket ball should have dropped into the sea between the ships. Instead it whipped across the deck of His Britannic Majesty's 24-gun frigate *Hebe*. The marine officer's head, nearly severed from the shoulders, dropped to one side. A great gush of bright red froth erupted from the devastated artery, covering everyone who stood close to him in a layer of foaming blood.

'Get that off my quarterdeck,' shouted Captain de Lisle, as though the body were no more than offal. 'Mr Markham, you will replace Mr Frobisher in command of the marine detachment. I intend to lay the ship alongside the enemy, fire off a broadside, and board in the smoke.'

'Aye, aye, sir,' Markham replied, raising his hat in the crisp fashion that was an absolute requirement of his present position. The slight breeze was welcome, acting as it did to cool the sweat that had soaked his light brown hair. The trickle of sweat that ran down the hollow of his spine seemed continuous; the desire to throw off his heavy red uniform coat overwhelming.

Inwardly he was troubled by all manner of conflicting emotions. An army officer, his grasp of marine tactics was near to zero, something Frobisher had failed to redress. And *Hebe*'s complement was a mixture that approximated to oil and water; half no-hopers from his regiment, the remainder marines who didn't know or like him. Could he command them at all? And even if they obeyed, what was he supposed to tell them?

A sudden piercing scream, a dark shape on the edge of his vision, made him duck involuntarily. The body of the falling seaman stretched the nettings above his head, the victim nearly impaling himself on one of his soldiers' bayonets. But the fellow bounced up again, his body twisting in desperation as the force of his own momentum threw him over the side into the sea.

'A little return fire with musketry might be of advantage, Markham,' snapped de Lisle. 'Otherwise, I'll have no topmen.'

Looking aft to the knot of men by the wheel did little to reassure him. The captain's round face, the glowering stare full of distaste and the sneer on his lips, was matched by every officer on the ship. It had been like that since he'd come aboard. And nothing on the long voyage south had diminished it. To their rigid naval minds it was bad enough being obliged to share the wardroom with a soldier. But to have as an enforced dining companion a man who was probably a Papist, certainly a rake, and bore the stigma of cowardice, was anathema.

Markham dragged his thoughts away from such contemplations and tried to concentrate on the task ahead. Frobisher had placed a third of his men in the tops, occupying the platforms that surrounded the caps. That vantage point, a third of the way up the masts, let them play their muskets on the enemy deck. He called up, ordering them to find a target and fire at will.

'Pay particular attention to the gun crews,' he shouted. That produced a snort of derision from the officer commanding the quarterdeck battery, the Third Lieutenant, Fellows.

'It's a good thing we're not under an admiral's eye, Markham,' he called, in a loud voice. 'Given such a lamentable performance, the whole ship's company might expire from embarrassment.'

He longed to ask why, prepared to display his ignorance if it would help. Fellows, inadvertently, solved the problem by barking at his own fidgeting gunners, telling them to keep their heads down. In that position they offered no target to the enemy sharpshooters, now peppering the *Hebe*'s deck planking, seeking to hit the officers arrayed in front of the ship's wheel. No-one moved to avoid them, it being a canon of a gentleman's existence that no officer, of whatever service, ever flinched under fire.

Fellows' strictures had little effect, being ignored the minute he looked away. The crews below, on the maindeck, were also peering through the ports. In a high state of exhilaration, they were eager to gaze upon the enemy, men they'd do their very best to kill as soon as they received the order to open fire.

Conscious of the sensations in his stomach, part apprehension, part excitement, Markham jerked slightly as the men aloft fired off their first volley, aimed exclusively at the enemy commanders, wondering if they might be indulging in calculated disobedience. But they were, very likely, just obeying some standard instructions about which he knew nothing.

He turned to the rest of his men; perspiring, crammed into the forward section of the quarterdeck between the companionway and the waist, exposed to the full glare of the sun. What a mixed bag they were; Lobsters and Bullocks, the only common factor amongst them the red of their sweat-streaked coats. The Bullocks were the dregs of his regiment; hard bargains, thieves and defaulters, dispatched by a grateful Colonel to make up the numbers demanded by a short-handed fleet. They'd come aboard under the command of a strange officer, which was just another element to add to their seething resentment at the service they were being forced to perform.

The Lobsters presented another problem. In different uniforms, carrying unfamiliar weapons somewhat shorter

3

than the regulation army issue, they'd let him know that any order he issued would be obeyed only if their own commander approved it. In this they'd been aided by Frobisher, who'd taken every available opportunity to insult him, and belittle the soldiers. None of the marines had even exchanged a smile with the men foisted on them. They kept themselves separate, aloof, and were thus even more a mystery. He had the right to command them, without the certainty that they would obey.

'Two paces forward, march. Present!'

'Damnit, Markham,' de Lisle yelled, 'what are you about? You're more of a threat to your own than the enemy.'

'It is my intention to aim at the French gunports, sir,' he replied, pointing with his sword.

'An action which will kill any one of the quarterdeck gunners who raises his head. Clearly you know as much about shipboard tactics as you do about the duties of an officer. Perhaps I should spare a midshipman to instruct you.'

The sudden boom of the enemy cannon, firing a rolling broadside, took everyone's attention. The *Hebe* shuddered as half the cannonade smashed into her hull. At that range, most of the balls hit the side of the ship, but one clipped the very edge of the bulwark right before his eyes. A great shard of wood, a splinter several feet long and shaped like an enormous spearhead, sliced across the deck. One soldier, a yellow-skinned, toothless sodomite called Perkins, took it right in the lower belly. His mouth opened, a black empty hole that was too shocked to emit a scream. His eyes stared in horror at the fractured wood that protruded from his guts. Half of those, a long visceral trail of tangled intestine, had come out at his back, entrails dragged through the flesh by the rough edges of the splintered timber.

He staggered slightly, his frightened eyes looking to his mates to help him stay upright. It wasn't discipline that

4

kept them in line, but indifference. Head bent, he saw the blood running down his legs to form a pool at his feet. Then, as the first piece of his innards slid into the gore, he began to scream. Two seaman grabbed him by the elbows and dragged him towards the companionway with such disregard that they left a long trail of his guts behind. By that time the screaming had ceased, the pain too much to bear.

The blistering late August heat formed a haze over the sea that, mixed with the billowing black smoke of the broadside, turned the approaching enemy frigate into a chimera. With little wind to disperse it, the smoke hung like a cloud. The two warships were closing at a snail's pace, and in Captain de Lisle the navy had an officer who believed shot expended at anything other than point-blank range was a waste. The whole scene had a dreamlike quality. But there was nothing surreal about the continuing crack of the passing musket balls.

'Get your men up onto the bulwarks, sir,' cried de Lisle, 'where they can see the enemy. And you, Lieutenant Markham, if you have a shred of honour, will join them.'

It was a foolish command that would offer his men as sitting ducks to anyone capable of responding, either with cannon, musket, or pistol. A half-decent broadside would decimate them. It was also a direct order publicly delivered by an officer with the ability to break him, so the temptation to comply was strong. No man likes to be perceived as a coward, especially when the suspicion existed, deep in his own mind, that the accusation might have some foundation. The men hated him, a fact which they demonstrated daily. But that didn't absolve him of responsibility. He was damned if he was going to have them butchered just to satisfy the captain's bilious temperament.

'My duty to my command does not permit me to comply, sir.'

'What!' de Lisle yelled. He opened his mouth to

5

continue, but the words were drowned out by the crashing roar of another French salvo. Two of the *Hebe*'s gun captains, no doubt inexperienced men shaken to the core by the noise, touched off their own cannon. The main-deck eighteen-pounders bellowed black smoke and shot inboard, rocked back on their carriages, their muzzles jumping skywards as they were brought up by the straining breechings. The quarterdeck gunners, fearing they'd missed the command, followed suit. And then the rest of *Hebe*'s larboard maindeck battery went off in a ragged discharge.

Captain Richard de Lisle, a man habitually reserved in his demeanour, had gone puce with passion. As the sound of the guns died away he could be heard screaming for names to be taken, so that the culprits could be flogged for insubordination. Only Markham, it seemed, had any interest in the result of their accidental efforts. Peering through the smoke he observed the great black balls smashing into the side of the enemy frigate. Even at that crawling pace it shuddered and slowed, as if slapped by some great hand. Screams came across the water to match those on *Hebe*'s deck, as Markham gave his men their orders.

'Aim careful now, my boyos,' he called, adding a knowing grin to the overstated Irish accent. 'Don't hit one of them gunners, or sure, the captain will be after stoppin' our grog.'

Intended as a joke, it was met with a stony silence. They presented on command, though in an undisciplined way that shamed him, followed by a ragged volley which owed as much to poorly-loaded weaponry as it did to their ineptitude. He felt the sense of excitement, which had come upon him at the moment of going into action, evaporate, to be replaced by one of extreme frustration. He tried to keep his face rigid, so that these feelings would remain hidden. But suppressing his anger was one emotion he'd never mastered. Every man in his party,

6

looking at those cold grey eyes, tight lips and clenched square jaw, knew that he was livid.

He wasn't alone. The volley attracted de Lisle's attention to the fact that Markham had blatantly disobeyed him. But with the ships closing, supervising the final preparations for the forthcoming battle, he could do little.

Both frigates were moving out of their own smoke, bowsprits angled inwards. In such close proximity Markham could see, for the first time, the faces of the enemy. The officers stood as rigidly formal in bearing as their British counterparts, their glittering uniforms marking them out as the men in command. This surprised him. In the four years since 1789 the Revolution had, supposedly, changed France out of all recognition. In the previous twelve months it had swept away the King and the aristocracy in the maelstrom of the Terror. He'd expected this to show, anticipated less of a distinction between officers and men. Whatever happened to *Liberté, Egalité* and *Fraternité*?

Ordered to step two paces back, his men were reloading their muskets, some fumbling with rammers and wads as their own sweat mixed with oil and grease. Silence had descended on both decks, broken only by the whispered sound of prayer. Markham might know nothing about the ways of the navy, but he'd been in battle before. Men were going to die, and in significant numbers. The French captain had guessed de Lisle's aim and was prepared to match it. He wanted a prize to take back to Marseilles just as much as the Englishman wanted a present for his commander, Lord Hood. So they crept towards each other, under topsails, hardly making anything in the way of speed, each ear cocked for the first hint of the command to open fire.

'Now, lads!'

De Lisle had stepped away from the wheel, far enough forward to see down into the waist, so that his voice would carry to the whole ship's company. The dark brown eyes in his pale, round face were steady and compelling. Never had he looked more like his nickname, 'Spotted Dick'. He was a short, compact man, with bland features that rarely showed emotion. The glare of the bright sun, which reddened the features of every other man aboard, gave him a bloodless appearance. That was heightened by the ghost of a grin which looked fixed, as though underneath that rigid exterior lay a degree of terror. But Markham guessed that the only thing the captain feared was disgrace. He'd die willingly, if only he could be assured of doing so with nobility.

'They're only Johnny Crapaud, who we've had sport with for fifty years. They ain't got the stomach for real fighting. So just you ply your guns at the right rate and we'll see them to perdition.' He paused, his eyes raking the deck. 'Any man runs, leaves his post, will answer to me, d'ye hear?'

Then he filled his lungs with air and, in a voice that could be heard a mile away, bellowed, 'Fire!'

The enemy commander must have issued his command simultaneously, since the gap was too small to register. Suddenly the air was full of flying death, as both sets of guns opened up. It was no odd splinter now. Great chunks of the ship's side were blown asunder and the wood sent in all directions. One of the ship's cannon took a direct hit on the muzzle, the clang of contact resounding like a hellish bell. The gun was blown inboard so hard its breechings parted, the flying, snapping ropes adding yet more terror to the dangers the crew faced. The cannon, including its carriage, slewed sideways, taking both the legs off the gun captain, who'd stood ready to haul on the flintlock. The barrel, flying apart, added metal shards to those of wood, and gutted the men closest with deadly efficiency. Through the gap that had once been the side of the ship, Markham could see the Frenchmen who'd done such damage, an enemy gun crew already straining furiously to reload.

'Fire through the gap,' he yelled, pointing his sword at the open gunport, less than twenty feet away. His men obeyed, but to little effect. Most shots went wide, with only one hitting home, striking an officer well to the rear of the intended targets.

'Reload, damn you,' he ordered. The ships were still twenty feet apart. Markham found himself staring right down the muzzle of a French cannon, which had been run out, ready to fire. He saw the man grasp the twine that would set it off and started to duck just as the *Hebe* slewed round to slam into the French ship. The crack of wood and breaking ropes from aloft, as the yards and rigging became tangled, was audible even over the din of battle. The long cannon, now just a few feet away, went off with a deafening roar, a streak of orange fire extending like a searing finger to engulf him. The sound was deafening and the fire struck his coat, burning his cheek and filling his nose with the acrid smell of spent powder and scorched cloth. Luckily the blast threw him sideways, onto his knees, so the ball, which would have cut him in two, sped past his left shoulder. It struck the mainmast and ricocheted along the deck of the ship, destroying everything, flesh, bone, and wood, that stood in its way.

'Boarders,' cried de Lisle, rushing down to where Markham knelt, the spittle shooting from his mouth a testimony to the violence of his language. All control had gone from a man who strove to be the epitome of calmness under fire. 'You damned Irish coward! What in the devil's name are you waiting for? Do your duty, sir!'

Fighting to control his outrage, Markham pulled himself to his feet. Standing nearly a foot taller than de Lisle he raised his sword aloft, and was about to order his men forward when the captain screamed again, pushing himself onto his tiptoes in an attempt to compensate for this junior officer's superior height.

'I'll not have any peasant general's bastard sully my deck again!'

9

Markham lost control. He swung back towards the captain, his weapon descending like a cleaver to decapitate the man. De Lisle's eyes nearly popped out of his head as the sword stopped an inch from his neck, the bearer screaming at him. 'Never use those words to me again. If you ever do and I'm sober, I'll call you out. In drink, I'll very likely kill you on the spot.'

Maybe it was shock that restored de Lisle's composure. Or perhaps he realised just how much he was demeaning himself. Hating to be overlooked, he took a pace backwards. With some difficulty he brought his temper under restraint, his face rigid, struggling to sound normal above the crash of gunfire. There was a quality of madness to this, the normality of the captain's voice, while all around him men wrestled with guns, received wounds, or dived to the deck to avoid shot.

'I have no time for your sensitivities, sir. We are in the midst of a battle, which will be lost by your inaction.'

Markham suddenly felt foolish and, with his back to the enemy, very exposed. But he would not break the gaze that held de Lisle's eyes, determined to stare him down. Vaguely, he registered the arrival of the midshipman, who was now tugging at the captain's sleeve, an action which forced 'Spotted Dick' to acknowledge his presence.

Released from contesting the stare, Markham turned and roared his commands, calling for his men to follow him. He ran for the jagged gap in the bulwarks, his heart thumping with exhilaration. The flap of the enemy gunport was open, and a lot closer than the side. Only a fool would have tried it. But his Celtic blood had been fired by De Lisle's insults, leaving Markham very close to madness. It dropped sickeningly as he landed, the ropes that supported it stretching with the increase in weight. He stood for a moment, heart in his mouth, his arms flailing as he fought to keep his balance. If he fell between the two battling ships he'd certainly die.

Another British broadside came to his rescue. As it

slammed into the Frenchman, it caused the frigate to heel just enough to lift his foothold level. With a roar he leapt for the deck, landing in amongst the terrified gunners. One swung a rammer, eight feet long, at his head. Danger heightened his already excited state, and he ducked, throwing up his sword. Sharpened for the engagement, it cut deep into the wood. The force of the blow ran up his arm with an instant jarring pain and the rammer carried on, taking his weapon with it. Knocked backwards he kicked out, and with that clarity of sight that only comes in a fight, he placed his foot right in the Frenchman's groin. The man doubled over, his long nose bending right into the punch Markham aimed at his face.

Leaping to his feet, Markham screamed a foul Irish oath, stepped over his victim and pulled a pistol from his belt. He fired wildly at the nearest face, clubbed at another with the empty gun, then leapt for the sword embedded in the rammer. It looked like lunacy, but he was very far from out of control. Every nerve end in his body was alive to both danger and opportunity. An axe scythed towards his unprotected head as he bent down, only a violent and painful dive against the bulwark saving him. The force of the blow caused his assailant to over-reach, so he fell over the feet of an enemy who was already halfway back to being upright. Markham was grinning as he grabbed his long hair, but it was the look of an executioner not a friend. He pulled him back, then drove his knee into the top of the man's spine.

The neck went with a resounding crack and with a triumphant scream, sword in hand, Markham leapt to his feet, chest heaving, eyes searching for his next victim. The sound died in his throat. The look he cast around produced first bewilderment, then anger, and finally a slight sense of panic. He spun round to look back towards the *Hebe*'s deck. The line of red coats, standing in exactly the same place as he'd left them, was mockery of the highest order. Not one of his men, Bullock or Lobster, had followed him onto the enemy deck. Worse, he could see de Lisle issuing frantic instructions to cut his ship free. Men were no longer serving the guns; they were running up the shrouds to disentangle the rigging, while others struggled to set sail.

'Monsieur?'

Markham span round again, his mouth suddenly dry, to find himself facing a row of angry faces; men holding pikes and axes, and a lieutenant with his hand outstretched. It was clear what he wanted. This mad British officer was being invited to surrender and hand over his sword.

There was an air of unreality about the whole scene, almost like one of those patriotic pieces they performed at Sadler's Wells, in which Britannia's enemies were humiliated. The costumes were right, and so were the expressions on the faces. Only this time, instead of a Frenchman surrendering, it was him. They'd take him to Marseilles, there to parade him before the populace. Given what he'd done, and their bloodthirsty reputation, they might even guillotine him.

Taking a breath so deep it seared his throat, Markham bowed, fighting to control his trembling, sweat-soaked limbs. As he stood upright, sword held out, he threw it at the Frenchman's head. He was over the side, standing on that same gunport flap, before the first pike could reach him. Now the stretching ropes came to his assistance. As the flap dropped, it took him just out of reach of those intent on spearing him. His feet began to slip and, frantic with fear, cursing every saint he knew, he leapt into the air. If the French hadn't shot away the side of the ship he'd have been doomed. As it was he landed badly, and fell at the feet of his own men. Looking up into the row of glistening, red faces, he saw nothing in their eyes but contempt.

# Chapter two

'Spotted Dick' was berating him again, first for his failure to board, then for his single-handed attempt to capture the Frenchman. Safe behind his desk, voice under control, his manner seemed slightly bored, as if he were recounting a particularly tedious anecdote to a rather dim child. Only his eyes hinted at the depth of his emotions, flicking occasionally as he fought the desire to be more forthright. While careful to avoid any reference to the nature of his antecedents, de Lisle had managed to include numerous facets of Markham's background that he found objectionable, not least his hot temper. A month before he had fought a duel in Finsbury Park, his opponent a French emigré, le Comte des Ardres, who'd caught Markham in bed with his wife. This seemed to provide de Lisle with ample evidence of his unsuitability both as human being and an officer. He professed himself amazed that even a regiment as uncultured as the 65th Foot should allow a man with such a background to purchase a commission. All this came together in a general condemnation of Markham and the military arm of which he was a member.

'First you won't damn well go, and then when the orders are to stay put you're off on your own. If this is the way the Army behaves, Lieutenant, thank God we've got a Navy.'

Conveniently, he forgot that Markham would not have heard the panicky orders to make sail, issued just as he leapt through the gap in the bulwarks. The captain himself had only found out about the approaching French three-decker because he'd been passed a written message by one of his midshipmen. Faced with a 74-gun warship that could blow *Hebe* out of the water, they'd been forced to run. Did that change in circumstances exonerate Markham's men, who'd so signally failed to support him? Or had they stayed put for another reason? To the captain's way of looking at things, it didn't provide an excuse for this officer.

'Is it the Irish in you, that damned contrary Celtic streak, that makes you do the very opposite of what you're told? Or is it, Lieutenant, plain stupidity?'

Markham wasn't really listening. His eyes never even flickered towards 'Spotted Dick's' pallid face. Mentally he was recalling exactly the same actions, trying to assess them objectively. He had tried hard, these last twelve years, to live down the stigma attached to his name. The accusation that he'd deserted his post while in command of his regiment, going off to settle a private matter. The memory of that day was burned into his consciousness, as well as the disdain with which his peers had subsequently treated him.

The *Hebe*'s officers felt the same. Judging by the way they'd responded to him throughout the voyage, his very name seemed to stink in their nostrils. All Englishmen, and subscribers to the Thirty-Nine Articles of the Protestant faith, they sneered at his Irish background, mimicked his accent, rehashing all the old Paddy jokes they could, which saw his race as either devious or stupid. They were convinced that his status, as the illegitimate son of a rich, retired general, had not only influenced his court martial; it had been used to disguise his Catholicism, thus allowing him to sidestep the statute that ensured no Papist was ever permitted to hold the King's commission.

There was a certain delightful irony in the way that none of his sire's wealth had found its way into the hands of the natural son. He'd come aboard at Chatham with the bailiffs on his heels, most of his possessions still ashore, unable to retrieve them while the fleet lay at anchor lest they clap him in Newgate for debt. George Markham wasn't prepared to discuss his past or present life. So they'd never know that his only asset, after four years spent fighting for the Czarina Catherine, was the commission bought and paid for by his father, one that he'd declined to exercise since the end of the American war.

'Your soldiers are a disgrace to their red coats,' de Lisle continued, this time with a force in the words that made his chest swell. 'Frobisher, God rest him, was right about that.'

'They didn't volunteer for sea service, sir. They were given this posting without the option to decline.'

'Volunteer!' De Lisle actually spluttered, his face betraying indignation despite his best efforts to contain it.

Markham derived some pleasure from his ability to rile 'Spotted Dick', cracking his studied demeanour. Something he'd never seen anyone else achieve, it made him feel less inadequate. Then he recalled the probable reason. It wasn't wit or sophistry that upset de Lisle, just his mere presence.

'Volunteers! You have the gall to name them that? They're the scrapings of the gaol, man, and you know it. There probably isn't one of them that doesn't deserve to be hanged.'

It was true, though he was loath to admit it. The way the British Army recruited didn't bring in anything but gaolbirds and vagabonds and he'd been saddled with the very worst apples in a rotten barrel. They'd stood fast when they should have advanced, leaving him in the lurch. Even as he opened his mouth to defend them, he was cursing himself for a fool.

'They are no better, sir, and no worse, than Captain Frobisher's marines.'

De Lisle's lips seemed to disappear as again he struggled

in vain to contain his anger, his efforts betrayed by the rush of blood to his cheeks. 'Rubbish! Properly led, the Lobsters are the finest fighting men in the world. I repeat, properly led. Someone who behaves as if he's participating in a costume drama, does not fit anyone's notion of a proper leader.'

That made Markham go red in turn. Partly because, deep down, 'Spotted Dick' had touched a nerve. He harboured a suspicion that the accusation might be true: there had been a theatrical quality to his 'death defying leap'. But he was still angry with his superior, even if he knew that to continue this dispute was to invite more insults like the one the captain had just delivered.

'I saw no evidence of that today, sir. They were no more keen to follow me aboard that Frenchman than my infantrymen.'

'What you saw today, sir, were men wisely disinclined to engage on behalf of anybody behaving like a fool.'

'I believe, sir, if you are dissatisfied with my conduct, I have the right to demand a court.'

'You have that right, Markham. But I should beware. This is the navy not the army, the Mediterranean not New York. This time you won't have a blood relative selecting who sits in the judging chair. In fact, if I were you, I'd worry about the state of your command rather than your already blemished reputation.'

Markham had to fight to control his voice. 'I resent those remarks.'

There was no passion in 'Spotted Dick's' voice now. His face was composed, bloodless, and he even managed a thin humourless smile as he delivered the *coup de grâce*. 'I do hope so, Lieutenant Markham. Now be so good as to get out of my cabin.'

The wardroom was no more welcoming. Every officer in that cramped space had mentally grasped prize money before that aborted fight. To see it taken away from them, when it was so nearly theirs, hurt badly. In the nature of things a scapegoat was required, and since de Lisle's dislike of Markham was plain, and self-criticism alien, he walked into an atmosphere that was arctic in its cold intensity. Bowen, the barrel-chested First Lieutenant, didn't even wait till he'd made it to the strip of canvas that acted as a door to his tiny, cell-like cabin.

'To think that Bullocks have to buy their rank as officers! You'd wonder at what they get for their money, when any bogtrotting Croppie prepared to deny his church can enlist.'

'The 65th are less fussy than most,' added Smyth, the purser. 'Even their regimental goat's poxed and manged, I've been told.'

'I've heard the animal is a-scared of sheep, never mind the vagabond types that they've sent us,' Bowen continued, adding an hollow laugh. 'Since they were getting rid of everything rotten, I'm surprised *Hebe* wasn't lumbered with that creature as well.'

Markham turned, the canvas lifted in his hand. 'The goat can handle sheep all right, and men if they stay the right end of him. But with the kind of whoremongers serving in this fleet, I wouldn't let him near a ship's manger unless I intended to sell him into debauchery, and that at tuppence a throw.'

The 'Damn you, sir!' was muffled by the dropping screen. More remarks followed, all aimed at the army, and in particular his regiment. These were hard to refute, at least for social cachet. The 65th was no more than a normal line regiment, with a former Colonel indebted enough to his father to allow young George a commission. Yet, newly returned from Russia, and hounded by his relatives to return everything his father had gifted to him, that had been his only tangible resource, suddenly worth something because of the outbreak of war.

The present Colonel had snarled with rage when he insisted on taking up his duties; had been delighted to see his back when the orders arrived that required him to provide a platoon for sea service. He transferred not only his most persistent defaulters but, in the officer required to command them, a potential embarrassment. In fact, he'd done Markham a favour, putting him in a place where no tipstaff, acting on behalf of his creditors, could touch him. Nor could the law, who were after him for duelling. As an added bonus, serving in a fleet on distant service placed him beyond the reach of his grasping blood relatives.

'We had that sod in our grip,' growled Bowen. 'If we'd boarded at the right time, instead of holding back, we could have taken her and still got clear.'

'How much d'you reckon she was worth?' asked the purser dolefully. As the money man on the ship he'd know better than most how much they'd lost, so the question was posed only to annoy Markham.

'Admiral Hood would have bought her in, no doubt about it. Then there was head money for the crew and gun money for the cannon.'

'And she was fresh from port, fully provisioned, I daresay, with her holds packed with fresh stores. That would have fetched a mint of money, Mr Bowen, a mint.'

There was a tired quality to their speech, as though this were something that had been said several times before, and was merely being repeated to rub salt into his supposed wound. He'd never thought about prize money himself. Loot and booty were more the soldier's way of supplementing poor pay. But in sea service, however unpleasant, he would have qualified for a share of the officer's eighths, a sum of money that would have been very welcome in his present circumstances.

He eased off his coat, relishing the sudden chill as the cool, lower-deck air acted on his damp linen. Habit had him feeling his chin, before he remembered that he'd shaved just before his interview with the captain. The screen was pulled back suddenly, and Frobisher's servant,

Briggs, appeared, his pinched features screwed up in exaggerated concentration.

'I need tellin' what to do with the late Captain's dunnage.'

'Sorry?'

'His sea-chest, clothes, weapons and the like.'

'Why in God's name ask me?'

'You're the marine officer now,' Briggs replied, not attempting to hide his annoyance. 'It be your duty to sort it out.'

'Is there a common method?'

'It's normal to auction.'

Markham conjured up an image of his late superior. Frobisher had served in the marines all his military life, and like all men who'd never seen action, hankered endlessly after glory. The very first ball of his very first engagement had killed him. Now he was sewn up in canvas, with a piece of roundshot at his feet, lying on the deck awaiting the moment when his body would be slid over the side.

'He hasn't even been buried yet.'

'Makes no odds to him, one way or t'other.'

'I suppose I'd be right in thinking that such an auction takes place in the wardroom?'

'Or on deck if it's clement. I've laid it all out on his cot, good an' ready. And at the end, it be the custom to slip some of the proceeds to the officer's servant. The rest goes home to his kinfolk.'

'Get out!' Markham snapped. 'I'll see to it after he's buried.'

The head disappeared, as though Briggs had been shamed. But that was just wishful thinking. Given his first personal servant as a fifteen-year-old ensign, he'd soon realised that most of the men who took the job did so because it allowed them better food, as well as a chance to steal. Nationality made no difference. Those he'd had in the Baltic, the Caucasus and Moldavia were just as bad.

Bowen hadn't provided him with a servant and Markham hadn't asked for one, happy to rely on the wardroom stewards to see to his limited needs, which had only added to the contempt of his fellow officers.

He stood up and lifted the screen. Ignoring the cold glares that came his way he skirted the narrow table that filled the centre of the room and entered Frobisher's cabin, a space only slightly bigger than his own, made to look much more spacious by the mirror on the bulkhead, and the lantern close enough to that to multiply the light.

Briggs had indeed laid out all his possessions, even going so far as to clean the bloodstained accoutrements in which his master had expired. Frobisher, when he heard the drums beat to quarters, had changed into his very best for the forthcoming engagement. His everyday uniforms, including his spare hat, were folded at the top of the bed. His best red coat, with its frogged white facings and twisted gold aiguillettes, lay flat above two pairs of doeskin breeches. The single white crossbelt shone, as did the silver buckle in the centre.

On top of the monogrammed sea-chest the brush and comb set, silver backed, gleamed in the dull light. At its base lay three pairs of highly polished officer's shoes, one with silver buckles, stuffed with fine stockings; a set of excellent riding boots; a map case and a field telescope. Briggs had arranged his sword and pistols at the foot of the cot, expensive pieces set to catch the eye. There were the muster and pay books, a prayer book and a Bible, well thumbed, plus a list of the items in the chest.

'You might fetch a price,' Markham mumbled to himself, fingering the dull metal of the pistol barrels. 'But who's going to buy red coats aboard this ship except me?'

That produced a thought. His army uniform, though not so very different from a marine one, was not only showing signs of wear; it had proved a liability. Yet that, for the little it was worth, identified him to his own contingent. He and Frobisher were much of a size. If he were to take over his late superior's uniform, then he might begin to convince the Lobsters that he was just as much their officer. The sword he would need to replace his own, and he felt no compunction about claiming it. The only two questions he couldn't answer were obvious; how much to pay, and where the money was going to come from.

'Briggs,' he yelled. 'On the double.'

The screen lifted within a second. 'I've no desire to cheat the late Captain's relatives, nor the means to buy such fine pistols, but I need to know how much his uniforms are worth?'

Briggs' face screwed up in a parody of the usurer's art. Markham could almost see him counting. 'Before you reply let me tell you that, even if I find it *is* a custom to reward a dead man's servant, it's not one I propose to subscribe to. So, since you will receive nothing from the sale of anything on this cot, you might as well be honest.'

'Ain't worth bugger all,' Briggs wailed, 'if'n you don't take 'em.'

'A price!'

'Twelve guineas to include the sword if anyone's feeling generous. But the pistols is worth a lot more.'

'They shall go home intact, on the next packet, with a letter from me informing them of how he died.'

'That's the captain's job.'

'The captain may write too,' Markham replied savagely. 'But perhaps my account might be more truthful. I might be tempted to say that he didn't expire with much in the way of gallantry.'

The distant cries of the lookouts brought the ship to life, the thudding of the officers' shoes as they ran for the deck adding to the air of excitement. Markham knew he should follow, but decided against. If danger threatened he would soon know. He untied the queue that held his light brown hair and picked up the brush, leaning forward to gaze into the mirror.

The eyes that stared back at him looked pale green in

this light; the unlined, slightly bronzed face familiar from thousands of previous encounters. He'd been told he was handsome, and wondered at the eyesight of those who'd said so. Of the many women who'd ventured such an opinion only his mother could be forgiven, allowed a parental mote in her eye: the face was too long, the cheekbones too pronounced and the jaw a bit too square for that to be true. His nose was no longer straight, though the way it had been broken tended to enhance the shape, not spoil it. Then there were the scars, some from childhood, others from adult encounters, the only really obvious one just visible above his left eye. Fingering that always produced a smile, given that it had come from a pretend fight, not a real one. He was lucky in his teeth, white, strong and all present, making it easy for him to smile. An interesting visage perhaps, but certainly not handsome. As if to emphasise that, he screwed up his features to produce a passable imitation of a gargoyle's face.

By the time he'd tried on Frobisher's coat, Markham knew they were within sight of Hood's fleet. A good fit, it was beyond his financial reach, so he replaced it and returned to his cabin to fetch his own. Flicking through the muster and pay books, he looked at the names of the men he commanded. There were faces to go with those, but precious little in the way of knowledge that would help him command them.

Suddenly sick of the confined space, he jammed on his hat and made his way on deck, joining the others in looking to the east. The great ships, over twenty in number, and including the hundred-gunners *Victory* and *Britannia*, were beating to and fro off Cape Sicie, which guarded the approaches to the French naval base of Toulon. Even to a landsman's eye, they presented a stirring sight. What a pity that the image of the King's Navy, as portrayed by the gleaming white sails aloft on these magnificent leviathans, was so very different from the reality.

*

Descending the companionway that led down from the maindeck, Markham wrinkled his nose. The stench below was something he'd never get used to. Several hundred men, most with a mortal fear of fresh air, slung their hammocks here, fourteen inches to a man. If they washed at all, it was in salt water, and they ate where they slept. Right forward in the forepeak was the manger, full of the stink of cooped-up animals. Most of the crew had gone on up to the foredeck, braving sunshine and breeze to catch a sight of the fleet. That's where he'd first looked for his men, only realising that they must still be below when he failed to spot them amongst the crowd of sailors.

Somehow he had to get on terms with these people. They would certainly see action again, given that they were in the Mediterranean, and that the French had a large fleet at Toulon, one that the Admiral was determined to bring to battle. Frobisher, in all the weeks they'd been at sea, had trained no one, instead spending his days boasting to all who would listen of his intention to smite the enemy as soon as they appeared. He hated the French with such a passion that it came as no surprise to Markham to learn that the marine captain had never met one.

His own experience told him that training was the key to success. If the two groups could be brought to act together, given time they would blend into one. And there was plenty to learn, even for the marines. They'd had no more idea of what to do in the recent engagement than he had. They might claim to be real Lobsters, but they were just as false as his soldiers. Lost in thought, and unable to see clearly by the tallow-lit glim, he walked straight into Yelland, the youngest of his troopers, an innocent blond-haired youth much put upon by his elders who, to his mind, had been included in the detachment by some error.

The boy was looking the other way, craning slightly to

see something ahead. Then his officer appeared. Habit brought the lad to attention. The low deckbeams did the rest. Hatless, he fetched himself a mighty clout right on the crown, and would have fallen if Markham hadn't taken a firm hold. Supporting him, he inquired after his condition. The boy mumbled something which included the word fight, and started to move away. That was when Markham heard the unmistakable crunch of bone striking flesh.

'Damnit, what's going on?' he demanded, rushing forward.

The line of red coats, all with their backs to him, barred his view. But there was no mistaking the sounds of bare-knuckle fighting, the thud of soft flesh and brittle bone being mauled. He'd heard it too many times, and grabbed hold of a pair of shoulders to haul them apart.

Schutte, the huge Dutch-born marine, was there, stripped to the waist. Completely bald, the only colour between his breeches and his pate the red of his face, he stood before Rannoch, the most fearsome of his soldiers, a Highlander with hair so fair it hinted at Viking blood. They were trading blow for blow, both faces already covered in blood, their bodies a mass of red weals that would soon turn to ugly black bruises. Toe to toe, not giving an inch, the pair were pounding each other, their breath coming in hastily snatched grunts.

'Enough!' he yelled, stepping between them. Both sets of eyes, filled with hate, determination and pain, turned on him. For a moment he thought that he was about to fall victim, that they would cease to pound each other and instead lay their punches on him. 'What in the name of Jesus, Mary and Joseph do you pair think you're doing?'

His hands slipped on blood and sweat as he sought to push them apart. All around him he could hear the growls of dissatisfaction as the audience, deprived of their sport and their wagers, made their feelings known.

Dornan, another of his soldiers, with a bovine face to match his character, was vainly trying to hide the money from the bets inside his coat. Several coins slipped and landed on the planking, which turned some of the glares away from Markham. It said everything about these men that they'd put a simpleton in charge of the one thing that, proving complicity, would bring on the heaviest punishment.

'Stand back, damn you!' The shouted order produced no movement, just the same look he'd seen earlier, a combination of hate and indifference. 'Two paces to the rear, march!'

Some had the discipline to respond immediately, but most hesitated. Markham, still between the two giants, arms outstretched to keep them separate, felt like Samson trying to bring down the temple. He knew that even if he pushed harder, he didn't have the strength to move them. Concentrating, he didn't see Ettrick, smaller and nimbler than the rest, in one swift movement scoop up the coins Dornan had dropped.

'What's going on?'

The strange voice caused the men glaring at Markham to turn to face the officer of the watch, Fellows. He stood with his hands on his hips, a grin that was half a sneer on his face.

'There's nothing going on,' Markham replied lamely.

'Is that you in there, Markham?'

'Mr Markham to you, Fellows. There was the risk of a fight, but I put a stop to it.'

Fellows threw back his head and laughed. 'A risk. Last time I looked they were at it hammer and tongs. I expected another canvas sack on the deck, with an addition to the burial service.'

'You knew this was happening and did nothing to stop it?'

'No I didn't, *Mr* Markham!' The emphasis on the Mister was even more insulting than its absence. 'But I reckoned Schutte to win. Why should I take a hand if he was going to spare the purser the need to feed a Bullock?'

'That way we find out who in charge,' Schutte growled, his hairless chest heaving. He stuck one finger in his own belly, then pointed it at Rannoch. 'Sergeant me or Sergeant Bullock.'

Markham pushed him hard, which was dispiriting since he only went back a fraction of an inch, thinking that was another thing Frobisher had ignored in his determination to keep the two groups separate: the status of the non-commissioned officers.

'There's only one person in charge, you great hairless oaf – me! If this happens again I'll have you all up at the grating and personally flog you till you weep. This stops now, and as for who will be a sergeant, that is something I will decide.'

Fellows was laughing in the background, his shoulders heaving with merriment. Markham walked up to him and, leaning over, stuck his nose less than half an inch from that of the naval officer.

'You! The captain's cabin, this minute.'

# Chapter three

'Are you a milksop, sir?' de Lisle sneered, shuffling the papers on his desk. The captain was clearly enjoying himself, half smiling, his head turning slightly to include the other two naval officers in his rebuke. 'Men will fight, even Bullocks. Damn me if that's not why we offer them the King's shilling. You're worse than I supposed, Markham, a stranger to that most necessary addition to an officer's equipment, the blind eye.'

'Sir, I . . .'

Without a look in his direction, de Lisle cut right across his protest. 'Silence! There's a hierarchy below decks, man, which is just as real as that of the quarterdeck. . You're a stranger to it who shows no sign of willingness to learn. All of which makes the order I'm about to give you more appropriate.'

Bowen, the premier, was grinning. Fellows, who should have been shaking in his shoes, had a blank, innocent look on his face. He'd been aware, before he'd even entered the great cabin, that de Lisle would not condemn his actions. Quite the reverse, his commanding officer approved. And by the tone of his voice, he was about to pay this upstart Bullock out for his damned cheek in interfering.

Another slight shuffling of papers, designed to underline his importance, was necessary before de Lisle continued. 'It seems that there's great support for the Bourbons in Provence. Marseilles has sent delegates and so has Toulon. The admiral has decided to take possession of the naval base, and is demanding contributions to

27

form a garrison.' He finally looked up, unable to resist a sneer. 'I was happy to inform his lordship that *Hebe* was in a position to dispense with its entire complement. You can go ashore, Markham, where you belong, and take that rabble you call your command with you.'

'Including the Lobsters, sir?'

'Yes.'

Nothing went well. His soldiers were happy to be going ashore, the marines less so. And when it came to getting in the boats, it only served to widen their divisions. The men of the 65th had been seasick in the Channel, useless lubbers in the storms of the Bay of Biscay, a damned nuisance at Gibraltar and hopeless fighters in the Gulf of Loins. Here, off Toulon, in their attempts to go over the side with some dignity, they excelled themselves.

The marines, led by Schutte, had got themselves into *Hebe*'s cutter before the sun rose. They'd then rowed to a position where they could observe the fun, before the men of the 65th emerged from below. As the other boats pulled alongside nearly every member of the crew had come on deck to witness the ineptitude of these lubbers.

The rope ladder was the first obstacle. Hanging by the open gangway, it dropped from the side of the vessel, an arrangement of hemp that seemed imbued with a life of its own. Pressure exerted on one strand produced a corresponding movement in another, so that even if the man descending could stay upright, difficult in itself, he tended to be spun round to slam into the planking. Wet and slippery, the soldiers' iron-shod boots produced an added handicap, as did the encumbrance of their equipment. The long Brown Bess muskets were the very devil, while the full infantry packs acted like dead weights.

The first contingent were invited to board the jolly boat, the smallest conveyance on offer, a target that from the side of Hebe looked to be miles away. Two grinning tars, with boathooks, were there to assist. Encouraged to add to the fun, they took a savage delight in making matters worse. Every time a man looked like falling, they pushed off so that he wouldn't hurt himself. This meant he landed in the sea. Then the boathooks, applied with no gentleness, could be used to fish him out.

Markham's order to remove their equipment improved matters, but only marginally. One or two managed it without difficulty, but most took an age to descend, spinning first, then slipping and dropping, emitting terrified yells. Every mistake produced a great belch of laughter from the assembled hands that de Lisle did nothing to inhibit. Finally the barge came alongside and, after it had taken on the last half-dozen soldiers, it was his turn.

Concentrating on the task ahead he didn't notice that Briggs had lashed Frobisher's sea-chest to the whip along with his canvas sack. The bundle was lifted up and out, sat there for a moment before the men holding the line let go. The chest dropped like a stone, and the boatmen pushed off. They held the line just as they reached the water, and, to a gale of laughter, they were hooked and loaded into the boat.

Markham realised the error just as he was turning to raise his hat in a salute to the quarterdeck. Not one of the officers responded, with a discourtesy so blatant it penetrated the thick skin he'd created to protect himself. Hurt, he could not speak. Turning quickly, he went over the side. The rope dipped under his foot and he tried his other leg on the next strand. That sank and pushed inwards, which left him hanging, his back out over the sea. Slightly panicking, he grabbed at the first rung with his hand, which, stretching, only increased the angle. He felt it begin to spin, then heard the first cackle of the laughter that was sure to follow.

Progress from that point was swift and terrifying, with Markham unsure of what rungs he hit or held, and how many he missed altogether. Out of the corner of his eye he saw the boathooks pressing against the side as the sailors pushed off. Fearing nothing more than an igno-minious drop into the sea he jumped, landing on top of one of the tars. The man fell back into the thwarts, cushioning the fall, nearly capsizing the boat. Only the action of the other sailor saved everyone aboard from a drubbing, as he pulled hard on his hook to keep them level.

Markham found himself staring into the pained eyes of the man he'd landed on, who looked as if he were about to tell him what he thought. There was nothing stagey about Markham's Irish accent now. It had all the passion associated with his race.

'One word, you stinking, pigtailed bag of shite, and I'll ram every inch of that boathook right up your arse.'

The hoots of merriment behind him were loud enough to carry to the whole fleet. In his fall, Markham had provided the icing on the cake of the day's humour. *Hebe*'s whole side was lined with grinning faces, some so taken with the farce that they could hardly draw breath. Likewise the men in the other boats, soldiers, sailors and marines, were convulsed with laughter. Insult was added to injury by the way Bernard, a midshipman who looked about twelve years old, skipped down nimbly to take command of the small flotilla.

'Man the oars and get me out of here,' he snapped, 'before I'm tempted to shoot someone.'

The oarsmen, and the midshipman, fought to keep their faces straight as they took their positions. Once in motion, the other two boats fell in behind and they made their way across the short choppy swell to enter the outer roads of the harbour. Within minutes men were hanging over the side, retching into the sea. Markham lifted his eyes, to avoid the chance that by looking, he might emulate them, and, since they'd cleared the St Mandrian peninsula, he caught his first sight of the land around Toulon.

The sun was fully up now, promising another scorching hot day. He could hear no gunfire, nor observe any evidence of fighting. Even the numerous anchored British warships, well out of range of shore-based fire, looked peaceful. It was as if the plans were still being laid, with the town yet to be taken. He'd been told that Toulon had surrendered, the citizens handing over the administration to British officers. But nothing he could see supported this, and the sudden thought occurred that they were being rowed towards a hostile shore, perhaps offered as a sacrifice to test the validity of the capitulation.

The bay consisted of an inner and outer harbour, the former smaller and better protected. As they rowed steadily along he took in the salient features. The town was surrounded by hills, the slope beginning almost from the shoreline, rising gently at first, before suddenly increasing in gradient. The highest was right behind the town, a massive limestone rampart topped with a green fuzz of vegetation. Whoever held that could dominate the inner harbour, and if there were any Jacobins about, that was where they'd be.

There were other *massifs*, all capable, in varying degrees, of dominating some part of the anchorage. They broke to the west, forming a valley which provided an easy route from the hinterland into the naval base. Inside the arm of the twin peninsulas that enclosed the Grande Rade, he could see several forts placed at strategic points, their embrasures bristling with guns which dominated the roads, with others aimed at the gap between the two headlands that formed the entrance to the inner harbour.

And he was being rowed right into that confined space, well within range of the artillery, in a boat that would fall apart if even nicked by a cannonball. Closer and closer they came, into an opening no more than a mile wide, with Markham's eyes jerking back and forth, from the stone fort on one side, to the round moated tower which acted as a signal station on the other.

'Stay close to the right-hand side of the entrance.'

Bernard, with his superior nautical knowledge, looked

set to disagree. But Markham's grey eyes brooked no argument, and he pushed the tiller to oblige. The place was so somnolent it smelt of a trap, with an empty boat bobbing in the watergate of the round tower as if no notion of war existed. Markham was holding his breath, alert for the first sign of movement on the cannon; the head of a gunner or a raised rammer, that would provide some warning. Nothing happened, and soon they'd passed that zone of maximum danger and entered the Petite Rade.

He directed Bernard to turn northeast and head for the town itself. The white and ochre buildings and the long quays were hidden behind the forest of masts that constituted the French Mediterranean fleet. Bernard directed his attention to another boat, which had put off from the eastern shore, quite clearly a wealthy captain's barge, judging by the uniform dress of the crew. He could see, sitting at the rear, an officer in a dark blue coat, white facings edged with gold. As the boat came near he raised and waved his hat.

'I'd be obliged if you'd come alongside,' he shouted, the strong Scottish accent apparent even at that loud level. Markham nodded to Bernard, and they changed course so that the two boats were on a parallel course. As soon as he was close enough, the officer called out, 'Elphinstone, *Robust*.'

'Lieutenant Markham, of the frigate *Hebe*, and Midshipman Bernard. Is the harbour secure, sir?'

'Och aye, laddie. The Frenchies are hiding in their barracks and houses, waiting to see what's going to happen.' Elphinstone's gaze ranged over the three boats as he replied, before coming back to rest on the barge. 'Have we met before, Lieutenant? Your face seems a mite familiar.'

'Not as far as I'm aware, sir,' he replied, giving Bernard a black look as the youngster coughed.

'Maybe not,' replied the captain, clearly showing by his

expression that Markham, not he, must be mistaken. 'Is this the entire complement from *Hebe*?'

'Yes, sir. Thirty-four men in all, not including the tars.'

Elphinstone looked over the men in the barge, then nodded towards the jolly boat and the cutter. 'Half your party seem to be in soldier's garb.'

'Sixty-fifth foot, detached for sea service.'

Some of the men were still hanging over the side, retching, even though their stomachs must be empty. 'And not enjoying it much, eh?' barked Elphinstone.

'I daresay some of those being sick are marines.'

'Fetch my wake, Markham. I've a wee job that needs attending to, and a file containing some soldiers is just the thing.'

'At your service, sir,' Markham replied. 'Just let's get them ashore.'

'I daresay,' Elphinstone responded, with a deep booming laugh. 'If you look yonder to the west you'll see the bay at the head of the valley. La Seyne, it's called. Join me there. You can leave your extra equipment in the boats.'

'May I enquire what service we're required to perform, sir?'

'Oh aye, laddie. The Jacobins have taken Marseilles and set themselves up to butcher the people. There's a portion of them on the way to do the same here. You and I are going to stop them.'

On land, before very long, the positions reversed themselves. Now, despite the discomfort brought on by the heat, the soldiers were in their element, with boots on their feet that were well suited to the hard dusty road on which they marched. The marines in their lighter shoes, so perfect on a planked deck, were less comfortable, able to feel every stone on which they trod. But it was no pleasure for anyone, especially since Elphinstone set such a cracking pace, not stopping till they were well away from the last buildings in the town. Markham ordered his men to rest, then went to join the naval captain, who was examining the road ahead.

'We need to buy time, Markham, to get some troops ashore.'

'I didn't see any evidence of haste amongst the fleet, sir. In fact, such boats as were in the water looked to be engaged in Sunday visiting.'

'These things take time to organise,' Elphinstone replied, slightly piqued perhaps that a soldier should disparage the fleet. 'If the Jacobins arrive in numbers too soon, they'll pitch us back on to our ships, no matter how many men we disembark.'

He reached into his coat. 'Take this map. It's pretty sparse and it only goes as far as the village of Ollioules. I'll leave it to you as to whether you think it prudent to push on from there.'

'How many of the enemy are we expecting, sir?'

'I don't have a clue, laddie. Could be hundreds, could be thousands.'

Markham tried to keep the surprise out of his voice, and when he spoke he was well aware of stating the obvious. 'There's a limit to how many I can hold with thirty-four men, even if I can find a good defensive position.'

Elphinstone frowned, looking at him closely again, as if trying to place him. ' I know that. I'll go back and see if I can muster some reinforcements. Your job is to make contact with the enemy, and give the men I bring up a position from which to fight, which I suggest would be better achieved at the double.'

There were dozens of questions. But Markham guessed, by the steely look in Elphinstone's eye as the Scotsman peered at him, that he would be wasting his time to ask them. He saluted slowly, and ordered his men back on to their feet.

'I've seen you somewhere before, I'm sure of it. I rarely forget a face.' Elphinstone shrugged when Markham didn't respond. 'You'd best be on your way.'

The Bullocks doubled smartly to annoy the Lobsters, not to please Markham. The marines, in turn, were determined not to lag behind. Rivulets of sweat streaming down inside his uniform, he didn't care. Nor did he look behind him to see how either were faring. He was too busy with his own worries, the greatest of which was the prospect of being required to lead these men into battle.

He was on land now, his element, without the burden of ignorance. He knew what to do. As a youngster, even before he'd put on a uniform, he'd received a depth of training denied to most of his contemporaries. Indeed, he'd grown up almost as a military brat. The break in his martial career hadn't dented that, and service in the Empress Catherine's army had only honed skills he'd first been taught in the Americas.

The heat was intense and getting worse, with clouds of dust thrown up by their feet making life hell for the stragglers. Good order was less important than speed. Elphinstone had made it clear, and this was proved by his map, that failure to hold the French at Ollioules would mean trying to stop them on the very outskirts of Toulon, which as yet had no troops to man the defensive perimeter.

The youngster, Yelland, was ordered to remove his coat and share out his equipment, then sent ahead to reconnoitre. When, after about an hour, in which he'd only allowed his men one stop, Yelland came back into view, Markham held up his sword to call a halt, fighting to stay upright himself as his men collapsed where they stood.

'You may drink some water, two sips each.'

Yelland was in a worse state, his face running with sweat and his chest heaving. Markham gave him a drink from his own canteen before he asked him to report.

'The village is about a mile ahead, sir. Not a soul in sight, that I could see. But it does have a well full of water.'

'Any sign of the enemy?'

'None, though there's a rate of abandoned equipment on the road leading to the village. I went clear to the other end, and it carries straight on until it disappears into a deep gorge.'

Markham looked at his map. Ollioules was just a hamlet, a post stop to change horses on the way to Marseilles. The problem was simple. He had no idea what lay further on, beyond the gorge that Yelland had mentioned. Perhaps, even though the youngster thought the village deserted, he could find a local inhabitant to tell him how matters lay. He held out his canteen again.

'Take this. Get to the other side of the village, no more than two hundred yards up the road, so you can keep an eye on the entrance to that gorge. Wait there till I join you.'

Yelland grabbed it and ran off, as Markham shouted to the rest to get to their feet. The curses and groans resurfaced long before they resumed their double march. It wasn't long before he saw the debris that Yelland had remarked on; cartouches, pikes, casks and the odd musket dropped by the roadside. Elphinstone had said nothing about the enemy retreating, only advancing, which was strange.

The double pace quickly brought the stunted church tower and the rooftops of the village into sight. Calling another halt, he scrambled up the nearest knoll and examined the terrain. The hillsides were low and undulating to the south. But just on the other side of the village a rampart of rocks formed an impassable barrier. To the north, on the inland side, they steepened considerably until they became an unclimbable escarpment. That accorded with Elphinstone's rough map, which showed that the only route an army could take from Marseilles lay through Ollioules.

He needed a defensive position on the Toulon road. That had to be on the inland hillside, and it had to overlook the road. There was some question about the range of the shortened marine muskets, but his soldiers, even if they were, as he suspected, indifferent shots, would be adequate at volley fire from a defensive position. He spotted what he was seeking ahead, a cluster of heavy rocks around the base of a gully. They could be levered closer together and provide some cover if he was forced into a hasty withdrawal. Really worrying, should the enemy appear in strength, there was nothing behind that: neither decent cover on the long straight Roman road, nor the security of more troops to provide support.

His men were spread out over a long stretch of road. Some of the marines had kept pace with the leaders, while a few of his soldiers, supposedly trained to this, were well to the rear. He called on them to close up, fretting while the most laggardly joined. These included the two pugilists, Schutte and Rannoch. He pointed to the spot he'd selected up ahead.

'Since you two are keen to see who's the strongest, get up that slope and shift those rocks to the head of the gully. I want them as a rampart at right angles to the road. And if you can clear any cover from the other side it will help.'

'Help who?' growled Rannoch.

He'd expected it, so there was no shock in the man's insubordinate response. Aboard ship he had thought he was going to have to train these men into submission. Now circumstances had changed. He was going to have to blood them, no easy task.

Everyone was watching him, seeing how he would react to the challenge from a man half of them considered a natural leader. He could shout, quite possibly to no avail. Yet to plead would prove fatal. So, without the faintest idea of the effect, he smiled, and spoke as quietly as his heaving chest would allow.

'Don't ever question my orders, d'you hear? It's not your place. But since this is all new, just this once, I'll tell you. There are Frenchmen coming this way, how many we don't know. The first place we're going to stop them is somewhere on the road past the village. Then we're going to make them pay to get through it, since it's the only available route to Toulon. And after that, we will block the road so that they have to outflank us. By that time, I expect we will be reinforced.'

Rannoch was glaring at him, in his mind no doubt working up to a refusal. Frobisher's sword sang as Markham swung it hard, gratified to see the sudden flash of shock in the soldier's eye. The tip sliced across the strap holding his musket, parting it so that the weapon clattered onto the hard surface of the road.

'You'll need to take that off,' he said, flicking the sword so that it was pointed to the buckle on his belly. 'Would you like me to remove your pack as well?'

They locked stares, Rannoch's eyes deep green and surprisingly feline for a man of his bulk. Markham felt like a fieldmouse about to be swiped by a great paw. But he held his own look steady, along with the slight, detached smile on his face, trying to convey two things; that he was not afraid, and that he was prepared to kill to be obeyed. He spoke to the Dutchman as soon as Rannoch's hand moved to undo his belt.

'You too, Schutte. And I want a result. If I find you've been scrapping, I'll break you on the first wheel I can find, with a thousand lashes per man. The rest of you, follow me.'

The village hardly warranted the title. On the far side of a dry riverbed, over an ancient stone bridge, it consisted of a single dusty street, located at the point where the valley narrowed to form a shallow defile. Half a dozen shuttered houses lined the dusty, rutted road on either side of the central square, all empty. The church, square and plain Romanesque, stood equally bereft on one side, the tower too low to provide a long-range vantage point towards Marseilles. The post house, the only other substantial building, stood directly opposite, with a well beaten track that led down an alley, the dusty paddock at the rear just visible. A couple of undernourished horses were up against the fence. The sound of the soldiers' boots, echoing off the stones around the well, startled them, and from somewhere close by, a mule brayed its response.

'Keep going,' he yelled, as the leaders stopped by the well. Others had done so before them, since the stone surround was stacked with debris. 'We'll send someone back for water.'

A few more houses, then the floor of the valley opened out again, onto a narrow, rising hill bisected by the road. The crest, three hundred yards from the village, was some hundred yards across, hemmed in by the steep surrounding hills. It looked a good place to defend, but with his limited resources, a shade too wide. The landscape provided little shelter, barring a couple of dry stone walls shaded by stunted trees on the northern side, about fifty yards from the point where the road topped the crest.

'Packs off, all of you. Get into the shade of those walls.'

He didn't wait to see them comply but marched on till he breasted the rise. The road led straight on, undulating slightly, with no sign of any enemy, until it ran into a narrow gorge in the massive limestone crags that rose up half a mile distant. The sloping lea, which widened out to form a circular pasture, was dotted with trees and edged with fallen boulders. But none of them stood close enough to the crest to provide decent cover. Anyone wishing to take this crest would require to advance, uphill, over several hundred yards of open ground, making it a place that could be held, easily, given adequate forces.

Yelland, seeing him against the skyline, stepped out from behind one of the trees and waved. The temptation to push on was strong. But his men were tired from double marching in the heat. To keep them going in this kind of weather, with the sun full up and little shade, might render even the good ones useless. Although the position he occupied was too shallow to be perfect, it might be better than anything he'd find off Elphinstone's map.

But there was another reason. All that equipment on the road, and around the well, indicated a force in retreat. Judging by the amount of abandoned kit, it was one that certainly outnumbered his own. It was hard to tell how long it had been since they'd passed this way, and with no-one in the houses of Ollioules he couldn't ask. But one thing he did suspect. If they discovered they were being pursued they'd turn and fight in a place of their own choosing, and that was a battle he couldn't win.

He waved to Yelland again, then span on his heel and made his way back. Halsey, the marine corporal, in the absence of Schutte, was now in charge of the Lobsters. He knew his name, but struggled to remember that of the taller man next to him.

'Leech,' Halsey replied, when he was forced to enquire.

'Make your presence known to Yelland, give him some water, then take up a position on the blind side of the crest. Stay low and keep him in view. If you see Yelland coming towards us, double back and get me. I'll relieve you both in an hour.'

'Water bottles off,' he snapped, his eyes raking the rest of somnolent men. 'Take a good drink now. Tully, Hollick,' he called to the two nearest Bullocks.

'He's Hollick, I'm Tully,' the man replied, without adding a 'sir' or making any attempt to stand up. Added to that his pock-marked, ugly face had a sour, insubordinate expression.

Markham thought hard, but then had to admit the man was right, which made him clench his jaw in anger as he issued his instructions. 'On your feet, both of you.'

'Christ, there's no peace,' Tully moaned.

But he'd begun to rise, so Markham let that pass.

Hollick, his fair skin burnt red, hesitated for a split second before doing likewise. He had them collect the water bottles, then led them back to the village to fill them. Once they were fully occupied, Markham turned to look around. It was odd that the place was deserted. Not that he imagined it ever bustling, but there should have been someone around.

The Provençal architecture was dissimilar, but it still reminded him of those small Loyalist townships in the Americas, hamlets that would empty as soon as a red coat was sighted on the horizon, the people taking to the woods until the soldiers had passed. He'd been told the locals, afraid of the Terror, had invited the British ashore. Perhaps that didn't apply to the people of Ollioules. Or maybe just the sight of one armed man, of an unknown nationality, was enough to send them into flight.

'Tully, I'm going to see what food there might be in the inn. Come and tell me when you've finished.' That was answered with a slow nod. Markham was tired and hot, and well aware that imbuing this lot with discipline was going to be an uphill struggle. All of which added real force to his response.

'The correct response is "yes, sir", and don't you ever forget to use it again. If we retreat, I intend to poison that well. The quickest way, I've found, is to tip a dead body into the water.'

What emerged from Tully's throat wasn't the right response, but it was close enough to satisfy a man more interested in a drink than the exercise of authority. Taking his hat off as he ducked under the low lintel, he could feel the coolness of the interior on the rim of sweat that circled the top of his head. It was dark, too, after the bright sunlight of the roadway, so his eyes took time to adjust. The empty flagons that littered the tables engendered curiosity, which was immediately forgotten as the assailant shot towards him.

# Chapter four

If they'd come at him together he wouldn't have stood a hope in hell, and he was glad that the first one tried to crown him with a bottle rather than get him with a knife. The backlift required to put any force into the blow slowed what was intended and gave Markham just enough time to duck under it, so that it took him on the shoulder rather than the head. He still felt a sharp pain followed by a spreading numbness, but the amount of effort used by the attacker knocked the bottle out of his hand, and it clattered onto the stone floor and shattered.

Markham had already managed one loud shout, praying that the combination of noises would bring him help. He could only see two men, but in the dingy interior there could be dozens. He got his arms round the waist of the bottle smasher and turned him towards the second man, whose access was impeded by a table. He was carrying a knife, of the small variety, sharp, vicious and curved, used for gutting and filleting fish. Frightened that he was about to skewer his companion, he pulled the weapon to one side, which, surprisingly, threw him off balance.

Loosening one hand, Markham struck viciously for the groin, jabbing first. Then feeling the loose sack of skin, he took a tight grip. His assailant shot bolt upright, emitting a scream, his lips pulled back to show a fine set of white teeth. Markham tried to get his free hand across to unsheathe his sword, but his own arm was in the way.

The man with the knife had staggered round the table and was coming at his unprotected side when help finally arrived. Tully, standing on the elevated doorstep swung his boot high and took him right on the side of the head. Markham had a fleeting impression of a swarthy complexion, dark curly hair and slightly glazed eyes, before the light went out of them and the attacker crashed to the floor. Tully stepped forward, his bayonet out, and dropped to one knee.

'No!'

The shout made his fist tighten even more, producing another scream from the man he was holding. But it failed to stop Tully, who in one swift movement jabbed forward with the eighteen-inch blade and cut his victim's throat from the inside out. Vaguely aware of Hollick standing in the doorway, Markham pushed hard, sending his attacker reeling across a table. The distance thus opened allowed him to get his sword out, and the tip, laid on the man's ribcage, just above his fine waistcoat, removed any notion of continued fighting from his mind.

'Hollick, take charge here.'

As soon as the trooper responded, his own bayonet replacing the sword, Markham walked over to look at the other assailant, now on his back with a stream of blood running from his neck on to the stone floor. He noticed that he was dressed like a servant, his clothing of quite good quality without being as fine as that of the man on the table.

'Damn you, Tully, there was no need to kill him.'

'Safest way, I reckon,' Tully replied. There was no passion in his voice, nor emotion in his pig-like eyes.

'Come with me. Hollick, keep that man still.'

There wasn't much to search. The place consisted of no more than a front parlour and a cramped backroom that doubled as a bedroom-cum-kitchen. The girl, more of a child really, was lying with her back to them curled in a ball, her naked body showing even in the grim light the marks where she'd been beaten and assaulted. Markham bent down and touched her, producing a fearful shudder which ran right through her body, accompanied by a whimpered plea to be left alone. Turning to the soldier, he saw a look in his eyes that, ranging over the slim, bruised body, spoke volumes about what touched his emotions.

'Out, Tully!' snapped Markham. 'Help Hollick get something round that fellow to restrain him.'

'What you got in mind for her?' Tully asked, his voice rasping and low.

'Protection, man,' Markham replied, reaching for a threadbare blanket. 'And something to cover her shame.'

'She's only a Frenchie, sir. I thought we was here to fight them.'

Markham stood up and faced Tully. 'The men, soldier. Not the women, and certainly not a young girl. Do as I say and get out!'

He was again faced with that look, the attitude of a man contemplating disobedience. If Tully thought himself a dissembler he was wrong. Markham could see, in his eyes, all the thoughts that flickered through his mind. The bloodstained bayonet was still in his hand. The man who stood between him and a chance to assuage his lust would be so easy to kill. Better still, the people to blame were to hand, one with his throat already cut. There was an air of desperation about him. Weeks at sea, without even the sight of a woman, had made him very dangerous indeed.

'Out,' said Markham softly. 'There'll be a whorehouse in Toulon for what you're after.'

Tully blinked and Markham didn't, and that was what made the difference. He took a pace backwards. 'There's a mule around somewhere. Find it, we'll need it to carry the water back.'

'Sir,' said Tully softly, before spinning on his heel and striding out. As he bent to reassure the girl that she was now safe, he heard him say something to Hollick. The walls made it indistinct, but it sounded remarkably like 'all officers are the same, right selfish bastards'. The girl's dark brown eyes, responding to the soft words spoken in her native tongue, fixed on his face. Whatever she saw there turned her whimpers to sobs, and tears streamed down the smooth olive skin of her face. Markham covered her with the blanket, and left.

Hollick was standing in the same place, the man still splayed on his back across the table. He opened a shutter, filling the room with light. There were flagons everywhere, some empty, others half full, and their prisoner was no longer an indistinct shape, but a formed human being. Black-haired, carefully curled, with a thin moustache, he had a narrow face with sharp features, and the kind of hooked nose that hinted at Arab or Levantine blood. His thin red lips were parted, with a fine line of dried saliva where they'd joined. He was breathing deeply, eyes shut tight, as if trying to draw moisture into his dry mouth.

The quality of his garments became even more apparent in the light; high quality linen, fine cambric waistcoat, good, if dusty boots and breeches so tight they were like a second skin. Markham saw a green silk coat and sword belt across a chair which he assumed to belong to his prisoner. In the inside pocket of the coat he found several official-looking letters, all addressed to a Pierre-Michel Fouquert. He was about to read the first one when Tully came back from his search for the donkey, his boots ringing on the flagstoned floor.

'There's a poor sod out the back lashed to the fencing with his balls cut off.'

'Dead?'

'Wouldn't want to be alive without his nuts, would he, sir?'

Markham jabbed the tip of his sword into the man on the table, which brought his eyes open. Black and bloodshot, they were nevertheless steady and full of hate, with an intensity that, allied to his other features, gave him a demonic look. What he'd seen in the back room, added to what Tully had just reported, indicated he might well be like that. He struggled, rather feebly, to move. Given the number of empty bottles in the place, it was a fair guess that he was suffering from the effects of too much drink, not all of which had worn off.

'Get him upright and take him outside.'

The Frenchman started moaning as soon as the soldiers grabbed his shirt-front, the supplication softening his features. The protests began as he was dragged outside. They were only halfway to the back of the building before he started sobbing, as though he'd worked out what was in store for him. The sight of the body, wrists and neck tied to the split wood fence, its feet splayed over the deep pool of mixed flesh and blood, brought forth the first hint of a scream. Tully hit him, a blow that swept across his moustachioed mouth, jerking his head to one side and producing an immediate flow of bright red froth from the split lower lip. Hollick, hanging onto another post, was trying not to retch.

'Cut down that poor fellow and put this sod in his place,' said Markham, his voice and manner as cold as ice. 'And as soon as you've done that, undo those fine breeches he's wearing and show him your bayonet.'

That instrument, dull gleaming steel playing tantalisingly around the curled black hairs of his exposed groin, had the Frenchman gabbling replies to Markham's question in a manner that guaranteed truth. He confirmed ownership of the letters Markham was waving, and that his name was Fouquert. He claimed to be a French naval officer, who'd been unsure which cause to follow, that of the Republicans or the Monarchists. The Royalist commander in Toulon, Admiral Trugueff, had been deposed. When Hood threatened that any warship which hadn't landed its powder would be treated as an enemy, Fouquert and his men had gathered muskets and pikes, then abandoned both vessels and forts. He'd brought the main body here, then sent them on to Marseilles while he waited for the stragglers.

'How far behind are these stragglers?' It was hard to shrug in that position, but Fouquert managed it. If they'd been on the road, seeing his soldiers approaching, they must have taken to the hills. 'How many men did you bring out of Toulon?'

The reply produced such a shock in his lieutenant that Tully's bayonet, acting like an extension of Markham's surprise, drew blood from the inside of the man's thigh. Both soldiers then looked at him hard, wondering what had produced such a response.

'According to this turd there are five thousand well-armed French sailors roaming around these hills, mostly in front of us, God be thanked, but some behind.'

The figure really wasn't that surprising. Hood's fleet, if you included tenders and supply ships, was manned by more than twenty thousand sailors. The French Mediterranean fleet would need that many, if not more, to be effective.

'I say we make it one less,' said Hollick, leaning forward so that his face was less than an inch from Fouquert's, the words delivered in a growling, manly fashion to cover his recent, retching response to the sight of dead man's blood.

Tully waved the bayonet before the terrified Frenchman's eyes, so close that Hollick had to pull back. 'You ain't got the stomach for cold death, mate. Best leave it to a man.'

Hollick, upright again, had his own bayonet out in a flash. 'Damn you, Tully, I can do it as easy as you.'

'Never,' the older soldier replied. Then he spat, deliberately, at the prisoner.

Fouquert, convinced he was about to be stabbed, protested, pleaded that what had happened here had been none of his doing. That even as an officer he could hardly be expected to control men who'd run away from their duty. Markham, unsure if he was lying, told him to shut up, then ordered Tully and Hollick to take a step

47

back. He continued to question him, noticing that as Fouquert answered his black eyes never left his interrogator's face.

There was intelligence there, that was obvious. With each question his fear was evaporating, to be replaced by a rather superior demeanour that began with those same eyes, but soon spread to his thin cheeks. Markham watched, fascinated in a detached way, as they relaxed, soon followed by the clenched jawbone. The lips, hitherto compressed, eased to become full and red. The Frenchman knew that for all the bluff, and the threatening behaviour of the men he had with him, this British officer was not going to kill or mutilate him. By the time he'd finished his interrogation, there was something very close to a smirk on those same red lips, a look which seemed to convey that should the positions be reversed, Fouquert wouldn't hesitate.

Markham had somehow surrendered the initiative, but was at a loss to know how to regain it. Short of torture, he had few options, and he was neither prepared to indulge in that, nor turn the kind of blind eye that would let Tully loose.

'Leave him tied up here. If we're reinforced and hold out, I'll send him back to Toulon. There's his own kind there to find out the truth and deal with him.'

'What if we have to run?' asked Tully, his eyes narrowed.

'In that case, soldier, I'll make you his keeper. He's an officer and a Republican, who probably cut up this poor sod, which in Toulon could well mean the rope. But to us, he's a prisoner of war, and will be treated as such. If he dies before we get back then you'll probably hang in his place.'

He was tempted to go on, to say that they were British soldiers, not renegade Republican sailors. To tell them of the effect of unlicensed and unbridled rapine on a local populace. To explain that he'd seen it in America, during a war so unpopular that the King, unable to field enough men from his own land, had been forced to recruit German mercenaries to fight the colonists.

That was when Markham had to shut his eyes, fight to block out the personal memories, those that only normally came to him at night, producing an overwhelming sense of failure and loss. He succeeded only by opening those eyes again, and observing in the faces of both Hollick and Tully an inquiring look.

'We need the locals to trust us,' he said, his eyes ranging around the high escarpments that hemmed in the village. 'Don't be fooled by those empty houses. The people who lived in them will be in the hills around here, perhaps so close they're watching us now. Killing their own kind won't make them trust us.' He kicked viciously, and suddenly, at the ground, sending a cloud of dust into the prisoner's smirking face. 'Even a shit like this.'

Spinning round, he saw that the donkey and the two under-nourished horses had retreated to the other side of the paddock, as far away as possible from the smell of blood. 'Get that donkey down to the well.'

Tully stepped forward and drew his bayonet gently across the Frenchman's throat, then laughed at the look his action produced.

'Move,' said Markham, softly.

The two soldiers headed across the paddock, spreading out to hem in the animals. Markham went back inside the inn to look for food. The girl was hunched by the blackened grate, still with the blanket around her shoulders, gently dabbing a cloth into a pot of water slung over the embers, trying to wash herself. Judging by the pressure she was applying to her skin, it wasn't only dirt she was trying to remove. The sudden realisation of his presence made her clutch the blanket tightly to her.

His questions regarding food, delivered to her partially hidden face, produced mumbled answers. More men than his two attackers had passed through from Toulon – this said in such a rasping, painful way that Markham should understand the true depth of her ordeal. In the course of her mutters he discovered that her name was Celeste. The men who'd abused her cleaned the place out, torturing and murdering her father in front of her to try and find if he had anything hidden. Contrary to his earlier belief, the other inhabitants of Ollioules hadn't fled to the hills. They'd been driven out of the village ahead of the deserters, herded like cattle carrying their meagre possessions, as a punishment for their lack of revolutionary fervour.

As gently as he could, he established that Fouquert was, indeed, the leader. She started to curse softly, and then a stream of words tumbled out. He listened carefully as she detailed how Fouquert had abused her, the pain he inflicted and the contempt he had shown. When he was finished, he'd handed her over to some of his drunken supporters. The temptation to confront him with his guilt was strong. Would he smirk at this girl if she had a bayonet in her hand? It was an alluring image, but pointless, since Fouquert well knew what he'd done.

'Where did they go?'

The girl waved a hand in the general direction of Marseilles. 'They drove off the livestock, as well, leaving the two horses for their companions.'

'Who continued drinking,' Markham added, looking around.

'The arrival of your soldiers woke them from their snoring, but then they found they were trapped.'

'You will be safe now, that I promise you,' he said.

She turned to look at him, dark luminous eyes set in the round, full cheeks of a girl not fully grown. Her thick black hair was wet from washing, and hung down, framing her face in such a way as to make her look even more pitiful and forlorn. He stood upright, patting her gently on the shoulder before turning on his heel and walking out into the sunlit street. His men had hard tack, salt beef and water, all supplied by the *Hebe*. That would have to suffice for now.

He relieved Yelland, Halsey and Leech, sending them back to the inn, but not before issuing strict instructions regarding their behaviour. Halsey, the marine corporal, seemed a steady sort, a trifle old for service, but clearly conscientious. On rejoining his men he'd checked that they were all well before responding to the orders Markham had given. He had presumably got his stripes, either from Frobisher or some other officer, because he could be trusted. He felt instinctively that this man, with his rather paternal air, would ensure that no further harm came to the girl.

'Bury that dead man behind the paddock in a proper grave. The other one can go in the ditch. When he's had a rest, send Yelland back to find Schutte and Rannoch.'

'Aye, aye sir.' Halsey replied, in the first expression of proper discipline he had from any of the Lobsters.

Markham looked closely at the corporal, at the eyes trained to avoid expression. He had the dry skin of a man unlikely to enjoy fresh air, with a nose that was soft and well spread out. It looked like an appendage that had been hit several times. The pepper and salt hair was neatly tied in a queue at the back of his neck. With his stocky build, Halsey gave the impression that, despite his lack of inches, he might be a fighter.

'Have you served with the colours for a long time, Halsey?'

'Since I was breeched, sir. Started out as a drummer.'

'Why was Schutte made sergeant?'

Halsey hesitated for a second before replying. 'He's a hard man to argue with. That keeps the men in line, which is what most officers want.'

'What's the range of your muskets compared to Army issue?'

There was no enthusiasm in either voice or face as he

51

responded. 'We don't care about range at sea. It all comes down to seein' if you can hit something. If you can't you've got no notion of where the ball goes.'

'Carry on, corporal.'

'Sir.'

Markham watched him as he collected his men and marched down the hill, wondering what he was really like. The bland look he'd seen many times, a perfect one with which to address an officer, hinting at no personal opinion, saying he was quite prepared to agree to whatever was proposed, sensible or stupid. Schutte struck Markham as strong but dense, the kind of bully a lazy officer might elevate to keep discipline. But what really mattered was what both men were like in battle. In his experience, brains were often more valuable than brawn.

Having set the new piquet, he had a good look down the still deserted road. His problem was simple; it was the same behind as it was in front. There was no way he could hold this position against a determined assault with what he had at his disposal. Assuming the worst, which was the safest thing to do, he reckoned that the men under his command would behave poorly under fire. And he could expect no acts of individual initiative that exceeded self preservation. His real worry was that at the first assault they'd break and run, with him waving his sword uselessly in an attempt to stop them.

The sun glinted on something just as his advance guard started to run back towards him. He turned and called for his men to prepare, not impressed by the lack of any sense of purpose in the way they put aside their food and reached for their weapons.

'Coach, sir,' called the marine he'd sent up the road, while he was still thirty yards away. Then the man stopped, put his hands on his knees, and bent over to try and get his breath.

'Attention,' Markham shouted, and, as the man pulled himself upright, 'report to me properly.'

The man lifted his musket and marched towards him, his face contorted by the effort of breathing. Two paces from the officer, after a quick sideways glance at the two men behind him, he stopped and stood to attention.

'Coach, a big one. Pulled out that there gorge. The horses look knackered and he's having to whip them to keep them going.'

'Any sign of soldiers?'

'No, sir. Coach is on its own. Road's clear behind it.'

'Name?'

'Gibbons. Sir.'

He needed his spyglass, which was still in his own army trunk, back in the inn he'd stayed at in Chatham. All he could see was a cloud of dust, billowing around an indistinct shape.

'Will they make it up the hill, Gibbons?'

'Can't say they will, sir. They're struggling on the flat, from what I can see.'

Markham stood, in an agony of suspense, as the shape inside that cloud of dust took form. It was a big coach, the kind that rich men used, spacious inside, well sprung and comfortable. The lead horses' heads were bent forward as the whip played around their ears, with the pair behind in no better condition. The man on the box was relentless in his efforts to keep them in motion, and Markham fancied he could hear him swearing.

The crack of the shot was distant, but still clear, a very different sound from that of the driver's whip. It was followed by another. Markham glared at Gibbons, then searched the hills to each side, looking for telltale puffs of smoke, but nothing showed. The shots must be coming from behind the coach, which had just reached the bottom of the slight incline. But if they were, he couldn't see those firing them for the dust. In fairness to Gibbons, now standing rigidly to attention awaiting a tongue-lashing, he probably wouldn't have been able to see them either.

'In future, Gibbons,' he said calmly, 'I require you to be more careful in your reporting. Do you understand?'

'Sir!'

'Now get off the crest.'

Gibbons looked at him with surprise, before snapping his eyes back to the required position. Then he was gone. Markham paid him no heed, since he had a difficult decision to make. If that was the enemy shooting at that coach, then he should help those inside. But to do so too overtly would give away his position as well as his numbers, and thus sacrifice the only thing, surprise, that might hold an initial assault. He had to assume that whoever was in that coach would have the good sense to get out and walk if it ground to a halt. But without any idea how close the enemy was, they might get caught in the open without protection.

He ran back down to the dry stone walls, tallying off the first ten Bullocks. 'Up to the crest. Five men each side. Stay below the skyline, and that means the tops of your hats.'

They definitely hesitated, but it seemed that no one wanted to take a prominent position to question his orders. But the way they dragged their feet was infuriating.

'Damn you, move!' he yelled. 'At the double!'

He directed his men into position on either side of the road, fuming at the way they exaggerated their confusion. The sounds of shots mingled steadily with the crack of the whip, seeming to increase in tempo as the first pair of horses' heads came over the lip. The white foam of sweat streaked their bodies and even in the heat the steam rose from their backs. The tip of the whip cracked above their heads, the driver standing to egg them on. All four animals looked as if their legs were about to give way, just at the moment when the lead wheels were at the top of the rise. The driver, his own mouth flecked with foam, was yelling and swearing. He raised his hand to hit them once more when a bullet took him in the back. He fell sideways, his eyes suddenly looking into the clear blue sky, dropping into the gap between the horses' flanks and the coach, then rolling clear of the wheels and down the blind side of the hill.

The animals, no longer pressured to move, stopped dead, with the coach balanced right across the crest. Markham leapt forward, calling to Gibbons, as the only name he could remember, to come and assist him. He grabbed the bridle of the horse nearest him and hauled hard, dragging it reluctantly forward. Gibbons, responding to his shout, had the other one. Dornan had stood up to help and between them they got the wheels onto the downhill slope. The horses, now required to hold the weight, seemed set to sink to their knees, but a thump on their flanks produced a final surge of energy. A glimpse of the shaded interior showed him what appeared to be a family group, one male, two girls and a young boy, all looking fearful.

'Gibbons, get this damned thing down to the village and out of sight. The rest of you men, fall back to the stone walls.'

# Chapter five

The coach rattled down the hill, with several men hanging on to the traces. Lying on the crest, Markham took stock of the situation. The dust began to settle, revealing those who had been in pursuit. They had slowed to a walk, indicating it was a target of opportunity, not something they were actually pursuing. Within minutes an untidy column of infantry appeared, led by half a dozen officers, mounted and plumed. One was waving, earnestly, ordering the men out in front to get back into column of march. If that was his instruction, it was being comprehensively disobeyed by a group of soldiers who looked as if they were out for a Sunday stroll. That delayed the need for an immediate withdrawal, allowing him some time to contemplate the options.

It would be impossible to stop the increasing number of soldiers spilling out of the gorge, at least a whole regiment. But could he find a way to delay them? They were marching without skirmishers, which was certainly foolhardy. Such a lack of even the most basic reconnaissance could only mean one thing; they believed they had nothing before them but the terrified citizenry of Toulon. If they knew that Hood had taken over the port, they had no intelligence regarding his intentions, and were in ignorance of the fact that he was prepared to come out and fight.

If Markham stayed hidden, the undisciplined rabble out in front would just come on, forcing him to engage them, thus throwing away, very cheaply, the only good defensive position between here and the naval base. If

Elphinstone brought up enough reinforcements they could hold it. The French would then be obliged to mount a major assault to dislodge them. Reduced to basics, what he must do depended on the quality of the forces opposing him.

With only a fleeting glimpse of the French and their commanders, he had hardly enough on which to base a sound judgment. But instinct counted. It told him that he had a chance to inflict some casualties, and slow the main body down, if he could only surprise them. Lacking discipline, at the sight of a red coat they might just rush the crest en masse, in which case he'd be forced to run. But that same vision, so unexpected, might bring the whole column to a halt. Time might be expended while they prepared an attack, an interval that might allow Elphinstone to fulfil his promise.

Common sense dictated that he look beyond that possibility. Without more men, his detachment would have to pull back. Facing just infantry, he could hold them up in the village, making each building a redoubt that would need to be taken individually. But he'd also need room to effect an escape across the bridge and a hundred and fifty yards of open road. That couldn't be achieved against a commander brimming with confidence. The best way to ensure he lacked that was to induce caution from the very outset, which in turn, required him to be bold to the point of madness.

He slid back down the slope, standing up as soon as he was out of sight, gnawing on the various alternatives, which really came down to the best way to handle his divided command. His preferred method, of explaining what he was planning to attempt, a must with well-trained men, might backfire with this lot. Yet leaving them in the dark could prove worse. Even within their own groupings there was little common purpose.

Halsey had rejoined from the village, and was being interrogated by Schutte, with the Dutchman's finger regularly poking the corporal in the chest. 'Line up the marines,' Markham barked as he approached the pair, deliberately aiming his instructions at both men. Close to, Schutte's heavy frame dwarfed the older man. His small eyes, in a shaven skull that was almost square, held a hostile stare designed to let Markham know that he was the senior of the pair. There was an ugliness about the Hollander that spoke of the kind of belligerence which bordered on stupidity. It was there in the reclining forehead, a furrowed narrow strip, well defined despite his bald head, in the heavy lobes and fighter's flat nose.

'You're improperly dressed, Schutte,' Markham barked, forcing the Dutchman to put on the tricorne hat he carried, a headpiece which had a grey wig sewn inside. 'How's your knowledge of infantry tactics?'

Schutte looked blank, but Halsey replied with an eagerness that stood in sharp contrast to his previous attitude. 'We did a bit at Chatham. Not much, but enough to get the root of the thing.'

He suddenly remembered himself; the faint hint of enthusiasm disappeared, and the look he gave Schutte had a trace of supplication, designed to show that he was only trying to be helpful. Markham, addressing him, only increased his unease.

'Fine. I want you to get your men up here and line them up in column. We're going to march over that hill like a pack of fools, deploy halfway down the crest and take on all the appearance of men preparing to stand and fight. There's a French force coming up that road, with men out front who're more like a rabble than an army. I want to give them a fright.'

'I lead,' snarled Schutte.

'No,' Markham replied coldly.

'I sergeant!'

'Only if I say so. Rank is something you earn by soldiering, not by using your fists. Captain Frobisher is dead. It's me you have to satisfy. If you don't, I'll break you back to private.'

The implication was obvious, even to the slow-witted Hollander. If he didn't perform, Halsey would replace him. Markham was sure Schutte was feared rather than popular. Certainly Halsey, a marine to his fingertips, was afraid of him. Such a demotion, and the elevation of a better man, might do something for his own standing amongst the majority of the Lobsters. He turned his back on the pair of them to cut off further discussion.

'Carry on.'

The temptation to look round was hard to resist, since some form of drama was being played out behind his back. Schutte, if he wanted to assault him physically, couldn't do so in full view of the entire company. And Halsey, if he wished to decline the responsibility, could hardly make such a request to the back of his head. There was a pause, some hasty whispering, then the crunching of shoes as they moved away.

Markham waited till that faded before moving behind one of the stone walls to address the men of the 65th Foot. Quinlan and Ettrick, an inseparable pair of skinny individuals whose self-assurance troubled him, were playing cards with the slow-witted Dornan. They stopped for a moment, checking to see how he would react. He ignored them, his words aimed at Rannoch.

'On your feet, sergeant.'

He rose slowly, hatless, and looked his officer right in the eye. Markham observed that in a face that appeared to have suffered as much punishment as Schutte's, the result was very different. The thick blond hair, nearly white in the sunlight, helped. He had a larger forehead that made him look perceptive instead of stupid, a nose that was broad rather than flattened. Certainly the eyes were not dead like the Dutchman's. They were lively, questioning, carrying a look at that moment utterly lacking in subservience. Markham briefly explained the position.

'Your job is to march just far enough up the slope on

either side of the road to show your bayonets or your hats. I want the enemy to think there are troops hidden by the crest. If they do attack us, fall back to these walls, and keep out of sight.'

He pointed to the marines, beginning to line up. 'We're going to try and get the French to chase us over the crest. I want you to surprise them. As soon as you have a clear field of fire, I need you on your feet giving three rounds per minute of steady, well aimed musketry. Who knows, if it's poured into the head of their ranks we might even drive them back.'

'What if there are cavalry?' Rannoch asked.

'I haven't seen any.'

'That does not mean they are not about,' he replied, lifting his musket and cradling it in his thick forearms. Rannoch had a slow, measured way of speaking, words delivered in a lilting Highland voice that would have been quite pleasing if he'd shown any respect. Vaguely, Markham noted that his weapon was gleaming, the metal clean and the stock highly polished.

'If there were horse soldiers around, that fine head of yours would already be atop one of their sabres. And believe me, if I see any approaching, you'll have to run like the devil to catch me up. Forget cavalry and just think about stopping the infantry. The Lobsters and I will turn to support you as soon as we can. If you are forced back we will cover your retreat. Good luck.'

He chose to ignore the long slow sound of a derogatory fart, as well as the silent amusement it engendered, which emanated from the card school. The marines were ready, in an untidy column, with Schutte at the front. He took station at their head and issued the order to advance.

Their appearance, marching over the crest, had an immediate effect on the enemy, the first sign a ragged volley of musket fire from the rabble out front. Having delivered that, they ran back towards the main body, creating quite a commotion.

Sabre blades flashed in the leading enemy ranks as the marines formed a line, the flat of the French metal being used to suppress the confusion. A bugle blew, seemingly in vain, as the plumed officers dashed about trying to control their men. They got them in some kind of order, but there was no headlong rush to attack. Markham allowed himself a smile. He had every right to feel pleased. With no more than eighteen marines, including himself, facing a force that numbered something like three hundred men, he'd achieved his first aim, to halt the advance.

The French commander was surprised and clearly intended to treat them with respect, not sure if they were the whole force opposing him, or bait for a trap. He rode forward to extreme musket range, the gold that fringed his uniform coat flashing in the sun. Markham saw him point several times to the left and right of his position, indicating that Rannoch was doing what he'd been asked. He didn't dare turn round to confirm that, lest by doing so he nullify their efforts. The other officers gathered round their commander when he rode back, colourful plumes mixing to form a tricolour whole as they conferred.

After some fifteen minutes they dispersed, riding back to organise the first units of an attacking force, detaching what looked like half the regiment and bringing them forward. The untidy lines made them difficult to count, but Markham reckoned they numbered around two hundred men, which produced much fidgeting amongst the marines. His voice was loud but steady as he sought to calm them.

'You will stand until I order a retreat, d'you hear me now? Which means that you're going to have to face several volleys. I have no intention of trading fire with the enemy. Our task is to draw them on, hopefully in disorder. The men behind those walls are just waiting for a target to present itself. And just in case you're feeling shy,

I did tell them if it's a single marine they can practise on him.'

As the front rank of the French began to advance he noticed the big Dutchman edging his way backwards. 'Schutte, take station beside me. Halsey, you inspect the weapons, then take position on the left of the line.'

The corporal moved along the row of marines, checking that muskets were loaded and cartouches open. Before them, the broad column, six men wide, over thirty deep, began its approach. They moved off in the proper prescribed manner, at a slightly oblique angle, taking them to the left of the road, the sound of a drum beating out a tattoo that kept them in step. Even at this distance, without the aid of a telescope, he could see the variegated uniforms of his enemies.

Some wore green coats, others blue, with many barefoot, in torn striped breeches. A perfect example of the *levée en masse* conscripts, brainchild of Lazare Carnot, they gave every appearance of being untrained. But troops like these had beaten Brunswick at Valmy and the Austrians at Jemmapes. Only when they turned to face his men, and musket balls started flying, would he know their true quality.

The first stage of column order marching was simple, and told him little. Would they attempt to deploy from their present formation into a three-deep line, a manoeuvre only to be attempted with highly disciplined soldiers? He prayed not, since such tactics, performed with precision, given the consequent increase in the amount of fire that could be brought to bear on his small detachment, would annihilate them.

They could, of course, stay to his right, in an attempt to draw forward any forces on the reverse slopes. Or if Markham moved to cover them, establish that they didn't actually exist. The steep sides of the escarpment, given the numbers they faced, meant they could be outflanked, so they could be forced to withdraw without firing a shot, just to keep a safe distance. On the other hand, they could deploy into scaled-down columns of division, perhaps to a depth of around twenty men, extend themselves to their right astride the road and try to rush forward and overwhelm the redcoats.

The waiting was agony, the point of decision a matter of guesswork. But if they weren't going to turn, why did the officer at the head of the forward column, dressed in a black coat and wearing a tricolour sash, have his sword raised? And why was he waving his hat in the air above his head, using the red, white and blue feathers that adorned it to encourage his troops? Any command would be indicated by that same sword, and Markham watched it, holding his breath. On and on they came, the head of the column now well to the right of his position. The sword came down, sweeping to one side to aim at Markham's chest. He opened his mouth to order the retreat.

What happened then was so far from what was required that Markham nearly laughed. The column, its head now no more than a hundred yards away, became a jumbled, untidy mass of bodies, with only the leading two files showing any sign of holding their formation.

'Take aim on the extreme right of the line.' He waited while the muskets swung round, let the men steady themselves to compensate for the long range, then shouted: 'Fire!'

Smoke, cocooning the bright orange flashes, billowed from the line of guns. If the French infantry drill was a shambles, the marines' musketry wasn't much better. Partly, as Markham remembered from fighting in the Americas, it was the weapon itself. The heavy trigger tended to make men open their hand in order to aid the action of the forefinger. This gave full scope to the recoil, notorious on the Brown Bess. Fear of that inclined the firer to throw his head and body back at the very moment of discharge. Not trained to aim, they also shut their eyes to avoid the flash of the powder igniting in the pan, leaving the direction of the shot more of an accident than a design.

Against well-trained troops, in such superior numbers, it would have proved useless. It was luck that the French were worse than their opponents. The officer, who should have stayed upright, dropped to his knees. What little control he had of his unit evaporated completely, as they enveloped him, spilling right across the road. The Frenchmen knew they had to advance, but they did so as a rabble, which meant that their fire was erratic. Some fired off their weapons then turned back towards their own troops, as though their task were complete, crashing into the men still trying to come forward. Some seemed to be threatening to fight each other. Muskets which should have been aimed at the redcoats were discharged uselessly into the air. And those who bothered to reload were just as unco-ordinated, with each man stopping as he saw fit, and facing in every conceivable direction, to perform the necessary actions.

At least Markham was favoured in that respect. Whatever training his men had received, it had included ordered reloading. Halsey at one end, and Schutte beside him, called out the instructions, too slow to be perfect, but steady and effective, so that he could swiftly order another volley. Despite the confusion, the majority of Frenchmen were still edging forward. The range had closed, and the second salvo had a profound effect. Those shots that hit threw their victims back amongst their companions, adding stark terror to the already fearful turmoil.

For those which missed, the spurts of dust affected the front ranks while the cracking noise of passing balls confused the mob at the rear. They didn't halt, but they slowed to a crawl, exacerbated by their need to advance up the steadily increasing slope. For a moment Markham thought they might break and retire, a fantastic result given that he was outnumbered by more than ten to one.

Then the officer with the tricolour sash reappeared,

pushing his way through the throng to the front, belabouring everyone he could reach with the flat of his blade. His face was contorted with passion as he yelled at his troops to move forward, taking the lead himself, jamming his hat onto the tip of his blade and running at the hill. Markham had his sword raised again, waiting for the last of his men to present. One marine, faced with the line of screaming Frenchmen, dropped his weapon, which distracted those close to him. Fearing a general loss of cohesion, he gave the order, and as soon as the crash of the weapons subsided, yelled for his men to run.

The line of redcoats, never perfect, dissolved, as those with either quick wits or overwhelming fear headed first for the crest. The triumphant yells from the throats of their attackers drowned out both Markham's bellowing and their own cries of encouragement. Two of his men in the centre of the line, too slow to move, took the full force of the ragged French volley, their bodies spinning and dropping. One managed to get back to his feet and stagger on.

'Leave him, damn you,' Markham yelled, as he saw Halsey hesitate beside the still body. At the crest he stopped himself, waving his sword at the stragglers, an act which attracted its own response. He felt one ball tug at his sleeve, while the others whistled and cracked around him. His sword took one right on the tip and was knocked clean out of his hand. He was halfway back to the dry stone wall when the thought registered that the ball had come from behind him, knocking his blade towards the enemy, not away from them.

There was no time to ponder on that as he followed his men through the gap that ran between the road and the walls. There he span round to shout at the crouching soldiers. What he saw in their eyes made him hesitate for a split second. It was fear, of course, the sight of a mass of French soldiers spilling onto the crest, the shock of a threat now visible instead of imagined. It made no difference that the enemy was a rabble, nor that the redcoats were in a reasonable defensive position. As the numbers in front of them increased to fill the skyline, so did the apprehension, with several of his men beginning to inch backwards.

'Sixty-fifth, on your feet, present, fire!'

What followed made the marines look like marksmen. All the same faults were there, this time made worse by firing uphill with longer barrelled weapons. It was hard to tell if they'd taken aim at all, judging by the amount of earth they dislodged. But at fifty yards some found flesh, driving those struck by a ball into the arms of men only too willing to drag them back out of danger.

'Reload,' Markham yelled, as chips of stone exploded off the wall, the balls ricocheting skywards; a small fragment hit the top of his cheek, drawing an immediate flow of blood.

That reloading was a shambles, with some of the men leaning their muskets on the wall so that they could open cartouches that should never have been closed. Rams were dropped, the powder from the cartridges going everywhere but into the barrels, so that it seemed like an eternity before they presented for a second volley, with those that had shown more dexterity, forced to hold their fire, swearing at their mates.

Again, it was only the inexperience of the enemy that averted disaster. They'd halted, shaken more by the sight of extra redcoats than their musketry. The marines, with Halsey yelling at them, had formed up and come forward again, giving an impression of a solid line of defenders. The French officer tried to rally his troops for the final charge, just as the 65th's second attempt was released. As he turned, sword raised, a ball took him right between the eyes, with a force that threw him back like a rag doll, causing those around him to stop in shock.

Nothing in soldiering was worse than facing fire, without cover, when standing still. That, the very essence of successful infantry tactics, required steadfast reliance on a collective will not to give way. The French didn't have even an ounce of such discipline. Before their leader's body had stopped twitching, they began to retire, running over the crest, retreat degenerating into a rout before the last man was out of sight.

His men should have cheered, should have had him yelling at them to stand still as they ran forward to drive home their success. That didn't happen. The silence that descended was total. Markham took a musket from the man nearest him and made for the crest alone, feeling the eyes of both Lobsters and Bullocks boring into his back. The road before him was dotted with more than a dozen bodies. Some wounded men were stumbling back. The rest were still running, ignoring the officers who were trying to halt them.

He stepped forward to examine the one red-coated cadaver, now bleeding from dozens of bayonet wounds. It was a young face, probably unblemished before being struck by French gun butts, one that he had seen from time to time on the *Hebe*. But he didn't know the boy's name, and that made him feel ashamed. Returning to the rim of the hill he stooped and retrieved his sword, looked at it meaningfully before turning to face his troops. The body of the French officer was right at his feet, the red-rimmed hole in his head dead centre, side to side, eyebrows to hairline. Deliberate, it was a brilliant shot; certainly better than the one that had been aimed at him, and had only managed to hit his blade.

Order was, at last, driving out the chaos in the French ranks. Their commander had ridden amongst them to find out what had happened, shouting at the top of his voice. Within minutes Markham saw the first lines form up, taking up positions to recommence the advance. No columns now. The man who led them had learned his lesson. He had his men in open order, like skirmishers, and was waving his sword to bring them forward personally to the base of the rise.

'Back to the crest,' Markham shouted, 'on the double.'

They made the French pay for the top of that hill, each man firing individually, with Markham moving amongst them, trying to encourage them to fire properly. A battlefield was no place for such instruction, even if he'd been capable of providing it, but the marginal improvement he managed was shown by the number of dead Frenchmen whose bodies were added to those that already littered the plain.

His frustration grew with every glance he threw back along the empty road to Toulon. And all the time French troops were arriving, debouching out of the narrow gorge onto the open ground, enough men to walk through his small detachment without raising a sweat. He had no idea what made them hesitate, his sole object being to stay were he was until the inevitable happened and he was forced to withdraw. As soon as the first artillery arrived, he was obliged to do so anyway. Only two six-pound field pieces, they were enough to make his position untenable, since without return fire they could adjust their range at their leisure, and fire case shot over the crown of the hill to kill men on the opposite side.

They had to abandon the dry stone wall as well. With the guns moved up and a spotter to guide their fire, they could become a death trap of flying rock splinters. He'd swapped positions with the French commander. Now Markham would be unable to see any developing assault on the reverse slope. He ordered everyone back to the edge of the village, and began to distribute them in small packets throughout the three houses which had walls facing the west. Holes were knocked through the soft masonry for each musket.

To each group, his instructions were the same. 'Make sure you have plenty of water. Eat now, because once they settle themselves on that hill, unless we're seriously reinforced, you'll have to be ready to retire. When the time comes, fall back to the well and I will allocate you new positions. When we get to the last houses and there's no more cover, you're to run for the gully where I left Schutte and Rannoch.'

He went back to the inn, stopping only to watch the artillerymen on the hill. They were hacking grooves in the rim that would act as an embankment, allowing them to fire on Ollioules undisturbed, destroying the buildings while lessening the risk to themselves of suffering from return fire. It would be a time-consuming business, requiring a rampart on the back slope to contain the recoil. Clearly the officer in command was prepared to indulge them, and had decided against a second infantry assault. He wanted to blast the redcoats out of the village, prepared to destroy the whole place rather than face the casualties house-to-house fighting might entail.

The coach stood outside the inn, horses removed from the shafts, the sweat on their bodies dried to a white line. Heads lowered, they munched greedily at the bale of hay that had been spread at their feet. Entering the interior, he was surprised at the heat. With the sun full up the room was no longer cool; instead it was warm and stuffy. He found Celeste in conversation with a small, rather plump man, red-faced and perspiring under his wig. His cheeks were half covered with a large white handkerchief, already limp from the amount of sweat it had been required to absorb. As her eyes strayed past his shoulder, he span round to face the British officer.

'Monsieur,' he cried, throwing up his hands. 'Is it true that Toulon has surrendered to your Admiral?'

'Yes.'

'Then I require you to instruct this wretch to surrender to me her horses.'

'It's not my place, sir.'

'I must get my passengers to Toulon.'

'If you've looked at the horses you're asking for, you might decide you'd be better off walking.'

'I have a child with me, who is delicate.' The man paused for a second before continuing. 'Not to mention my daughters.'

'If you were running from the revolutionaries, I must tell you that they could be here within the hour.'

'Do you not intend to stop them?'

'I don't have the means. They have artillery and numbers. I have neither.'

'Then it is even more imperative that we get away.' He gestured towards the doorway. 'You will have observed my own animals. They will require to be rested. I can only proceed by using two for a short time.'

Markham turned to the girl. 'Celeste. What I just said is true. And I don't have any reason to suppose the men who are going to take over the village have any more respect for property than those renegade sailors who came here earlier.' That produced a sudden look of alarm. 'In fact, you'd be better off in Toulon, as well.'

She searched his face then, as if to ensure that he was telling the truth. The older man, wiping his brow with his handkerchief, missed her quick nod of consent.

'I must insist.'

'I think, sir, if you offer to take this young lady with you, she might agree to let you have them.'

He looked her up and down then, taking in her bruised face, as well as the badly mended rips in her dull-coloured dress. 'I cannot consent to have such a filthy creature mix with us. We are people of some quality.'

'Then they shall have to walk, after all.'

'Oh, all right,' he snapped. 'If it must be so, I can be consoled that the journey is short. Can you provide me with one of your men to drive them?'

'No sir, I cannot. You will just have to drive them yourself, which will at least spare you the need to share the interior with this girl you so loosely refer to as a wretch.'

# Chapter six

The bombardment started sooner than Markham had hoped, the first ranging shots dropping well short of the buildings that edged the village, with each succeeding salvo creeping ever closer. The baking, midday heat had killed what little breeze had existed. But now, in the late afternoon, the air began to stir again. Soon the first house, on the very edge of the village, was hit, sending up a great cloud of dust as the walls were breached.

There was only one way to stop them: attack, and either take the guns or force them to limber up and withdraw. Outnumbered, that was not an option. To leave men in position when they could not return fire was absurd, so he began to pull out those who stood in greatest danger, leading them out through the village to the ancient stone bridge and instructing them to make for the last defensive position.

Despite his best efforts, this evacuation didn't go unobserved. One of the guns was elevated to fire over Ollioules on to the road leading back to Toulon. The first shot struck lucky, an inspired guess, given that the gunner couldn't actually see the target. He caught the heavy coach just as it cleared the end of the bridge. The shot hit the road, bounced under the body, narrowly missed the spring and struck the wheel on the point at which it was fixed to the axle. The wheel flew off and the coach dropped sideways, tilting at an acute angle. The horses, scared by the noise, reared up, pawing the air in a frantic bid to get clear. The old man, who was no great shakes at horse driving, was tipped off the box to land heavily on the roadway.

Markham ran forward and dragged the door open, calling frantically for the occupants to get out. If the French fired another salvo at the same range they might score a direct hit. He was greeted by two women screaming their heads off, Celeste sobbing quietly and a calm boy of about twelve, handsome and pale, who seemed totally oblivious to the mayhem going on around him. Reaching in he grabbed the heavier of the two women, and hauled her forward, fighting the desire to curse her as she resisted. He heard the swish of the balls as they passed, ducking instinctively as they struck the road some forty yards ahead. The gun layer, unable to see the effect of his first shot, had raised the range, hoping to catch the fleeting defenders.

'Sortez, Madame. Vite!'

Halsey and a couple of his soldiers had helped the man to his feet and brought him to assist. With a strength that surprised him, Markham was barged out of the way, which broke the grip he'd taken on the lady's wrist. Her resistance collapsed in the face of parental commands, as the older man yelled at her. Meekly she allowed herself to be led out on to the road, followed by the others. Markham was briefly conscious of the other girl, the slim one. Her face, especially white with fright, was rather pretty. Then good sense, combined with pressing danger, overbore his inclinations. The last person to alight was the young boy.

'Get them off the road.'

'Somebody's coming,' said Halsey, in a voice that had Markham looking towards Ollioules in panic. 'Not that way, sir, the way we came.'

Looking down the Toulon road, he saw the men pulling the guns, teams of sailors on long lines with nine-pounder naval cannon, still on their carriages, lashed to carts. Elphinstone appeared on a horse, kicking it to get ahead of his men. De Lisle was behind him, also mounted, though somewhat less secure in the saddle. A deep file of marines, in all about two hundred men, who brought up the rear, were ordered to halt by their officers.

'What are you about, man?' de Lisle yelled at Markham, driving his mount forward to pass Elphinstone.

'We were withdrawing, sir.' The sound of cannon fire, which had resumed the assault on the opposite side of the village, made him pause. 'Without artillery we couldn't hold, and the French have at least a thousand infantry.'

'Spotted Dick' looked at Elphinstone, stony faced and clearly displeased, before replying. 'You've got guns now. Might it be an idea to turn around and get back where you came from?'

Markham ignored his captain, concentrating instead on the Scotsman. Elphinstone's manner had changed, judging by the look he was giving the foot soldier. At their previous meeting he'd been brusque, but not unfriendly. Now he was glowering at Markham as though he and not the French were the enemy. De Lisle, of course, would have told him who he was dealing with.

'Most of my men are still in Ollioules, sir. With those guns set up I can go ahead and signal the range from the church.'

De Lisle answered again. 'Captain Elphinstone has fetched up a midshipman to do that job.' He gestured to a youngster who stepped forward and produced a blue flag, then a red one. A mere stripling of about fifteen, with a spotty, sweating face, he stood very erect as Elphinstone gave him his orders.

'Driberg. Up into that excuse for a church tower, laddie, so we can see you. Red to increase, blue to reduce, and both flags crossed to show on target.'

'Aye, aye, sir,' replied Driberg, as he ran off to comply.

'I'll get my men into position.'

'I should damned well hope so, Markham,' snapped de Lisle, his colourless face carrying an expression of manufactured shock. 'I wouldn't want the reputation of the *Hebe* dented by a want of application on the part of the man in charge of my marines.'

'I want those Frenchmen running this time, not you,' added Elphinstone, his voice every bit as unfriendly as his countenance. 'Spotted Dick' favoured his fellow captain with a thin smile of approval.

Stung, Markham replied with real anger. 'We drove them back once, before they brought up the cannon.'

De Lisle's disbelief was very evident. And inexplicable, in a situation where he could have claimed some credit, the defenders being from his ship. 'Over a thousand men?'

'They were no more than a single regiment then.'

'That's just as well,' barked Elphinstone, 'otherwise we'd probably have met you on the outskirts of Toulon several hours ago. Take the marines I've brought up through the village and deploy them on the other side as soon as the guns open fire. Wait for me, and their own officers, there.'

He swung his horse round before Markham could respond, calling to the other marine officers, both captains, to send their men after Markham, and attend on him to confer. The leading sailors had come abreast and Elphinstone ordered them to halt. They spun the carts and tipped them so that the guns could be run down onto the hard packed earth of the road. Others were unloading shot and powder, while still more were fixing up a wooden brake that would act to contain the recoil. Someone, who was able to see far enough down the road, had told the French gunners about these reinforcements. They lifted their range again, trying to hit the column of redcoats who were now passing the naval gunners.

'Corporal Halsey, round up our men as best you can and get them back through the village.'

'You'd better tell us how matters are placed over yonder,' demanded Elphinstone. Markham explained to the assembled officers the position of the guns, plus the theory that the enemy infantry were probably deployed on the reverse slope waiting to attack.

'Which they will do immediately you open fire, sir. There's no advantage to them now in keeping their infantry out of the action. I would . . .'

He got no further, and the way Elphinstone responded brought a real, full-blooded smile to de Lisle's lips. 'Don't try to teach me to suck eggs, laddie, just get on with the orders you've been given.'

Markham flushed angrily as Elphinstone turned his back on him again. But hierarchy demanded he bite his tongue, salute and obey. The marines' column from Toulon was ahead of him, and he ran to catch up. The cannon were in place as he left, and with a precision that would have shamed the gunners of the *Hebe*, they were loaded and made ready to fire, booming out just as he re-entered the village. He had a vague impression of faces cowering in a doorway, and called to Halsey to find out who they were.

'That frog and his women. He wouldn't go the right way. Said he felt safer in a house.'

'The man's an idiot.'

Once the two batteries engaged he began to form up the men on the Marseilles road, marching them into the open as soon as Elphinstone's cannon began to range. At the first shots, the French commander moved what infantry he'd deployed back from the crest. Self preservation demanded that, regardless of the tempting target assembling in front of them, the French gunners ignore the infantry and try and destroy the opposing cannon. But they were outclassed both in the rate of fire and its accuracy, as the British guns, ranged from the church tower by Midshipman Driberg, steadily removed their protective earthworks.

The first balls, falling short, hit the stone walls, sending deadly showers of broken rock whizzing around the artillerymen's ears. The next was closer, sending up great clods of earth that hung suspended in the light of the fading western sun. The third salvo overshot, landing on the reverse slope that, Markham guessed, would be full of French soldiers. Driberg signalled the reduction and the naval guns at last found the range, landing right on the crest of the hill and blasting it apart. Several balls seemed to hit together, just to the right of one of the French cannon, taking with it several tons of their protective earth. When the dust settled Markham could actually see the men working the cannon. But they weren't loading shot into the muzzle, they were frantically throwing their equipment onto the limber.

Markham looked back, but could see no sign of Elphinstone, de Lisle or the other marine officers. If they were still behind the guns they were now in the wrong place, negating any advantage the bombardment had given them. Having made the French run once, here was a chance to do so again, by retaking the crest before they brought up their infantry to defend it. Driberg had certainly spotted them pulling out, and had shown the red flag to increase the range. The balls from the naval guns were landing out of view, behind the French artillery, perhaps cutting swathes through their supporting infantry.

The long black snouts disappeared, withdrawn to their horse teams to be taken out of danger. He was desperate to attack, well aware that would be taking the kind of risk that would see him broken if he failed. These men were not his to command. They had their own officers, still on the other side of the village, who would be furious if he presumed to lead their detachments into battle. But everything he'd ever learned, added to what he'd already observed during the day, convinced him that he was right, that the time was now, or never. That to adhere too strictly to the chain of command would throw away a golden opportunity. His tongue, which had been dry before, felt like leather now as he issued his orders.

'Bayonets!'

The deadly lengths of steel, eighteen inches long, scraped out of their scabbards at his command, to be fixed to the front of nearly two hundred hot muskets. He looked along the line, trying without much success to identify his own men in the fading light. His sword was up, and as it dropped he stepped forward, which set the whole extended line into motion. All that was missing as they marched up the slope was the sound of a drum to control their pace: that, and any hint of musket fire from the top of the hill.

The defenders, expecting to occupy a safe position, arrived when they were twenty feet from the crest, strung out in a long line. The shock when they saw the marching redcoats was palpable, a ripple in their ranks which was underlined by a moan that sounded like a collective cry of fear. Markham's command to halt and present was crisply obeyed, in sharp contrast to that of the enemy silhouetted against the last vestige of the sinking sun, thrown by sight of the thin red line. The single volley of musket fire, delivered within five seconds, cut the French to ribbons.

'Charge!'

As he crested the ridge, stepping over writhing bodies, for the second time that day, Markham saw the enemy in full retreat. The whole field in front was a milling mass of scruffy men, many surrounding the guns, the drovers frenziedly lashing the animals in an effort to break through the crush. Those retreating down the hill had infected the men to the rear, most of whom could not even know what they were running from. But fear gripped them just the same, and nothing the officers could do stemmed the tide. The temptation to pursue them was strong. But it had to be resisted.

About twenty yards from the rim, a trio of Frenchmen were staggering along, the individual in the middle hanging on to his companions, clearly wounded. Some of his men began to fire at them, which sent up spurts of earth around their feet, bringing them to an abrupt halt. Markham called on them to cease fire as the small party turned to face death. The wounded man, an officer of artillery, was injured in the groin, with blood covering the entire lower half of his body. Markham waved his sword to indicate that they could proceed without danger.

'It would be nice to let them know we've won, lads,' he shouted, as the trio turned again and staggered off.

This time there was a proper cheer to celebrate the victory. Looking round and smiling, Markham saw, out of the corner of his eye, the flash of red behind him. The men of the 65th were meandering up to the crest, obviously having taken no part in the advance. Somebody must have either heard or seen the horses, since they broke into a run as Elphinstone and 'Spotted Dick' appeared, and so joined the main body before the navy.

'You were ordered to wait, Markham,' barked de Lisle. 'Do you know the meaning of the word?'

Behind him, Markham could see the two marine captains, rushing up the hill to join them. Judging by the looks on their faces they were no more pleased than their superiors.

'If I had, we would have lost the advantage. And since we stand on the crest with the enemy in full retreat, sir, I submit that my appreciation was correct.'

'Your appreciation,' Elphinstone spluttered.

'Having already fought them, sir, I knew their calibre. Thankfully, it was even easier than the previous encounter.'

Elphinstone scowled, unsure if he was being goaded, examining the terrain and the enemy strength as a way of avoiding the look of certainty in Markham's eye. There wasn't really much that he could say, given the undoubted success his small force had achieved. The French had slowed down, still fleeing, the only thing holding up the rout the narrow entrance to the gorge.

Elphinstone pointed at them. 'How long is that gorge ahead?'

'I don't know, sir,' Markham replied. 'We had neither the time, nor the strength, to find out.'

'Pity,' he replied, though he made it sound the precise opposite. 'Holding that, we'd have avoided a fight altogether.'

Markham was seething, judging this to be just the usual 'Johnny come lately' attitude of a man determined to pick holes. He could have, and no doubt would have, led the charge up the hill himself if he'd arrived sooner.

'And if we'd failed, sir, we would have found ourselves retreating across the only piece of true open ground for miles. In which case I doubt I'd be here talking to you now.'

Elphinstone flushed furiously, and glared at his fellow captain. 'You allow your officers too much freedom, de Lisle.'

'With respect, sir, I do not,' de Lisle snapped back. Then, seeming to have realised his mistake, his voice softened immediately. Clearly, if the Scotsman chose to rebuke him, it was because he had the power to do so. 'I will not be called to answer for those the Admiralty foists on me. I am accustomed to choosing my own officers, and I can assure you, had I been indulged, I would not have the likes of Lieutenant Markham aboard my ship.'

Elphinstone nodded, seemingly mollified, as though the person referred to was elsewhere, and that little speech explained everything. He sat silently for almost a minute, before speaking again. 'Dig in here for the night, Markham. I'll take my marines back with me to continue work on the perimeter defences around Toulon. I'll send another officer, and orders, at first light.'

They should have relieved him and his men, leaving some of the others they'd brought up in their place. But insolence had its price and Markham was paying for his. He considered arguing, but put it aside, knowing that he couldn't plead. But he did know that for the next twelve hours he had precious little strength if anything developed.

'If you leave the guns, sir . . .'

He got no further, Elphinstone shaking his head as though the proposition were stupid. 'Of course I can't leave the guns, man. We need to get them in position to defend the town.'

'Then I must warn you, sir, that I may be forced to abandon Ollioules.'

'We will be doing that anyway, Markham. What you've seen today is only the advance guard of the Armée de la Bouche de Rhône. The rest are to the rear, some fifteen thousand men, who left Marseilles this very morning.'

'Spotted Dick' produced one of his humourless smiles. 'Fifteen thousand men. I don't think even your brand of insubordination will hold that number.'

'There's another French army,' Elphinstone added, 'from Savoy, approaching from the east, which makes any position outside the Toulon perimeter untenable. But the longer we keep this lot away from the port the better.'

'I'm sorry, laddie,' he continued, though he signally failed to sound so. 'All we've bought here is a wee bit of time.'

'Come, sir,' said de Lisle, giving Elphinstone an admiring look that lit up even his bland face. 'Let's not be too self-deprecating. You must admit that you have fought a brilliantly successful action, given your limited means. The enemy, a superior force, have been compelled to withdraw.'

This piece of outrageous flattery was taken without a blush. Markham, already displeased, was made doubly so. Again, their own captain didn't see fit to praise the men from the *Hebe*. Clearly Elphinstone was well above him on the Captains' list. More than that he had influence, so much that de Lisle was prepared to absorb a rebuke, even to grovel in order to gain some regard.

The object of this sycophantic praise called out his commands as he swung round on his horse. His marines fell in smartly behind him and marched off in his wake. De Lisle followed, leaving Markham's small party of just over thirty men in possession of the hill.

The sun dropped lower, with the sky, indigo above their heads, turning gold behind the limestone crags. 'Entrenching tools. Schutte, get a party together and carry the French wounded and dead down to the bottom of the hill. They'll want a truce, and we can't let them see how few in number we are. Halsey, tally off four men. I want a piquet to the rear just in case they try and slip some men round behind us. Rannoch, get some fires ready, enough to make it look as though we're still here in strength.'

'I don't quite get the lingo, sir,' said Yelland, who, with his piping voice, sounded even more youthful than he looked. 'But I think he's after some help to fix his wheel.'

'Why, in the name of God, didn't they go with Elphinstone?'

'What do you want me to do about it?'

Markham, who'd lain back to rest by the dry stone wall, pulled himself to his feet, slapping at his uniform and sending forth a cloud of brown dust into the warm evening air. 'I'm not even sure it can be repaired,' he said.

'It's not as bad as all that,' Yelland replied eagerly. 'I had a look. The ball took the wheel off clean enough and only one of the spokes is stove in.' His eyes dropped as Markham stared at him, the look full of curiosity. Yelland, when he spoke again, adopted a defensive tone. 'He offered money for to have it done.'

Markham laughed, which surprised the youngster, who'd prepared himself for at least a verbal drubbing, if not two dozen lashes. 'Well you deserve something for all that running you did today. Make sure you charge a decent fee.'

'Thank you, sir.'

They began to walk down the hill, watched by the men Markham had set to stand the first sentry duty. The last of the light was fading, with a promise of a clear starlit night ahead, one so bright that it should preclude a surreptitious approach by the enemy. They, having retrieved their dead and wounded, had moved forward again, and were now encamped across the Marseilles road.

'Tell me, Yelland, how did you come to be in the regiment?'

'No choice, your honour,' he replied, without embarrassment. 'It was that or transportation.'

'For what?'

'A bit o' fish poaching. Went back to the same spot too often. Thought the bailiff was as stupid as me.'

Markham laughed, with just a trace of bitterness. 'I doubt you're alone amongst the Hebes.'

'I ain't, sir,' he replied, adding a sneer. 'And don't you let those Lobsters fool you, neither. They're as destined for the fires of hell as the rest of us.'

They entered the inn, to find the family gathered round a table, eating from the supplies they'd brought in the coach. Judging by the feast before them they'd been determined not to starve. There were hams and cold chicken, beef and pork, fresh looking bread and ample wine. Celeste, now dressed in a cleaner, less tattered frock, stood in the background, her eyes ranging hungrily over the laden table.

'Lieutenant, you will join us, I hope,' said the father, beaming, his hand sweeping over the food.

The women at the table nodded in agreement, while the boy stared straight ahead. Then the Frenchman saw Yelland, who'd stopped in the doorway, and he gave the soldier an inquiring stare. Markham, for the first time, had a chance to look at him properly; a squat, thick-set individual, his high colour was exaggerated by the candlelight, and quite probably by the amount of wine he'd consumed. He had lost his wig when he came off the box, and the close-cropped hair made his cheeks look much fatter.

'I have not introduced myself, monsieur.' He bowed his head as he continued, 'Guillaume Rossignol. Will you oblige me by a loan of some of your soldiers to repair my wheel?'

'Loan, sir? I understood you'd offered to pay hard money.'

The split-second pause was enough to establish that he'd hoped to avoid the charge. Markham lifted his eyes to Celeste, standing in the shadows, her hands clasped together in front of her, as though she were cold. She'd brushed her hair, which made her look even younger than she had earlier.

'I certainly hope you've paid for the use of this table.'

Rossignol's eyes swung round, to look in the same direction. His voice, when it boomed out a reply, had an air of falsehood. 'Of course, before we depart.'

'I think she would prefer to be paid out in kind,' said Markham, looking at the food on the table. 'If you can't spare the victuals, then she may have that you wish to bestow on me.'

'Come, sir, there is enough for everyone.' The two men stared at each other for a moment, Rossignol's eyes taking on a sad look. 'I have offended you, Lieutenant, have I not?'

He held up his hand to stop Markham replying, which was unnecessary, since the Irishman had no intention of doing any such thing. 'Please don't deny it. I've been thoughtless and you have, quite properly, checked me for it. Girls, a plate of food for this unfortunate, with some wine if she wishes it.'

That had Markham raising an eyebrow. Only a few hours before he had referred to Celeste as a wretch. His eyes took in the rest of the family as the girls complied, with their father fussing at them to add more to the plate. None shared common features. The elder daughter was plump, quite heavily powdered with dark brown eyes. But the other, whom he'd caught the briefest glimpse of earlier, had her father's blue eyes, his fair skin, and was fortunately free from any trace of his bulk. Indeed, as she half stood to fill the plate, he could see that she was slim and graceful. Earlier, she'd worn a cloak. Now, her low-cut dress revealed a becoming décolletage. Her sister, with a greater endowment of flesh and a similarly low-cut garment, looked overblown. Both girls had smooth hands, and showed an elegance in their movements that denoted a decent upbringing.

Rossignol, satisfied that their work was progressing properly, turned back to Markham, and observed the direction of his gaze. 'And here I find I have failed to introduce my daughters, Eveline and Pascalle.'

Since both curtsied in unison, he had no idea who answered to which name. He was just about to blurt out the question when Yelland, who had not understood a single word of the exchange, coughed loudly to remind them of his presence.

'Tell Sergeant Rannoch to light the fires,' he snapped. 'You can then start work on the coach. I'll see you get your fee.'

'It'll take a few of the lads, sir.'

'I'm sure there'll be enough payment to go round.'

As Yelland left Markham swung his eyes back to the table. Rossignol was beaming at him, which might mean that he'd noted the confusion. So he looked at the boy sitting at the end of the table: pale-skinned, expression-less of face, he had large luminous brown eyes which were utterly uninterested in his surroundings.

'Jean-Baptiste, a friend of the family, Lieutenant,' said Rossignol. 'Whom we have taken under our wing for protection. I'm afraid that recent events in his life have affected him. He is, you will observe, rather witless.'

'Deaf?'

'No. Nor dumb. Just cocooned in a world of his own.'

The pretty daughter had taken the heaped plate, plus a cup of wine, to Celeste, who looked like a waif by comparison. As she turned to come back she raised her eyes and smiled at Markham. At the same moment, Rossignol solved the problem of her identity.

'Thank you, Eveline. You have helped to save your father from being a boor. Now I must apologise to our guest, and hope that he will allow that panic can affect a man's natural behaviour. Come Lieutenant, join us. You must, after such resounding victories, be famished.'

Markham might have said something modest if the words had produced a look of admiration from Eveline. He sat down opposite, accepting a cup of wine without taking his eyes off her. That earned him another smile, repeated several times as her father explained to his distracted guest how they had come to be here.

'The murder of the King was a tragedy, and I cannot tell you how much I fear for the poor Queen. Separated from her children these last months and kept alone in a cell, she is constantly threatened with a similar fate. If an entire nation could be consigned to hell, that punishment would fit such a crime. Those madmen in Paris wished to kill any person of quality, especially those who owned land.'

'The newspapers in England have reported every gory detail, monsieur. And since you are fleeing, in such a handsome coach and with such elegant creatures, you are, I presume, at risk.'

The words were addressed to both women, but he made sure that Eveline knew they were intended for her.

'Certainly, monsieur, though not because of my personal worth. I am a maître, a lawyer, who had the good fortune to represent some of the most elevated families in France. I had hoped that my daughters would give a lustre to our family that I could not gain myself.'

'They are certainly lustrous enough, monsieur,'

Markham replied, which produced a bowed head from Eveline and a simpering response from her sister.

'You are most gallant,' said their father.

The door crashed open as Halsey burst in. His face, instead of being the smooth visage Markham remembered, was lined with worry. 'There's men moving down through the hills behind us!'

Markham's wine went flying as he jumped to his feet. 'Have the French outflanked us?'

'I don't think it's soldiers. They ain't fired off a single shot. They don't want to be spotted, I reckon. And they're dressed wrong. It might be them deserters. All I know is there's a rate of 'em. I left Leech and the others to keep an eye out.'

Celeste shuddered just as he said the word 'deserters'. Rossignol had gone pale, and his daughters had their hands to their mouths. Markham was cursing himself for a fool. He'd forgotten to mention deserters to Elphinstone. Not that it would have made much difference. The Scotsman's opinion of him, since their original meeting, had been reshaped by de Lisle. Both men would probably have dismissed such information as irrelevant. It was anything but now.

'Tell Rannoch, if he's lit those fires, to douse the damn things. He's to pull the men off the crest and get them back down into the village. And Halsey, inform them that this is no time for anything other than their very best. If they fall into the hands of these fellows, they could end up suffering the fate of this girl's father.'

# Chapter seven

The night, apart from the sound of the crickets, had been silent. But it came alive as the first shot was fired by one of the marines Halsey had left behind. Markham cursed the uncertainty that left him unsure of where to go. He needed to both see the threat and try to evaluate it, but he also had to be sure that those dug in on the hill facing west obeyed quickly the instructions he'd sent with the marine corporal. Exiting from the village he came across Yelland, Dornan, Quinlan and Ettrick. They'd stopped work on the coach and, alerted by Halsey, were staring in the direction of this new hazard.

'Yelland, get that damned thing fixed if you can. We might need it to get the women out of here.'

He passed on, pulling out his pistol before cutting up into the hills to the northern side of the Toulon road, tracing the path he'd used earlier to set the guard. The noise of a large party, seemingly oblivious to any threat to their safety, floated over the night air. The clink of a bayonet scabbard, a few feet away, alerted him to the presence of the men Halsey had left to shadow them. Kneeling down he called out 'Hebe', which was returned from a point just to his left. Looking closely he could barely make out the crossed white bands of the marine uniform.

'To me,' he whispered. The man slithered over immediately.

'It's Leech, sir.'

'How many are there?'

'Hundreds of the buggers, and not a bit bothered

about noise an' the like. It's as if they don't know we're here.'

'Did you see if they were armed?'

'They looks to have muskets and pikes. If you get close enough you can see them set against the night sky.'

Markham went forward, half crouched, till he could observe for himself what he meant. The French were using the top of the hill to make their way, their numbers more obvious by the noise rather than anything he could actually see. But he did observe the silhouetted weaponry attached to each human form. According to Fouquert (who, to spare the ladies blushes, had been tied up in the back room of the inn), the revolutionary sailors had escaped with everything they needed to fight. He was nagged by several questions. Having taken to the hills, why were they now coming back down to the valley? Did they know about his detachment holding the village? Perhaps, having seen Elphinstone withdrawing, they assumed the road to be clear. But then why not use it?

'When sorrows come,' he said quietly to himself, 'they come not single spies, but in battalions.'

'What?' asked Leech, who had sidled up to join him.

'Nothing. Where are the other men?'

'In the bushes right in front of you,' the marine replied, in a manner which was well short of that required for a ranker addressing an officer. But this was not the place to reprimand him, nor was there time. The landscape ahead, narrowing into the steep-sided valley, meant that these French sailors would have to descend to the road soon to pass through Ollioules. They couldn't do so without discovering his presence, and since the British were behind them, and freedom lay to the west, it was very likely that they would fight. That would leave him trapped between two forces, in a situation where the noise of one battle could very well alert the army encamped on the Marseilles road.

There was no reason to assume that these men would prove any better than their fellow countrymen. But, if they were French sailors, they had one thing the soldiers lacked, and that was a purpose born of desperation. The ill-trained men who'd set out to march to Toulon had the option to withdraw to relative safety. These sailors could not. Security for them lay beyond those who would oppose them, which would make their attempts to break through more dangerous. And he was going to be faced with a defensive night action commanding men who'd shown scant ability to either comprehend or obey his orders in full daylight.

'Gather the men,' he whispered, 'and follow me back down the track. When we get down to the road, double back to the village and find Halsey. Tell him, if he hasn't managed it already, that he has about twenty minutes to carry out my last instructions.'

It was hard to know what alerted the French. A clink of metal, or the flash of something bright? One man, closer than the rest, shouted and that was taken up by the others. Suddenly there was a hail of muskets balls flying about British ears.

'Hebes! Out of here. Move!'

Markham shouted as he stood upright, firing off his pistol wildly, more for effect than with the hope of actually hitting anyone. Then he turned and ran, vaguely aware of the slithering sounds of his own men right at his heels. There was a sudden cry of alarm, which quickly turned to pain, that overlaid by the sound of a fall and a bone breaking. Markham stopped as another marine cannoned into him, knocking him into a thick bush that scratched as much as it supported him. He shot out a hand and grabbed at a second Lobster running past, hauling him up short.

'Who's down?'

'God knows,' the marine panted, the whites of his panic-stricken eyes very obvious in the moonlight.

'We can't leave him, not after what they did to that poor sod who owned the inn.'

They heard the whimpering as soon as they stopped talking, faint over their heaving breath. Markham pulled the reluctant marine up the slope towards the sound, ears tuned to the noise of their pursuers crashing through the undergrowth above them.

'Fire off your musket,' Markham said as they found the fellow who'd been injured.

'I can't see no-one.'

'Just do it, man, never mind if you hit anything!'

The whimpering, as he knelt down, was drowned out by the crash of the Brown Bess over his head. From above them came a cry of pain as the ball took someone. Suddenly the sound of pursuit ceased, a brief respite while the French checked that they were not in danger too. Markham grabbed the wounded Lobster's musket and fired it through the scrub. There was no sound of it hitting flesh and bone, but it produced many an anguished cry as the Frenchmen vied to tell each other to stay low, that they were at risk, and to call out to their special friends for reassurance.

'Take my arm,' Markham said to the man on the ground, vaguely aware that the other marine was reloading. When he leant forward he realised that it was Leech.

'Can't walk. Leg's gone,'

'Then I'll have to damn well carry you,' he hissed. 'Take my bloody arm.'

As the man complied the musket above him crashed out again, producing another series of shouts. He couldn't be sure if he'd heard right, but it seemed to him that several of their pursuers had identified not only their position, but now knew that they were only facing one weapon. The shouts were changing from those urging caution to others calling for a renewed attack, with only the fear of being first acting as a brake to their efforts.

Markham hauled hard to raise the marine, and once he was upright lifted him on to his shoulder.

'Stay at my back,' he gasped, to the other man.

They stumbled down the hill, slithering and sliding on the bone-dry, rock-covered scree. As they emerged on to the roadway, Markham emitted a breathless curse. Ahead, on the road, stood a milling group of the enemy. Some of his pursuers, who'd probably been ahead of the main body, had got there before him. Their gaze was fixed on the indistinct shapes of the houses of Ollioules, and very likely the retreating backs of the rest of Halsey's piquet, who ran on well ahead of their officer. Without stopping he plunged into the scrub on the other side of the road, praying that the man covering his back would have the sense to follow. In amongst a group of olive trees he came to a halt, falling to his knees, his breath searing his chest. As gently as he could he laid the wounded man on the ground, only realising when he rolled over that the marine had passed out with the pain.

'What's your name?'

'Dymock.'

'Stay with Leech, and keep out of sight.'

'There's a rate of them frogs?'

'They're not interested in you,' Markham replied testily, covering his own uncertainty. 'They're interested in getting to safety, which means going through the village.'

'What about the rest of the lads?'

'I've got to get them out of there. Which I intend to do. We'll pick you both up on the way through.'

'And what if you don't manage it?'

'Sir!' snapped Markham, finally exasperated. 'If we don't make it, get back to Toulon and tell them to come and bloody well get us.'

'Sir,' the marine replied softly.

But Markham didn't hear him. He was already gone, half crouched and running, praying that his sword wouldn't hit some tree or stone that would alert those on the roadway to his presence. The bright stars showed him the gnarled tops of the olive grove, which provided some point of reference. That also enabled him to move swiftly through the trees, until he saw the black outline of Rossignol's coach. He shot up onto the *pavé*, then ducked as someone raised a musket to take aim at him.

'Hold your fire,' he called, as he slithered over the patch of road and dived under the coach. It was only when he came up the other side that he realised it was now resting on four wheels. Yelland confirmed that it was repaired, and that the two other marines who had been with Halsey were back in the village.

'Get on the shafts, you men. Push this damned thing back across the bridge. If they attack I want it close enough to the first pair of houses to block the road. Leave just enough room to get the horses through for now.'

While he was talking, he kept his eyes on the steady flow of sailors, nothing but dark shapes, emerging from the undergrowth to swell the ranks of those he'd have to face. He started to walk backwards himself as the coach began to move, its metal-rimmed wheels grinding loudly on the surface of the road, a sound which carried, judging by the sudden number of ghostly white faces looking in their direction. He had to fight the temptation to borrow a musket and shoot at them, since the last thing he wanted at that moment was that they should disperse.

More importantly, they didn't follow, giving him time to work out what to do next. Markham had the distinct impression that they were a mob without a central directing authority. Everything about their behaviour on the hillside, as they'd shouted to each other, indicated that. He could hear the buzz of much conversation as various opinions were stated as to what course of action they should adopt.

Once the coach was close to the narrow gap between the buildings, practically blocking the route, he ran back towards the main square. Rannoch had evacuated the crest, as ordered. The men were arguing noisily when he appeared, duplicating what was happening with the deserters on the Toulon road. Those who'd run before him had spread a degree of alarm and despondency. The silence that fell as he walked amongst them was nothing to do with his rank, more a measure of their curiosity about this officer, who should by all accounts be dead, and what he was up to now.

'Get the horses out from the paddock,' he shouted, 'and that bugger Fouquert who's tied up in the back room.'

They were looking at each other, in that way men do when they assume a task to be another's responsibility. It was Schutte, perhaps stung enough by his preferment of Halsey to assert himself, who saved him repeating the orders. Markham heard him tallying off men to the task as he burst in through the inn door. Rossignol was standing by his hampers, now repacked, he and his party ready to depart.

'The coach?' the Frenchman demanded.

'Is repaired. I've called for the horses.'

Quickly, he explained their predicament. The men on the Toulon road might wait for daylight. But he, with an army on the other side of him, dare not. They had to break out or risk capture, and the best time to achieve that was by using the darkness to aid them against what he hoped was a rabble.

'My men will secure the road ahead. As soon as they do so you are to drive through as fast as you can. Your horses are rested now, so they should manage some speed.'

'But they will be bound to fire on us, monsieur. We will present such an easy target compared to your soldiers.'

Markham nodded, spun on his heel and walked outside, calling to the first two men he saw. 'Ettrick, find some hay, a length of rope and a couple of torches.

Quinlan, go and tell Yelland that I want the doors taken off the coach.'

They moved out with a discipline they'd not shown since coming ashore, such was the threat these French sailors posed. Rannoch was issuing crisp, clear orders to keep his men in place. There'd not be a single member in his unit who had not heard of the fate of Celeste's father, and such knowledge kept them tight and alert. On the narrow roadway they couldn't deploy, so he arranged them in ranks of ten. As soon as he saw the crowd of Frenchmen, who were still milling around and arguing, he opened fire. As the front rank discharged their muskets he brought forward the second and gave the men before them another salvo.

The first had shocked them; the second, no more than ten seconds later, added to the surprise. The third caught them as they started to run and the fourth made them scatter. Many didn't make it. Firing along such a narrow causeway into such a mass of flesh, even the most inept musketry was effective, and the cries of men wounded and dying rose above the crash of the guns. As soon as they had dispersed he broke his men into two files, each to take one side of the road and provide a screen for the coach, with Schutte leading a party along the causeway to clear any bodies. Yelland, lying on the roof rather than sitting on the box, held the reins tight. There was no need to steer the beasts on the old, straight, Roman route, only to hold them steady and keep them moving. Lying down he made less of a target.

Behind him the twin torches flared and flickered as the coach increased speed. Grabbing two men, he crashed into the undergrowth to the right, calling out for Dymock, and firing high and wild to keep the enemy on the move. Dymock's strangled tones rose above every other sound. Recognising the gnarled profile of the tree under which he'd left them, Markham headed for it, ordered those with him to lift the wounded Leech, and then covered the retreat as they made it back to the road. The coach was rattling along, nearly abreast, and he halted it for a second to load on the wounded man.

Fire began to pour down from the hillsides as the renegades, having found some cover, started to play their muskets on the men beneath them. Two went down immediately, and he called for them to be lifted aboard, which was swiftly followed by the command to run. Every man in his detachment had already been told to stay ahead of the coach, if necessary to hang on to the traces and be pulled along. The wounded were thrown through the open doors, inside which the passengers cowered behind thick bales of hay.

Markham himself jumped up onto the step, then threw himself across the box, wondering what the Frenchmen would make of his little surprise. The quantity of fire, which had been extreme, suddenly began to fade away. In the space illuminated by the twin torches the renegade sailors could see Fouquert, lashed to the rear of the vehicle, screaming his head off, a perfect target for any man who didn't care whether he hit friend or foe.

They couldn't keep up the pace for any length of time, and it wasn't long before Markham had to order Yelland to slow the horses. The men ahead slowed too, some so out of breath that they nearly collapsed where they stood. Jumping down, Markham ordered them to keep moving, waited till the noise of the wheels faded, then gazed back down the road. The night was clear and warm, though with a slim moon he could see little. But his ears told him more than his eyes. There was no evidence of any pursuit.

Fouquert was covered in the dust thrown up by the wheels of the coach, his face caked so that he looked like a pierrot, the curly black hair, eyelids and thin moustache doubly coated. When he begged to be cut down his voice was cracked, partly from the dirt, but more, Markham suspected, from shouting at his compatriots. His wrists, where the ropes had rubbed against them, showed angry red, made more obvious by the still flickering torches. Disliking needless cruelty, Markham was tempted to oblige. But if he did, Fouquert would have to walk, and that would mean putting some of his exhausted men to guard him.

'There's no room in the coach,' Markham replied, checking his bonds to see that they were still secure. 'Besides, you are such a useful talisman, I would be loath to surrender the protection you provide.'

Fouquert tried to spit on him, though he lacked the saliva to do so. But his black eyes held enough hate to render the liquid unnecessary. Loping round to jump back aboard, he saw that both Lobsters and Bullocks were well ahead. A last glance to the rear killed any temptation he had to call them back. Jumping aboard, Markham called for the interior lantern to be unshaded and passed to him.

He examined the wounded. Leech had a broken leg, though it looked clean enough. One of the men shot on the road, a Bullock called Firman, was dead. The other, a marine, had a shoulder wound which didn't appear too serious. He spoke to the older of Rossignol's daughters, as he removed the injured man's belt, bayonet and pouches.

'Mademoiselle, you must help me tend to these men.'

'I cannot, monsieur,' Pascalle Rossignol replied, cowering even further behind her hay. 'I swoon at the sight of blood.'

'I shall assist you, Lieutenant,' said Eveline. Leaning forward, she immediately removed her cloak and knelt to cover the man's legs. As she did so, her beautiful face came full into the light, and Markham smiled at her. She returned the smile, which broadened as his eyes, of their own volition, fell to take in the slim neck, the pale skin beneath it, and her proud breasts.

'I must warn you, I am not equipped to nurse, monsieur.'

Recognising it for what it was, a *double entendre*, Markham's face broke into a grin, that followed by shared laughter. It took a supreme effort to drag his mind back to his responsibilities as an officer, and he gingerly started to remove the wounded soldier's coat.

'Torches ahead, lieutenant,' called Yelland from the box. 'Lots of them.'

'That will be the Toulon defences,' Markham said, to reassure the passengers. 'We're safe now.'

The first hint of the new dawn was edging over the eastern horizon before they'd finished. Markham, under the watchful eye of her father, saw Eveline seated and covered her with her cloak. Then, exhausted himself, he lay across a bale of hay to try and snatch a brief sleep.

A runner had been sent back into Toulon as soon as they were sighted. De Lisle, still ashore, had been roused out of his bed and dispatched to investigate. Halsey shook his officer awake as soon as the captain came into view. De Lisle, typically, made no attempt to disguise his feelings in front of the civilians. His countenance was livid as Markham, suppressing a yawn as well as a curse, climbed down from the coach to report.

'What is this?' he demanded. 'You were given clear orders to stay in Ollioules.'

'I had to pull back, sir, or risk losing everyone.'

'Why, damnit?'

'French deserters, sir, sailors from the Toulon fleet. They were coming out of the hills. I suspect our initial approach to the village drove them up there in the first place. Having seen Captain Elphinstone heading back here, they probably thought it was safe to come down.'

De Lisle had stretched himself as Markham spoke, his haughty features showing increasing disbelief. 'I know nothing of French deserters?'

'I've been told that they number near five thousand, all armed. I have the man who informed me of this. He, it seems, is one of the officers responsible for their flight. He took part in the insurrection which so nearly scuppered our landing.'

'This is more nonsense, Markham.'

'It is not, sir. Fouquert . . .'

He got no further, since de Lisle repeated the name with a great explosion of air. 'Fouquert?'

'You know the name?'

'The whole of Toulon knows the name. He's a damned Jacobin and a bloody butcher, who hanged several dozen loyal naval officers the day Trugueff offered to surrender.' The captain poked his head into the coach, turning first left, then right, his eyes alighting on Rossignol. 'Is this he?'

'No, sir. I tied him to the back,' Markham replied. He couldn't help smiling, or adding a small, ironic bow, as he invited his superior to follow him.

De Lisle did so reluctantly, like a man who expected he was about to be made to look a fool. That was heightened as he looked at the back of the coach. The sinking feeling Markham experienced made him wonder if his blood was emptying into his boots. The ropes were there, as were the torches, now extinguished. But they hung loose, with no sign of the prisoner.

'He was there,' he stammered. 'Not two hours ago.'

'Where?' demanded de Lisle, confused.

Markham felt like a schoolboy, advancing an excuse that though truthful, was never likely to be believed. And he was aware, as he spoke, that such a feeling was evident in his voice.

'We tied him to the back of the coach, between these torches, thinking his men would recognise him and stop shooting at us. It worked brilliantly.'

De Lisle could have shouted at him, and probably if he had, Markham would have accepted even so public a rebuke. But the captain wasn't like that. He hissed his response, his voice dripping with well controlled distaste.

'Then I must assume you tied the knots, sir, which would just about match the competence of every other task you've undertaken.'

'I resent that, sir. I have told you that I was forced to withdraw. If I had not done so we could not have avoided being captured.'

'It's very easy to avoid that, Markham. All you have to do is behave properly, perhaps even act like an officer and a gentleman, something which is clearly alien to you.'

# Chapter eight

Toulon was crowded, not only with its own inhabitants, but with British sailors and marines, and those people from the hinterland who were afraid to face the possible arrival of the Terror and its bloody mistress, the guillotine. The anchorage was packed with shipping, the original French fleet in the inner basin by the dockyard, while the outer roadstead was choked with Hood's fleet, plus the recently arrived Spanish contingent under the command of Admiral Don Juan de Langara. But for all the bustle there was a peaceful air in Toulon itself, more like a town on a busy market day than a city facing an imminent siege.

Unable to find the equipment they'd left with Elphinstone, and bereft of orders, Markham was obliged to ask for the use of Rossignol's coach. So it was a heavily-laden conveyance that made its way round the Petite Rade, first to the hospital, then towards the bakehouse, where the detachment was entitled to collect some badly needed supplies of food, bread and biscuit. Markham, noticing that confusion reigned in the commissary, took enough of those fresh commodities to supply the Rossignols and Celeste. They then made their way to the arsenal to indent for powder and shot, and possibly to receive further orders. That was where they encountered the first manifest signs of confusion. There were no orders, and neither was there accommodation.

'It's fend for yourself,' said the officer, a naval lieutenant, charged with billeting the troops, who, in looking at his filthy army uniform, and his haggard face, had confirmed a prejudice without stating it. 'The barracks are full and the Dons have taken over the rope walk. All the major buildings have long since been filled by marines, so it's down to haylofts and warehouses for your lot. Still, it's what the army's used to.'

The news that Markham was leading a detachment of marines was met with incredulity. What it didn't produce was a place to lay his head. 'My men have spent the last twenty-four hours without either sleep or decent food, having been damn near the first troops ashore. They need proper rest and somewhere to cook up a hot meal.'

'Then you should have sorted out your accommodation first.'

'I'm sorry,' Markham, making no attempt to soften the irony in his tone. 'We had the small matter of a battle to fight.'

'What battle?' he asked doubtfully.

'Ollioules.'

'Ah!' said the lieutenant, suddenly brightening, 'You mean Captain Elphinstone's victory. Damn my eyes, I wish I'd been there to see him lead the charge.'

'Charge?'

'It's the talk of the town! A naval officer mounted on a horse, sword in hand, leading the Lobsters forward and routing the frog guns almost single-handed.' He suddenly looked suspicious. 'But if you were there, you must have witnessed it.'

'I was there all right, Lieutenant, and I can testify that Captain Elphinstone never led any charge. Indeed, since he stayed very close to his own cannon till the French were beaten, he barely got within half a mile of the enemy.'

The billeting officer's face went red. 'Damn you sir, for a lying dog! How dare you come in here and say such things? I've a good mind to report you.'

'Don't fret, sir, I shall make my own report. That is, if the good Captain is to be found anywhere close to the conflict.'

The lieutenant's tone was icy. 'You will find him at the French Admiral's old headquarters, Fort de la Malgue.'

'Powder and shot?'

He flicked a finger towards the open doorway. 'The arsenal is right across the yard.'

'And what about a billet?'

There was a palpable degree of satisfaction in the man's reply. 'I told you, fend for yourself.'

'I shall,' Markham replied coldly.

Then he spun on his heel and marched out. Inwardly he was seething: having twice seen off the French, the credit was not to be his. That wasn't an uncommon thing in any military enterprise. Whole reputations, including those of very senior officers, were based on good fortune rather than leadership or bravery. And any officer who saw his glory stolen was bound to feel aggrieved. All the same, there was a part of his mind, nagging him, wondering if his reaction would have been quite so extreme if he hadn't arrived on this campaign carrying the baggage of his own chequered past.

The coach stood where he'd left it, in the yard, with the sun beating down. His men had found a patch of shade by the wall of the arsenal building, and had stretched out to rest. Seeing them, he cursed the billeting officer even more roundly. Amongst the many yardsticks that men used to judge their officers, about the highest was the ability to find a decent billet. Food and freedom from risk were secondary. A good body of troops would accept privation and possible death with an equanimity they'd never show when deprived of a place to sleep.

'Rannoch, Schutte, Halsey,' he shouted. The last called was first to his feet, with the two 'sergeants' taking their own sweet time to respond. Schutte was reluctant to arrive before Rannoch. He, busily cleaning his musket, seemed disinclined to put the task aside. Markham waited, his limited stock of patience rapidly evaporating, while the Highlander finished working on his weapon.

Only then did he stand up. All three then came over to where he stood.

'That is the last piece of insubordination I am ever going to put up with,' growled Markham, his eyes ranging over the three men. 'And it won't be your stripes I'll take away, it will be your lifeblood. I'll have you transferred, and when I do it I'll make sure that you end up on a duty that not even Lucifer himself could survive.'

He looked at them each in turn. Halsey, the least troublesome, was at attention, gazing at a point above Markham's head. Schutte dropped his eyes the second he made contact. Only Rannoch held his gaze, the stare steady and the very slightest of smiles playing round his lips. It was a 'do your worst' look, for which many an officer would break a man. Indeed, he felt he was being challenged to do so. The image of Rannoch cleaning his weapon came into his mind. None of the others had seen fit to do so, not surprisingly since he had issued no such order.

'Fetch your musket,' he snapped.

That registered; a small move of the eyebrow and tightening of the lips denoted his surprise. He spun on his heel and walked back to the point where he had leant it on the brick wall, picked it up, and after a quick examination came back. Markham held out his hand for the weapon, which Rannoch surrendered. It was spotless and smelt of fresh gun oil. Each metal part shone in its own way, the barrel, flintlock, and trigger guard grey and gleaming, the brass on the firing plate and butt sparkling. The pan, normally encrusted with a deep residue of burnt powder, was scraped clean. The wood of the stock looked like a well polished piece of prized furniture.

'You take good care of this.'

'I do at that.'

'Are you a good shot as well, sergeant?'

'I manage.'

Their eyes locked again. 'When I was on the crest at

Ollioules, my sword was shot out of my hand. The ball wasn't fired by the French, Rannoch, and I don't suppose it went exactly where it was intended.'

'Would that be right, now?' Rannoch replied, with the kind of mockery in his voice that practically admitted responsibility. Markham fingered the strap, a replacement for the one he'd cut with that same sword before they'd entered the village.

'And someone took out that French officer with the tricolour plumes.' Markham raised his hand and put one finger in the middle of his forehead. 'The ball took him right here.'

'Then he would not survive it, would he?'

'Remarkable shooting, don't you think?'

'It is not my place to put forward an opinion in the presence of an officer.'

If Rannoch knew what he was implying, nothing registered in his face. And neither Halsey or Schutte so much as moved an eyebrow. What had happened, where the shot that had hit his sword had come from, would remain a mystery. And, in truth, given the poor quality of the musketry, it was more likely an accident than deliberate.

'It is when you're asked to, sergeant,' said Markham. 'And you will oblige me by never forgetting that. I have to find us somewhere to lay our heads, since while we've been fighting all the other men who've come ashore have had the chance to pinch the decent accommodation.'

'Bastards,' said Halsey, then realising he'd spoken out, as well as what he'd said, he looked flustered.

'A very accurate description, corporal. And damned awkward for us. But I've no intention of letting such a thing bother us. First I must indent for powder and shot to replenish our losses.'

Markham looked back towards Rannoch. The man's natural authority made any other choice foolish. Schutte could match him for size, but was all muscle and no brain. Halsey had been a marine all his adult life, and was a good subordinate. But this sergeant of the 65th foot was a man apart.

'As soon as I've done that, I want you to take charge. Distribute the ammunition and then get every man to clean his musket. And Rannoch,' he added, handing the man's weapon back, 'I expect them all to look like this.'

Still that stare, which was very close to contempt. 'Should any of you fancy deserting, you have a fine choice. Castration inland, or a hanging at sea.'

Having signed for the supplies, Markham went over to the coach to explain to the passengers what had happened. He found Rossignol eating again, the same hampers that had occupied Celeste's table now occupying the space between the seats. Yelland, who'd acted as driver, was sitting on the blind side, consuming his fill.

'You must have a glass of wine, monsieur. I had your soldier chill it in the sea, and while not cold, it is quite palatable.'

'Obliged,' Markham replied, unable to avoid shooting a glance at Eveline. After a welcome sip he explained about his problems with billeting, adding that the town was exceedingly full. 'In your case, it is not something with which I can help. My first task is to find accommodation for my own men. Of course, should I happen on anything suitable, I will inform you.'

'It strikes me, Lieutenant,' said Rossignol, his mouth full of the bread Markham had supplied, 'that I might have more luck than you. After all, I am a Frenchman, as you are not, despite your facility with the language. And if all the barracks and dockyard buildings are already gone, it stands to reason that anything left will be in the grasping hands of the locals. Together, with your uniform, which will terrify them, and my knowledge of their wiles, we might succeed where individually we would fail.'

'That's most kind, monsieur, but I rather think that

what I'm in search of would hardly suffice for your daughters.'

'That may be so. But neither do I wish to drag these poor weak creatures all over the town on such a hot day. Shall we try first as a pair, just to see what we can find? At the very least it may speed up your own search.'

It was the last thing he wanted to do. But faced with such a direct offer he couldn't really refuse. 'I would be most grateful for any assistance.'

Rossignol threw the rest of his bread out of the opposite side, narrowly missing Yelland's ear, drained his cup of wine, smacked his lips and beamed at Markham. He then grabbed his hat and a large stick from the rack above his head.

'Then let us be off.'

Rossignol's tactics first embarrassed Markham, then amused him, and finally, quite frankly amazed him. There was no supplication in his approach, which was peremptory and very close to being threatening. He brushed aside the idea that something suitable might be found outside the old town walls, and was loath to contemplate any accommodation that did not have some view of the harbour. The stick was first banged on any likely looking door, and when a servant appeared, Rossignol entered, brushing him aside. The owner of the property, naturally nervous at the turn events had taken in Toulon, wilted before his air of authority, made so much more potent by the unkempt British officer at his side. Having got Hood's name from Markham, he acted as though he were the Admiral's personal representative.

And he was fussy, inspecting both the public rooms and the bedrooms, as well as the outbuildings and the view of the inner harbour, then interrogating the occupants to see how much space they were prepared to sacrifice to the common purpose of fighting the revolution. Dismissal, or even a stated intention to think about it, after his verbal onslaught, seemed to induce feelings of guilt and disappointment in those he chose not to immediately favour. After looking at two dozen houses, all with major or minor defects, they happened on the home and business premises of a certain Monsieur Picard, who made a substantial living from supplying the French fleet.

The exterior was unprepossessing, a flat-fronted, detached building with no windows on the ground floor and only a double-doored loading bay with a hoist on the first. The main, ground floor entrance, a narrow door, was of sturdy oak, warped with age and heavily studded. But the interior was quite a revelation. Once through the dingy warehouse that fronted the quay, they entered a courtyard with a central fountain. The building at the rear, though old, was large and graceful, timber-framed in antique style and graced, like the surrounding walls, with climbing, sweet scented vines. The owner who, judging by his property, must be one of the leading business men of the town, was interrogated by Rossignol in the same manner he applied to all the others. As soon as he saw the rear courtyard and entrance, with a set of doors big enough to take the most substantial coach, the Frenchman pronounced himself satisfied and went back to beard the owner in his own salon.

'These are difficult times, Monsieur Picard,' said Rossignol, addressing the tall skeletal figure who stood before him. The man's plump wife was just behind, scowling at what she probably saw as her husband's cowardice. 'And you have so much space that you may occupy a whole wing of the house and not even notice your guests. Why, with such an abundance it will be hard to remember we are here.'

'No!' said Madame Picard.

Her husband held up a hand to stop her, which only served to make her scowl even more. Yet Markham had the distinct impression that he intended to turn them down as well, albeit in a manner less brusque. Rossignol responded to Madame Picard's abrupt refusal with a gesture of despair. Then he turned to Markham, who was doing his best to conceal his own embarrassment.

'Lieutenant, would you mind leaving us alone for a moment?'

'Happily,' he replied.

Outside the salon door, in a cool hallway lined with expensive tapestries, he heard Rossignol speaking quietly, but insistently. He also heard numerous questions posed, some in a male voice but more from Madame Picard. After about ten minutes the door opened and Rossignol, smiling, invited him to re-enter.

It was like walking into a different room. Certainly the furnishings were the same, rich pieces heavy with age and deep beeswax. But the owners, by their change of mood, seemed to have altered the effect. All was now light and welcome. Monsieur Picard looked as though he'd added another pair of inches to his already decent height; while his wife was somewhat swollen, clasping and unclasping her hands, and actually smiling at this strange, handsome, but rather dishevelled British officer.

'As you see, Lieutenant,' said Rossignol, his round red face beaming with pleasure, 'our hosts' fears are laid to rest. Monsieur Picard has kindly agreed to allow your men to occupy the first floor of the warehouse, while you will, of course, join us in the selection of the premises they have so kindly given over to our use. The girl, Celeste, will be accommodated in the servants' quarters, with a modicum of work to compensate for her keep.'

Picard bowed and his wife was very near to a curtsy.

'Why, that is very decent of you, sir.'

'The very least we could do, Lieutenant,' Monsieur Picard replied. 'France would not forgive us for anything less.'

'That is settled then,' said Rossignol quickly. 'And since you're here as allies and protectors, our hosts have agreed to supplement your rations so that your men will have plenty to eat.'

In the absence of any other suitable response, Markham bowed.


'I can't think what you said to them that made them change their minds so quickly.'

Rossignol spread his hands, his smooth white palms reflecting the sunlight. They were walking along the commercial quay, by the inner basin, heading for the Vielle Darse, which housed the arsenal. The great ships of the French fleet, warped in close to the dockyard, towered above them.

'What does he see as he looks up from his ledgers, Lieutenant? His own nation's ships, indeed the major part of his livelihood, lying idle while the harbour is full of the vessels of England and Spain. What does he hear from outside Provence? I mentioned the name Fouquert to him, and what little blood his body contains ended up in his feet. He knows that should the Revolution triumph in Toulon, and he is still here, his head will be lopped off his shoulders, along with that of his wife.'

'But he knew all that before he arrived,' said Markham.

'True. But he had not considered that, even with the port under British control, he might not be safe.'

'Who would threaten him?'

'There are thousands of idle sailors in the town, thrown off their vessels. And while I have no desire to denigrate the profession of arms, monsieur, even you must acknowledge that in the best trained army there are those whose standards of behaviour fall somewhat short of perfect.' He must have mistaken the look Markham gave him, because he continued hurriedly. 'I refer of course to the Spaniards.'

'Of course,' Markham replied, with deep irony. If Rossignol had cared to look carefully at the men he commanded, he'd have seen just how right he was.

'What better for a rich man, in these troubled times, than to have a detachment of troops under his own roof, armed and comfortable, able to deal with anyone who seeks to trouble him?'

'You offered us as an armed guard?'

'Nothing so absolute. Let us say the lesser of two evils.'

'Let us hope you're right.'

'I think I am. And I know that my daughters will feel much safer knowing that you are there to protect them.'

Markham stared at him hard then, but Rossignol was looking elsewhere; judging by his face, seemingly content. Could he really not have noticed the looks that his daughter Eveline had thrown in Markham's direction, glances that had been returned with compound interest; could he really believe that she would be safe with him under the same room?

It was an exhausted contingent that finally arrived at the Picard house, with Rossignol taking the conveyance round to the back of the building, while Markham and his men entered the warehouse from the front. One of Picard's servants showed them to the vacant first floor, where they were ordered to rest. Markham left the organisation of the billet to the men themselves, too weary to take any notice of their internal dissensions, and followed the same servant to the room that had been set aside for him.

This was at the far end of a corridor that housed all of Picard's visitors. Rossignol's room was the closest to the stairs, while his daughters' room lay opposite that which was given over solely to the young boy. Markham stopped briefly there to thank Madame Picard, who was fussing about the room, ordering a serving girl to tidy this and remove that, watched all the while by the silent Jean-Baptiste. Finally satisfied, she turned to face the boy, a most peculiar gleam in her eye. She extended her hand and touched his cheek, recoiling almost immediately as though stung. Seeing her occupied, and aware that something private was happening, Markham responded to the servant who tugged his sleeve, and moved on to his own room.

Sleep should have come to him instantly, but instead he lay for what seemed like an age, tossing and turning, the events of the last two days played over and over again in his mind. Each time he examined any of his actions, he could see how flawed they were, driven by his own demons rather than either bravery or good sense. That impulsive desire to be better than other men, examined when alone, depressed him utterly. And as for his command, they were probably more divided now than they had been throughout the entire voyage.

Things looked very different when he woke, the momentary unease at the strange surroundings set to rest by those same recollections. It was dark, and until he made it to the candlelit hallway he had no idea of the time. A tray lay outside the door, the cold collation and bread covered, only the carafe of wine showing. They'd let him sleep throughout the day, and judging by the tightly shut door of the girls' room, and the untouched trays outside, they'd done the same. But Jean-Baptiste's door was ajar, just like Rossignol's, both rooms vacant.

He grabbed a hunk of bread and a slice of ham, munching them greedily as he washed them down with the rough wine. Taking a candle into his room, and placing it before the mirror, he saw just how wretched he looked. Several days' growth of stubble covered his chin; his eyes were red-rimmed and bloodshot from exposure to sun and dust, and that same commodity caked his face. He needed hot water, a razor and soap, plus hazel twigs to clean his teeth. His uniform, hat, coat and breeches and gaiters, were filthy, needing to be sponged and brushed, while his boots required a strong application of blacking and polish. Still munching, he set out to look for the servants' quarters. In the main hallway, the sound of voices behind an open door was too tempting to pass, and he knocked gently before opening it.

Rossignol was there, heading for the door, hand extended as though intent on keeping it shut. But Markham swung it wide before he could get there, leaving the Frenchman looking rather foolish. The tightness of his facial muscles was fleeting, immediately replaced by a bland look, as the extended arm swung to introduce the other occupants. Markham could see that the Picards were there, standing well away from the two strangers who crouched before Jean-Baptiste, one examining the boy while the other watched his every move.

'Forgive me if I don't introduce you, Lieutenant,' whispered Rossignol. 'But matters are at a crucial stage, and to disturb the doctors now might be regressive.'

It was that final word, so unfamiliar, which alerted him to what was happening. But Rossignol carried on with his whispering, just in case he hadn't understood.

'They are examining the boy, to see if they can find the seat of his malaise. The very best doctors in the city, I do assure you, renowned far and wide. They were employed by Admiral Trugueff himself before the surrender.'

The boy began to sing, so softly that the words were incomprehensible. But the effect on everyone present was electric. The doctors shot back to take a long look, Picard clutched his wife, and Rossignol started to clap his hands, only stopping himself when he realised that the sound might alter things. One of the doctors leant forward again, lifting Jean-Baptiste's eyelid and peering closely into the still orb. His other hand touched the boy's neck at the side.

'An improvement in the vital functions,' he declared, in a hushed but insistent voice. Then he moved back to allow his companion to examine the patient. That, when accomplished, produced a confirmatory nod. And all the while Jean-Baptiste sang. The senior doctor turned to Rossignol. 'It is too early to claim success, and several more tests will have to be conducted.'

Rossignol looked at Picard, who nodded, before addressing the doctor. 'Please, spare no expense.'

Then Rossignol spun round, took Markham by the arm, and led him out into the hallway, pulling the door shut behind him.

'Have they found out what ails him?' asked Markham.

'If they have, Lieutenant, they would not say, since to do so might depress their fees. But they have got the boy to respond, and with luck they may bring him back to normality.'

'Then let us wish them luck,' Markham replied.

'Yes indeed,' replied the Frenchman, with passion. Then his voice returned to normal. 'Were you in search of something?'

'Water with which to shave, the wherewithal to make my uniform more presentable. What little kit I came ashore with is still in the possession of Captain Elphinstone, and the last thing I want to do now is go and find him.'

'Return to your room, Lieutenant. I will ensure that all you require comes to you.'

'The Picards won't mind?'

'Of course not. Now do as I say.'

# Chapter nine

The following morning found him standing rigidly to attention in the senior officers' quarters which lay inside the massive stone walls of Fort de la Malgue. Through an old glassed-over embrasure, he had a fine view of the Grande Rade of Toulon. The outer harbour, bathed in brilliant sunshine, was full of ships unloading men and supplies. The atmosphere in the elegant room was, however, somewhat chilly as the men around him discussed forthcoming operations.

Earlier, kicking his heels in an ante-room, Midshipman Driberg had brought him up to date about the siege and those engaged. The Bouche de Rhône Army was under the command of General Cartaux. He was rated a fool but his troops, despite their ragged appearance, were numerous and buoyed up by the surrender, then the subsequent sack, of Marseilles. The Army of Savoy, under Lapoype, was closing in from the east. Given the topography, they'd seek to occupy the surrounding heights, especially Mont Faron, thus cutting Toulon off from the interior. But it would be a hard nut to crack. The features of the landscape, plus the permanent fortifications built by the French themselves, made it a natural stronghold. Unless the French could dominate the harbour with gunnery, the fleet could sit there till doomsday.

Driberg was even more loquacious on the subject of his commanding officer. The Honourable George Keith Elphinstone was not only very well connected, he was also high on the captains' list, close to the promotion that would allow him to hoist his flag as a Rear-Admiral. The midshipman insisted he was fair but firm, a strict disciplinarian who cared for his men, an opinion Markham found hard to accept. He was certainly short-tempered, which Markham discovered as soon as he entered to make his report. And it wasn't just his failure to hold his position that got him into hot water. The captain's florid complexion and grey, bushy eyebrows, atop a heavily muscled body, gave him the appearance of an avenging Biblical prophet.

'You had in your hands a man who deserved to be hanged.'

'I accept full responsibility for Fouquert's escape, sir.'

'I should damn well think so, laddie.'

'I checked on the pursuit, personally. But I was looking for a large body of men, not one or two of his sailors. If they came after us, staying off the road, I could not have seen them.'

'So they were free to sneak up to the coach in the dark and release the blackguard, is that what you're saying?' Markham nodded, but kept silent. Elphinstone's eyebrows drew together to form one single entity. 'You had no notion to post a guard? Any officer with a half a brain would have thought of that.'

'My men where exhausted. Besides, sir, I had no idea he was so important. To me, he was just another sailor.'

The captain slammed the table. 'He was a damned murderer, and that, laddie, is in your own report.'

Markham opened his mouth to protest, but his list of seeming errors was not yet complete. 'I'm informed that you also passed up the opportunity to capture a French artillery officer.'

'Hardly, sir. He was so severely wounded he had to be carried by two of his men.'

'Yet you didn't see fit to bring him in?'

'If you'd seen the wound, I think you would have judged, as I did, that his best hope of survival lay with his own surgeons.'

It sounded lame, said like that. And Markham hoped his face didn't betray the truth. It had been the bravery of his gunners, who'd very nearly sacrificed their own lives to save their officer, which had affected him so deeply. The contrast between that and the attitude of his own men in the recent frigate action was not something he could easily explain.

The Scotsman put his hands on his hips, leaning forward slightly to emphasise what he was saying. 'You will oblige me in future, Lieutenant, by killing the enemy instead of releasing them, wherever you encounter them. Do I make myself clear?'

'Sir.'

Elphinstone picked up a set of maps from his desk and gestured with a peremptory wave. 'Come with me.'

Markham had followed him through a door, to the larger room he now stood in, dominated by a long dining table covered in maps. A group of Spanish officers stood round the table, one of them clearly of Admiral's rank. He knew, because Driberg had told him, that Lord Hood had no intention of taking command ashore himself. But instead of handing over that task to the only person Driberg thought fit to hold it, Elphinstone, he'd agreed that the Spaniard, Rear-Admiral Gravina, be appointed to the office.

The conversation that Markham witnessed, carried out in a polite but strangled way, demonstrated quite clearly that a fissure had already appeared in what was supposed to be the united allied front. Gravina himself, being reluctant to debase his Spanish honour by taking part in the discussions, left most of this to a yellow-faced army Colonel called Serota. Tall, thin and hollow-chested, this officer clearly considered Elphinstone an imbecile. He had a hacking cough to go with his sallow complexion, one that interrupted the flow of every single sentence he uttered. The discussion ranged back and forth, as various matters were aired. What it boiled down to was simple enough. The Spaniards wanted to attack, while Elphinstone insisted that they must stay on the defensive. Finally, having stood in the background for an age, Markham was called forward to relate what had happened at Ollioules.

'I think Lieutenant Markham will bear witness to the low quality of those troops opposing us,' said Elphinstone, as soon as he'd finished, pacing back and forth, his stocky legs making his heels dig into the flagstones. 'Certainly we can drive them back if they encroach too far. But even the worst soldiers, in such numbers, will cause us casualties we can ill afford.'

'I have brought ashore the flower of the Spanish army,' said Serota, his concave chest puffing out enough to make him look normal. Elphinstone's eyebrows shot up, and he had to rub his hands over his face to hide his reaction to that remark, since his opinion was that the plants at the Spaniard's disposal were more like weeds. Obviously neither Gravina nor Serota noticed, since the latter, after a deeper and more serious bout of coughing, carried on in the same flowery tone. 'They are proud men and will not be content merely to act defensively. The admiral and I intend that they should fight like lions, not dig like dogs.'

Elphinstone addressed Gravina directly, which brought a touch of rouge to Serota's cheeks. 'We must find more men, Admiral. We cannot undertake offensive operations without reinforcements. If we control the heights, with additional redoubts built to withstand whatever the French send our way, the town is safe, just like a little Gibraltar.'

That made Gravina flush angrily, and his officers growled amongst themselves at the mention of that name. Being allied to the British was strange enough for such men, who'd more often found themselves fighting alongside the French. The mention of that island bastion, vehemently claimed as an integral part of Spain, only reminded them of how much the world had altered. Realising immediately that he had made a gaffe, Elphinstone shot Markham a hard look, as though the mistake had been his fault.

'Let us look to the future. Toulon will act as a vessel into which we can pour the forces necessary not only to fight the Republicans, but to beat them. If we can tie down Cartaux and Lapoype until Spring, then the countryside could well rise behind them. That is the time to break out, when they raise the Royal standard. Attack then, and the whole of Provence will be ours.'

Elphinstone had said these last words with the same kind of exaggerated flourish as the Spaniard had used moments earlier. Now he swept his arm in a great arc, his eyes aimed at a point near the ceiling. 'Imagine the rewards a Bourbon monarch will bestow on the men who achieve such a thing! Why, Admiral Gravina, he will very likely make you a Duke.'

Driberg entered during this little speech, his face registering shock at seeing such a display from a man normally taciturn. 'We have a British army Colonel outside, sir. He was in Leghorn, taking passage home in the same vessel as your niece. He heard about events here and wishes to offer you his services.'

'Splendid,' cried Elphinstone. 'That's just what we need. You told him that Brigadier General Lord Mulgrave is on the way?'

'I have, sir, and Colonel Hanger has acknowledged that he is happy to serve under such a distinguished officer.'

'Hanger,' said Elphinstone. 'I know the name.'

'Augustus Hanger, sir. Second son of Lord Coleraine. Served in America with Banastre Tarleton's British Legion.'

Markham hoped that no-one observed his reaction to the name. His body actually shook. In a second his mind had replayed the events of a dozen years ago. The vivid image of the flames leaping above the Imrie house, the screams of the burning inhabitants mingled with the bloody face of Augustus Hanger. His hand closed involuntarily, as though he still held the broken sword blade he'd used to scar him. But overriding all of that was an ache that filled his chest, a pain so penetrating he thought his heart would burst. The whole edifice collapsed as he heard, for the first time since that night, the gravelly voice of the man he hated most in the world.

'At your service, Captain Elphinstone.'

'I'm overjoyed to see you, Colonel Hanger. You've no idea how much we require an army man to oversee the creation of proper defences. We sailors know our way on water, sir, but the finer points of land fortification are a soldier's preserve.'

This was said quickly, in English, to avoid offending the Dons, who manned their ships with soldiers, not marines. It also flew in the face of the well-known truth that sailors considered Army officers buffoons. But if he was going to work with a fool, he wanted a British one called Hanger, not the Spaniard, Serota.

'Allow me to name Admiral Gravina, who has the honour of overall command. Colonel Serota leads the men he brought ashore.'

'Delighted, sir.' Hanger's response, given with what sounded like a growl, conveyed anything but delight. But Markham knew that to be his habitual voice, one that sounded ill-mannered even when he was grovelling. He listened as Elphinstone went round the room, introducing each officer present. As the junior, he would be last, and with his back to the doorway, Hanger wouldn't recognise him till he turned. He fought the temptation to do so before his introduction was made. But he spun quickly enough when it was, in time to see the shock of the name, doubled by the recognition of the face; an emotion so sensational that the livid, rough-edged scar that covered half Hanger's face stood out like a beacon on his pasty complexion.

'Sir!' Markham snapped, his eyes boring into those of his superior. What he saw there almost eased the pain of remembrance, the shock and confusion of a man who wanted to swear but could not, a creature whose dignity and personality were in conflict. Officers of his rank rarely acknowledged lowly lieutenants, and to show that he even recognised Markham would call for an explanation. But he couldn't help the careful way he examined Markham's face, as if he expected to see it as bloody and bruised as it had been the last time they'd met.

'Wait outside, Markham,' said Elphinstone. 'I'm sure the Colonel will want a word with you when I've appraised him of the situation.'

'Oh I shall, Captain Elphinstone. I shall.'

Once back in the ante-room, he wasn't sure if he was shivering with fear, shaking with cold or trembling with rage. A wave of misery swept over him as he collapsed into a chair; the feeling that his decision to take up his commission in the British army, after a gap of a dozen years, was turning out to be a curse.

While not following Hanger's career, it had been impossible to avoid picking up snippets of information about him, especially since he was a crony of the Prince of Wales, and shared with that royal sibling an ability to provoke unflattering gossip. He knew that after the peace he'd gone to India as an aide to General Cornwallis, rising to become a member of the Governor's council, enriching himself in the process.

Returning to England on leave, Hanger had bought a colonelcy in a fashionable regiment. Thinking about that made him even more depressed. Hanger had cut quite a dash with his spendthrift ways. An ugly man, he was not, and never could be, classed a pleasant companion. His squat, gross figure and unappealing features were made worse by that scar Markham had given him. And once observed, they were merely a foretaste of his coarse manners. He treated men he considered his inferiors with disdain, and women of whatever station as fodder for his misplaced vanity, insulting them by the crude level of his attentions. Yet with all these faults he was courted by a section of society, where gold, liberally sprinkled around, spoke for more than looks and manners. And he was exceedingly careful not to insult anyone who had influence.

How different for Markham, who finally had only those two ephemeral qualities with which to trade. He should have come back from Russia with ample funds, but his attitude to the recent partition of Poland scuppered any chance of that, leading to rows with his seniors, both British and Russian, which had forced him into a hurried exit through Riga. While he'd been away, his father had died. His relatives not only wished to disown their bastard brother, but insisted that as a condition of his father's bequest he return every gift the general had ever bestowed. Naming each endowment a loan, they used every legal device available to them to deny him the right to see the will.

Some of his limited funds went to a lawyer. He agreed the idea of repayment was monstrous, but added that, being illegitimate, George Markham had already had more than his share. Appeals to charity fell on deaf ears. Frederick Markham, the general's son and heir, was weak and quite malleable. The real problem was Hannah, who would have dearly loved to cut all knowledge of him and her father's indiscretion out of the canvas of her life. Her sole concession, extracted in exchange for a promise never to darken her door, was to leave his mother in the small house his father had given her, a place she despised, and within whose walls she was steadily drinking herself to death on a diet of remorse and rough poteen.

After a brief stop in Dublin, he headed for London, that being the only place where a man like him could hope to secure a prosperous future. A wiser head would have taken cheap lodgings, and conserved his limited resources, realised his predicament and patiently sought opportunity. But soldiers rarely possessed that attribute, and George Markham was no exception. As an officer in the Russian army, when not actually campaigning, he'd lived in some style. Habit combined with inclination. He believed that in order to achieve prosperity, it was necessary to show some.

He'd always had an attraction to the theatre, though never the boldness to appear professionally, and that brought him into contact with some of the leading players of the day. These people, with their lack of hypocrisy regarding birth or fortune, seemed natural companions, and opened doors for him that might otherwise have remained closed. That stratum of social London was only too happy to embrace George Markham. Tall, good looking and an excellent mimic, gifted with an Irish tongue, and the wit to match. Credit and good company were readily available to a man who'd just helped Great Catherine defeat the Turks. There was gaming, eating, drinking, riotous companionship and, of course, in a world full of aspiring or successful actresses, women.

'If you'll wait in here, Miss Gordon,' said Driberg. 'I'll tell your uncle you've arrived.'

'You are kind, sir.' Markham sat up straight. The female voice was light and sweet, redolent of an English summer, roses, apple trees, the buzz of insects in a field of corn; the ingénue, perhaps, in a comedy of manners.

'I cannot say how long Captain Elphinstone will be,' Driberg continued. 'He's engaged in a conference of some importance.'

'It is exceedingly warm. If I could trouble you for some form of liquid refreshment, something cool, I am happy to wait.'

Markham was on his feet before she was through the door, tugging and brushing at his uniform in a vain attempt to remove the creases caused by the heat, and the stains that even the best efforts of Picard's servants had failed to eradicate. She stopped as she saw him, her pale eyebrows raised in delicate surprise, her lips slightly parted. With his practised eye he took in the attractive quality of her clothes, the chaste nature of their cut, and made a fair guess at the graceful figure they concealed.

'Lieutenant Markham, Miss Gordon, at your service.' Her eyebrows went up a fraction more. 'I heard Midshipman Driberg address you so. Have I made an error?'

She smiled slightly. 'No sir, you have not.'

'And did I hear him refer to Captain Elphinstone as your uncle?' She nodded, as he continued. 'A fine sailor, ma'am. It is an honour to serve under him.'

Her eyes took in the state of his apparel in one swift glance, seeming to register each point where dirt or sweat had stained it. His face was examined by pale blue eyes, the small, fresh cut from Ollioules first, then the more obvious old one above his eye, finally coming to rest at the poorly-sewn tear in the sleeve made by the French bullet.

'Might I suggest this chair to you? Being by the window, it takes whatever breeze is to be had from the sea.'

For the first time, she frowned slightly. 'I'm content to occupy another, Lieutenant.'

'I feel I must insist, just as I also need to apologise for the state of my dress, which I'll own, is pitiful.' He tugged at his coat again. 'I have come straight from fighting the enemy.'

'You have been in battle?'

'As soon as I came ashore your uncle ordered it so. We stopped the French at Ollioules and forced them to withdraw.'

'How splendid, Lieutenant,' she cried, clasping her hands.

'I might add, that we would not have enjoyed quite such a successful outcome if it had not been for the timely support of Captain Elphinstone himself.'

Markham was operating on instinct, Hanger and the problems he portended suppressed by the sudden arrival of this attractive creature. Her skin was pale and her hair fair, the whole set off by the deep cream of her hat and dress. The blue eyes, under their near-white lashes, were of a startling intensity, her nose straight above the full, slightly moist lips. He felt alive as well, the thrill of the chase taking over from whatever worries had preceded it. Nothing demonstrated that more than the way his remark regarding Elphinstone, the complete opposite of his true feelings, tripped glibly off his tongue.

'That is a most gallant thing to say, sir,' she purred, her bosom drawing his gaze as it heaved with pride. But the eyes didn't linger, Markham sensing that this girl was too chaste to appreciate such attentions. 'I shall tell my uncle that you said it, which will please him, I'm sure.'

'I admit to some surprise at seeing you here, Miss Gordon. Toulon, under siege, is hardly the place for such a gentle creature.'

Her eyes flashed slightly. 'I am not to be deflected by a few Jacobin rogues, Lieutenant Markham, any more than you are. When my ship was diverted here I could not countenance passing on to Gibraltar without seeing Uncle George.'

'Why, Miss Gordon, your uncle and I share a name, something of which I was unaware.'

He leant much closer as he said this, but was forced to withdraw quickly as the door opened. Driberg returned, followed by a servant bearing a tray. He looked from one to the other, as though sensing, in the way that interested parties sometimes do, a form of connection. Such a thought didn't please him, and he frowned as he directed that the tray be placed on the table. The servant departed, but the midshipman showed no signs of doing so, stopping to pour the drink. Markham had spared him no more than a glance, eager to see how this development affected the girl. He felt a thrill of satisfaction as the two thin lines appeared just above her nose. But they soon disappeared, to be replaced with a ravishing smile as Driberg delivered the drink, a smile that made the young man blush to his roots.

'Lieutenant Markham has been telling me about his battle,' she said, turning to smile at him. 'At Ollioules, did you say?'

'I was there too, Miss Gordon,' the youngster replied eagerly, 'ranging the guns from the church belfry.'

'Indeed?'

'Why if it hadn't been for my efforts, I beg to represent that there would have been no victory.'

Markham had to suppress a grin as she frowned, this time heavily, adding several more grooves to the lines that had previously creased her forehead. 'That is a touch at odds with what I've heard already, sir.'

'I do assure you it is the case, Miss Gordon.'

The way she looked at his pristine uniform, then glanced at Markham's, spoke volumes. 'Odd, sir, that this officer, who so nearly sustained a fearful wound by the look of his coat, was good enough to praise my uncle.'

'I was under his command, of course.'

'Which,' she snapped, 'makes the victory his, not yours!'

Markham felt a stab of guilt as he saw Driberg's face fall. Eager to impress, he'd been both boastful and forgetful.

'Midshipman Driberg behaved most gallantly, Miss Gordon. His ranging of the cannon was masterly, and contributed greatly to the ease with which we routed the enemy.'

The eyes that swept his face, as Driberg looked at him, contained such a depth of gratitude that he felt like a louse, a feeling made worse by the reaction of the girl.

'That is a most noble thing to say, Lieutenant,' she added in an arch tone. 'One that sets an example for others to follow.'

Driberg bobbed rather than bowed, his cheeks even redder, and shot out of the door, leaving Markham to speculate that the youngster probably thought his attempt to aid him had been a ploy to further undermine him. The episode had dented the feeling of burgeoning intimacy that had existed before Driberg entered. Markham set himself to recreating it, content to listen while Miss Gordon recounted her recent adventures.

'Naples itself is a cesspit, yet the surrounding country-side is delightful, full of antiquities.'

'Did you visit the excavations at Pompey?'

'I would have done, sir, had they not been recommended to me by that odious creature, Lady Hamilton. I can only assume, that if she recommended them, they must be of such a lewd quality as to be unfit for the decent to peruse. She disports herself semi-naked to be viewed by any passing rake or poltroon, in what she calls her attitudes. How someone who acts as His Majesty's Ambassador could have brought himself to wed such a creature escapes me.'

'I know the lady by name, though I've never met her.'

'Then, sir, you are fortunate, for she is nothing but a common whore. No amount of finery or education can disguise it.'

Emma Hamilton sounded, to him, like a diverting creature. He was just reflecting that the seduction of such a prig as Miss Gordon would add a great deal of spice to the contest when the door burst open. Hanger stood there, his eyes fixed on Markham with a look full of hate.

'Why Colonel Hanger, allow me to introduce . . .'

'I know this man, Miss Gordon, thank you,' he growled. 'And you, Markham, obviously require to be reminded of the custom of standing up in the presence of a senior officer.'

Markham got to his feet with slow deliberation, determined to convey to Hanger that his action was mere convention. The girl was slightly flustered by the turn matters had taken, and spoke, when she really should have stayed quiet.

'The good lieutenant has been in the thick of things.'

'He has that,' snapped Hanger, his eyes still on Markham. 'And in twelve years nothing has changed. He was a coward then and he's still one now.'

'You will withdraw that,' said Markham coldly.

'I will not, and before you threaten to call me out I would remind you of our respective ranks.'

'If you wish to take refuge behind your commission . . .'

Hanger cut right across him, his voice rising to a shout that made the girl cringe. 'Don't use that word to me! Not you. The only commission you deserve is to lead a detail digging latrines. And since I intend to stay here, I'll make sure that shovelling shit is all you get!'

'Colonel Hanger,' Miss Gordon spluttered.

'Your pardon, ma'am,' he replied, without a trace of apology evident in his voice or manner. 'But this specimen before you deserted his post.'

'But he told me . . .'

'Lies. He was ordered to hold at Ollioules, but he ran before a bunch of disorganised deserters. If you don't believe me, Miss Gordon, you may ask him yourself. And while you're at it, ask him about a place called Guilford, in North Carolina.'

He was gone before she could open her mouth, her eyes on the empty doorway where he had stood. 'Well. I must say I shan't be sorry he's no longer aboard our ship.'

'No.'

She turned to look at him, and he could see she was dying to ask him if what Hanger had said was the truth. But her nerve didn't hold and she took refuge in an aside. 'Mind you, for all his coarse manner, he is said to be exceedingly rich.'

With that, she turned and looked out of the window, effectively killing any atmosphere, or vestige of familiarity, which had existed.

# Chapter ten

For the first time in an age, Markham and his men were not required to dig at some point on the Toulon perimeter. The material might not have been as Hanger described, but the shovel was in use for weeks after the remark. It was backbreaking work, hacking out soil that had turned to a rock-like consistency after the long, hot summer months. When the sun wasn't shining it was cloudy and humid, often with a hot southern wind to add to their discomfort. Only the arrival of full darkness brought the longed for orders to return to their billets. But all that toil had one positive advantage. It served to level out some of the ongoing differences between the two groups of men, their mutual antipathy tempered by shared exhaustion. That this did not include their officer, whose task it was to supervise and direct their efforts, was only to be expected.

Markham drove them hard. They were up before dawn, and on their way to the workings with the sun still low in the eastern sky. When not digging trenches, throwing up glacis or building revets with lengths of timber, they were called upon to haul naval guns, these heaved out of the French arsenal and manhandled up to the various bastions nearing completion. With too few men, Lord Mulgrave, who had arrived to take command of the British troops on the ground, could mount no offensive operations.

Nor did the Spaniards, for all their bellicose statements. Gravina's troops showed as much inclination to dig as their commander did to fight. They also caused mayhem in the city, robbing civilians and assuming any Frenchman who looked them in the eye deserved a sword in the guts. But it was their treatment of the women which led to numerous heated exchanges between British and Spanish officers, some of which, at the lower levels, threatened to come to blows. At ranker level, fuelled by cheap drink, they often did. Hanger, who had been given equal status and a shared responsibility with Colonel Serota, had the pleasure of stringing up several men of both nationalities. A Neapolitan contingent, brought in by Captain Nelson, proved even more of a liability. Indeed, only the dilatory nature of the French advance allowed the allies time to complete their outworks.

Events at the Picard house proceeded in their own way, though fortunately all their kit, including Frobisher's trunk, had arrived. During his fleeting visits, Markham heard that the doctors continued to make progress with Jean-Baptiste, but never catching sight of the boy he had no way of knowing if this was true or false. Contact with the other members of the family consisted of nothing but the polite exchanges attendant upon an officer who was either consuming a hurried meal, sleeping, or leading his men off to their labours. His conversations with Rossignol were snatched affairs, his glimpses of Eveline momentary, both laced with moans from Monsieur Picard about the various infractions, real or imagined, made by his men.

But this morning was different. He had time to take more care about his dress, raiding Frobisher's possessions to ensure he turned out at his best. While shaving he noticed that his face had thinned, some of the fleshiness he'd acquired in London now gone, making his nose, high cheekbones and square jaw slightly more pronounced. The stone that had hit him at Ollioules added another small blemish. Touching the tiny scar revived the memory of that battle and the consequences.

He still wasn't on the kind of terms with those he

commanded that he would have liked. Some of the things he'd done – saving Leech, getting them out of Ollioules, and his care of the wounded – had softened the outright hostility of most of the men. They moaned continually, as soldiers do, but sometimes aired their complaints within his hearing, which was a very good way of indicating that they didn't see him as the cause. Some, like Yelland, were quite friendly, though in his case it was in his nature. Halsey was efficient and Schutte cautious, both of them working the men hard. Rannoch had emerged as a natural leader, a man whom even some of the Lobsters responded to.

'And he,' he said to his image in the mirror, 'wouldn't give George Tenby Markham an inch. And sure, why the hell should he?'

Hair trimmed and freshly washed, he donned clean linen, snow-white breeches, the long waistcoat and the shoes with silver buckles. Frobisher's red coat was of the finest material, thick, smooth and perfectly tailored. He put the bronze gorget around his neck, adjusting it so that it sat right between the broad white lapels. The burgundy silk sash was tied around his waist with special care, so that both ends hung down an equal length from the knot. He used one of the dead marine's cambric handkerchiefs to give a final polish to the royal device on the silver buckle, before slipping it, and the sword it carried, over his head. Gold-trimmed hat under his arm, he took one last look at himself, and left.

Wearing good clothes put an extra spring in his step, so he was slightly disappointed that no-one else was about when he came down to take breakfast. The servants informed him that Madame Picard was with the boy, her husband down at the quay supervising the unloading of a newly arrived cargo, while the Rossignol girls were still abed. Their father had, it seemed, left the house at the very crack of dawn.

As he made his way to the Fort de la Malgue, there to

receive his orders, he was aware of a slight chill in the clear morning air, an indication that autumn had arrived. Before entering the portals of the fort, he stopped to adjust his hat and coat. Perhaps because of its newness it seemed very strange, and felt a good deal heavier than his own. He'd appropriated the uniform without being absolutely sure that he was entitled to wear it, even with the rank tabs adjusted. Yet he soon discovered he was not likely to stand out in the unfamiliar apparel. The entrance to the military headquarters was full to overflowing, with well-dressed officers of all three nationalities crowding into the corridors, eager to find out anything they could about the state of the siege.

The sight of Rossignol, edging his way through the throng, was a surprise. The Frenchman stopped when he saw him, his eyes holding a startled expression. Then those same eyes took in the uniform, so much more becoming than the grubby clothes he'd appeared in these last weeks. A small bow followed, and he pushed his way past some gorgeously clad Spaniards to talk, as expansive and confident in his manner as Markham had ever seen him.

'I have just had the good fortune to be appointed as a sutler to your forces. I am, of course, acting as an agent for our host, Monsieur Picard. Am I to assume by your finery, Lieutenant, that you too have prospered, that your life as a mole is over?'

'I wouldn't swear to it, monsieur. It very much depends on what your fellow countrymen do.'

'Please do not refer to them as that,' Rossignol replied, with some distaste. 'Those Republican canaille are scum. It is my fond hope that you and your allies will drive them back into the gutters whence they came.'

'That's rather unlikely,' said Markham.

Rossignol frowned. 'But I've just spoken with two of your officers, one a British colonel. He and the Spaniard, Serota, assured me that Toulon is safe. That troops will be poured in over the next few months and that you will, when ready, take the offensive.'

Markham hesitated before replying. His first thought was that the only British army colonel in the city was Augustus Hanger, a man he'd managed to avoid since the day he arrived. His only sighting had been the distant one of the man on his horse, supervising a multiple execution, which all troops had been obliged to attend as a form of warning. The next thought was that Hanger had lied to Rossignol. Though it was never openly stated, the British were not here for either Toulonais or Bourbon honour. It was the fleet that provided the bait, and if Admiral Hood could have manned the ships, he might just have sailed out of the anchorage and left the city to its fate. But he couldn't. The sailors didn't even exist in England to provide crews for the seventeen line-of-battle ships that the French had ready for sea, let alone the other fourteen either refitting or under repair. And if the sailors were not available, neither were the soldiers. In its long history of conflict between the two countries, Britain had never had enough men to invade and conquer France.

Despite his loathing of the man he had to admit that, given the military situation, it was a perfectly natural thing for a soldier to do. The last thing the occupying army wanted was despair or panic amongst the inhabitants, most of whom had adopted a wait-and-see attitude. Reasonably safe, they were in for a long haul. But telling them that would not keep them calm, secure, co-operative and prepared to advance goods on credit.

But most curious of all was the simple fact that Rossignol had got to see people as elevated as Hanger and Serota in the first place. A glance around the courtyard showed numerous officers of a higher rank than himself waiting to be ushered in to see some staff member. Yet this Frenchman, with no official position that he knew of, who was merely seeking a trading concession, had taken precedence over the lot of them.

'I'm afraid the officers you spoke with have been too sanguine, monsieur.'

'How so?' Rossignol snapped.

Markham ignored the rude tone, enjoying the sensation of undermining Hanger too much to care about that or the consequences of replying. 'We're outnumbered at present, by a margin of perhaps eight to one. I admit that the enemy have not been active, but that is a situation which cannot continue. They have access to the whole of France for supplies and reinforcements, while we must fetch everything we require by sea.'

'But we are close to them, Naples and the like.'

'I wouldn't go putting too much store in the Neapolitans. If their ability with a musket is anything like their use of a shovel, they may prove more of a liability than an asset.'

'There will be troops from England.'

'Did Colonel Hanger tell you this?'

'Yes.'

Markham shrugged. 'He is, of course, privy to information that I do not have. But I would point out to you that England is many hundreds of miles away, and may have commitments that are more important than the retention of a French naval base.'

He knew he'd gone too far and opened his mouth to. say so; to remind the Frenchman that Toulon, given the topography, was near impregnable. Rossignol didn't give him the chance. Spinning round, he barrelled his way out into the courtyard, then stopped outside the gates for a moment, examining the harbour full of shipping. Then he slammed his cane angrily into the cobblestones, before stomping off in the direction of the Picard house.

A commotion behind him made Markham look round. The knot of officers had parted to allow their commanders through. Judging by the scowls on their faces, and the distance they seemed determined to maintain, they had little common purpose. Markham tried to shrink back into the stone wall as he saw Hanger, more through dread of what he might do or say than any physical fear of the man. But Elphinstone spotted him. His face creased as though he were trying to place Markham, then, recognition seemingly dawning, he walked over and addressed him. That didn't bother him half as much as the fact that Hanger followed.

'You've changed your coat, as well as your breeks!' barked the Scotsman, looking him up and down. Then he leant forward, brow knitted, to examine the coat buttons, which bore the fouled anchor device of the marines.

'I have, sir. It is my understanding that I have been transferred from the army.'

Elphinstone's thick eyebrows shot up in surprise, though he looked amused rather than angry. 'Never in life, laddie. It takes more than a scrawl by some Bullock colonel to make a marine officer.' He must have realised that Hanger was close by, within earshot, and that the words he used were rather insulting, since he continued quickly. 'Have you and your Hebes been assigned any duties?'

'No, sir. That is why I came here this morning, to receive my orders.'

'If I could have them for my mobile reserve, Captain?' said Hanger, stepping forward, his cold eyes fixed on Markham's face. 'I'm sure I can find them suitable employment.'

He opened his mouth to protest, but Elphinstone, unaware of any reason to refuse, was too quick. 'Make it so, Colonel.' He made to walk away, then turned back to face him, his eyes suddenly as cold as those of the soldier. 'I understand you made advances towards my niece, Markham.'

'Hardly advances, sir. We engaged in a brief conversation.'

'That is not the way it was told to me. Miss Lizzie Gordon is a bonny creature, and a trifle unworldly. Not for the likes of you, upon my word. Your reputation as a rake is as public as your other handicaps, sir. You will kindly assure me that, should your paths cross in the future, you will stay out of her orbit.'

He opened his mouth to deny both the accusation and the restriction. But Elphinstone wasn't finished, though he spoke so softly that only Markham could hear him.

'"That drop of blood that's calm proclaims me bastard." Laertes to the king, I believe. I told you I never forget a face. And I well remember the way you got that scar above your eye.'

It spoke volumes, that line from *Hamlet*. He racked his brain for a reply. But Elphinstone had already turned away, exposing, behind him, the bland innocent look on the spot-covered face of Midshipman Driberg.

'Take your Hebes to the Fort Malbousquet, Markham,' snarled Hanger. 'Wait for me there.'

'Upon what duty, sir?'

The green eyes bored into his. 'Whatever I choose to command. But it will be warm, that I do assure you.'

Picard caught him before he'd made it to the warehouse door, his thin frame shaking with rage and his hands held high in a gesture of apparent despair. It had been like this ever since they'd taken up residence, a constant stream of complaints directed against his men and the way they behaved. Markham didn't miss out on the irony, didn't tell this ageing French merchant that, though many of them had mellowed, any strictures from him were more likely to be ignored than obeyed. Really, he couldn't comprehend why Picard didn't throw them all out, leaving them to find another, more suitable billet.

From amongst the stream of near incomprehensible babble, he understood that the problem this time was a fire. Picard dragged him through the doorway, his voice now turned to a whine as he explained that his men had lit an open fire within the warehouse, which, given the timber construction, the age of the building, and the fact that the wood was dry, was dangerous enough. But as Picard had supplied the French navy with combustibles, gunpowder, flares and inflammable spirits, which were stacked on the floor above the soldiers, such an action threatened to blow them all to Kingdom Come.

Markham made his way to the stairs, requesting the civilian to wait for him, and ascended to the first floor. The smell was obvious before he'd climbed a single step, a fragrance of burning wood, hot gun oil. Then, up closer, what seemed like the acrid odour of fiery metal.

Emerging on to the first floor, he was struck, once more, by the way that his men had turned it into a version of their own favoured accommodation. The Bullocks had constructed a replica barracks on one side of the double doors, with beds made of boxes and straw stuffed into empty sacks, while the Lobsters had slung hammocks on the other, and lined their limited possessions neatly against the wall. Given a day of rest after all their toil, it ·was hardly surprising that most of the beds and hammocks were occupied. Nor did it shock him that none of the occupants saw fit to leap to their feet just because he'd arrived.

The glowing brazier stood between the two sets of accommodation, by the open double doors that overlooked the quay. Rannoch was bent over it, working on something, his broad back drenched with sweat that stained his calico shirt. Markham approached gingerly, curious to see what this man was doing. At his feet lay a short metal tube, very like part of a musket barrel, and a primitive pair of scales, with a rod attached to a tripod, an empty pan at one end, and a brass ball at the other.

Schutte and this Highlander still occupied their respective ranks. If they were going to return to being soldiers instead of navvies, that needed to be sorted out. The Dutchman had come into the marine service as an alternative to residence in a prisoner-of-war hulk. As dense as he was bald, prone to sulk, with only his uncommon strength, added to a brutal nature, to recommend him, he would never earn the respect of both sets of men. But Rannoch was different. He was certainly insubordinate, but there was nothing bovine about his actions or his words. They were calculated, always just on the edge of an unpleasant truth. Markham was sure he could discern, in those green eyes, the workings of a brain, without being sure whether he was seeing evidence of mental prowess or low cunning.

'You will not mind if I do not get to my feet,' said Rannoch, in his slow, clear way.

'I've long since given up expecting any disciplined behaviour from the likes of you,' he snapped in reply, wondering how the Scotsman had known, without turning round, that it was him. 'It's my misfortune to be burdened with you, something I intend to change at the first opportunity.'

'If you can make it on solid earth, I will not complain.'

Markham had come close enough to see over the sergeant's shoulder. He'd placed a tin ladle into the brazier, with several musket balls. Markham watched as the lead slowly melted. As soon as it was liquid, Rannoch lifted it out and poured the metal slowly into a hinged mould, which had half a dozen bowls on either side. The spare lead was tipped into a tin mug, and after waiting for a moment until the metal started to set, Rannoch gingerly picked the first hot ball out with a pair of pliers, then plunged that into a bucket of water by his leg. The metal hissed, sending a cloud of steam into the low rafters. After a second, the sergeant took it out, opened it, exposing the now formed ball to view, before tipping it into the bucket, there to cool completely. He repeated this until the main mould was empty.

'Monsieur Picard is somewhat upset about the fire.'

Rannoch, who was loading more musket balls into his

tin ladle, looked round and grinned. It was the first time Markham had seen him show any pleasure, let alone smile, and the change was pleasing. But it didn't last. It was a fleeting thing, soon gone. He reached into the bucket, produced a dull grey ball, scraped the flakes off the edges and held it up.

'Well tell him that when his friends come to chop off his head at the neck, on that infernal toy they use, he might just be thankful for me doing this.'

'Douse it,' snapped Markham. 'Get the men on their feet and downstairs.'

Rannoch picked up the metal tube lying at his feet, and as he stood up he slipped the musket ball into it, holding it up to the light. Then he tilted the tube so that the ball ran through it, to land in his waiting hand. The bellow that followed, delivered so close to Markham's ear, achieved what was intended. It roused the soldiers, and made their officer jump.

'On your feet, you lazy, heathen bastards! We are off to the war again.'

'Schutte, Halsey,' shouted Markham. 'You too. I want you downstairs in full equipment in five minutes.'

Rannoch was gathering his tools, in a leisurely and infuriating way. After a quick glance below, to make sure the quay was clear, Markham hooked his foot around the leg of the brazier and tipped it out of the open door.

'If you don't get a move on, the bucket will follow.'

The Highlander suppressed his anger very well, pulling himself slowly to his full height. For a moment Markham thought he was going to hit him, and prepared to jump back out of reach. But Rannoch just looked at him hard, and spoke in a voice devoid of emotion or respect.

'It would be a pity to do that, now. Those balls, they are measured to perfection, barring the weight. They have a home to go to in the flesh of some poor soul.'

The way the sergeant was looking at him, Markham suspected that some of the flesh might be his. He spun on his heel and made his way downstairs, reassuring Picard on the way that his warehouse, as well as his combustibles, were now safe from a conflagration. Crossing the inner courtyard he caught sight of Eveline at one of the upstairs windows. She waved to him and smiled invitingly, which made him curse the duty that removed any opportunity to follow up and find out just what lay behind the look.

As he passed the small salon he heard Madame Picard talking slowly and deliberately, as if to herself. Curiosity made him push the door open further. The boy sat on a stool, looking at her with that bland lack of expression that he'd had the day he'd first seen him. She, with a reverential air, was kneeling in front of him, holding a large book of colourful drawings to the boy's face, saying 'mama' and 'papa' over and over again.

With no children of her own, Madame Picard had taken to the boy, spending much time in his company, no doubt engaged in the very same activity he was now observing. Such maternal feelings in a woman who lacked, to his knowledge, much natural compassion, was good to behold, proving that even the most hardened breast was home to finer feelings. Markham found himself staring at the embossed gold and red background of the book's cover, thinking that both she, and the doctors, had made very little progress.

Suddenly aware of his presence, Madame Picard spun round, her puffy, pale face full of consternation. She snapped the book shut with a resounding thud and started to get to her feet. The boy looked round slowly, his handsome, sallow countenance registering no emotion as he too saw the soldier in the doorway. Markham opened his mouth to apologise for the intrusion.

'Pardon, monsieur.'

He reacted to the voice behind him, for all that it was soft and respectful, like a man caught at a keyhole. Celeste stood with a tray in her hand, a steaming bowl of soup lying alongside a hunk of bread. Markham had seen even less of her than he had of the others these last weeks. She had lost some of the hunted air he remembered from the day they arrived, and any physical scars she bore had long since healed. But she was painfully thin, her olive skin rather translucent, giving her an undernourished air.

'Celeste. Are you well?'

She curtsied, her body moving while the tray stayed still, her long dark hair dropping to her waist. 'Perfectly, monsieur.'

'And you are comfortable?'

'Yes.'

He decided to take the ritual reassurance for what it was, a desire to avoid discussion. He stood aside to let her enter, his eyes following her as she passed him. Her body was beginning to develop, though fate had made her a woman before nature had the chance. Her hips seemed larger, swaying under her loose dress, something which he realised he was examining with surprising dispassion. One day, he thought, she'd be an attractive young lady. Not a beauty, but very pleasant.

For the first time, as she approached the centre of the room, he saw the boy react to another human being. His lips moved in the merest ghost of a smile. But the deep eyes, so much more expressive than any other part of him, looked pleased. And they followed Celeste as she passed by to lay the tray on the table, in such a way that Madame Picard could not avoid barking at her. Celeste put the tray down and bobbed a hurried curtsy before running out. Looking back into the room he saw that the old lady, her position challenged, was angry. But he noticed that the boy, for just a fraction of a second, looked sad.

The distant clash of boots and equipment reminded him of his duty, and he rushed off to change into his army uniform coat. He had no idea what Hanger had in mind for him and his Hebes. But it would be unpleasant and very likely dirty work, not something that would do Frobisher's best outfit much good.

# Chapter eleven

'If you look over yonder, Markham, you'll see a pair of masked cannon.' Hanger turned to include Serota, who sat on a horse by his side, in the conversation. 'That is the newly constructed Batterie de Bregaillon, manned with field guns that have a part of the harbour in range.'

Serota coughed softly, covering his yellowing face with his hand, as Markham swung Frobisher's small telescope in an arc from the hill called La Seyne to the south, through the freshly dug defences in front of the northern heights, to the great bight of water to his rear. He'd met plenty of emigré French officers in Russia who'd waxed lyrical about the advances their country had made in the use of artillery. The armies of the Revolution had certainly surprised everyone by the ferocity and mobility with which they used their guns at Valmy. But none of that applied to what he could observe in front of him now.

'I can see that they don't have a hope of either bombarding the dockyard, the basin, or closing off the entrance to the Petite Rade, sir. And even if they did, two field guns hardly constitute a serious threat.'

Hanger glowered at him, not wishing to hear the obvious. That, in truth, Cartaux had sited this artillery too far away from the centre of activity to do much harm. Any ship that wanted could engage these emplacements by shifting their moorings. But for all practical purposes they were offensively useless.

'The only thing they have done,' Markham continued, 'is to deny us a site we had no intention of occupying anyway.'

'How do you know that?' asked Serota. The answer was so obvious that Markham merely shrugged, throwing a glance past the Spaniard's horse to the regiment of soldiers he'd brought forward from Fort Malbousquet. Caught between coughing and speech, Serota's next words, which he tried to deliver with a flourish, exited his throat in a wheeze. 'They impugn our honour.'

'We can't have the buggers getting the wrong idea.' growled Hanger, more prosaically. 'I think they should be taught that if they leave themselves exposed, they'll be punished.'

'With respect,' Markham replied, trying hard to keep his voice even. 'It's a bad idea to throw away men's lives. The best way to show the French we're not fools is to leave that battery alone. And since we're in range, and not under fire, I daresay the man commanding those field pieces thinks exactly the same.'

'If you wish to decline the honour, Markham?'

The hope that he would shone in Hanger's eyes. For Markham it would be a further loss of face. As an officer he had every right to reject such an order, and if admonished, ask for a court of inquiry to vindicate him. But with his past that would be a sure way to invite retribution for what many perceived as his past errors. It would allow Hanger to air, publicly, every detail of what had happened at the Battle of Guilford, to say outright that any other group of officers than one convened by his natural father would have found him guilty of cowardice.

But he was not being asked to assault these positions on his own. The Spaniards, a Catalan regiment, he could do nothing about. But the Hebes would have to attack with him. Even a military novice could see that such an assault couldn't be undertaken without risking serious casualties. To give himself time to think, Markham re-examined the ground. Between the shoreline and the guns, it was dotted with gentle hillocks, making it, by

Toulonais standards, relatively flat. But it was still nearly a third of a mile of open country, with little in the way of cover. On the extreme left, it was grassland, and that ran right across the front of the embankments protecting the guns, providing a perfect avenue for an attack by cavalry. Where the ground began to break up there were a series a small hillocks, a few trees and some gorse.

To the very right, where his men were assembled, lay bad infantry country, rising steadily towards the mountains inland, broken and hilly, dotted with fallen rocks, which would make an ordered advance impossible. Ideally, they should have brought forward artillery to subdue and distract the guns, thrown out a cavalry screen to the left to suppress any mounted counter-attack, and brought up enough infantry to convince the French commander that discretion, and withdrawal, was his best course.

A pure infantry attack would only convince the same fellow that his enemies were mad. Advancing in line, they would have to cover over half the distance without firing a shot. Then, at extreme musket range, they could open up with a volley that might do no more than make the gunners duck. To stand still and reload would be marginally less hazardous than rushing the guns, always assuming that enough men survived to attempt it.

'Why the delay, Markham? Is this the way they do things in Muscovy?' That made Markham turn around sharply. He'd kept very quiet about being on foreign service aboard the *Hebe*, and since Hanger had come from Naples he could hardly be aware of any gossip prevalent in London. The Colonel was grinning at him, glad to see that his remark had caused surprise. 'I know all about your Russian service, Markham. And it's the right place for someone like you.'

Clearly Hanger didn't know everything, how that service had ended. 'It will give me great pleasure to hand your men over to another officer, one who has a little fire in his belly, a proper soldier who will not embarrass me in front of our allies.'

As Hanger stared at him, Markham was trying to work out more than a method of attack. He was wondering why he should care about his mixed command of Lobsters and Bullocks, who had so comprehensively undermined him when he was forced to take over from Frobisher. At Ollioules he suspected that someone had taken a shot at him. And in the final assault their tardiness, up against a better equipped opponent, could have cost him everything. The improved atmosphere that had surfaced when digging trenches was no guarantee that when called upon to fight, they wouldn't revert to their previous behaviour.

Occupied with his own thoughts, the words he heard were slow to filter through. But they did eventually, and the conclusion was sobering. The same men would be used to attack the batteries regardless of his participation. Hanger would sacrifice them, and the life of another officer, just to see him damned.

'Well?'

Markham looked at Serota, hoping that in those eyes he might see some common sense. But the face was expressionless, leaving him to wonder if this madcap idea, in which the Dons would suffer many more casualties than the British, had been his or Hanger's.

'I accept.'

Serota coughed, which in another man would have sounded like surprise. Had he hoped that Markham would decline, giving him an honourable way to do the same? Hanger grinned, his pleasure so profound that it turned the long, ragged scar on his face white.

'It's an interesting reflection on the nature of cowardice, Markham, that a man can actually be more afraid of a refusal than a bayonet in his guts.'

'I'm always willing to follow you, Hanger.'

'Colonel!' he yelled, startling the Spanish officer at his side, busy signalling for his own men to get to their feet.

'Not to me.' Markham replied coldly. 'I think of you as a bully and a murderer, a man who's a disgrace to the uniform you wear. I don't suppose Salisbury was the only town you burned. No doubt you're fit for service in some Maharajah's Indian rabble.'

'I see your game,' said Hanger, struggling to control his temper. 'I'll not call off our portion of the attack just to see you court-martialled for insubordination.'

'I never thought you would.'

'Line up your men.'

'My orders, if you please?'

Hanger pointed his riding crop towards the French guns. 'You're to attack that position, taking station to the right of Colonel Serota's Spaniards. And if you cannot capture the cannon, destroy them.'

'In writing.'

'Most happily, Markham,' said Hanger, reaching into his saddlebag for the necessary materials. He scribbled quickly, tore off the page, and handed it over. Markham took the slip of paper, turned on his heel and marched over to where his men were gathered. As usual the marines were in one group, the soldiers in another, but both were eyeing their allies warily, as the Spanish officers bullied them into untidy lines.

'Gather round, all of you. I want to talk to you.'

They looked at each other, suspicion evident in almost every eye. In the world they inhabited, afloat or ashore, officers shouted at them, if they bothered to address them at all. They certainly didn't engage in cosy chats like this one was suggesting. Markham waited patiently, watching the nudging and shoving that was needed to make some men move.

'Come along, Lieutenant,' shouted Hanger, 'get them lined up. We haven't got all day.'

Markham ignored him, his eyes still on his reluctant command. Because of that, he picked up the first sign that they had a common purpose. Every eye that flickered

145

in Hanger's direction held a degree of hate in it that, undisguised, surpassed anything he'd ever had directed at him. He'd been about to issue some words of encouragement, but that suddenly decided him to tell the unvarnished truth.

'Both those Colonels over there, the British one especially, would like to see us killed.'

'Then he is no different to most officers,' said Rannoch, the lilt of his Highland tone so at odds with the venom of the sentiment.

'No,' Markham replied, looking straight into his eyes. Instinct told him that if he could convince this man, he might at least carry the soldiers with him. The marines, especially Schutte, were another matter. 'I don't suppose he is. But his particular reason for doing so is to spite me, not you.'

'That is none of our concern.'

'Unfortunately it is, Rannoch. He's selected us to take part in an attack on those French guns. If I don't lead you then another officer will, someone who hasn't got the sense to see that the whole affair is unnecessary, nor the wit to realise that the ground between us and them is no good for a standard infantry assault. Any line trying to march across that terrain will be in tatters before they get halfway. It's a job for skirmishers.'

'Which we are not trained for, in case you had not noticed.'

'Then you'd better damn well learn,' Markham snapped. 'And just in case you're thinking of being shy, then I can tell you that redcoat Colonel is aptly named. You've seen him in action. He loves to watch a hanging almost as much as he likes the idea of seeing me dead. He'll dangle the lot of you from a rope, and grin from ear to ear while he does it. And that will be after he's treated you each to a thousand lashes.'

'Fuckin' officers,' said Tully, ducking his head to avoid being seen by Markham.

Markham mimicked Hanger's gravelly voice, so accurately that half his men looked at the colonel, wondering how he could sound so close. 'How right you are, Tully. I've no time for most of the sods myself.'

Several of his men gasped audibly. Those who'd been looking at him turned away. Yet they declined to engage any other eye, lest by doing so they indicate agreement. But underneath that were one or two faint negative murmurs, which might just mean that perhaps they were beginning to see him differently.

'There is of course one way to get out unscathed. Put a ball in my back and trust that your retreat will be seen as a panic instead of cowardice.'

'Are you going to be much longer, Markham?' Hanger shouted. The Catalan regiment was lined up, ready to begin the advance.

Markham's reply was even louder. 'If you'd care to lead us yourself, sir, I'm sure my men would, like me, consider it an honour. They admire valour in an officer.'

Rannoch laughed, a clear indication that he understood the nuances of what was happening better than his fellows. They, less sure, joined in only to avoid being seen to have missed a joke. Markham was grinning himself as he turned back to face them.

'That shut his trap, sir,' said Yelland.

'We have no choice, sergeant,' he said to Rannoch, the grin turning earnest very easily.

'I do not suppose we do,' he replied, fingering his musket.

Markham's hand swung and his finger jabbed as he issued instructions that might just keep some of them alive. 'We're not going to form a line, but move forward in two groups. Stay off that clear ground to the south. Let the Spaniards occupy that, so that they draw the defenders' fire, as well as any cavalry. Use the terrain and stay low. They won't ignore us, no matter how tempting a target the Dons provide. Hide when you feel you can, then advance when the fire shifts to another target. Above all, keep moving forward. Any man who gets stuck, and tries to avoid the fighting, I'll probably hang myself. We've got to cover at least four hundred yards before we can fire a shot. I will signal extreme range. Don't blaze off at anything you don't think you can hit. If you haven't fired a musket lying down before, you'll find it's actually a lot easier to aim it. Use the ground to rest the muzzle. Don't reload until you can find cover to stand upright.'

His mind was racing, trying to convert a complex military operation into a few simple orders. Really, it would come down to common sense. Those who had the wit to see the way to fight would employ it, those who didn't would either take refuge or die. At least, dispersed, they might not be subjected to salvoes of case shot, something they'd certainly face if they attacked in line.

'Right, we're going to move off in two groups, the Sixty-fifth to that run of hillocks on the left, marines to that dip at the foot of the hill nearest the guns. Rannoch, you will lead the Bullocks, and I'll take charge of the Lobsters.'

There was a pause, with Markham wondering if Rannoch was considering refusal. But his expression, followed by the slow nod, demonstrated that he saw the sense in what was being proposed. The men Markham had brought to France were a rum bunch. But whatever training they'd had, it was in land warfare, which was not the case with the bulk of the marines.

'And Rannoch, when we get close enough, see if you can make those balls you were so busy fashioning do some damage.'

'Oh, they will do that, all right, never fear.'

'Dammit, Markham,' Hanger shouted, 'what are you about! Get your men in line.'

Rannoch looked over Markham's shoulder, his musket shifting slightly. 'It might be an idea for that fat fellow to get out of range. Him and that yellow-skinned Spaniard.'

'You leave them be, Sergeant. If anyone is going to exact retribution for this piece of stupidity, it will be me.'

Suddenly both cannon opened up, their shot pitched just short of the Catalan soldiers. The lines before the point of impact dissolved in fright, with men diving left and right, or falling face down on the ground to avoid the balls that ricocheted off the hard-packed earth. Markham wondered if they'd done it to concentrate the attackers' minds, to point out the futility of what they seemed set to undertake. Those Frenchmen had no more desire to die than he did himself.

Their next salvo seemed to have a similar aim, since they raised the range, the black balls screaming over the heads of the infantry. One landed within feet of Hanger, sending a huge plume of earth skywards, before the bounce took it whistling past his ear. The horse reared with fright but he held it well, forcing the animal back down onto four hooves and steadying it expertly. Serota's mount had skipped away, and he had to ride in a long circle before he could calm it enough to bring it back to its original position. His sword was aloft and he shouted, hoarsely, for his soldiers to advance.

'Go!' shouted Markham, pushing the men at the front.

Rannoch's voice bellowed out beside his ear, giving clear instructions to the men, then he ran ahead of them to lead them to decent cover. Markham turned to the marines, noticing that Schutte was well to the rear of the leading section, but there was no time to correct this. Nor was this the moment to raise questions of rank and responsibility.

'Corporal Halsey! Two lines, well spread out. You take one section, I'll take the other.'

The small, greying corporal reacted in a manner that pleased him, taking his men forward by example rather than cajolery. The enemy were, naturally, still concentrating on the Spaniards, three hundred strong. What had been two untidy lines had now broken up slightly into disjointed groupings, because of the terrain. With only two cannon to bombard them, the Frenchmen seemed content to inflict limited damage. That, he guessed, wouldn't continue. Once the Catalans were halfway to the Batterie de Bregaillon they'd employ case shot and decimate them. And they couldn't have failed to see the redcoats to their left, moving like skirmishers, or failed to understand the threat they presented if they reached the nearby foothills.

'Rannoch,' he yelled, as he saw the leading Spaniards come abreast of the sergeant's position. 'I'm going to take the marines to that pile of rocks about two hundred yards from the guns. If there's any fire we should draw it. Don't wait till we arrive. Move out beforehand. You mustn't give them any time to settle on your range.'

Markham was gone without waiting for a reply, sword in one hand and pistol in the other, crouched low and moving from side to side, the Lobsters at his heels. Rannoch and the Bullocks came out from cover when they were halfway to their goal, sprinting for the clumps of gorse which would put them about the same distance from the target.

The French still concentrated on the Spaniards. The first explosion, denoting case shot, followed by the screams of the wounded, came sooner than Markham had expected. Subjected to that, the Dons could easily break and run, leaving the redcoats to face the salvoes alone. That added a dollop of dread to his pace, so that when he reached the rocks, he dived behind them gratefully.

'Over halfway and no casualties, I think,' he gasped. 'We're doing well.'

'Poor sods,' said Halsey, pointing to the open, southern plain.

The Catalans were suffering now, and in seeking mutual protection they were bunching together, providing the French with better targets. But that wouldn't last long, and despite their bravery, and the efforts of their officers, their forward motion had slowed, and they looked very close to giving up. Logic dictated that having got this far without drawing down fire, the redcoats should avoid attracting attention. But seeing what was happening to the exposed Spanish infantry defied reflection. Even at extreme range, if they could divert the French gunners, they might save the Dons from being forced to retreat.

'Present,' he shouted, his eyes searching the landscape for Rannoch and his Bullocks. He saw them, only halfway to their goal, lying in the open, presumably having taken cover from the same doses of case shot peppering their allies. Being close to the Spanish right flank put them in some danger, and underscored the need for him to create a diversion.

Dymock had got himself in a mess, his gun facing the wrong way. Markham grabbed it and hauled it round, steadying both it and the marine as he issued instructions, his hand slapping down on the rim of a rock. 'Muskets on these, and take aim on the earthworks around those cannon. Try to keep the barrel from kicking up and your eyes open as you fire.'

Markham stood on the biggest rock and waved his sword, shouting to the Bullocks to go forward. As soon as he saw the first movement of a red coat he called down to the marines to open fire. Fifteen men were never going to stop the French from discharging their guns. But he saw the heads above the earthworks, which were ranging the cannon, disappear, one of the muzzles being heaved round towards them, and he tried to calculate the timing as the men below him frantically reloaded.

'Rannoch,' he yelled. 'Those gunners are going to give us a salvo. As they discharge, I want a volley over the top. With luck you might get one of them trying to observe the fall of shot.'

Not knowing the exact range, the commander of the

battery was taking a calculated risk in halving his ability to break the Catalans. They'd have to fire at least once to see the result, and Markham intended to be gone before they could get in a second. He ducked down just in time. The gun was suddenly shrouded in a cloud of black smoke, the red of the discharge just a spot in the centre. As he hit the shale behind the rocks, face down, the shell exploded to the front of their position, and a whole raft of balls then whistled past.

Markham was on his knees, yelling at his men to move, taking the lead himself and heading for the next piece of cover, the dip in the landscape he'd spotted from their starting point. Once there, he stood on the edge, screaming at those behind him to hurry. At the same time he was desperately trying to check on Rannoch's progress, ignoring the sudden fusillade of musket balls that cracked as they passed overhead. He could see the Highlander moving forward, slowly now, encouraging men now subjected to musket fire themselves.

And still the guns boomed out, both back on their original target, sending shrapnel into the Dons, who'd lost all forward motion and were crouching down to try and escape their fate. As he watched they broke, which had Markham searching for cavalry. But it wasn't that which had defeated them, it was the losses they'd suffered by advancing in lines. The number of yellow-coated bodies that covered the landscape testified to that.

Not that retreat saved them. The French elevated their guns, pouring more case into their huddled, scurrying ranks, probably inflicting more damage now than they had when the Catalans were advancing. Should he retreat too? As a course of action it had almost as many risks as going on, especially for the Bullocks, who had been left high and dry. In fact, from what he could see Rannoch was using the enemy's concentration on the retreating infantry to move forward to a better position.

'Where's Schutte?' demanded Halsey, raising his head to look for the Dutchman.

'He's still back behind those rocks,' said Dymock.

'Wounded?'

'Afeard!' Dymock spat as he said that, his face curled up in a sneer that turned to consternation when he heard Markham's shout. What he couldn't know was that by using that word he fixed his commander's resolve. There was no way he was going to fall back and allow Augustus Hanger to use that word about him.

'Forget Schutte. We're on our own now, which means that we've got two of those cannon to contend with. Every man to move out as soon as they fire the next salvo.'

He pointed his sword in the direction of the enemy, his mind registering the darker slash of what looked like a ditch right ahead, as well as the twin muzzles of the cannon being heaved round to take aim on them again.

'They're getting ready to fire,' shouted Halsey. Markham threw himself down once more as the guns belched flame and smoke. It was a good shot, certainly better than anything they'd experienced at Ollioules. Both balls of case exploded within thirty feet of the rim of the depression. One Lobster, who'd dropped back to the rear slightly, had sacrificed his cover in doing so. Several of the small balls, blown out of their metal casing, peppered his uniform, making him jerk like a rag doll. But the rest of Markham's party, hugging the ground, were protected by the top of the dip. Earth flew off the rim, covering them in a layer of dust.

'Out of here now!'

He wasn't so much leading by example as he jumped up, more galvanised by terror. The cannon would be reloaded in thirty seconds or less, and the next salvo would be right above their heads, making mincemeat of anyone caught underneath. He heard the shoes pounding behind him. Those gunners had shown some skill, and that changed the odds, which were never very good, even more in the favour of the French. He was suddenly surrounded by sliding, slithering bodies, as those who'd come to join him scurried to get some protection behind individual rocks.

'Halsey, for God's sake spread your men out!'

Only half his mind was on what Halsey was doing as he ordered his marines to split up. The French had swung their pieces onto Rannoch's group, who were huddled amongst the trees and clumps of gorse. If they stayed there they would die.

'Forward at the next salvo, Halsey, and fire on the run. There's something that looks like an irrigation ditch running right towards the northwest. Get into that before you reload. Then move up until you can play on the French flank.'

He was on his feet before the guns spoke a second time, running flat out to the knot of redcoats, men who scrabbled so hard at the ground they looked as though they were trying to bury themselves. His hat flew off, removed by a wayward ball, his ears full of shrieks of a man wounded as the rest of the case shot, fired high, found flesh. By the time he reached them several men were writhing in agony, calling out to God and their mothers to come to their assistance.

'On me,' he shouted, running past them, his sword waving the air. Frightened they certainly were, those still fit to run, but they knew that to stay still was worse than moving. His eyes searched ahead for a place to hide, and he heard his own voice screaming at those running with him to spread out, his hasty shouts identifying places, trees, tussocks and dips where two or three attackers could take cover. Men fell, some shot, others merely stumbling. His heart was pounding in his chest as he made it to the base of a gnarled oak tree right at the edge of the clear ground in front of the guns, Rannoch cannoning into him as he did so. Pieces of wood flew about their ears as every musket, now firing at no more than fifty yards, seemed to single them out. That was followed by a cannonball, which hit a tree close to their left, smashing it to pieces.

'If you do not put aside that sword, you are a dead man,' Rannoch gasped. 'That ball was aimed at you.'

Markham replied, equally breathless. 'It makes no odds. The uniform tells them I'm the officer. And I don't suppose they like the breed any more than you do.'

Another ball swished by above their head, lopping off several branches in its passage. Rannoch managed a ghost of a smile. 'What now?'

Markham searched the landscape to his right, in vain, it seemed. Halsey and his men were out of sight, and he was stuck here until the marines were in place. Thankfully, the merest ghost of a red coat showed on a hunched back as it moved along the ditch which had been their destination.

'There's fifty yards of open ground before the guns. Halsey and his men are in a good position to our right that might actually overlap the French defences, which will allow them to give us covering fire. What we have to do is wait until they are ready, then give them something to cover.'

'So it will be death or glory you are asking for?'

'I'm afraid so,' he replied, pointing his sword towards the marines, now coming above the edge of the ditch, well forward, muskets sliding along the ground, ready to fire. The French tried case shot again, firing beyond the Bullocks in the hope of wounding them in the back. They overdid the range, but that just meant the next attempt would be more dangerous. Rannoch replied to Markham's conclusion in his usual deliberate way.

'Then we had best be about it, or we will get the death part where we stand.' He was on his feet before Markham finished nodding, his huge frame visible to everybody, shouting at the top of his voice. 'On your feet, and fix bayonets. Run like the hounds of hell are on your tail.'

They screamed like banshees, from a combination of fear and excitement, Rannoch's Highland battle cry louder than the rest. The gunners were stymied. Case shot fired on an enemy at such close range risked their own lives, since fuses too short could explode in the barrel. Only those with muskets could beat back the assault. But the men they were trying to kill were well spread out, coming at them fast over that swathe of open ground, leaving them little time to reload.

The air of calm behind the embankment had evaporated, as it dawned on the defenders that they might be taken, and any thought of firing cannon was put aside in favour of increasing the number of muskets. The braver souls amongst them fell to Halsey and his marines as they stood up to take aim, half their bodies above the parapet, presenting a large target for carefully aimed guns. Turning to engage the Lobsters allowed those Bullocks with loaded weapons to take aim on men no more than ten feet distant. Bodies spun left and right as the Frenchmen were caught between two fires. Rannoch had to dodge when he reached the base of the earthworks, as one wounded defender thrust forward desperately with his bayonet. He parried, then pinned his opponent, pushing his own blade into the space between the hunched shoulder and then neck, then pulling the trigger when it was embedded, to blow his enemy's head off his shoulders.

Markham only saw that act on the very edge of his vision. For him time and sound had ceased to exist. He felt that he was in a cocoon, a shell that insulated him from everything around him but the scream from his own dry throat. It barely registered, the increase in the slope as he charged up to the fascined edge. Below him, frightened faces looked up, jabbing at him with bayonets that he swept aside with his sword. He cut, parried and thrust without a conscious thought, reacting to flashes of flesh and colour as they appeared on the periphery of his vision.

It was crowded, red coats mixed with blue and green, men swinging muskets as clubs, and using detached bayonets as knives. It took no more than a minute for the redcoats to get down to ground level, more to drive the enemy back. The wheels of the cannon provided some of the defenders with what they thought to be a slight shield, until they found themselves being speared through the spokes. Men fell, to be trampled on regardless of the colour of their coats. Blood flew from new wounds, spraying those around as one man was stabbed in the throat, another sliced wide open by an officer's sword. Markham registered that and turned to face it. The Frenchman was as eager to get to him, and they clashed with their weapons across their chest. There was no room for swordplay and Markham head-butted him viciously, sending a fountain of blood streaming from his smashed nose, to cover the blue facings of his coat. As soon he staggered back Markham stabbed him in the groin, twisting the blade as the man doubled over.

The crush was easing. He had a vague impression of Halsey's marines among the attackers now. They'd sacrificed their cover and come to aid the Bullocks, the weight of their attack driving the remaining Frenchmen backwards. Without any word of command, more from a collective realisation of defeat, the enemy broke and ran. Suddenly Markham found space in front of him, a chance to suck in a desperately needed breath, as he realised that, despite the odds, he and his mixed bag of indifferent Lobsters and undisciplined Bullocks had just won a battle.

# Chapter twelve

The dread word 'Cavalry!', despite their exhaustion, made every head snap up. Markham, who had just sent a party of men back to see to his own wounded, jumped up onto one of the limbers to take a look. It wasn't difficult to pick them out, a whole squadron, some fifty men, off to the right on the other side of the Marseilles road, wheeling round to face him. Whoever was in command of that detachment would be in trouble, forced to recapture a position which should never have been lost. Had they been mounted earlier, and ready to charge, they would have made mincemeat of the retreating Spaniards. And if Markham had come on, his rush across the open space before the guns might have ended in death, with every Bullock mown down by a cavalry sabre.

But their appearance forced him to make a much quicker decision about his next move. He'd never doubted for a moment that the French would try to retake the emplacement, if only as a sop to their pride. But an infantry attack, which would take time to prepare and execute, would at least have allowed the tattered Catalan regiment to reform and offer support. Any attempt actually to hold the battery, without a major commitment of force, was doomed. But with enough time, it would be possible to fetch up some horses and remove the guns. Nothing hurt an artilleryman more than the loss of their cannon, an event that cheered the successful foot soldier even more.

It would take a lot to cheer up the Catalans, even if they could see that their sacrifice had not been entirely in vain. For every redcoat casualty that Markham could see

158

to his rear there were a dozen in yellow, some bunched together in bloody clumps where one shell had taken its toll, their compatriots moving amongst them to lift and take in the wounded. Serota would be trying, he was sure, to send what remnants he had forward. But the time for that was past. Demoralised, out in the open, and at the mercy of cavalry, they wouldn't be able to stand.

The idea of taking the guns was so tempting he was loath to let it go. Searching his mind, for a solution, he remembered that half his men were marines, all of whom must have worked the cannon on board *Hebe* at some time.

'Halsey. How many of your Lobsters are trained gunners?'

'Every man jack's handled a piece at one time, sir. But there's not a gun captain among us. It's mostly hauling on ropes that we were set to.'

'But you've seen them loaded and fired at close quarters?'

'Aye,' the corporal replied, guardedly.

'Good.'

'That don't mean we can fire 'em.'

'You're going to have to learn. Can we get them turned round to face those cavalry?'

Halsey peered at the horsemen. 'Not if they charge now.'

'Stand by to spike them if they get into a gallop. If we're forced to run we can tip them off their carriages as well, so get some men ready with axes to smash the wheels.'

'What about a charge put in the supply of the powder?' Halsey asked, slapping the caisson at the back of the limber.

Markham nodded, still keeping his eyes firmly fixed on the enemy. They'd sorted out their line and the officer, probably impatient to rescue his honour, raised his sword to order the advance. He had to do something to slow them down.

'Rannoch, what are the odds on hitting the man waving the sword?'

The Highlander jumped up to join him, holding a wetted finger up to feel the wind. The change in his attitude to Markham was obvious. There was no scowling or insubordination now. 'I can do it, maybe, if he comes on. But there is a breeze, and you know how that affects a Brown Bess.'

'I want to stop him before they get into a canter.'

'It is worth a try.'

Rannoch jumped down, pulling the base of the small metal tripod he'd used as makeshift scales from his pack. He rammed it into the loose earth that the French had built up at the rear of their emplacement. The second piece, inserted in the tube, was V shaped and spun easily on the main assembly. It was a neat way of turning an ordinary musket into something very like a swivel gun. He ignored the men working around him, heaving, hauling and cursing as they sought to reverse the cannon. Halsey had men standing by with powder, shot, water buckets, swabs and rammers, so that the cannon could be loaded as soon as they were in place. The French officer's sword dropped, and the men behind him began to walk their horses. Rannoch, now lying down, wriggled to adjust his position.

'It has to be now,' said Markham softly.

He wriggled some more, as if his officer hadn't spoken, stating quite clearly that he had no intention of being rushed. Markham watched as his hands manipulated both trigger guard and muzzle, saw him pull the brass butt of the stock tight into his shoulder. The French began to canter as his finger slowly squeezed the trigger.

It needed a strong man to pull on a musket trigger with just one finger, in such a way that the gun didn't move off true aim. Rannoch was such a man, and with the tripod to help him he never wavered as the trigger came back. Suddenly the flintlock crashed forward, sending the spark that lit the powder in the pan. The flash singed his hair, and left a black mark along his cheek. But that didn't register. What did was the ball that took the French officer in the upper leg, knocking him sideways off his horse.

Leaderless, and not yet in a headlong charge, the rest of his men hauled on their reins and came to a confused halt, milling around in disorder as they tried to see where the shot had come from. Markham's men had stopped work, and stood silent in the final few seconds. Several jaws, not least those of the Lobsters, dropped open when they saw what Rannoch had achieved. Most of them had never consciously hit anything they'd aimed at in their lives, certainly not at what looked to be over three hundred yards. Nor had Markham. He'd never really thought such a shot possible, even with a musket resting on a makeshift swivel.

'Well done,' he said, with deliberate understatement.

'I was aiming at his bloody horse,' Rannoch replied, slamming an angry fist into the ground.

Markham turned to the sweating marines. 'Right, lads, let's see if we can put some hot metal in amongst them.'

As they went to work he ordered Yelland back to Hanger and Serota, with instructions to tell them about the presence of the cavalry, and his desire to bring in the guns. 'We have the limbers and the wheels; what we need are horses with enough wind to tow them. And impress upon Colonel Hanger that, even if we can keep the cavalry at bay, we only have an hour at most before we're subjected to an infantry assault.'

'Wine, for the sake of Christ,' snarled Rannoch, spitting the liquid out of his mouth onto the packed earth. He held the straw-covered bottle up in disgust. 'Do those damned heathens not know about God's good water?'

'There's water in the butts,' said Dymock, heaving alongside Halsey. 'An' it's just right for Bullocks.'

Even under such exertions, that made the marines

laugh. Artillerymen commonly pissed in their swabbing butts, the contents of which were already covered with a thin film of burnt powder from the barrels of their guns.

'This will serve,' said Markham, dragging the flagon out of the sergeant's hands and taking a swig. 'When everybody's had some, I want you to break a hole in that embankment facing the harbour, so that we can get these guns through.'

'It is as dry as bone,' Rannoch growled, kicking at it.

'Just detail some men to do it, Sergeant,' Markham said, handing him Frobisher's small telescope. 'And get your musket back on that tripod.'

'Will I have your permission to fire at will?'

'Fire at anything you think you can hit. Just try and stop those horses from charging.'

'Tully,' Rannoch shouted, 'over here and load for me.'

'Guns ready,' said Halsey. Markham turned. The marines had removed their jackets, and each man had tied a bandana around his head and ears so that the noise would be muted. And they were looking at him, waiting for orders. The crack of Rannoch, firing off his first round, was the only thing to break the silence.

'I know less about aiming artillery than I do about sailing a ship, Halsey. So I'll leave the ranging to you. See if you can .get those cavalry to retire beyond the Marseilles road.'

'There is something stirring further back,' shouted Rannoch, halfway through swapping muskets with Tully, his finger pointing to the long valley that led to Ollioules and Marseilles. 'There. A big cloud of dust. Could it be infantry coming up on us?'

'I daresay,' replied Markham calmly, with a display of confidence he certainly didn't feel. But his words were drowned out by the cannon going off. The balls were arcing through the air, clearly going nowhere near their intended target. Indeed they were more of a threat to the distant infantry than they were to the cavalry. His response, eyes facing firmly forward, was deliberately laconic. 'Down half a mile and right several hundred yards.'

His calm tone clearly needled Halsey, who, for the first time since they'd come ashore, allowed his discipline to crack, positively growling at him. 'These ain't naval cannon. They're field pieces, and I ain't never even seen their like a'fore.'

From where Markham was standing that was fairly obvious. So was the effect. The cavalrymen, who'd been milling about, sorted themselves out and began to prepare for a renewed assault.

'Just do your best,' he said quietly. 'And hope that Yelland is a fast runner.'

The crack of Tully's musket followed hard on those words, and Markham heard Rannoch curse a second time as he missed whatever it was he was aiming at. Looking back towards Toulon, above the heads of the men hacking at the embankment, he could see no evidence of any activity, no hint that Hanger was even interested in his progress. He'd half expected the man to ride forward once they'd taken the guns. Yet, on consideration, that would be the last thing he'd do. Markham dead would have had him spurring his horse in pleasure. Markham triumphant was a very different affair.

'Sergeant sent you this, sir,' said Tully, loudly, holding out his telescope, his pock-marked face split with a wide grin. 'Says, with the Lobsters shooting the way they are, you need it more'n he does. Might aid you in discoverin' where they land.'

Several of the marines swore at Tully, but Markham didn't respond to them or the soldier, merely holding out his hand to take the telescope.

'Any sign of help comin'?' Tully asked softly.

'None,' he said, looking down. 'But don't worry. I've no intention of staying here for some useless sacrifice.'

'The lads'll be pleased to hear it, sir.'

'Then make sure they do, Tully. And tell them to be ready to run like the devil if I give the order.'

Halsey's next salvo, while a vast improvement, still didn't trouble the cavalry. He looked at Markham to see if he was to be exposed to another jibe, his pasty face screwed up in anticipation, only to be greeted with a reassuring nod.

'Better, corporal. Much better.'

Markham's thoughts were elsewhere. Having got ready to begin their advance, he couldn't understand why the cavalry were hesitating. Common sense told even the most foolish soldier that under an artillery barrage it was best to be moving, either forward or back. Rannoch took out one of the horses with his third musket ball, aided by the fact that they were in close order. Still, at the given range, some three hundred yards, it was remarkable shooting. Was it that, or an order from another source, which suddenly made them turn to the right and trot off? He watched them as they rode parallel to his position for a while, then observed the lead rider wheel round.

Putting the telescope to his eye, he looked beyond the dust-covered road. The infantry marching in his direction were clear now, men in such numbers that they would overwhelm his puny force in a single charge. With the cavalry on the southern flank, ready to cut across his line of retreat, the position, which had never been secure, was rapidly turning into a death trap.

'Yelland coming,' shouted Dornan, who was standing on the top of the earthworks. 'On his bloody own, an' all.'

It was true. The youngster was staggering with the effort of running, sucking in great gulps of air in an attempt to keep moving. The ground behind him was clear of everything but a few mendicant monks working among the Catalan wounded with neither infantryman nor horse in sight. The reasons for that troubled Markham, but not so much that he failed to concentrate on the consequences. Those cavalry would come after them as soon as they moved. Out in the open, especially retreating, he was about to be exposed to the foot soldier's greatest fear. Even in the broken terrain the horses would have the advantage over men who could not present to them any kind of solid front, able to pick off individual targets at will. But to stay still was even worse.

'Halsey, one more salvo at maximum elevation, just to see if we can slow up the French column, then pack the guns with everything they will hold and hammer in the tampions. You men digging, stop at once and get these limbers alongside the cannon. Rannoch, once Halsey is ready to fire take your men back to a point halfway between here and the shoreline. Get into that broken ground and form a line facing south, bayonets fixed, and prepare to receive cavalry.'

There was more than a trace of the old Rannoch in the way he posed the obvious question. 'And when they come?'

'I will be there with you. The marines will retire to a point behind us. We'll give them three rounds when they charge and run for it. Let's just hope those sea service muskets the Lobsters have got are accurate enough to fire over our heads.'

'Do you hear those words, Halsey,' the Scotsman snapped, addressing the whole group of sweating marines. 'If one of those balls of yours comes anywhere near me I will, by my own hand, stick my bayonet up your arse.'

Halsey's pepper and salt hair had come undone, his face covered in perspiration. There was nothing bland about his manner now. He positively spat his reply. 'Go drink your own piss, you tartan toerag.'

'Form the men up, Sergeant,' Markham snapped, seeing Rannoch's fists begin to close. 'At the double.'

That earned him a portion of the glare which had been aimed at Halsey. But he obeyed; the whole area was now a mass of frantic activity. Halsey let fly with his last attempt, achieving more with that than any previous salvo. It didn't reach the French column, which looked to be over a thousand strong, but it did hit the road ahead of them. As soon as the guns were clear he got busy, he and the other team shoving charge after charge into the cannon, with Halsey rubbing earth over a metal sphere. Once it was full he jammed the dirt-covered ball in the barrel, followed by the tampion. He then grabbed a hammer and started to swipe at that, ramming it home, as hard as he could, into the muzzle. Gibbons was poking a long piece of slowmatch into the touchhole, the entire operation being duplicated on the second gun. Others, mysteriously to Markham, were emptying the brackish water butts onto twin sections of loose earth right before the cannon, and jabbing at the darkened earth to break it up.

'When you're ready, Corporal.'

'Not yet, sir,' Halsey croaked, reversing the angle on the elevating screw so that the cannon now pointed down towards the ground. He called for a solid heave and the marines ran the guns forward so that their muzzles smashed into the wet, softened earth, adding another seal to the already blocked cannon.

'On your way, Rannoch.'

The sergeant yelled for his men to follow and headed up over the remaining earthworks. Markham swung his telescope to take in the cavalry, watched as they reacted very swiftly to this development, swinging round and breaking into an immediate trot as they saw the redcoats retreating. Halsey and his men were struggling into their coats, grabbing their weapons, and forming up. The dishevelled corporal came up to him, a spluttering piece of burning slowmatch in his hand.

'The honour is yours, sir.'

'Thank you, Halsey. Get your men out of here.'

'Aye, aye, sir,' he replied, tugging at his shoulder straps.

When the last man was gone, Markham dropped the

smoking twine to the piece protruding from the first gun. As soon as that took he moved to the second, watching as that spluttered into life with a kind of deadly fascination. Jerking himself out of such a suicidal reverie, he quickly fired the fuses to the caissons, leapt up onto the top of the embankment and ran.

Needing to keep an eye on the cavalry, he also had to be careful where he put his feet, even on this, the smoothest part of the ground. Any kind of serious fall would be fatal. Ahead, Rannoch was beginning to form up the men, shouting at them as he shoved them into position.

Even with everything occupying his mind, he had room to wonder at the sergeant's ability. Ever since they'd commenced the attack he had been like a rock Markham could lean on. The assumption that he'd been assigned to service at sea because he was useless as a soldier was plainly erroneous, just as wrong as the notion that he was a sergeant merely because of his physical prowess. Judging by what had happened this day, he held his stripes deservedly, and was a man any colonel, in any line regiment, would want to hold on to. So why was he here?

He responded to the shouted warning immediately, though the sweat running into his eyes made it difficult to see. Two of the swifter cavalrymen had detached themselves from the mass and turned to intercept him, using the smooth rising pasture to speed their passage. The next few moments were spent in an agony of suspense. He was running as fast as he could, but aware that his lungs, never mind his legs, were past the point of maximum speed. At the same time he was trying to calculate the relative distances, the shortening one between him and the line of redcoats, as compared to the more rapidly closing gap to the horsemen.

Suddenly he knew he wouldn't make it, so his decision to stop running made sense to him. That it didn't to the men of the 65th Foot was obvious by the yells of encouragement that floated across the hot dusty landscape.

But that was being drowned out by thudding hooves, and he turned, his first vision the great bursts of dust being thrown up as each equine foot struck the earth. Markham pulled out pistol and sword, keeping the latter in his left hand while he aimed the former at the leading cavalry-man. A standard sea service affair, it was famous for being useless at anything other than point-blank range. But he couldn't wait. He needed time to transfer his sword and prepare to defend himself. So he blazed off more in hope than expectation, disappointed despite himself that it had no effect.

The gun was cast aside and his sword was in his hand, a slight fumble making the whole action too slow. Again time changed its dimension, slowing so that every feature, every move, had an astonishing clarity. The flaring nos-trils and the foam round the horse's curb chain were so close he felt he could reach out and touch them. He could see the moustachioed face of his first opponent, the eyes and mouth wide open with anticipation.

That light of battle, of approaching success, died as the ball took him, slamming him sideways and forwards across the withers of his mount. Markham scrambled to the left, narrowly avoiding the horse's shoulder as the animal swerved. There was no time to see if the rider was alive or dead. The second horseman was upon him, and only a frantic slice with his sword deflected the sabre from his exposed chest. He slashed as the cavalryman went by, cursing as the point of his blade missed the man's back. The Frenchman hauled on his reins to bring the beast round, so Markham went after him, catching his opponent before he swung through more than a quarter of his turn.

The sabre slashed down viciously, narrowly missing Markham's head. His sword was jabbed into the horse's flank, which caused it to rear, reducing the rider's control and balance. He thrust forward again, luck helping him to push his weapon up under his opponent's arm. The wound he inflicted wasn't deep enough to do more than gash the skin, but in trying to avoid it the horseman slipped out of his stirrups, one foot waving close to Markham's ear. He cut hard, sweeping upwards, the sharp blade going right through the leather of the boot, in through the flesh, to crash against the leg bone. The impetus added by this blow tipped the horseman right out of his saddle. He'd have been safe still if his horse hadn't spun, exposing his unprotected back. Markham put all his body weight behind the thrust, producing enough effort to take the blade through almost to the hilt.

The falling horseman landed right on him, knocking him to the ground, with his animal's hooves rising and falling dangerously close. Vaguely, over the mass of sounds around him, he heard, in the background, the staggered fire of ill-disciplined musketry. Struggling hard, he managed to get the man's dead weight off his chest, and with several heaves he got his sword clear. In his death agony, the Frenchman still held the horse's reins, clutched tightly in one clenched fist. Markham grabbed them as he cut at the wrist, releasing the fingers. The animal, terrified, spun round in a tight circle as he sought to mount it, flecking his uniform with foam from the mass that covered his mouth.

Markham, like every Irishman, knew his horses, and having seen action with Russian Cossacks, had learned even more. He punched the animal, as hard as he could, on the nose. As it stopped in shock, he jumped without any sure knowledge of success, just hoping to get enough of his body weight over the saddle to stay on board. The animal bucked as it felt him press down, jumped in panic so that his search for one stirrup seemed doomed. Suddenly, instead of hauling on the reins, he let them loose, pressed his knees together and the horse took off. Galloping, it was a steadier platform than when bucking, which allowed him to get his feet in the stirrups. With the reins tightened to pull on the bit, he began to feel that he could, at last, exert some measure of control.

That evaporated as soon as he lifted his eyes. He found himself charging straight for a disordered group of French cavalry. To his left, Rannoch was retiring fast, yelling furiously at the men, keeping their bayonets pointed towards the enemy so that they couldn't mount an over-whelming attack. Markham heard him shout and the red-coats broke and ran. As soon as they did Halsey opened up, firing over their heads, hoping that the higher elevation of the horsemen would provide him with a target.

But all such thoughts had to be put aside as his mount's forward motion took him right in past the enemy flank, several of their number spinning to engage him. Slipping the reins into one hand he slowed the horse, knowing that the animal could not be made to perform properly at anything like his present pace. But it was a cavalry mount, trained to battle, and he deliberately took it close in to the enemy, relieved that when he sent the right signals with reins and body, it skipped sideways.

The move was no more than six inches, but it took him, by a fraction, out of the reach of the first sabre slash, while his forward motion allowed him a swing of his sword that deflected a second. Now he had the enemy both in front and behind him. Reins centred, pulling hard while standing in the stirrups, he got the animal spinning round and round, his sword flashing to keep men out of his orbit. Then, dropping back into the saddle, he jabbed again, this time with both knees together, pleased in spite of the danger with the way the animal reacted. It shot forward, the rider now over its neck, egged on by his growling encouragement and the slap of his sword blade on its hind quarters, which took him clear of those sur-rounding him at a full gallop.

The gap between them opened swiftly, and he found himself overtaking his own soldiers before the ground, getting steeper and rockier, forced him to slow. He also came under fire from Halsey's marines, and it was only luck that saved him from falling to his own side. Rannoch had already arrived and began to form his men up, yelling furiously at the numerous stragglers. Slewing to a halt just in front of the marines, Markham slid off the horse, slapping its rump to send it on at the same time as his feet hit the ground. Then he ran to the right of the line, and took charge of the firing. After one round the French wheeled away, the right thing to do considering that the ground precluded attacking at anything other than walking pace.

Just as they began to withdraw, the first cannon went off. Earth, along with pieces of wood and metal filled the air. The second gun went straight after, setting off the caissons full of powder. A huge plume of dust rose up, and as it settled, the emplacements for the Batterie de Bregaillon completely disappeared.

# Chapter thirteen

Hanger, faced with an inquisitive superior, looked a lot
less assured than he sounded. 'Colonel Serota and I both
agreed the attack was essential. Indeed he insisted, and
since he was prepared to back his judgment with a whole
regiment of Catalan infantry, I could hardly refuse him
an additional thirty men.'

'The cost was high,' said Mulgrave, 'especially
amongst those same Catalans. What were our losses
again, Lieutenant?'

'Remarkably light, sir, considering.' Markham wondered if he was replying to a question designed to
embarrass Hanger, since the answer was in his report on
Mulgrave's desk. 'Three dead, a dozen wounded, two of
whom will most certainly not survive. Half the others
will be invalided out.'

Hanger flushed slightly. 'If the French had been left in
peace they would have pushed forward to a position
which would have threatened Malbousquet, the redoubt
now building at La Seyne, as well as the anchorage.'

Lord Mulgrave was small, with an air of tight control
about the way he maintained his features, an image
heightened by the bright eyes and tight white wig; the
way his skin showed every bone, and the close-fitting
nature of his uniform. A hero of the American war, he
wore the bronze medal struck for his success at Germantown. There, surprised by General Washington, he had
repulsed an attack in the fog that, if successful, could
have jeopardised the whole British position in America.

To Markham that meant two things; that he was a

proper career soldier, and that having served in the former colonies, he might know all about the man who, having finished his report, had stepped back to allow Hanger his say. He wondered if he needed that tight control now; was curious to know if Mulgrave had any inkling that what Hanger was telling him was utter nonsense. If he did, it wasn't to be allowed to show. He listened with the same air of concentration he had shown to Markham himself.

. 'We felt the need to teach them a lesson, sir,' Hanger continued, 'and we succeeded. As to Lieutenant Markham's decision to withdraw, without specific orders, I have already given you my opinion on that. If you wish, I'm more than happy to repeat it.'

'That won't be necessary, Colonel,' Mulgrave replied.

It wouldn't be a flattering one, that was certain, otherwise why make any observation at all? And it made little difference. There wasn't much that Mulgrave could say, even if he did consider the action rash. He could hardly castigate Hanger for agreeing to attack the enemy, that being the very stuff of the zealous warrior. Nor could he question the fact that he hadn't taken part. Staff officers weren't supposed to get themselves killed in search of glory. To admonish him would imply a degree of displeasure which, of necessity, must include Serota, impacting on his already strained relations with the Spaniards. After a full minute, with Mulgrave drumming his fingers on the desktop, and occasionally stroking the bronze medal, he finally spoke.

'It's fair to say that while the action wasn't perfect, in either conception or execution, it will serve to encourage the rest of the garrison. A little bit of offensive spirit is to be admired. Lieutenant Markham, you must be weary. I suggest you return to your billet and get some rest and refreshments.'

'Sir,' Markham came to attention. Mulgrave had decided to sit on the fence which, if it showed a lack of leadership, was at least common sense.

'That Hollander I took into custody,' said Hanger, glaring at Markham. 'I suggest that the drop is a fitting punishment. Done publicly, it will serve as another lesson to the garrison.'

Markham felt his hackles rise. Hanger had arrested Schutte, whom he'd found wandering amongst the shattered Spaniards, without even an acknowledgement that he was his responsibility. The idea of this man demanding that the Dutchman face the noose was anathema. He screwed his face up, looking perplexed.

'Punishment, sir?'

'Damned coward refused to go forward,' Hanger growled, looking at Mulgrave, 'which I think you'll agree qualifies him for the Tyburn tippet.'

'He obeyed the orders I gave him, sir.'

'What orders?'

'To stay to the rear and look to the wounded. Had you hung around long enough, or even risked riding within musket range, you might have noticed that I lost several men to enemy fire.'

Hanger opened his mouth to shout at Markham, but Mulgrave, quiet and controlled as ever, beat him to it. And in doing so, made it perfectly plain that he'd not been fooled either by Hanger's explanations of the day's events, or Markham's sudden inspiration regarding his orders.

'He is your problem, Lieutenant, and will only become mine if you choose to draw my attention to it. Now, Colonel Hanger and I have other matters to discuss, so I bid you good day.'

Mulgrave continued speaking to Hanger as Markham exited. As he began to close the door he heard the opening remarks, which slowed his actions considerably. 'It requires someone of your standing to go to Genoa and Piedmont. I'll not have the tars fetching in all our reinforcements. God knows, after today we need them badly. Those blue-coated bastards are unbearable enough. Never did like working with the Navy. The salt gets into their skulls and rots their brains.'

'What brains?' demanded Hanger.

Markham heard Mulgrave laugh as he finally closed the door.

Schutte was languishing in the guardhouse, a well-constructed affair set into the walls of Fort de la Malgue, right beside the main gate. Clearly the previous incumbents, the commanding admirals of Toulon, with thousands of sailors to man the fleet, had need of such a place. Markham had a look at him through the peephole, before ordering the guard to unbolt the door. The Dutchman looked up tentatively as it swung open, his pale blue eyes wide with fear. Markham entered and stood silently, waiting for the marine to stand up. This came slowly, almost reluctantly, like a last act of surrender that he wanted to save. But eventually he was on his feet. Still Markham waited, until the Hollander came to attention.

'Guard. Return the sergeant's equipment to him.'

Schutte's eyes, which had been looking above his head, dropped suddenly, betraying a mixture of hope and confusion as he looked at the officer before him. Markham stood to one side, revealing the open door.

'Move. I haven't got all day.'

The hesitation was caused by disbelief, and it was short. Schutte practically ran out of the cell.

'I need him signed for, sir,' said the guard.

'Of course.'

They were out of the gates before Markham spoke, pushing his way along through the teeming alleyways between the numerous works and warehouses of the Toulon dockyard, and that was to tell Schutte that he was no longer a sergeant. There was no activity in the area they were crossing, only knots of men standing around talking, groups who would cease speaking when the redcoats got close. The dockyard workers and French sailors, though not prepared to express support for the Revolution, could not be persuaded to undertake repairs or victual ships that might be stolen by the British. Emerging on to the more open area of the Vieille Darse, Markham spoke again, deciding that before they re-entered the billet, Schutte should know why he had behaved as he did. But first he told him about the action.

'That colonel wanted to hang you, and he was right to think like that. Don't get the notion that I've saved you out of any finer feelings. I've done it because the men performed well today, better than I could have hoped. I'll not have that sullied by your disgrace.' He stopped about a hundred yards from the door to the Picard warehouse, forcing the huge Dutchman to do likewise. 'One more mistake, a single piece of insubordination, and I'll hand you back to Hanger, to do with what he will.'

The look on Schutte's face angered him. The man, it appeared, wasn't even listening to what he was saying, more interested in what was happening over his shoulder than the threat he was delivering. When his huge hand shot out, Markham ducked, cursing himself for a fool. But Schutte didn't punch him, and the guttural cry that he emitted was designed to concentrate his attention. Markham spun round, following the Dutchman's finger. The glimpse he got of the bottle-green coat and the shocked, levantine face was fleeting, but enough. He was running before his quarry disappeared, chasing the man into the alley from which he'd just emerged, wondering what Fouquert, who risked certain death if he was recognised, was doing in Toulon.

Schutte was right on his heels, his feet pounding hard on the cobbled *pavé*, as the two of them sped from the bright sunlit quay into the narrow, dark space between the warehouses. Markham saw Fouquert's heels as the Frenchman ducked to the left, taking another one of the alleys that formed a labyrinth behind the main buildings on the waterfront.

Markham's voice echoed off the walls as he shouted to Schutte. 'Go straight on to the road that runs to the rear of the Picard house. See if you can spot him trying to get across it.'

He was still talking as he turned left. Schutte ran on, his heavy footsteps fading till all Markham could hear was his own. The alley he was in, high walls broken by an occasional doorway, ran for some distance straight ahead, and it was empty. There was no way that Fouquert could have opened up such a gap. So when it swung to the left, he followed it round, and ran full tilt into a bent figure, carrying a huge covered bundle on his back, sending him flying. He spun backwards, emitting a terrified scream, and calling on every saint in the canon to come to his aid.

Markham grabbed one of his hands and hauled him to his feet, ignoring the pleas which had turned to curses, looking back the way he'd come. Fouquert could no more have got past this fellow than him, yet he hadn't gone straight on. Retracing his steps slowly, with curses still ringing in his ears, he tested every door he passed. None yielded to his efforts, yet the Frenchman must have used one of these to escape. Unless, that is, he'd suddenly sprouted wings.

He knew that a return to the quayside was probably futile, but he made it anyway, searching the milling crowd for any sign of Fouquert's dark green coat. Schutte, hatless, standing head and shoulder above the crowd, appeared several hundred yards ahead. Markham stood on a bollard, so that the Dutchman could see him. The shake of the great bald head told him that he had also failed. Markham signalled that the Hollander should stay put, and walking towards him peered into every open doorway he passed.

The futility of what he was doing was soon apparent.

Each warehouse was half full of chandler's goods, barrels and boxes, bales and great wynds of hempen rope. If he wanted to search them he'd need to call out all his men, and for what? Just to catch a committed Republican in a city that was probably awash with them. If he was here now, then it would be to visit Jacobin sympathisers. That meant he had a secure way through the lines, a fact that those in command would want to know. He turned round when he reached Schutte, and gave each doorway another inspection, unwilling just to let it go. But common sense told him that Fouquert could be anywhere by now; that if he had found a way into the rear of one of these warehouses, then he could have exited at the front and got lost in the crowd long before Markham returned to the quayside.

'Schutte. Back to the Fort de la Malgue. Get a message to Elphinstone. Tell them who we saw, what happened, and where.'

Schutte nodded curtly then hurried off along the quay. Markham watched his broad back, wondering if he'd ever see it again, all the while knowing that if Schutte harboured any desire to desert, he'd rather have him go now than at some critical juncture which might threaten other men's lives.

A few minutes later he entered the Picard house. The owner was, once more, complaining about his men lighting a fire in his warehouse. But this time his reaction was different. Instead of sympathy, Picard got short shrift. Lieutenant George Markham knew, even if Sergeant Rannoch hadn't told him so, that one of the musket balls produced from that glowing brazier had, that very afternoon, killed that first cavalryman and saved his life.

It was also pleasant, later on, to hear that Schutte had returned, to be greeted, in silence, by the men he'd once led. And Rannoch, sensibly, made sure that none of the Bullocks took the opportunity to make jokes about the Lobsters. The Highlander had heard his conversation with Picard, and without comprehending the words, knew that his officer had taken the side of his men. That, when Markham gave him his orders for the following day, earned a smile, if not an acknowledgement of his status. He also accepted that he and Halsey would keep their respective ranks.

'Permission to issue an extra tot of rum?'

'By all means, Sergeant.'

'What a pleasure, Lieutenant to finally have you share our table. I have to say that it is something that I'd anticipated happening before this. After all, we have been here for nearly a month.'

Markham, weary, had tried to get out of the invitation, but he'd refused so many that another 'no' seemed churlish. Eveline, despite the presence of her father, had come very close to him, adding a plea for him to attend, laying a pressing hand on his arm that sent a restorative thrill of pleasure through his entire body. She was wearing a loose dress of shimmering silk, which, advisable on such a warm, humid day, did little to conceal her figure. Markham would have pulled her closer still, if her father hadn't been standing right beside them.

So, despite being exhausted from the day's efforts, he accepted, changed into the marine uniform once more, and was now describing the attack on the battery in terms that made it sound like a matter of no importance, praising his men and the way that they'd behaved. But as he spoke, he was mentally replaying the events of the battle for those guns. Only now, with time to reflect, did he begin to understand just how lucky he had been.

He wondered why the Picards didn't react when Rossignol said that, a guest claiming their property as his own. If they'd noticed, it didn't show. Indeed, Madam Picard was nodding vigorously.

'A day's digging does not make a man fit company, monsieur.'

'But surely,' asked Eveline, her lovely eyes wide with disbelief, 'you did not actually handle a spade yourself?'

'Of course not,' said her older sister, Pascalle. 'The good Lieutenant is a chevalier, not a paysan.'

Markham demurred, not wishing to admit that his claim to the title chevalier was suspect, and that at one point he had done just such a thing. As an attempt to bond with his men it was an abject failure, not least because when it came to trench work he was, compared to them, useless, so what he'd intended as camaraderie was seen as condescension. Thinking back on it made him wonder why they'd followed him into battle today. But they had, which had a great deal to do with Rannoch. For the first time, thinking about the Highlander, he had no sense of anger or frustration, but that train of thought could not be pursued when he had a question still to answer.

'Even supervising spadework, in the hot sun, is exhausting.'

'Such a pity,' said Eveline, looking at him from under her dark eyebrows. 'Life here has been so dull.'

Rossignol clapped his hands. 'With the perimeter works complete, that will improve. A formidable obstacle, wouldn't you say?'

'I doubt the perimeter is as sound as any of us would like.'

Rossignol frowned. 'How so?'

'Do you remember that Jacobin fellow in Ollioules, who we tied to the back of the coach?'

Rossignol looked up slowly, his face creased, like a man searching his memory. 'Was his name not Fouquert?'

Both the Picards responded to the name with a sudden intake of breath. So when Markham gave a positive reply, he included his hosts, adding a brief and filleted account of how they'd met. 'He was quite a catch, which I only found out afterwards.'

Picard's long face was grave as he cut in. 'He nearly

prevented Toulon from surrendering. He might even have chopped off Admiral Trugueff's head if the British hadn't come ashore.'

'So I was told. You'd certainly think he'd be glad, once he reached Republican territory, to stay out of the city.'

'He has not done so?' asked Rossignol.

'I saw him today on the quayside.'

Picard barked in disbelief as Rossignol fiddled noisily with the food on his plate. 'Did he see you?' demanded Picard.

'He ran as soon as he recognised me. I gave chase, but he disappeared.'

'He certainly sounds a dangerous fellow,' said Rossignol, his eyes flicking anxiously between Markham and the Picards. 'But that does not render the whole of Toulon defenceless.'

Markham knew how much effort Rossignol put into sustaining the Picards' fluctuating morale. And since he found his billet comfortable, he too had a vested interest in that commodity. But he was unprepared to lie, or to pretend that Fouquert's presence didn't matter. 'If a man like that can come and go, we must presume at will, the defences are a bit porous.'

'One man, Lieutenant,' Rossignol replied.

'Just the mention of his name makes me feel as if we are in danger,' whispered Madame Picard.

'No!' he replied, with a look of assurance. 'Toulon is a natural fortress. As Monsieur Rossignol says, he is but one man. For an army it would be very different.'

'And when does our army arrive, Lieutenant?' asked Picard, 'The one that will drive Jacobins out of Provence.'

'Soon, I'm sure,' said Rossignol, before Markham could reply. He leant forward and frowned, adding a slight shake of the head and a gesture towards the others present. He didn't want Markham to repeat, in front of them, what he'd said about the garrison's shortage of numbers, or the unlikelihood of reinforcements. The true state of affairs, that they were in for a long and bitter siege, would be bound to depress them.

'We none of us actually saw this Fouquert, Lieutenant,' he added. 'Perhaps you should describe him to us.'

'Shorter than me, and thinner. He's careful about his dress. He was wearing a good quality bottle-green coat, high boots and tight white breeches, both today and when we took him.'

Rossignol smiled, nodding to Frobisher's best uniform. 'A man may change his coat.'

'Thin face,' Markham continued, 'very dark, nearly black eyes. Not much given to blinking, wears a thin moustache, also black, like his curled hair which looks carefully barbered. His nose is hooked enough to give him the appearance of a Moor.'

'You studied this man in some depth, Lieutenant.'

'No. I recognised what I saw there, especially in his eyes.'

'And what was that?'

'Certainty. A knowledge of his own superiority. And cruelty. I think he enjoys death, destruction and inflicting pain.'

The whole table had gone quiet, the mood quite spoiled. Rossignol, seeing this, changed the subject abruptly, talking of happier times. Both his daughters aided him in this, and the atmosphere began to lighten. Markham needed no encouragement to participate. The idea of Fouquert could not compete for his attentions with Eveline. On the brief occasions he'd spied her, he'd been forcibly reminded of her beauty, as well as her knowing look. Here at table, sitting right opposite her, was hard to bear. Moving the conversation on, in a way that satisfied Rossignol, he set out to charm her, including her sister and their hostess so that his attentions shouldn't appear too obvious. In a besieged city full of soldiers, both the girls were disappointed at the dearth of social life. Markham pleaded that those in command be excused on similar grounds to himself.

'Now that matters have eased somewhat, Lord Hood will see the need for a ball or two in order to raise civilian morale.'

The boom of the cannon, rolling across the harbour, made them all jump. Picard, Rossignol and Markham were on their feet, making for the front of the building. The quay, now that it was dark, was less crowded than during the day. Several people had emerged from other buildings, or stopped to look. The orange glow, slightly to the south beyond the Fort de Malbousquet, lit up the night sky, the boom of the guns following after a second. With a sinking feeling, Markham realised that the shots, whatever they were aimed at, were coming from the same position he had destroyed earlier that day, the Batterie de Bregaillon.

'Does this signify danger, Lieutenant?' asked Picard.

'No, monsieur. It is just General Cartaux flexing his muscles. All he's doing is churning up some seawater.'

'You're sure?' demanded Rossignol, peering at him in the darkness, observing the sad look on his face. Assaulting those guns had killed nearly half a regiment of Spaniards.

'I am. And I think we can safely go back to our dinner.'

The boom of the cannon accompanied them through the meal. The depression it induced, plus the wine he consumed, made it ever harder for Markham to maintain any semblance of wakefulness. Try as he might, yawns came frequently, and his head felt as though it were hollow, with each sound magnified by an echo.

'I fear we have overtaxed you, Lieutenant,' said Madame Picard.

'Inexcusable,' snapped Rossignol, standing up. 'Eveline, fetch the lieutenant a candle.'

The girl stood up, and seeing her body move so easily

in her loose dress sent a surge of energy through his tired limbs. It was so easy to imagine that garment removed and, for a man to whom women were a weakness, hard to put from his mind. He stood up abruptly, aware that if he didn't move his breeches would fail to disguise the way his thoughts were developing. He bowed before he was fully upright, muttering fulsome thanks to the Picards for their hospitality.

Eveline was in the doorway, holding the silver stick with the flickering candle on top. That made him stretch to his full height, and renewed the ache of desire. Markham had no wish to disguise his amorous state from her. Nor she from him, judging by the way she shuddered as he passed her, taking the candlestick from her. He leant over to kiss her hand, sure that the words he whispered hadn't fallen on deaf ears.

He climbed the stairs with a stiffness that had more to do with his condition than any of the day's exertions, a feeling of lassitude only adding to the mental anticipation of his invitation to Eveline. The soft singing he heard added to the sense of unreality, and as it grew louder he couldn't resist following it. Celeste was sitting on Jean-Baptiste's bed beside the boy, holding his hand, singing him a lullaby. He lay back on the pillows, smiling, the whole scene one of such tranquil beauty that for a moment Markham forgot all about Eveline Rossignol. Celeste turned her head, and spying him in the doorway put her fingers to her lips. He nodded and carried on to his room.

He had no idea of the time at which Eveline Rossignol slipped into his bed. He hadn't even heard the door open and close. All he knew was that she was beside him, naked, and as eager as he was. He registered some surprise at her lack of inhibitions, as well as her expertise. Eveline was no novice at love-making. She was either promiscuous or had enjoyed a long-term relationship with an experienced partner. This thought was fleeting, overborne quickly by a desire she fully shared.

Markham loved women; their company as much as their bodies. And nothing pleased him more than the intimacy of a conversation carried out in the dark with someone to whom he'd just made love. There were no barriers of convention to debar honesty, no need for formal manners that disguised true feelings. Candour was pleasant, even if some of the things he told her were less so. It was easy to talk about his life, and tell stories of disaster that made her shake; to admit that his excellent knowledge of her language had come, not from schooling, but from an amour of long duration with a French woman, plus his service in Russia were it was in daily use.

That country, so remote and full of mystery, fascinated her. So he talked of St Petersburg, of the near oriental splendour of the Czarina's court, confirmed to Eveline the fact of her unbridled libido, told tales of the fantastic Prince Potemkin, of the patience of the long-suffering peasants and serfs he'd commanded, their willingness to die just to please their little mother, Catherine. Mention of the Turks made her shiver, though the frisson of fear was mingled with fantasies of the seraglio.

And he spoke quietly of his family, including his own illegitimacy, in a way that established the difference between gentle, kind Freddy and Hannah, though he made his half-sister sound like an amusing villainess instead of a hard-hearted termagant.

'Hannah craves respectability, of course.'

Eveline raised her head from his chest a fraction, her voice full of feigned shock. 'Are you not respectable?'

'Certainly not,' he replied, gently stroking her nose, adding with an amused sigh, 'I'm a blot on the Markham escutcheon. My mother is Mary O'Connell, the daughter of an Irish doctor, who never quite got round to marrying my father.

'You see,' he added with a deep yawn, 'Hannah worries

about how she is perceived. Her main aim in life is to make a good marriage. She has the money to attract a noble husband, perhaps even a peer. Someone like me, hanging about, doesn't do anything to further that ambition.'

'She doesn't need a husband, this sister of yours,' she murmured, her hand moving down over his lower belly. 'She needs a lover. Then she would learn that to be generous has its own reward. Perhaps you should hand her over to the Turks.'

Markham turned slightly, pulling her warm, pliant body close to his. 'I'm not sure I dislike them that much.'

The commotion woke him, as it had everyone in the house. The first thing to register was that Eveline had gone, leaving him asleep. The noise, coming from the hall, made him get up. Wrapped in a sheet, he went out, strode along the corridor and stopped at the top of the stairs. The Picards were there below him, dressed in their nightclothes, the old man who owned the house, tall and thin with a lantern in hand, looking like some low comedian. His wife was crying copiously, snuffling loudly and emitting low moans. Eveline was halfway down the stairs with Pascalle, her hand to her mouth. Picard turned to Markham as soon as he appeared.

'They have murdered the Queen, those barbarians, taken her to that damned guillotine and chopped off her head.'

Rossignol stepped forward, to pat Madame Picard on the shoulder, which exposed the shadowy figure behind him. 'If the good people of Toulon needed to be convinced of the evil of the Terror, this is the very thing to do it.' He turned to face Markham, a gleam in his eye. 'It will stiffen their resolve.'

'Oh my God,' sobbed Madame Picard, walking towards the staircase with her arms outstretched. 'Who will . . .'

Rossignol cut her off, both physically and verbally, his voice sharp and insistent. 'Monsieur Picard! Take your wife back to bed, and let sleep restore her.'

'Of course,' Picard replied, pulling at his wife's arm with a force that seemed to Markham a trifle excessive. As he spun round the lantern in his hand lifted to reveal the yellow-skinned face of Colonel Serota, his hand covering his mouth as he coughed. Then he was plunged into shadow again, so swiftly that Markham wondered if he'd truly seen him.

Then Rossignol spoke quietly. 'Thank you, Colonel, for personally bringing us this terrible news.'

# Chapter fourteen

The inactivity of the French Republican generals, particularly Cartaux, was Hood's greatest asset. Only a ponderous engagement between the reconstituted Batterie de Bregaillon and a couple of line-of-battle ships aided by gunboats broke the calm. That useless exchange lasted for several weeks, against a navy more stung than threatened. Eventually the action was broken off, with the French still in place and the Royal Navy back at its moorings, in an area of the harbour well out of danger.

The whole siege settled down into a desultory exchange of occasional fire just for the sake of morale, though it served to remind the inhabitants of Toulon that they were cut off from anything but help from the sea. Every time a salvo was fired, people would stop and look around, checking that the enemy had not moved closer, putting them in personal danger. The French were quiet because of half-hearted generalship, the Allies because of necessity. Mulgrave, the true military commander even though Gravina held the title, prayed daily for more reinforcements. The Neapolitan troops brought in by Captain Nelson were worse than the Spaniards, lacking in discipline, addicted to wine, and such a nuisance they were kept in the trenches, away from temptation, which served to destroy what little morale they possessed.

Markham, temporarily relieved of any specific duty, was determined to use the time to drill the remainder of his men, now only twenty-three in number. If they still resented him, it was now more the endemic attitude of any serving man to authority than personal dislike. And instead of being mere faces, they took on names and personalities, a great number of which were, to say the least, uninspiring. Hardly one of the Bullocks came without the blemish of a criminal conviction of some kind. The marines, though less forthcoming, could not aspire to virtue either. Through occasional contact with other soldiers of the garrison, they got to hear the gossip about their officer. Markham wasn't sure if his reputation as an illegitimate rake and known duellist stood to his advantage in such company.

He knew enough about the common soldier to be aware that they liked their officers aristocratic, wealthy or both. The government rarely paid wages on time, forgot that uniforms and equipment wore through, and were singularly inept at treating and caring for those who were wounded. So a rich, well-connected commander, particularly one who felt a responsibility to his men, was a definite advantage. In that respect he failed completely, and if the gossip about him was comprehensive enough they'd know it only too well. His indebtedness was common knowledge, so any man who hoped that Markham could lend him money or buy him equipment was doomed to disappointment.

He had slipped some of his meagre purse to the surgeons on the hospital ship, to ensure that those wounded during the recent action received decent treatment. Fortunately, with so little activity, the medical branch had scant work to do, most of their patients suffering from venereal ailments, rather than wounds. Only one of the men shipped there looked likely to recover enough to resume his duties and Leech, hobbling about with his broken leg, had been left behind to see to his needs.

As to accusations of cowardice, he hoped, should his men hear of them, his own behaviour had rendered them false. Not that he was sure himself. He was able to recognise a grain of truth in what Hanger had said about the differing levels of fear, having had cause to examine himself in that regard many times. In reality, what his mixed bag of Lobsters and Bullocks thought of him should have been an irrelevance. He had the command of them and they must obey. He was inclined to berate himself at the slightest hint that he cared about their opinion, good or bad.

Relations with Rannoch, particularly, were hard to pin down. But they had certainly improved from the days before the assault on the Batterie de Bregaillon. The Scotsman had no time for officers as a race, but now seemed to accept that, stuck with Markham, he had to make the best of it. Was it that hint of the Viking, apparent in his physical appearance, that gave him a contrary streak, friendly one minute and resentful the next? He particularly disliked any probing into his past, or any casual assumption of superiority by his officer. Markham soon learned that a form of meticulous politeness served best, clear instructions given in a way that denoted a degree of respect.

In return, Rannoch disciplined the men who'd come to sea with him, and had the good sense to work through Halsey when he was required to treat with the marines. Schutte had become very subdued, his initial gratitude for the gift of his life seeming to weigh heavily on him. Markham wasn't sure if resentment was building up in the Hollander, caused by anger at him, or a degree of self-loathing brought on by his own failure to attack with the rest. Taking their lead from Halsey, the Lobsters stayed out of his orbit, leaving him to his brooding, glad that at least he seemed submissive enough to obey any instructions he was given.

Practice at musketry was a priority, and having captured the entire arsenal of the French Mediterranean fleet, the supply of powder was plentiful. In this respect, Rannoch was a far superior instructor to Markham. As an officer, he knew all about the problems of musketry, but it was a knowledge that came to him more through conversation than actual use. Rannoch was just the opposite. The man was a crack shot, adding to his ability to aim and fire the Brown Bess a care for his weapon that bordered on love. He was particular in the selection of his musket balls and the quantity of powder he used, and that made him, on a windless day, deadly even at long range.

Before he lectured the men, he felt it necessary to teach his officer the inherent problems of the weapon they needed to use. Even though Markham knew, he listened intently so that the sergeant would not assume he was taking the matter lightly. Rannoch talked knowledgeably about the gun itself. The Brown Bess had been in service with the British army since the time of Marlborough. Originally the barrel had been fifty-four inches long, but that had been shortened in the 1770s to the standard weapon in use, the so-called Land Pattern Musket with a barrel four inches shorter. And in the nature of things, their weapons had come from several different gunmakers in London, Birmingham and yet more from Ireland. The marines had an equally mixed bag of the Sea Service Pattern. They'd been deprived of a further six inches of barrel to facilitate the problems of firing and reloading aboard ship, a deletion which had done nothing for the accuracy of the weapon, though it had helped with the fearsome recoil. Rannoch had fired them all, and could tell, without looking at the markings on the firing plates, how old each gun was. As he spoke, his lilting Highland voice made him sound like a particularly pedantic schoolmaster.

'It does not matter what length it is, Sea Service or Land Pattern. Brown Bess is big in the barrel, half as much again as a French musket, and while that means a ball that will take a man's head off, or give him a body wound that will tear his innards apart, it also produces a kick that most men cannot hold steady. It also happens that if the ball does not fit in the proper manner, once it's fired off it can go in any direction.'

'Which is why you cast your own?'

'Not only cast them,' Rannoch replied, holding up the short length of tubing. 'Barrel sizes can vary a wee bit too. This is a piece from a true gun, a Long Pattern that saw service in the Forty-five rebellion. After I have cast the balls, filed them and rolled them in a touch of gun oil, I slide them down here. They have got to go through without sticking at all. And when I hold it up to the light, if I see a glint I throw them back to melt.'

Markham took the barrel from him, selected one of his musket balls and tried it for himself. The grey lead sphere was slippery to the touch, and the smell of the clean oil rose to his nostrils. Suddenly his mind was cast back to Finsbury Park, to that cold morning when he faced the emigré French count across that damp patch of grass. He'd inspected the ball before his second loaded it, and that same odour had been present then. How much easier it would have been if the Count had withdrawn. But he could not countenance giving way to a man he'd nearly caught *in flagrante*, in his very own house, with a wife half his age.

'Most of the men in this army,' Rannoch continued, cutting across his thoughts, 'are using French musket balls in British guns. And it will not do for accuracy, not ever. They try to compensate by increasing the wadding, thinking that will make the ball fire true. But they are fooling themselves. If they hit anything at all, it is only luck.'

'It would help if they'd just take aim, sergeant.'

'It's hard not to blink, with that flash of powder right by your eye. And the trigger is a devil, as you know.'

'Can that be eased?'

'Never. It has to be stiff so that the pressure on the flint gives you the spark. I have known men file them down for ease, and misfire five times out of ten even on a dry day.'

'So how do you overcome that?'

'Only by practice, and some of the men we have will

never manage it. They lack the strength. But if they pull hard on the butt end, and keep it well into their shoulder, then they might just send a ball in the direction they are pointing.'

Markham looked him straight in the eye, for once abandoning his tone of rigid politeness. 'If you inspect most of the guns we have, Rannoch, Lobsters or Bullocks, you'll see as I have that, unlike yours, most of them lack any sights.'

For once Rannoch didn't bridle. Safe on his own subject, he could afford to smile. 'Nor will they profit from what I have, which is a stock that has been fashioned to suit my own size. The army cannot accept that each man is a different shape, and the gun needs to be made to fit him if it is to aim true.'

'Are you saying sights don't matter?'

'Not much point in fitting them, fiddly things they are, too, if you are not going to be aiming.'

'I want them to aim,' Markham growled. 'I want them to fire steadily and I want them to hit whatever it is we're trying to kill. We could have fought that squadron of cavalry to a standstill with accurate fire. Instead we had to run.'

'That is so,' said Rannoch softly. 'It must have been galling, with that colonel you like so much looking on.'

Markham was stung by Rannoch's gentle admonishment, intimating that his only reason for wishing to improve the performance of his men was to impress Hanger. He wanted to refute it, to say that more men would have survived if they'd been better shots. But to do so would sound like a lame excuse.

'I'm less concerned about the why, more about the solution.'

'Training, only training,' said Rannoch, pulling his lead mould to from his pouch. 'And perhaps a few more of these to make enough true musket balls.'

'Is that enough?'

'You would be amazed how it cheers a man to really hit something for the first time in his life. It makes him want to do it again. It is a bit like winning a wee skirmish.'

Markham looked at the Scotsman hard then, but the irony was masked by a bland look that conveyed nothing.

They found a gunsmith close to the dockyard who could make moulds, though deflecting his attempts to sell them other weapons took half of the morning. Some of the pieces he offered, originally made for the French naval officers, were handsome. But they were also expensive. And when Markham had paid for the castings to be made, and also the huge tub of beeswax that Rannoch demanded, there was little left for luxuries. On the way back to the Picard warehouse they stopped off at the arsenal to order powder and shot for the morrow, and pick up a barrel of gun oil, which Rannoch hoisted on his shoulder and carried back.

Getting permission to set up a training range was much harder. Markham only managed to persuade Lord Mulgrave to agree because Hanger was away from headquarters. In such a confined and crowded area, with refugees from all over Provence occupying every available space, that commodity was at a premium. But the General allocated them a piece of ground in the reserve trench system that had been dug to the north of the city.

Markham watched as Rannoch set up the targets, straw bales covered in painted cloth, while the rest of the men sorted out positions on the firestep. The sergeant was fussy about their placing, demanding exact measurements of the distance from the trenches. He was likewise adamant, in the face of all precedent, that it was a waste of time to try and teach them standing musketry until they had mastered the art of shooting recumbent.

'No man comes to a gun as anything other than a bairn,' he explained. 'No more than he is born to walk, is he born to shoot. Let them lie on their bellies for a while, then get to their feet. When they have put a ball or two into yonder straw they will do the standing in a willing fashion. That is how I was taught, and it is the right way.'

'Where did you learn to shoot?'

The reply was quite fierce, a reminder that inquiries about the Scotsman's past were unwelcome. 'In a place where there was room to do so, and something other than men to aim at.'

'Deer, rabbits, wolves?' Markham persisted.

'The targets are set. It seems fitting that we get started. Otherwise the day will be gone and nothing worthwhile done.'

Rannoch's limited supply of balls meant that little could be achieved anyway. But he took each man individually, had them tie a piece of canvas, which acted as a cheek guard, round their head, then set them to practise pulling the trigger with one finger until their hand ached. The canvas at least meant that when they succeeded, using the French musket balls, their faces weren't blackened and burned by the discharged powder in the pan. The sergeant then gave them one of his own true balls to fire. The results were mixed, with some still blinking and lifting the barrel as they fired. The sky had clouded over, presaging rain, and the Scotsman suggested an early stop. The skies opened as they marched back through the town.

'That is another thing we'll need to take care of. A musket is of little use if the flints are wet. And dust in the barrel is no friend to good shooting, which our lads are about to find out. I do not expect them to be happy about it.'

The truth of that remark, given the moaning that followed their arrival at the Picard warehouse, when the men were put to cleaning their weapons, was amply borne out. Rannoch was not to be moved. No-one ate until their musket was cleaned and inspected. Several were obliged to change their flints. Others were put to tightening up the restraining screws on the firing locks as well as merely polishing them. Finally, at the very moment when Picard's servants brought the steaming pots containing a handsome stew, Rannoch produced his tub of beeswax.

'Now polish the wood, all of you. Make them gleam so you can see your face as clear as day. Then, and only then, you can eat.'

He managed to spend most of the night with Eveline, a pair whispering happily to each other in between their love-making. Her curiosity about his past was in sharp contrast to her own unwillingness to divulge much, but that didn't bother Markham. He was happy to talk, to tell stories that made her laugh. But she did describe a life of some ease, in a Paris which, before the Revolution, hadn't paid much heed to King Louis.

'Versailles and the city were like two different countries. One stuffy and packed with idiots, the other alive.'

The word 'alive' moved her body in an enticing, uninhibited way that had him wondering once more about her previous liaisons. 'Then tell me about it.'

'Have you ever heard of a man called Beaumarchais?'

The question surprised him, since it was not what he'd expected. Not so much a change of subject as an acute tangent. Having mixed with many of the leading figures in the world of theatre, people who naturally had an interest in what happened in Paris and Vienna, he was no stranger to the name.

'Who could fail to know the man who inspired a Mozart opera? He's one of the few Gallic writers respected outside France.'

Eveline stiffened at that, and thumped his chest with her fist. 'What about Molière and Racine?'

Since Eveline didn't strike him as an erudite creature, that too engendered slight surprise. But it was fleeting, overborne by an uncomfortable sense of condescension, made more acute by the silky way he avoided the second question by answering the first.

'*The Marriage of Figaro*. I heard it caused quite a stir.'

Eveline sat up, the light from the unshuttered window playing across her naked body, which made it hard for him to really listen to her words.

'The King's ministers wanted to ban it. But they were too afraid of the Parlement of Paris. Beaumarchais was such a rogue. He knew that a story in which a servant outwits his fool of a master was dangerous. There are those who say it led directly to the Bastille, which tickled his vanity.'

Her voice had a tone he recognised, one that hinted at familiarity, if not actual intimacy, Markham leant forward, nibbling at one of her nipples. 'You sound as if you know him.'

She pulled his head up suddenly and kissed him hard.

'Do you know him?' he asked, when he was finally permitted to draw breath. He was again confounded by the way she avoided a direct answer.

'We Rossignols always seek out amusing company, wherever we are. I thought you would know that by now.'

'Does your sister know what you're up to at night?' he asked, pushing her away so that he could look into her eyes.

'Pascalle?' she replied, with a slight chuckle, twisting onto her knees. 'Once in bed she hears nothing.'

'And what about your father?'

That reduced her to a fit of giggling, which, given that she was being deliberately enigmatic, threw him into more confusion. But not enough to distract him from the attractions of her quivering body, which was now straddling him.

Markham was first up in the morning, awakened by the bright sunlight of a crisp autumn dawn. Normally a man to relish that soporific moment of waking in a warm bed, he rose and dressed, eager to get to the range. Coming downstairs he saw Rossignol, fully dressed, crossing the hallway and heading for the Picards' study, a sheaf of papers in his hand. The Frenchman stopped dead at the sound of his footsteps, and faced the stairs.

'You're as bright as the lark this morning, Lieutenant.'

'I have work to do,' Markham replied, wondering why his voice held a slightly apologetic tone.

Rossignol held up the papers, which appeared to be drawings of buildings rather than script. 'So have I, monsieur, so have I. The doctors are with us once more.'

On ground level, Markham could see the door to the study was slightly open. The drift of suppressed voices came to his ears, one of them, he thought, female. But there was a male voice too, which stopped speaking long enough to emit a consumptive cough.

'Besides that, Monsieur Picard and I are hard at it. He and I are as one, that we must not allow the war to deflect us from matters of business.'

Rossignol gave him a weary smile, meant to convey that while Markham had slept, he had not. Then he went through the door. As it swung shut he heard Picard's voice begin speaking, only to be overborne, in the split second before it closed, by an insistent female voice. He made his way to the kitchen, finding that Celeste was up, and already engaged with the other servants in making the family breakfast. She fed him on fresh bread, a conserve of plums and strong coffee.

'Are you comfortable here, Celeste?' She shrugged, her sad eyes and lack of response killing off his attempt to engage in cheerful conversation. 'Well if there's anything you need, you can always ask.'

Once, he assumed, she'd been a bright, lively girl, whose long dark hair would have been used to frame a becoming smile. Not any more. Her cheeks looked more drawn than he remembered, the olive complexion wan rather than healthy. Too much time spent indoors perhaps, since she never went out into the city. He suspected she still hadn't recovered from what had happened in the back room of her father's inn.

Going through to the warehouse he found Rannoch and the men up and making ready to depart. The sergeant had set the brazier, and the charcoal to heat it, ready to be carried. Beside it were two water buckets full of musket balls.

'We will not get the rest of the casts until tomorrow at the very soonest, so I thought we could use some of the time up on the range to make the balls we need.'

'Have the men been fed?'

'We are taking rations with us. It will do no harm to have a day or two back on soldier's commons, after the soft life they have been leading in this place.'

Markham felt a slight twinge of annoyance at that. Rannoch had issued that order without consulting him, which wasn't strictly correct. But it would be churlish of him to stand on his dignity when the sergeant seemed so keen to oblige him in the matter of musketry.

The chill in the air, as they marched up through the steep slopes of the town, was very evident, a sign that even in these warm climes the nights were cold. When they arrived at the trenches, his men indulged in a great deal of foot-stamping and hand rubbing, accompanied by the usual moans of soldiers dragged away from a warm stove.

Schutte lit a fire which attracted them like moths, while Rannoch produced a fair quantity of musket balls. These, the product of his nocturnal labours, were laid out for inspection. Then he set off to check that the target was still at the correct distance while Markham ordered the men to breakfast. As they sat eating hard tack and dried beef, washed down with warm water laced with rum, he detailed the firing order. Strictly neutral as always, it was one Lobster followed by one Bullock. Rannoch returned, loaded his own musket, filled the firing pan with powder, and handed it to Markham. The look he gave him made the words that followed superfluous.

'Little point in asking men to do what you cannot do yourself.'

Markham jumped on to the firestep and leant forward, his elbow and forearm brushing the hard, cold ground. The smell of the weapon, a mixture of oil and wax, filled his nostrils. He was vaguely aware that behind him his men had stood up to observe, still clutching the canteens of mixed biscuit and salt pork in their hands. Rannoch's mouth was close to his ear, the voice soft and almost caressing in the way that he issued his quiet instructions. As his hand came forward to touch the front of the weapon Markham saw the brand on his thumb, something which caused him to stop breathing. The letter 'M' was etched into the skin, a deeper red than the surrounding colour.

'Take a firm grip with both hands, then turn them as if you were wringing out your smalls. As much pressure as you can both ways. Now pull the musket right back into the shoulder. Remember this is no sporting gun. When you pull the trigger it is going to come back and hurt you if it gets any chance to move. And the barrel is going to want to go up, so pull that front forearm down hard and aim the gun a wee bit low. The target is at one hundred and twenty paces, and you can fire when you like.'

The polished metal was cold against his cheek as Markham obeyed. But his mind was elsewhere. That mark on Rannoch's thumb meant that he had been found guilty of manslaughter, that he'd killed someone in a fit of violence so great that he'd escaped hanging by a whisker.

'You need to concentrate.'

The finger on the trigger, tugging hard, seemed to make no impression at all on the hanging hook of gunmetal. As he pulled, Rannoch spoke again. 'Do not let that hauling on the trigger upset any of your other hand positions.'

Markham realised that his grip, in all areas, had eased a fraction, and he sought to compensate. But that made the pulling of the trigger harder still. He could feel his hand getting stiff as the unaccustomed grip induced slight cramp. That brought forth a surge of effort. He was being watched. The idea that he might take his hand off the weapon and flex it was not, for him, an option. He concentrated on firing, putting to the back of his mind that brand on his sergeant's thumb. The trigger eased back; Markham's face was screwed up with the strain. But it passed the point he needed, and began to act on the arm of the flintlock. The hammer shot forward, striking a spark.

'Eyes open!' hissed Rannoch.

He did as he was ordered, saw the spark flash, then felt the blast of air and the singeing pain as the powder in the pan detonated. A streak of blinding light shot across his vision as the weapon fired. The brass butt slammed his shoulder back and the barrel, taking on an uncontrollable life of its own, started to lift. But the musket ball was gone before it shot in the air. Concentrating on controlling it, Markham didn't see the wisp of straw fly off the top corner of the target bale. But Rannoch and the others did, and that produced a spontaneous murmur.

'A splendid shot, Lieutenant,' said an unfamiliar voice from the rear of the trench. Markham spun round as the man, a naval captain, crouched down. He had piercing blue eyes, a pale complexion, and a warm and engaging smile. 'Nelson; *Agamemnon*.'

'Sir,' Markham replied.

Nelson pulled a large white handkerchief from his coat pocket and handed it to Markham. 'I fear your hair is singed, Lieutenant. I'm surprised you can't smell it.'

He rubbed at his cheek, which doused what remained of the singeing, wondering why Rannoch hadn't given him a piece of canvas to protect his face. Unfortunately, it also covered this captain's handkerchief with the soot from the firing pan.

'I'm afraid that I've rather done for your linen, sir.'

'Never fear, Lieutenant . . .?'

'Markham, sir.'

'I'm having a look around the fortifications,' said Nelson, standing upright. 'Would you say they are sound?'

'Sound enough, sir. Given the troops to hold them, that is.'

Nelson looked up at the top of Mont Faron, where a trace of the French outworks was just visible, a brooding reminder of the tactical prison they occupied. The smile that followed lost none of its warmth, but the voice had a wistful quality.

'That's the rub, Mr Markham,' Nelson sighed. 'Not enough men. Forgive me, Lieutenant, I am distracting you from your practice.' He touched the rim of his hat and turned away, eyes still raised towards the hills, his arms behind his back as he walked along the rear of the trench. A blue-jacketed sailor, probably his coxswain, fell in behind him.

'Right,' shouted Markham. 'Breakfast's over. Let's have the first of you lot on the step.'

'That was good shooting,' said Rannoch softly. Then, in a voice that made it sound as though it was dragged from the depth of his bowels, he added, 'Sir.'

Tired, dirty and hungry, they marched back to the Picard House. There was a certain amount of jocularity, which for the first time crossed the divide between Lobster and Bullock. The shooting, individually then in teams, had given them a common source of scorn. Each bad shot was recalled, the perpetrator subjected to endless ribbing. Not all of it was being exchanged in the right spirit, but that it was happening at all was welcome.

As Markham crossed the courtyard, he encountered

Rossignol in conversation with the two doctors who'd been attending Jean-Baptiste. Judging by the looks on their faces, it wasn't a pleasant experience for the two physicians. Rossignol, pacing up and down, speaking to them in a harsh tone, stopped both as Markham passed by. But he resumed as soon as he thought him out of earshot. Markham slowed his pace as he crossed the hall, his curiosity getting the better of him. Even if he couldn't make out many of the words, he knew that the man who'd employed them was less than happy with the results of the doctors' endeavours.

At the top of the stairs, Rossignol's voice became an indistinct growl, whatever he was saying overborne by soft singing. Putting his ear to Jean-Baptiste's door, he heard Celeste. He also heard the boy, his high-pitched voice very different from hers. He wasn't in tune, but the words of the simple song were being enunciated quite clearly, much more so than he'd achieved with the doctors several weeks before.

# Chapter fifteen

Hanger was back in Toulon in time for the ball at the Bishop's palace, bringing with him a welcome detachment of Piedmontese troops. Genoa, his first destination and the best hope for a substantial increase in strength, was too close to the borders of France to assist with anything other than stores, too fearful that should Republican Terror triumph in Provence, as it had in Savoy, then their city state would be first on the list to face retribution.

The French disposed of the two commanders Cartaux and Lapoype, replacing them with General Dugommier, reputedly more energetic, so an assault of some kind was expected hourly, which added to the air of increasing gloom in the town. Several voices raised doubts about going ahead with this public entertainment, which would, of necessity, require the attendance of most of the garrison's officers. But Admiral Hood was adamant. The palace, lit up like a defiant symbol of Royalist fervour, served to boost morale and the citizenry took their cue from that, so that every major building in the town was equally dazzling.

All this to disguise the truth that the Allies were still heavily outnumbered. The circle of works they held was some fifteen miles in length, which tied up most of their available troops. That made it impossible to mount offensive operations, an increasing source of friction with the bellicose Spaniards. Rumours abounded that Gravina, backed up by Colonel Serota, had threatened Hood with a complete withdrawal if his men were denied a chance to attack.

But the figures spoke for themselves. Of a nominal strength approaching 17,000, of which 2,100 were British, the Allies could only field two-thirds of that number. Dugommier outnumbered the beseiged by three to one and was receiving a steady stream of reinforcements, both men and material, on a daily basis. The few soldiers who had arrived from Malta, Naples and Sicily, while welcome, hardly did much to redress the imbalance, though the multiplicity of uniforms, of nearly every colour imaginable, added an air of greater gaiety to a strictly social gathering.

Markham, who might have avoided such an event, was badgered by the Rossignols into acting as their escort. Wearing Frobisher's best uniform again, and shaved by Picard's own valet, his dark brown hair glistening and tied back with black silk, he awaited the family in the hallway. As they came down from their various rooms he could not help but judge their appearance. Rossignol had set aside the normal solid grey of his profession to don a bright red velvet coat, fringed with gold. His eldest daughter wore elaborate, rather old-style garments, all heavy silk and petticoats. Only Eveline had the figure and looks to carry off the latest fashion. She'd piled her hair high, and had it formed into a mass of tight curls. The Burgundy dress was of a light material, slightly pleated, low-cut and tight-fitting around the bosom and flowing from there to the floor. The whole impression was of some creature from classical antiquity.

The Bishop's palace stood back from the waterfront at the top of the largest square in the port, a magnificent three-storey building in the classical style, the brilliant illuminations seeming to pierce the air of increasing Toulonais gloom. The steps leading up to the entrance were lined with guards dressed in fifteenth-century uniforms. On being announced, Markham could not be sure, when heads turned, how many had reacted to his name, and how many to Eveline's beauty. Certainly the men they passed seemed eager to ignore him and extend their greetings to her.

Miss Lizzie Gordon, acting as hostess on behalf of her uncle, was close by the entrance. The contrast between her and the French girl could not have been more striking. Her dress was discreet and primrose yellow, which with her fair hair and pale complexion made her look the very image of Anglo-Saxon sobriety. Only her turban, of heavily patterned yellow and blue silk, and fixed to her head by a large pearl-encrusted pin, hinted at extravagance. When he bent to kiss her hand, he took his time, gently rubbing her fingertips between finger and thumb. The action, a clear signal of interest, was not reciprocated, but he smiled nevertheless as he stood upright, an air of amusement reflected in his eye.

'I fear your uncle was given a jaundiced report regarding our previous meeting.'

'He pointed out to me, Lieutenant, that having been in Italy for so long, I was not privy to the latest happenings in London.'

He could just imagine what Elphinstone had said to his niece. Serving in the Russian army wouldn't do anything for his standing either, since that was generally considered to be a refuge for scoundrels. He would have been condemned utterly, with every detail of his liaisons and his duel laid out in all their gory detail, underpinned by a reflection of his status, both his lack of wealth and the old accusation of cowardice. Certainly not a suitable companion for one such as Lizzie Gordon.

'Such things can be much exaggerated.'

'Indeed?' she replied, as though eager to hear how that could be so.

'Close to, I'm as dull a creature as the next man. I do hope you have space on your card to permit me a dance, Miss Gordon, so that I can prove this?'

'Of course,' she replied, flushing slightly. He could almost see her lack of propriety fighting with her sense of decorum. Part of her was afire with curiosity about the man in front of her. Yet she was also alarmed by his presence, fearful that her knowledge of his reputation as a rake would not protect her. The hint of rouge in her cheeks made his smile even more marked.

'Good.' He came forward a fraction, enough to smell the scent wafted upwards by the warmth of her body, his eyes boring into hers. 'Now, if you will permit me, I have undertaken to escort a family of French refugees. I cannot, regardless of my own inclinations, leave them to their own devices.'

The flash of anger cheered him immensely, hinting as it did at an independent spirit, a person who, regardless of their upbringing and education, could be expected to rebel against convention. 'If they are the people you arrived with, I hardly think the word refugee appropriate.'

That was a statement it was hard to argue with, given their evident affluence. Nor did they lack the social graces. Eveline was surrounded by men eager to catch her eye, and Rossignol *père* was in a heated discussion with Hanger. The Picards were walking around the room, introducing Pascalle Rossignol to the leading citizens of the town, which effectively left him at a loose end. He walked over to fetch a drink, aware that people, seeing him coming, tended to avoid his eye. All except one.

'Markham, is it not?'

'Captain Nelson,' he replied, with a slight bow. He turned to the man with Nelson, a bull-like individual whose ruddy countenance was screwed up in evident disapproval.

'Allow me to name Captain Troubridge, of the frigate *Castor*.'

'Sir.'

'You're off the *Hebe*?' he said abruptly.

The tone was unfriendly, the look damning. 'I am, sir.'

207

'De Lisle told me of you. We had dinner, him, myself and his officers, not two nights ago.'

The sarcasm was unnecessary and probably a mistake, but he couldn't help himself. 'Alas, sir, as a mere soldier, I can't hope to dine in such elevated company. Nor could I pretend to match the wit of the *Hebe*'s wardroom. Why, I'm all envy.'

A small growl started in Troubridge's throat, but was overborne by Nelson, who spoke as though the nuances of that short exchange had completely passed him by. He patted Markham reassuringly on the arm.

'I came across this fellow showing his men the art of musketry, Troubridge. He's a damn fine shot, who'll see off any Frenchman who comes within range. I daresay he's a dab hand with pistols too.'

Markham looked at Nelson, to see if there was some kind of warning there for his fellow captain, that Troubridge should not react to the quite blatant way this marine officer had put him down. But Nelson's pale blue eyes held no expression other than a degree of regard.

'It was edifying to see that,' he continued. 'Just as I was delighted to see you taking instruction from your sergeant. You are, I believe, an army officer, despite your coat.'

'He is that,' said Troubridge sharply. 'Your notoriety precedes you, sir. I doubt you'd be still commissioned in the navy. That is, if you'd ever had the wit to achieve it.'

'Hush, Thomas,' said Nelson. Then he turned back to Markham. 'I fear we sailors hold ourselves a cut above Bullocks.'

'So I have observed,' Markham replied, glaring at Troubridge. 'Though nothing I have experienced warrants it.'

Nelson laughed. 'We do have some cause. We're all obliged to serve our time as mids', studying the art of what we do. And we're examined, which makes us feel very sure of ourselves.'

Markham was just about to list the fields of battle on which he'd been examined, but the other naval officer spoke first.

'Hood,' said Troubridge softly, responding to a sudden commotion by the door.

The commander-in-chief stood there, surrounded by all the senior officers, admirals British and Spanish, and generals from all the nationalities, surveying the room. Mulgrave was missing, having been indisposed for days by a bilious attack. Regardless of the splendid uniforms that surrounded him, his air of authority was obvious. After a few bows to those he recognised, he stepped forward into the throng, the good burghers of Toulon rushing eagerly to engage his attention.

'Like pigs at the trough,' said Troubridge.

'An unkind allusion, Thomas,' said Nelson before turning back to Markham. 'My good friend has little time for our hosts.'

'They're Frenchmen, aren't they? God knows, Nelson, I've heard you curse that race enough.'

'We must, I think, count as a friend any man who resists the Revolutionaries. They, after all, are the enemy.'

'You're dissembling,' Troubridge growled. 'You've no more patience with our presence here than I have.'

'Captain Troubridge maligns me, Markham,' replied Nelson, without rancour. 'He is of the opinion that we should never have landed in the first place. He feels that rather than defend the place we should have destroyed it, burnt every ship that we could not man, then sailed away.'

'An opinion I thought you shared.'

'I admit a degree of ambivalence.' He indicated Hood coming their way, and finished his sentence quickly before turning to face the admiral. 'And since the responsibility does not rest with me. I'm content to obey my orders.'

'Nelson, Troubridge,' said Hood, before turning to look at Markham, standing to attention by their side.

'Good evening, sir,' Nelson responded, following the

admiral's look. 'May I present Lieutenant Markham, of the *Hebe*. He is the fellow who destroyed the guns at Bregaillon, the first time the enemy set them up.'

'Are you, indeed?' demanded Hood, which made the object of this abrupt question turn back to face him. His eyes had been on Nelson, who'd behaved, up till now, as though he didn't really know George Markham from Adam. Clearly that wasn't the case. And if he knew about the attack of the Batterie de Bregaillon, he knew about everything else.

'The operation failed,' said Troubridge. 'The Dons lost half their men and the guns were back in place before nightfall.'

'But it was exceeding gallant, Thomas, was it not?' These words were spoken without Nelson taking his eyes off the admiral for a second.

Hood nodded. 'I suppose it was, Nelson.'

'I think that sentiment would be best conveyed to the officer involved, sir.'

'I daresay he can hear me at this range,' growled Hood.

Markham was embarrassed as Hood passed on. Clearly he'd responded reluctantly, which left Nelson beaming with pleasure. Sam Hood was notoriously reserved, and apparently not given to praising anyone if it could be avoided. Nelson had forced the remark out of him for what seemed like his own amusement.

'If you will forgive me,' Markham said, as the band struck up, 'I have several dances booked.'

'How lucky you are, Markham, to be so accomplished that the fair sex queue up to dance with you. It is not a skill that I have mastered.'

He nearly blurted out the question of which skill Nelson was alluding to. But the warm smile, at once both so ingenuous and deep, stopped him. He bowed again and turned to leave, finding himself hemmed in by the crush that followed in Hood's wake. As he eased a way through he heard Troubridge admonish his friend.

'You baited Hood, there, Horatio, and he won't forget it.'

'Good!' Nelson replied emphatically, in a voice very different to the one Markham had heard up until now. 'Perhaps he'll learn that a little recognition goes far, and cease to be so damned stiff.'

'What do you think of this rumour about a Bourbon Prince coming to help us hold Provence?'

The reply Nelson made to that was lost in the babble of conversation that surrounded Markham. On the other side of the crush he saw several men leading ladies onto the dance floor, Eveline and Miss Gordon amongst them. He also noticed a party of Spanish officers leaving, and wondered idly where they were off to. Several brothels existed in Toulon, as they did in any port. For all their rigid decorum, and deep religion, it looked as though these men preferred such places to an organised ball. Normally he was of the same opinion, and in his mind's eye he could not avoid conjuring up the memories of some of the better bawdy houses he'd visited. On balance, London was better than St Petersburg. Madrid, he suspected, being a pious Catholic city, was the most comprehensively served in that respect.

'What are you smiling at, Lieutenant?' asked Pascalle Rossignol.

'The music, mademoiselle,' he responded hurriedly, well aware that his true thoughts would shock her to the marrow.

'It affects me in the same way,' she replied, adding a coquettish look.

Markham was too much of a gentleman to miss the allusion. 'Then might I have the honour of this dance?'

Her hands went to her ample bosom with theatrical surprise 'Me, Lieutenant Markham?'

'It would be a pleasure,' he replied, since there was nothing else he could say.

The reaction, when he took to the floor, was intriguing.

The Picards nodded approvingly, but Rossignol was frowning. Eveline gave him a look that was at once friendly and understanding. But Lizzie Gordon, dancing with Augustus Hanger, responded differently. Not sure if he'd seen correctly, he looked hard, ignoring her partner's glare, when the dance took Pascalle close to the primrose-clad English beauty. The twin lines that appeared above her nose, the same as he had seen the first day they'd met, clearly indicated equal disapproval. Was she, he wondered, questioning why a man like him should be partnering a lady like Pascalle when he could have been dancing with her?

Pascalle prattled on endlessly, seeming quite deliriously happy to be in the arms of such a handsome officer. Markham thought her a little silly, but nevertheless put all his effort in to covering up her inability to dance. His liking for women extended even to scatterbrained ones, and he could not bring himself to do other than his best. The fatality of such an approach was brought home to him as soon as they stopped. Pascalle, ample chest heaving, brought forth her card and signed him up for several more dances.

He partnered Eveline on his next outing, welcoming the admiration that was directed at her, the way that she swayed revealingly inside her loose dress. And the degree of intimacy they enjoyed as the steps brought them into close proximity was even harder to disguise than her beauty, manifesting itself in dozens of different discreet gestures and smiles. Miss Gordon found this even harder to bear, and hardly took her eyes off the couple, much to the chagrin of Midshipman Driberg, busily boasting to her. The poetic justice of that made Markham perform at his very best.

Yet he wasn't solely concentrating on Eveline. Lizzie Gordon had appeared to him an almost unassailable target for seduction. Being English, and from the stratum of society in which she moved, he reckoned that nothing short of a miracle would be required to get her into bed. But her behaviour tonight, reacting first to Pascalle and now Eveline, denoted a degree of jealousy that hinted at a different character from the one he had supposed. The sirens, which should have been ringing in his head, warning him of the danger he was courting were, as usual, drowned out by the thrill of the chase. Elphinstone's niece was a stuck-up prig with no notion of what pleasure she could have. Nothing, not even Eveline's presence, could stop him from imagining what it would be like to change that.

He danced with Pascalle again to add to her annoyance, before making his way across the floor. The stony face cheered him immensely, being so much more encouraging than indifference.

'Miss Gordon, I have belatedly come to claim my dance.'

'Have you, sir,' she snapped.

'And the crowning prize of the evening, of course.'

The smile on his face clearly infuriated her. The way she snapped her fan shut had several heads turning in their direction. If Markham had cared to look, he would have noticed that two of them belonged to Elphinstone and Hanger. But he had eyes only for her when she held out her hand. As he led her on to the floor, she spoke, seeking by a change of subject to deflect his unnerving attentions by putting him in his place.

'This must seem uncommon dull after London.'

'Sure, at this very moment, it is anything but.'

'Oh come, Lieutenant. The attractions of the metropolis are obvious. Gaming clubs and the like. I believe you moved in rather raffish circles, that Mr Sheridan was a friend.'

'An acquaintance would be a more accurate description, though he did secure me a box at Drury Lane once or twice.'

'You are fond of amateur theatricals, I hear.'

That was a very revealing remark, one that demonstrated just how much Elphinstone had imparted. One of his father's friends in America had been Clinton's Adjutant General, Major André. A great lover of spectacle, he'd roped in young George Markham to play several, mostly juvenile, parts in the plays he put on for the garrisons. In one production of *Hamlet*, the naval officer playing Laertes was too drunk to perform. Thrown on into a strange part, Markham had been given a deep cut above the eye by the lead actor in the fight scene, something obviously witnessed by Lizzie's uncle.

Not that the accident dimmed young George's pleasure in performance. But it was ended when, one night in Philadelphia, André had cast him as a girl, a young beauty in some danger of seduction. Markham had enjoyed himself hugely. But such a performance, given the dubious inclinations of his son and heir Freddy, had nearly brought on an apoplexy in General John Markham. It would have ended anyway. André, having secured the betrayal of Benedict Arnold, was caught on his way back from West Point, and hanged by the Americans as a spy. Nevertheless the theatre was a bug which, bitten by once, was hard to shake.

'I had the privilege of seeing some fine acting,' he replied. 'Certainly Siddons and her brother, Kemble, were very fine, though I thought the child actor Master Betty somewhat overblown. Calling him Young Roscius is too flattering.'

'I saw Sarah Siddons perform in Bath.'

'How lucky you are.'

'Do you really think so? I am given to understand that she's rather a low creature.'

The smile never left his face, but the tone of his voice was hard. 'Then I can only suppose, Miss Gordon, that you sat in the Theatre Royal with your eyes shut and your ears closed.'

The sharp intake of breath caused her to hiss. 'I take it you admire her, sir.'

'I do. Both as an actress and as a friend.'

That was gilding it a bit. He did know Sarah Siddons, having pursued her eldest daughter for several weeks, not truly intimately enough to term her a friend. However, it had the desired effect on Lizzie Gordon, forcing her into an abrupt change of tack.

'There is a rumour that a Bourbon prince is on his way from Aachen. Imagine, the Dauphin here.'

Troubridge had said the same thing. Artois and Provence, the late King's brothers, had led the flight of the nobles after the fall of the Bastille, an act which had done little to help their eldest brother. Artois hungered after the crown, but couldn't claim it since no-one knew the fate of the heir.

'King Louis is dead, and who knows what has happened to his poor son. Whoever comes to Provence, it is unlikely to be the Dauphin. And given their past behaviour, I doubt if the late King's brothers will put themselves in any place where they perceive themselves to be in danger.'

Her lips pursed. 'I think you malign them.'

'Would that you were right,' he replied with deep irony.

The orchestra started playing, and the first dancers began to move. 'But it would be natural for Provence, at least, to come here. These are his own domains, the one place where the Revolution has been defeated.'

'Hardly defeated, Miss Gordon.'

'Deflected then,' she snapped, her hand waving imperiously. The evident passion made her look so much more beautiful than her pose of English reserve. 'Stopped, avoided, deferred.'

'Please, Miss Gordon, my poor Irish wits don't run to such a lesson in wordplay.'

'I dislike your condescension as much as I disapprove

of your being obtuse. You behave as if any notion, in a female head, must be mere fancy.'

He bowed slightly. 'Then I must make amends with my feet, for the mistakes from my mouth.'

'Imagine if they were both to come here.'

'Neither of Louis' brothers will stir from their retreats, I'd take money on it. Even if they were titled King of France.'

There was a twinkle in her eye as she began to move, a look that hinted at secret knowledge. And added to that was just a touch of triumph. 'Don't be too sure about that, Mister Clever Dick Markham!'

His attempt to ask her what she meant was interrupted by the commotion at the door. An ensign, covered in dust and clearly out of breath, was scanning the room. As soon as he saw Elphinstone he ran towards him, pushing the dancers out of the way. Since the Captain had moved closer to the dancing couple, so as to keep his eye on Markham, they were able to hear the message very clearly.

'The Dons, sir. They launched an attack on the batteries opposite the Fort de Malbousquet.'

'Damn Spaniards,' growled Elphinstone, ignoring the fact that many were still present. Markham was vaguely aware of Hood and his party pushing through the crowd as the ensign continued.

'They've been thrown back, Captain, with heavy losses. Some of them are abandoning the defences, and taking the Neapolitans with them. If the French take advantage of their reserve, the whole line will crumble.'

Elphinstone's voice rose, as Hanger took station by his side. He first commanded the band to cease playing, then every officer to return to his post. His eyes swung round to Markham, still holding his niece's hand.

'Markham,' he demanded, 'what's your strength?'

'A mere two dozen, sir.'

'But not occupied in the line?'

'No.'

Hanger cut in. 'I suggest they be sent anyway, if only to give a semblance of resistance.'

Elphinstone was looking at his niece when he nodded.

'Get your men up to Malbousquet at the double,' Hanger ordered. 'Hold the trenches before the sally port until the Spaniards can get you some reinforcements.'

'Sir.'

'And Lieutenant,' added Elphinstone, 'this is an emergency. You cannot fall back. You're to die there, this time, if necessary. No more of your damned retreats.'

The only thing that made the insult bearable was the way his niece swooned.

# Chapter sixteen

It was cold, and before an hour had passed the rain began to fall. A light drizzle that seemed to work its way through the necks of the rankers' oilskin capes, it produced muted moans and curses even though Markham had ordered complete silence. The poorly constructed trenches close to the river bed, so recently occupied by Spaniards, stank, with all the filth that an army could produce beginning to float around their boots. Markham spent more time looking back towards Toulon, still lit up like an invasion beacon, than at the enemy. If they wanted to come, then he had neither the force to disrupt their preparations, nor the men to stop them. And there was certainly insufficient flow in the river to do more than wet their feet.

He was more concerned that the promised reinforcements hadn't arrived. Out in no man's land, scavengers were picking over the bodies of those soldiers who'd died there, as well as the wounded. The cries for some form of succour, which had filled the night air when they arrived, tended to be short-lived. Those who desecrated soldiers' bodies were not the type to balk at dispatching to perdition someone whose property they desired.

'We have got to get the men out of these trenches, sir,' said Rannoch, as soon as the rain stopped. 'The air is mortal with all this filth. And the rain will only make it worse. Half of them will be down with a bloody flux in a matter of days.'

'We can't , Sergeant. As soon as we put our heads above the parapet they'll be silhouetted against the lights from the town.'

'They should have been doused ages past.'

'Someone forgot,' Markham replied bitterly. 'Just like they seem to have forgotten that we are here in the first place.'

'Then let us go back to the rear. It is not going to make much difference, two dozen men. If those French devils come, we will have to run.'

'I have strict orders to die here, if necessary.'

Rannoch's harsh reply was a complete throwback to his behaviour when they'd first come ashore. 'Then I hope you have got the sense to tilt a deaf ear to such nonsense.'

'Pull the men back through the supply trench and get them above ground between here and the redoubt. I'll keep watch.'

'Sir,' the sergeant replied, after a loud exhalation of breath. Markham wondered what he'd have said to him if he hadn't agreed, indeed was almost tempted to ask. But he was gone, slipping along the line, whispering to each man in turn, urging them down off the firestep, with orders to follow him. The slightest noise earned the perpetrator a hissed curse. Soon Markham was alone, in the Stygian darkness, wrapped in his heavy blue cloak with only his thoughts as company, thoughts which centred on how he'd come to end up here in the first place.

His silent profanities against the Spaniards were partly due to the situation, but more to do with Lizzie Gordon. The opportunities to tumble someone like her would come rarely, if ever, outside a marriage bed. But he'd had her in retreat, mentally conceding an interest in him, manifested in her obvious jealousy, that made anything possible. She knew she was a beauty, and resented the idea of some other woman taking precedence over her in any man's eyes. And in his experience, that lever of envy was often enough to make even the most chaste creature reckless.

Such thoughts were no good for a man in his position,

stuck in a badly constructed trench reeking with the putrid odour of human filth. Nothing in his experience had prepared him for this. In America and Russia, apart from a brief period before the surrender at Yorktown, he'd fought wars of movement, in the former country hemmed in by a dense landscape, in the latter over the vast expanses of open steppe. Darkness itself held no terrors, but the feeling of being constricted did.

A slight scuffing sound brought his mind back to the present. He peered forward, trying to discern some shape in the unrelieved blackness of the night. With a vivid imagination, it was all to easy to conjure up outlines and profiles that dissolved as soon as he seemed to have them fixed. But another sound, of something hard like metal knocking on wood, had every nerve in his body stretched taut. The French might have sent a party forward to see if the trench was still occupied. That in itself was scarifying enough. But worse was the notion that it might be the scavengers. Somehow the idea that he'd have his throat cut by one of that breed made his flesh crawl. They'd strip him of everything, perhaps even mutilate his body, and leave him naked to be found by his men at first light.

His hand, holding the pistol under his cloak, was clammy with sweat. The rain began to fall again, light, thin stuff that blew into his eyes. The hairs on the back of his neck were standing up, adding to the feeling that someone was close to him. In his imagination he could hear them breathing, even the pounding of an adjacent heart, until he realised it was his own.

Suddenly, the French sent up a flare, and there right in front of his eyes, silhouetted against the stark blue light, was the unmistakable shape, wrapped in some kind of scarf, of a human head. The figure rose swiftly, an arm coming aloft with the outline of a vicious-looking blade catching his eye. He struggled to pull out his pistol, conscious that it was caught in the folds of his heavy, damp cloak. Aware that he was too slow, he set himself to jump backwards as the thin flash of steel flashed by his head, and took the crouching figure in the chest.

He could hear Rannoch cursing in his ear, twisting his bayonet in his victim's guts as his pistol came free. Another figure rose to his left, beyond the sergeant's arm, black against the blue-lit sky, raising a club with which to smash out his sergeant's brains. The flash of Markham's pistol showed the face, swarthy, snarling and, though as ugly as sin, quite definitely female. She jerked back as his bullet took her in the head, and her screams were added to those of Rannoch's prey, sounds that died away as both expired.

'They were women,' Markham gasped.

'And poor souls they will be, too. The kind of men they bide with will be the sort to send them out to do the dirty work, then drink the proceeds when they get home.'

'Thank you, Rannoch,' he whispered, adding after a slight pause, 'that's not the first time I should have said that.'

'We cannot have you getting killed, Lieutenant Markham. We might get a real Marine officer in your place. Then we would be totally in the shit, instead of just up to our ankles.'

In the dark, it was hard to work out Rannoch's exact meaning. The irony in his tone was easy to detect. But the words, even then, had the capacity to diminish, even wound him.

'Have I just been complimented or damned?' he asked.

'You are alive, are you not?'

'D'you think more of these wretches will try to take us?'

They might at that. The riverbed in front provides a place for them to hide, and we have got no blue lights to send aloft. When I saw the Frenchmen put one up I expected to hear the sound of a charge.'

'That wasn't put up for an attack. More likely the

scavengers are near their trenches as well. I suppose they tried the same thing on Johnny Crapaud.'

'They are not the kind to care whose body they strip, that is for certain.'

Markham didn't want to think about that. 'Was there any sign of help on the way?'

'None that I could see.'

'It'd be best if we were back to back. That way we will reduce the chance of getting skewered.'

Rannoch complied, the broad shoulders in his oilskin cape providing more security to Markham than he did to the Highlander. He thought about reloading his pistol, but that would require some form of light, which would be certain to attract the attention of anyone still grubbing about in no man's land. The rain had stopped again, and overhead he could see that the cloud cover had broken, which produced a modicum of starlight and allowed them a few feet of vision. It also dropped the temperature quite drastically, and he shivered inside his cloak.

'We're in for a long night, Sergeant,' Markham whispered.

'And a cold one,' Rannoch murmured in reply.

The risk of one, or even both of them, falling asleep, was acute, so the conversation which followed, carried on in an undertone, was an aid to staying awake. It wasn't long before Markham understood how little they had to talk about. The subject of improving shooting was soon exhausted, and he didn't really wish to inquire as to the man's opinion about his qualities as an officer. Nor was the sergeant the type to respond to personal questions, even of the most vague nature, which threw Markham back upon his own history.

'What do you and the men know of me?' he whispered suddenly. 'Of my past?' Rannoch stiffened, hesitating, clearly aware that reply with a negative would fly in the face of all logic. 'You may speak the truth, Sergeant.'

'I know about what happened at the Battle of

Guilford,' Rannoch said slowly, his voice deeper than normal. 'Or, at least what was said to have happened.'

'I was fifteen at the time,' Markham said suddenly, aware that he was speaking of things he never disclosed. 'We'd tried to assault the courthouse three times. The regiment was in tatters, casualties screaming for help. And they were looking to me, the only officer still standing, for guidance.'

He couldn't bring himself to explain that he hadn't run away, but had left his post because he'd been told what the British Legion were up to in Salisbury, a hamlet where he'd been billeted for a week before the battle. In terms of atrocities, the British army in America was bad enough. But when it came to rapine, the cavalry of Tarleton's British Legion were in a different class. There wasn't even a semblance of restraint on their behaviour, with their commander positively encouraging them to rape, murder and burn.

'I stayed, for a week before the battle, with a family in Salisbury.'

'And that is why you left the regiment?'

'I thought we'd be rested. It never occurred to me that Cornwallis would ask us to go back into the battle. If I had, I would have stayed, regardless of my feelings.'

Rannoch's voice was suddenly even softer than his previous whispering. 'A girl, then?'

The quiet laugh that preceded Markham's positive reply had more despair in it than humour. 'Flora Imrie.'

'The same age?'

'Older by a year. I found out she'd been raped repeatedly before being thrown, to join the rest of her family, into the flames of her own burning house. The soldiers of the British Legion boasted to me of what they'd done – watched, encouraged, by one of their officers, Lieutenant Augustus Hanger.'

'Christ,' said Rannoch.

'He was so drunk he could barely stand upright. Laughed in my face when I demanded they be punished.'

'That scar on his face,' Rannoch prompted, which led Markham to believe he might know more than he was saying.

'I paid for that. There was no one to stop him taking revenge.'

'I wonder you are still alive.'

'The surgeons of the British Legion were bigger drunkards than the men. They didn't sew up his face very well. But I reckon I only survived because they gave him rum to dull the pain.'

'They won at Guilford without you.'

'Yes, Sergeant. But the cost was so high we had to retreat to Williamsburg. The thing I remember most is the carts full of wounded men, none of them receiving any attention. We were passing through a land inhabited by the same people as us. They spoke the same language, had the same customs, some must even have been related. But they shot at us. And after Salisbury and a hundred places like it, who can blame them?'

'Kin against kin usually turns out to be the worst.'

'You sound as if you know. Did you serve in America?'

'I did. In the Twenty-ninth Foot.'

Markham nearly blurted out 'Where?', but stopped himself just in time. That regiment had been in America for decades, fighting throughout the Seven Years War with little distinction, so ill-disciplined that they were damned by General Wolfe before, during, and after his Quebec campaign. Responsible for the Boston massacre of 1774, in which half a dozen protesters had been shot down, the 29th Foot were credited with igniting the spark that started the whole bloody conflict that became the American Revolution. Some of the men who had fired that day had been convicted of manslaughter, which resulted in their being branded with the letter 'M' on the thumb.

'Then you would have come home with as much credit as me.'

Rannoch snorted, angrily. 'Rankers do not get credit. They get half-starved, beaten and robbed of their pay. They are lined up by men who are rich and stupid, and ordered forward in line so that they can be killed. When their lords and masters err, it is the bloody soldiers who pay. And when those poor souls return to their homes, they find the land they grew up on taken away.'

'Why are you in the army, Rannoch?'

The ripple of anger was discernible through the man's back, a feeling so intense that he was actually trembling, and Markham thought he heard something that was like a cross between a snarl and a sob. Rannoch too was being forced to remember, and perhaps experiencing a pain similar to that Markham had suffered when he realised that Flora Imrie, the first love of his youth, was dead.

'Half starvation is a muckle better than the thing whole. I come from a place where keeping a sheep alive is more important than the life of a man, woman or child. I know, because when I have had to bury them, I was barred from using land that was fit for grazing.'

'I was no more glad than you to get home,' Markham murmured quickly.

Rannoch merely grunted, clearly unwilling to be any more open. So Markham kept talking, aware as he painted the balanced picture of the intervening years just how much he was leaving out. His mind was working on two levels, one recalling the truth and the other filleting it into a cheerful story. Not that he lied exactly, just that he indulged, as all people do, in the right to keep some things hidden. Thus his love of the bottle, after his return from America, was recounted as manly and amusing instead of destructive; the failures of his various ventures blamed on circumstance instead of stupidity.

Likewise, his decision to join the Russian army as a mercenary officer sounded romantic, when in truth it had been more to do with an empty purse and unbridled libido. Rannoch knew nothing of Muscovy, which filled an hour while Markham shared his knowledge of a nation whose love of drink outshone even that of the British; of soldiers who lied comprehensively and often, but laughed when exposed; of officers and men who were brave, romantic, clever and downright stupid, all at the same time, soldiers who could endure hardships of campaigning that would make any European wince.

He recalled part of the conversation he'd had with Lizzie Gordon, so talked of Major André. But Rannoch knew nothing of *Hamlet*, or Shakespeare, or even a modern playwright like Sheridan. It brought home to him just how narrow a world he'd occupied, and how far it was removed from the lives of ordinary mortals. And it was impossible not to compare his conversation with the more intimate words he'd spoken to Eveline Rossignol. He realised, not for the first time, how much easier he found it to talk to women than men. Was that because they were less inclined to judge him harshly, or because dignity was not so important as it was to his own gender?

'You actually got up there in Philadelphia, dressed as a girl, and performed?'

'I did.'

'It is hard to see you prancing around in tight hose.'

'My legs were much admired,' Markham replied, which made Rannoch laugh, his shoulder pressing against those of his officer. The absurdity of the remark, standing back to back in a filthy trench, struck him too, and soon he was heaving, trying desperately not to chuckle out loud. Yet even laughing he could see the dark layer of truth under those reminiscences, things that had brought him back to this; serving in the British army as the sole alternative to Newgate gaol.

'It is getting light,' said Rannoch, who was facing the hills to the north.

The sound of a trumpet floated across no man's land as the sky turned from grey to blue. Able to see the rest of the trench system, they inched their way along to a revetted observation point. Taking turns to look through the slit in the logs, they examined the space between the lines, dotted with the pale white bodies of the naked casualties.

'Fetch the lads, Rannoch,' said Markham, ducking back down. 'And send Yelland back to find out where those damned reinforcements are.'

They arrived at full daylight under the command of Colonel Serota himself, the Spaniard offering no apologies to the despised British for having left them in such a perilously exposed position for the whole night.

'What have you done about removing the dead?' Serota demanded, talking to him as though he were only fit for the bottom of the trench.

'I haven't done a thing,' Markham spluttered, too shocked to be angry.

Serota, his yellow face going several shades paler, actually shouted at him, his black eyes flashing with a look that in another set of circumstances would have had Markham reaching for his sword. 'It is the first duty of an officer to look after his dead,' he said, looking out over the churned-up field that was no man's land.

'You stupid, pompous, Spanish arse,' said Markham, a remark that was greeted by a gale of laughter from his men. Serota spun round to look as Markham repeated what he'd said, adding, 'The first duty of an officer, sir, is to keep his men alive.'

'Truce flag,' said Rannoch, jumping back from the observation point to land between the two officers, effectively killing their dispute.

Able now to look across the area in front of them, with trails of mist being burnt away by the rising sun, they saw a French officer approaching the riverbank, accompanied by two soldiers. The crisp white flag caught the light as it was waved back and forth. Serota was out of the trench in a flash, followed by Markham, striding towards the approaching enemy. Salutes were exchanged, and the formalities completed quickly. The Spaniards had one hour in which to remove their dead, before hostilities would be recommenced. Given the number of bodies dotting the area, and the limited time available, Markham knew that he'd have to stay to help.

It was a gruesome task, moving bodies that had stiffened overnight. Quite a few had been mutilated by the scavengers, ears and fingers that had worn rings sliced off. Those who'd been wounded, the men they'd heard screaming for help, had expired when their throats were cut. Several French soldiers took the opportunity of the truce to get out of their own trenches and stretch their legs. Markham looked at them closely, observing the way that their dress was complete, unlike the soldiers he'd faced at Ollioules. Gone were the ragged coats and trousers, now replaced with proper uniforms. They had boots on their feet and standard weapons. That meant they were not only receiving more men, but proper supplies, which would make them a much more formidable instrument in any future battle.

'Sir!' said Halsey, his pasty face worried as he passed him, carrying one end of a rigid cadaver. 'It might be of interest for you to get as close to the Frogs' trench as we've just been.'

Nonchalantly, pulling his cloak tight to ward off the chill, he wandered over to the point at which the bodies were thickest, the dip just before the enemy position where most of the assaulting troops had come to grief in a withering hail of musket balls. Behind the trench he could see a pair of artillery positions, each with embankments to protect the guns. Standing just near the top of one of them was an officer, a general by the gaudy quality of his attire, surveying the pleasing prospect of a victory. But it was the sight of the man beneath him, still sitting on his horse, that stopped Markham's breathing.

'Fouquert!'

It was as though the act of whispering the man's name

228

was enough to turn him round. He spun on his mount and their eyes locked as he spotted the solitary figure in the long blue cloak. Spurring his horse he came forward, barely nodding to the commander of the French troops who saluted him, reining in on the opposite side of the ditch. His clothes, for all the severity of their cut and colour, were well made and new. But the most obvious fact about Fouquert was that his attire was that of a civilian, not an officer. Yet a French infantry captain had been punctilious in the way he'd saluted him.

'Lieutenant,' he said coldly, before pausing. His thin face had lost none of the cruel look that the Irishman remembered, and not even the chill of the morning air had given it colour. 'Markham, is it not?'

'What do I call you, Fouquert?'

'Try Citizen Commissioner.'

'I'd rather refer to you in a manner that suited you. "Cochon" comes to mind, though you're so thin you have the appearance of one who's been left to suck the hind tit.'

The reaction to being called a pig, and a skinny one, was in the eyes, not the face, which was held rigidly steady. When he replied, he surprised Markham by doing so in very good, if heavily accented, English.

'In five minutes, I could have you calling me master, and begging for me to be merciful.'

'You'd be dead first.'

'Perhaps we can put that to the test, when Toulon falls.'

'There's an expression in English, about counting your chickens before they are hatched.'

'I know it. Just as I know that the position here is hopeless. Toulon must fall, and if it does so in the right way, then I shall do my very best to make sure that in any surrender, you do not march out with your dignity intact.'

'And just who are you?'

'Something a great deal more important than a mere mercenary. When the city is once more French, the civil administration will be in my hands for as long as I need to deal with the traitors who still support the Bourbons.'

'Then I'll tell the inhabitants what's in store for them, Fouquert, women and men. That way they'll never give in. And if you'd like to meet me in the middle of the field once the truce is concluded, I'll be happy to wait for you.'

Fouquert threw back his head and laughed. 'No, no, Markham. But rest assured we will meet, and that you won't have to wait too long.'

He hauled his horse round and trotted off, leaving Markham wondering why he'd used the word mercenary.

# Chapter seventeen

The attacks started halfway through November, within days of the Spanish débâcle at Malbousquet, and lasted for two whole weeks. Pinpricks in the main, all along the perimeter, they were designed to test out the defences and to keep Mulgrave's slim mobile reserve on the move. Being part of that, Markham and his men were in almost continuous motion, shifting from redoubt to trench, one day atop Mont Faron, the next force-marching to the boats, then shifted across the harbour to defend the batteries on the St Mandrian peninsula, at the very southern end of the defences, facing what appeared to be the enemy massing for an attack.

The advantage of operating on interior lines was nullified by the sheer weight of French pressure, something their general applied with great cunning. It was as if Dugommier always knew just where to attack, which bit of the line Mulgrave had denuded to shore up the defences elsewhere. Such a sequence of events produced much talk of spies, a suspicion that all the sailors of Republican sympathies had not left Toulon. Hood had them rounded up, loaded into their own ships, and shifted out under a flag of truce, bound for La Rochelle and Brest.

The effect of this move was welcoming and immediate. The next massed infantry assault from the enemy ran straight into a well-defended position, a specially built redoubt on the Hill of Caire called Fort Mulgrave, manned entirely by British marines, which protected the western arm of the Petite Rade. A sharp defeat was inflicted on the French, partly with the assistance of naval gunnery, which outflanked the enemy to both north and south of the fort. A counter-attack was launched against the French artillery positions on the 29th which, being mounted and executed with some care, saw several guns successfully spiked.

This cheered the inhabitants, who needed a boost. The sound of warfare had become constant, with cannon in play at every major installation in the semicircle of the line, the corresponding French guns adding to the air of increasing desperation. But the situation was not as grim as it sometimes appeared, since for all their efforts, the enemy had made no inroads into the defences.

After the defeat before Fort Mulgrave, with the weather becoming colder and the sky almost uniformly overcast, Dugommier seemed to realise the futility of carrying on with such tactics, and the pressure eased. The guns fell silent, and a calm, which seemed unnatural, settled over Toulon. That left Markham and his men with time to repair the ravages of endless movement, not least the cuts, sores and abrasions from fighting, plus the boils brought about from living on hard rations eaten in damp uniforms. Time to brush and clean their thick red coats, wash and mend shirts and undergarments, and to see to boots and weapons that had suffered from unavoidable neglect.

Markham was lucky in that regard. Not only did he have an alternative uniform to wear, but Celeste was available to take on the burden of repairing his army coat, and with her delicate fingers, much more likely to do a decent job than he could. It was wonderful to have a day's rest, to bathe his aching, grimy limbs. And, after a proper dinner, to anticipate a rekindling of his relationship with Eveline. This was a desire she shared, which she made obvious by her attentions to him before the meal.

It was hard to credit that the Rossignol family didn't know what they were up to. Judging by the frowns of disapproval which came from Madame Picard, which commenced before the soup was served, their liaison was no secret. But the other two members of the family treated him as they had previously, and if they noticed the myriad signs of their intimacy, the touches before they took their seats, the smiles full of secret understanding exchanged across the dinner table, they were ignored. Rossignol *père* was drinking more heavily than usual, which made him talk loudly, his conversation full of curses aimed at the Republicans, in between colourful descriptions of his past life. Openly prepared to admit that he been born in somewhat reduced circumstances, he was proud of his achievements. Some of his comments about the late Louis XVI made Madame Picard frown even more, and brought forth a burst of indignation from her husband.

'No purpose is served by violence, Maître Rossignol.'

'Agreed. But you must admit that it was only the prospect of revolt that brought movement from the boneheads of Versailles.'

'You call our late sovereign a bonehead?'

'Never, Monsieur Picard. But he was surrounded by them, fops to a man, more interested in the details of their toilette than the state of the nation.' Seeing the unhappy look on his host's face, he continued quickly, 'The King himself was a good man who, better advised, would have made the concessions necessary to stave off revolution. In Paris, one could not fail to see how such advice as he was given operated against his interests.'

'And the Queen?' asked Madame Picard sourly.

'Maladroit, Madame. To be accused so often of infidelity, even if she was innocent ...'

'If, Monsieur?' Madame Picard cut in. 'How can you say such a thing in this house ...'

Rossignol interrupted her in turn, dragging Markham into the dispute. He, addressed suddenly, had to tear his eyes away from the man's daughter, a requirement made harder by the way she was running her shoeless foot up his lower leg.

'Free speech,' Rossignol said, emphatically. 'That is the greatest benefit you English have, is it not, Lieutenant?'

'So it's said,' Markham replied, without enthusiasm.

'That is what we lacked in France. What nation, so near to a new century, could prosper with laws that belonged to a medieval kingdom?' Markham nodded automatically as Rossignol continued, his words aimed at Madame Picard. 'Mind, it must be said that too much free speech can be a bad thing.'

Markham was aware that some drama had been played out before his eyes, but he could neither understand it, nor bring himself to care. Days of marching all over Little Gibraltar, cut off from female company, had sharpened his appetites to a point where little else intruded into his thoughts. After dinner, he had the excuse of weariness to cover an early retirement. Rossignol, announcing that he had much to do, was happy to depart the table. Monsieur Picard, still with a business to run, however curtailed, rose as well. But his wife, probably sensing what would happen if the females retired, did everything in her power to keep the Rossignol girls at the table.

Arriving in his room Markham found Celeste in the act of laying out his army coat. It had been brushed, stitched and pressed with a hot iron, and looked better than it had since the day he left England. She would have darted out of the door if he hadn't filled it. As it was she stood still, arms by her side, eyes fixed firmly on the floor. He smiled at her, trying to breach the reserve the girl had shown since that first day at Ollioules, silently cursing the fate that put such a kind creature in the path of so dreadful a fate.

'How is Jean-Baptiste?' he asked gently.

'As well as can be expected,' she replied.

'I can't help noticing how the sight of you cheers him.'

Celeste raised her eyes, for the first time showing a hint

of passion.'Perhaps that is because I want nothing from him.'

'Is that why you succeed where the doctors fail?'

She fought hard to conceal her shock. 'He does not require doctors, Monsieur. He requires to be left in peace.'

'Come now,' Markham replied, stepping forward. 'Rossignol has shown great kindness to the boy. To take on a child who is not actually a relative.'

'He has his purpose,' she snapped.

'Of course he has. He wishes to effect a cure.' She looked at him with disbelief. Markham shrugged and moved to lay a reassuring hand on her shoulder. 'I'm sorry. You seem confused.'

She ducked and darted past him; as she went through the door he heard her reply. 'Nothing is as it seems. Not in this house.'

He waited impatiently for Eveline, wondering what had delayed her. Surely Madame Picard couldn't have kept everyone at table this long. Unable to stand the frustration any longer, he slipped out of the door and along the corridor towards the Rossignol rooms. As a precaution, he passed that which the girls occupied and put his ear to the old man's door. The sounds he heard, low moans, intrigued him; loud enough to carry through the panelling. He listened as they increased in both frequency and level, until they crescendoed in the unmistakable sound of a woman reaching climax. That brought a smile to his lips, as well as deep curiosity to his mind. It was quite definitely Rossignol's room. Who was he with? Some bawd slipped in for the purpose, or even one of the serving girls? Either would be unlikely to get past the eagle eye or meet with the approval of Madame Picard.

He dismissed the thought that it was the lady herself out of hand, just as he heard the floorboards creak on the other side of the door. He scurried back towards his own room, stopping at the bend in the corridor to peer back into the gloom. The door opened and Rossignol came out, his dishevelled state exaggerated by the light from a lantern just behind him. He was tugging at his coat, seeking to smooth it out, when Pascalle came out behind him, lantern in hand, dressed only in her nightclothes, bearing a cloak which she then held out for him to put on. Markham suppressed the cry of surprise that welled up in his throat, then checked to see if he could have made an error. But the sound of a woman enjoying such pleasure was one he was too familiar with. No wonder neither of these two remarked on his relationship with Eveline Rossignol. Any man prepared to debauch his own daughter was in no position to cast a pebble, let alone a stone.

The whispered endearments the pair exchanged pointed to no sudden seduction, more to a relationship of some depth and length. Rossignol, cloak around his shoulders, made for the top of the stairs, clearly, given the way he was dressed, intent on going out into the night. Intrigued, Markham was determined to follow him, but Pascalle was heading his way. He shrank back out of sight as she came along the corridor, waiting till she opened the door of the room she shared with Eveline before risking another look. Suddenly, as she shut it, the corridor went dark.

Returning to his room, he flung on his breeches and coat, then, holding his boots in his hand, scurried along to the top of the stairs. The hallway was in semi-darkness, the gentle snoring of the servant who slept by the door to the interior courtyard the only indication of human existence. But that noise meant that Rossignol could not have exited by that route, since to do so would mean waking the man up. Markham stood above him, to check that the door was indeed locked and the servant was still asleep, before removing the shaded lantern that sat behind his head. A quick check of the public rooms proved they were empty, so he made his way to the back of the house.

The rear doors, wide enough for a coach, could hardly be opened without disturbing Picard's coachman and his wife, who slept in the loft above. The heavy chain that secured them was still in place. A quick check of the stables showed the owner's coach, shafts empty. Rossignol's, still without doors, filled the yard, as it had since the day they'd arrived. Markham sat on the runner, pondering the implications of this. If Rossignol wasn't in the house, then he must be outside. Yet if that was the case, he'd used some form of exit that Markham knew nothing about. And given that, what was he doing out at this time of night?

Certainly it wouldn't be legal, if it involved all this sneaking about. And what did he really know about Rossignol, apart from what the older man had told him? He certainly hadn't been aware of the relationship he had with his own daughter! Shivering slightly, he stood up and made his way back to the house, turning over in his mind all the things that had happened since he'd met the Parisian lawyer; the way his coach had arrived just ahead of the soldiers; his singular way of finding a billet. Just what had he said to Madame Picard that turned her attitude from downright refusal to an almost simpering acceptance of their presence?

Standing in the hallway, he remembered meeting Rossignol on the morning he'd taken his men to their firing practice. He'd been heading towards the study, a sheaf of papers in his hand, covered in what looked like drawings. There was slight pang of guilt in trying the study door, which opened noiselessly; a feeling of trespassing not only on private property but the Picards' hospitality. The room was small and circular, lined with bookshelves which went all the way to the ceiling, dominated by a large round table covered in papers which nearly filled it. Markham put the lantern down on the only clear space, and the first thing he saw was the great red and gold bound book with which Madame Picard had been attempting to coach young Jean-Baptiste all those weeks before.

He opened it and leant forward, unshading the lantern fully so that he could see the pictures. There was no need to try and guess the identity of the figures portrayed, one per page, as each had a subscription at the base. The clothing was different, as was the quality of the artwork. Charlemagne was there, as was the first Capet king, St Louis, and Henry IV, the Protestant king who'd said that Paris was well worth a mass. Catherine de Medici glowered out from the preceding page, her dark eyes seeming still to carry the menace of the secret poisoner. The great Sun King was shown young, middle-aged, and in all the glory of his last years. But the pages which interested Markham the most had several drawings stuck between the leaves, sketches of palaces one of which was unmistakably Versailles. And the twin portraits underneath those sketches, on pages which seemed well thumbed, were of King Louis XVI and his recently guillotined wife, Marie Antoinette.

He made more noise than he intended shutting the book, a thud which seemed to rebound off the ledger-lined walls. Quickly he reshaded his lantern and slipped out through the door, laying it at the head of the still sleeping servant. It was only when he re-entered his room that he remembered Eveline. Had she come to him when he was out, and if so, what would she deduce from that?

He lay back on the bed, his mind in turmoil. There was a mass of questions he could ask, but would he receive either truthful or satisfactory answers? Celeste wouldn't speak to him, though she had the ability to answer questions. But that would mean interrogating her, and somehow that seemed wrong. Eveline Rossignol was the only person in the house he was really close to, the only one who could give him the truth. Still thinking of her, and how difficult she'd find it, naked and in his arms, to do otherwise, he fell into a troubled sleep.

If Rossignol had been up late, it didn't show in either his face or his manner. Nor, for all his consumption of wine, did he appear to have a hangover. He was as hearty as ever at breakfast, gabbling away at Markham and the Picards, whose presence hindered any form of interrogation. This left him wondering where the girls had got to, while another layer of his thinking ran over the events of the previous night. The cold light of a November morning made everything seem less suspect.

Toulon was a seaport, therefore there would be smuggling. Lurid articles appeared in the English and Irish papers about smugglers; their collective will and desperate methods to avoid taxes. Of how every port in the land was honeycombed with tunnels and secret doorways so that the Excise officers could be evaded. How even the most apparently upright citizens in the town would be at the heart of the trade, prepared to murder to keep their secrets. Why should France be any different? Looking down the table at the tall, skeletal figure of his host, he saw Picard in an entirely new light.

And Rossignol, full of bluster and confidence, who'd taken on the task of dealing with the Allies on Picard's behalf. Did that include the provision of scarce luxuries? Little imagination was required to guess at the level of nefarious trade going on in an occupied naval base. There were many commodities at a premium, and that was a sure recipe for underhand trading. With half a dozen nationalities, this would be a busy market. The British were no saints, officers or men, but they paled in comparison to the Spaniards when it came to corruption. And they in turn couldn't even begin to hold a candle to the Neapolitans.

And what about Eveline? Had she found his room empty Was that why she and her sister were so late to the table? Pascalle entered at that very moment, wafting in all directions her usual cloud of heavy perfume. Her eyes were bright and her smile, somewhat enigmatic, was aimed at him, which made his heart jump. But she turned and spoke to her father.

'Poor Eveline is indisposed, Papa, and has asked to be allowed to stay abed.'

'A doctor?' he inquired.

'No doctor is needed. It is but a woman's thing.'

Rossignol sighed with understanding, as Markham cursed under his breath. Was Pascalle telling the truth? It seemed unlikely, given that the previous night at dinner, Eveline had done everything in her power to indicate what the pair of them could look forward to. He struggled to remember the last occasion on which she'd been indisposed, but the date eluded him. Why had she encouraged him, when he'd been without her charms for over ten days? It seemed cruel, a thought which was immediately followed by remorse. In his experience, many women showed their greatest desire just before the peak of their cycle.

Reluctantly, he realised that he must either quiz Celeste, or put some direct questions to Rossignol. Of the two he preferred the latter.

'Time for me to be off,' said Rossignol, pulling himself to his feet. When he saw the look of surprise in Markham's eye, he clearly mistook it for inquiry and responded accordingly. 'I have taken to daubing a painting, which will stand as a representation of the siege. From the very top of the Grosse Tour, the whole of the landscape, harbour and hill, unfolds as a perfect panorama.'

'Indeed?' Markham replied, recalling the sketches he'd seen last night.

'Land and water are not a problem,' Rossignol

continued, 'but the ships, with their intricate rigging, are the very devil. I'm a total amateur. But it provides pleasure and passes the time agreeably. I hope that the day provides you with as much joy.'

'I was wondering if I could have a word with you.'

If Rossignol picked up the tightness in Markham's voice, he didn't respond. His voice was full of a warmth that precluded evasion. 'As soon as I return, Lieutenant. You will, I trust, be coming back here this evening?'

'Yes. Today will be taken up with further training.'

'My word, Lieutenant,' asked Pascalle. 'Are your soldiers not proficient enough?'

The reply was emphatic. 'No, mademoiselle, they are not.'


There was no sign of Rossignol at dinner. Picard informed him that the Frenchman had been called to the Fort de la Malgue to discuss future supplies, and intended to dine there. Nor was Eveline at the table, and he anticipated another solitary night.

'What happened last night?' he said, as soon as she appeared in his room.

'That old witch was watching.'

'Madame Picard?'

'Who else?' She rushed forward to embrace him, but he held her off slightly. 'Is your father up to something, Eveline?'

He felt her shoulders tense, saw the worry in the eyes, and heard the sharp intake of breath. Suddenly the indelicacy of alluding to what he'd seen and heard on the landing the previous night was too much. And his confusion made him stutter slightly.

'Sneaking out of the house at all hours of the night.'

'You were spying on him.'

'I was looking for you.'

'And here I am, chéri.' She leant forward and blew out the candle.

'I want to talk to you.'

'Not now.'

Unfortunately, the guns on Mont Faron began firing almost at precisely the wrong moment. He did everything he could to shut out the sound, and might have succeeded if the whole city of Toulon had not come awake. The church bells were rung, the agreed signal for a general alarm, which in his case was a standing order that he should proceed with his men to the Fort de la Malgue. Haste, plus the prospect of imminent peril, gave their lovemaking, already frantic, an added piquancy. But there was no time for post-coital inquests. He struggled into his clothes, jammed on his hat, grabbed his sword, coat, and pistols, and with his shirt still flapping outside his breeches ran through to the ground floor of the warehouse.

Rannoch had the men lined up and ready to move out as he clattered across the flagstoned floor. Every eye turned to take in the state of his dress, until a sharp command from the sergeant brought them to attention. While it removed their gaze, it failed to eradicate the smirks they wore on their faces, or entirely to suppress the laughter that was bubbling up in their breasts, making some of them shake uncontrollably. Rannoch stepped towards him smartly, his bulk cutting off the men's view.

'If we are not about to surrender, sir, it would be an idea to stow the white flag.'

'What are you . . .?'

Markham was in the act of putting on his coat, but his eyes followed the sergeant's downwards to where his shirt tail flapped. Rannoch would have seen him blush if the light had been strong enough. But he heard him curse, so he knew his officer was berating himself for a fool. Markham was still doing that as they doubled along the quayside. Having spent weeks trying to gain the respect of these men he'd thrown it all away, and made himself look like an complete idiot. It wasn't the first time in his life that the presence of a woman had been his downfall. Not that he blamed them. The fault, he knew, lay with him.

They barely paused by the fort, ordered towards the guns, booming and flashing at the top of the great sweep of hills that dominated the town, to the flat, featureless plateau of Mont Faron. Marching uphill at such a serious pace meant that when they arrived, he and his men were near to exhaustion. But the situation was too serious for any hope of respite. The French had confounded expectations by launching an attack before standard military logic said they were ready.

They should have sapped forward for weeks from their redoubts above the village of La Valette, inching obliquely upwards across the scrub-covered ground for a hundred yards, then constructing a defensive line that, once secured, allowed them to move forward once more. But Dugommier eschewed this and attacked with the whole Army of Savoy from half a mile distant. Ten thousand men in great infantry waves, ignoring the rules of war and manoeuvre, bugles blowing and tricolours waving as they advanced uphill towards the trench lines between the Forts of Faron and L'Artigues, under murderous shellfire with precious little artillery support of their own.

Musket fire, concentrated and deadly at short range, didn't slow them either. These were the tactics of the Revolution, mass assaults in overwhelming numbers, which had proved so successful in the north. But here on Mont Faron, with a clear view of the French lines, it looked like folly. At that distance from the defences, they should have been repulsed with ease by the men holding the perimeter, leaving free the British marines who'd been brought up to act as a reserve. But they were thrown into action at soon as they arrived.

Again, it was the allied troops that had failed to hold, Neapolitans and Spaniards, and the British who were called upon to take back the defences they had lost. Even as he cursed their inability to maintain their ground, Markham could sympathise. They were badly equipped and led by men who stole everything they could from their soldiers, officers who were often the first to retreat at any sign of danger.

That, at least, could not be said of those leading the marines into action. Elphinstone and Mulgrave were everywhere, shouting, cajoling and leading confused charges to throw back pockets of Frenchmen who'd established themselves in the casernes and redoubts. No longer moving forward to the sound of their bugles, some of their revolutionary fervour deserted them. And any cohesion the enemy might have had was gone after stumbling, in the gloom, up over half a mile of uneven scree. Content to try and hold what they'd taken, they looked to those still coming from La Valette to finish the battle.

He might hate Augustus Hanger, but no-one could doubt the man's courage. Sword waving in the ethereal glow from gun flashes, flares and blue lights, he led one counter-attack after another, always at the head of his men, in the position of maximum danger, taking the attacking French detachments in the flank and driving them relentlessly back down the hill, then turning to traverse the slopes so that he could slash into those Frenchmen who'd been cut off by their earlier successes.

Markham and his men, shifted from command to command, were ordered to clear one section of trench after another, with no idea, as they entered a new part of the line, how many men they would face. Night fighting in such a constricted space was deadly, with nothing but the light of the occasional flares and the orange glow of spitting cannon to show an enemy silhouette. Silent at first, screams soon drowned out the blaring trumpets as the enemy tried to reinforce their gains. Success below ground level was swiftly followed by an order to form up and advance, never knowing who was to the left or right as they did so.

Both armies struggled for advantage, aware that the loss of these heights could break the siege. All the musketry practice of the last few days was useless. In trenches, on the loose marl slopes and shallow earth of the limestone plateau, this was hand-to-hand work; stabbing with bayonets, clubbing with butts, gouging at the faint glow of an opponent's eye, biting any hand that was laid close enough to the mouth. Cursing, swearing, sometimes crying, they fought each other like demons, stepping over their own wounded and dead to engage.

Still more men came on, only the occasional blue light to show their progress, each advancing wave at least a thousand men, with double that amount already engaged, the whole easily outnumbering the defenders. The enemy established themselves around Fort Faron, then attacked the lower defences around L'Artigues, for once with the sloping ground to their advantage. British reserves, scraped from all over the battlefield, were sent in, piecemeal, to try and hold the line. Risking everything, Mulgrave denuded the defences around the other forts, St Catherine, Rouge and Blanc, plus the high western redoubt at Des Pomets, to stop up the gaps that inevitably appeared.

How they drove the French back, Markham didn't know. But they did, time and again, with confused bayonet charges that looked doomed but somehow succeeded, ragged volleys of musketry that imposed just enough of a check on the enemy to permit a counter-attack. All through the night the battle raged, until sheer exhaustion took over on both sides, and like two pugilists driven to their knees, they ceased to inflict any telling punishment.

As dawn broke the French withdrew, leaving at least a thousand of their fellows as casualties on the hillsides. The guns behind their lines, which had been sporadically active throughout the night, began a steady cannonade, churning up the ground between the positions, blowing already shattered bodies of friend and foe into tiny fragments.

Food came, with water to drink, and a chance to dress the innumerable wounds that every man had sustained. Then the bugles blew and a flag appeared, with an officer from each side to agree the obligatory truce. Markham dragged his men to their feet, and pushed and shoved them unmercifully, as they mingled with the soldiers they'd just fought, helping to clear the field of the thousands of casualties. Elphinstone and Hanger rode along behind the lines, bloody, bandaged and haggard, showing evidence of their own endeavours. Dragged away from his work, Markham stood to attention beside their snorting mounts.

'We stay here, Markham,' said Hanger hoarsely, too tired to sneer. 'We can't trust these positions to our so-called allies, so we must hold them ourselves.'

'Sir.'

Elphinstone, his thick, grey eyebrows twitching, looked at the damaged trenches, at the casernes destroyed and exposed, at the earthworks cast down, the timber and stone walls they'd so recently toiled to construct. His florid face was covered by a thin coating of dust, which in the light from the fires made him look ethereal. 'Get your men to work on those defences as soon as the truce ends. I want them back to what they were before a day is passed.'

'The men are exhausted, sir, and carrying a number of wounds. And I doubt the French are in any better state.'

'I don't care if they are on one leg,' he yelled. 'Just do as I say.'

It was a stupid thing to do. He'd made enough enemies without adding to the list. But he couldn't resist it, couldn't entirely subsume his natural personality into the military role that wearing his uniform demanded.

'Aye, aye, sir,' he replied. 'And when you return to the comfort of your quarters, after you've had a good sleep, be so good as to give my compliments to your niece. She still owes me one or two dances.'

The black look that received, added to the tired smirk that Hanger managed, convinced him that he'd struck home. Elphinstone hauled on the reins angrily and trotted off.

'Right, my boyos,' he shouted, laying on the brogue. 'We're back on the bloody shovel.'

'That's a job for a Paddy.'

Markham spun round to see who had shouted. Quinlan and Ettrick were just behind Dornan, and that was the direction from which the sound had come. But he knew that the man they'd pushed to the front was innocent. He always was.

'Sergeant Rannoch.'

'Sir!'

'I want the name taken of the man who shouted that.'

'And the charge, sir?'

'Stupidity. He must have already seen me with a shovel.'

'If stupidity is the charge, sir, you'd be looking at your entire command. There is not a brain amongst the lot of them.'

Markham grinned, and tried, with his sleeve, to wipe some of the grime off his face.

'So that's why they put me here.'

# Chapter eighteen

After the failed and costly assault, the French on Mont Faron reverted to proper siege tactics, though the hard, shallow topsoil made sapping forward a risky affair. Now it was obvious why Dugommier had taken such a risk with his attack. Given the shallow topsoil it was impossible to dig deep, angled trenches, which meant that most of the work was above ground. They would build a parallel with stones and earth, and work to make it impregnable before sapping forward again.

Their only advantage lay in numerical superiority. But they also benefited from the poor gunnery of the Allied artillery, which was manned in this sector by Neapolitans. As far as possible the best gunners, British sailors, were kept aboard their ships, being too valuable a commodity to risk ashore. Hood considered Toulon important, but compared to the integrity of his fleet, in an area where he could not make up his losses, it counted for nothing. The marines were needed as infantry, and could not be spared to man the guns.

Despite the wishes of their commanders, they were soon called upon to move from the top of Mont Faron. Admiral Gravina, more for the sake of his pride than out of any military sense, insisted that his troops be allowed, once more, to take over these defences. Hood, determined to keep intact the little tattered unity that remained, acquiesced. Like everyone else, he thought Toulon near impregnable, given the forces Dugommier had at his disposal.

Markham and his men were dispatched to the western

end of the defences. They were reinforced by another company of marines, men from a line-of-battle ship, *Alcide*, both of whose officers were aboard the hospital ship. They'd fared better than the NCOs, who were buried in the cemetery. The expanded unit, eighty strong, was sent to the forward trenches in front of the Hill of Caire and Fort Mulgrave. This commanded that portion of the Petite Rade and masked the coastal defences at l'Eguillette and the Tour de Balaguier which, standing opposite the Grosse Tour, dominated the narrow approaches to the inner harbour.

Denied leave to return to their comfortable billet, they were back on army rations, stuck in trenches with no respite, which made them moan. And with the balance of Bullocks to Lobsters now heavily altered, some of the tensions that had so recently subsided resurfaced. But it was nothing like as bad as it had been before, with the Hebes unwilling to allow the taunts of the newcomers to pass without a response. Rannoch, with the help of Halsey, so established his authority, leaving their officer little to do. And given that the sole French activity seemed to be in the construction of numerous battery positions, Markham was free to wander the entire length of the western defence line.

He also had time to pursue other things, such as Guillaume Rossignol. Talking to Eveline was possible, but he thought he would achieve more by asking the man himself. Once he'd established that he was not at the house, this aim took him along the foreshore past Fort St Louis, then on to the promontory that formed the eastern arm of the inner harbour. At the very tip of this stood the Grosse Tour, ancient, round and stone built, surrounded by a moat, which had once served to defend the harbour. Now it acted as a signal station, primarily for ships approaching the anchorage, but also as a base to repeat orders from *Victory* to those elements of Lord Hood's fleet that had difficulty reading her flags. Looking past it, he could see clearly the forbidding fortifications of L'Eguillette, less than a mile away.

The guard on the gate, an immaculate marine, presented arms with crisp efficiency as Markham crossed the drawbridge. Inside he noticed the mechanism for raising the heavy wooden platform. It seemed to be well lubricated and was obviously in working order, which was more than could be said for the rest of the tower. The lower chambers of the old fortress were empty of furnishing or people, the sound of his feet echoing off the walls a testimony to the way time had rendered it redundant. He passed the watergate, which lay on the seaward side, the waves lapping against the old stone walls adding to the line of green slime that denoted high water mark. A longboat, pulled back and forth by the current, creaked as it strained on its ropes.

A circular staircase ran up the outer wall. As he ascended he heard a babble of voices, high-pitched and excited. Emerging from the darkness of the stairwell he found himself on the battlements, a flat stone area, surrounded by heavy embrasured walls, and dominated by a copy of a ship's mast. Rossignol stood at his canvas, his back to Markham, dabbing repeatedly, then looking through the telescope set up by the side of his easel.

Flags flicked in the stiff breeze, as a midshipman read off the orders on the *Victory*'s yards. These detailed a ship's number, followed by a message that the Commander-in-Chief wished to convey. Another pair of mids pulled the required flags from the lockers, handed them to a couple of sailors, who tied them on and hauled the signal aloft. The folded flags, at the flick of the wrist, burst open and streamed to windward.

'Monsieur Rossignol,' he said quietly, after passing and acknowledging the salutes of the chattering midshipmen.

The Frenchman spun round, an alarmed expression

on his face, brush extended defensively, which forced Markham to lean back to avoid a stain on his uniform.

'Lieutenant Markham.'

'I fear I startled you, monsieur.'

'Yes, yes,' Rossignol replied breathlessly, moving his body to hide the canvas on the easel. 'I was so taken with my work.'

'Would I be permitted to look?' asked Markham.

Rossignol's loss of composure evaporated, to be replaced by a demeanour as blustery as the wind which tugged at his coat.

'Please, Lieutenant. No artist likes his work to be observed while still only half-completed. But I promise you, when I am done, you will be one of the first to be granted a view.'

'Of course.'

'What brings you to the Grosse Tour?'

'I had arranged to talk with you, do you remember? But circumstances have contrived to keep us from that appointment.'

'You came all the way out here just to talk to me?'

Markham shrugged. 'It's a part of the defences I've never visited, and since I needed to walk and think . . .'

'I sense you are troubled by something?'

Markham was about to tell Rossignol exactly what that was. But in order to avoid glancing at the painting, he'd looked at the view instead. That caused him to remain silent. The whole of Toulon was laid out before his eyes. Without a telescope, and with a mere turn of his head, he could see most of the defences, all the way from the tip of the St Mandrian Peninsula, past the Tour de Balaguier and l'Eguillette, round to Malbousquet, the old town and Forts St Louis and de la Malgue. Most of the forts on Mont Faron were hidden by low cloud, but not the steady stream of men and materials inching its way up the steep road to the summit. And by turning round, he knew without looking that every ship in the fleet was visible from this position.

'If I was to burden you with my troubles,' he said with a wry smile, 'it would ruin your mood as much as it has affected mine.'

'I hope you know, Lieutenant Markham, that in me you have a friend with a ready ear.'

'Of course,' Markham responded. Then he turned away. 'Forgive me for interrupting your labours.'

He made his way to the other side of the terrace, to where the senior midshipman stood, leaning out through an embrasure, his telescope fixed on the flagship. Sensing his presence the youth came smartly to attention, then went back to his task when Markham told him to carry on.

'How do you feel about sharing your loft with a civilian?'

'It was awkward at first, sir, what with him wanting to chatter with us, and lacking much in the way of English. He was inclined to get in the way, and we tried to persuade Colonel Hanger that it weren't on.'

'Hanger?' Markham snapped, unable to control his surprise.

The youngster sounded aggrieved as he replied. 'I got a flea in my ear and no mistake, which was galling with that Spaniard consumptive, Serota, standing right by him.'

'The Colonel is not one to spare anyone's feelings.'

'You know him, sir?' asked the mid, looking closely at him, trying to discern what he thought of the Colonel. Markham pulled a grim face, which served to reassure the youngster.

'Only too well.'

'I hope he ain't commissioned the work, for if he has, he's in for a shock.'

'You've seen it?

The midshipman rolled his eyes, then lifted the telescope, pointing it towards Rossignol's back, almost inviting Markham to have a look. At that moment, a signal gun boomed out and flags started shooting up the *Victory*'s mast. The invitation was withdrawn as the youngster set about his duties. In an even voice he read off and called out the message.

'Flag to shore, repeat to *Bulldog*, make private signal and inform that it is safe to enter inner harbour. Captain to repair aboard Flag when anchored.'

Markham was about to observe that, with the Grande Rade full of Allied shipping, such a reference to safety was obvious. But he bit his tongue, knowing, even from his short acquaintance with the Navy, that they were sticklers for the rules.

'I don't think I'll ever understand messages sent by flag.'

'It ain't difficult, sir, once you get the basics.'

'What happens if you make a mistake?'

'Why, sir,' the midshipman replied, his eyes rolling, 'if we did that, we'd be stretched across the gun and given fifty of the best. And *Bulldog* would spot it right off, up her helm and be back out to sea in a flash.'

He stood for an age, apparently watching the activities of the signal station, but in a deeply pensive mood, even more worried now than he had been earlier. To place a civilian, and a stranger, at the very top of the Grosse Tour was singular enough. To allow him the use of a powerful telescope bordered on stupidity. Nothing that happened on land would escape his notice. Not a single gun could be moved, nor a unit redeployed, without being seen. Had all those pinprick attacks, in which Dugommier had always known where to strike, really been the fault of the now absent French sailors? Or was it all Guillaume Rossignol, with his easel and his telescope, atop the Grosse Tour?

He couldn't bring himself to believe that, partly because he liked him, and even more for Eveline's sake. Rossignol had a bluff and hearty manner which he used to disguise a shrewd brain. His relationship with Pascalle, of which Markham had perceived no hint, meant he was capable of deep dissimulation. He was up to something at night, either on his own account or on behalf of Picard. And what of his relationship with Hanger? The Honourable Augustus might be a bully, with a gross and disobliging manner. But he was no traitor, and much as Markham despised the man he could not bring himself to think of him as a complete fool, duped into letting a French spy occupy such a sensitive spot. Then there was Colonel Serota, whose sense of his own importance was extremely profound, yet who had personally delivered the message of Marie Antoinette's death on the guillotine to a mere tradesman.

What was going on in the house that had Madame Picard permanently on tenterhooks? And what was she doing coaching Jean-Baptiste with that book of portraits? What did Celeste mean when she hinted that nothing was as it seemed? Perhaps if he'd paid more attention he would have seen more. Looking back over his time spent in the house, when not sleeping and dealing with the needs of his men, he'd concentrated almost entirely on Eveline, and his attentions to her had obscured whatever undercurrents existed between the rest of the occupants.

Yet there could be a perfectly innocent explanation, or, if not entirely above board, one that was acceptable to him. The atmosphere in Toulon was febrile in the extreme, something only to be expected in a city under siege. British and Spaniards totally distrusted each other, while the rest of the allies were, at best, indifferent in their support for the cause. Even with an open door to the sea, supplies of certain things were naturally scarce, and thieves or looters, where they had been found, had been summarily hanged. Talk of spies, when Frenchman was pitted against his own countrymen, was endemic. And justice, if it could be called that, was swift. An accusation placed against Rossignol could see him at the end of a rope before he had a chance to offer an explanation, and that was not something Markham was prepared to contemplate without proof.

'I'm sorry to disturb you further, Monsieur Rossignol.' The older man spun round again, if anything faster than he had before, his eyes locking on to Markham's, in a challenging way that seemed designed to put him off his stride. 'There are certain things troubling me, things that require explanation.'

'Such as?'

Markham, now that he was actually embarked on his quest, didn't quite know where to start, so he decided to go right back to the beginning, referring to the moment when he'd first sighted the coach. 'You never actually explained to me why you were fleeing in the first place.'

'I should have thought that was obvious.'

'I don't mean that. Where had you come from?'

Rossignol's eyes narrowed. 'Marseilles, and before that Lyons. Both cities sacked by the revolutionary mobs.'

'And from Paris originally.'

'Yes.'

'A couple of nights ago I heard a noise in the corridor.' The look of alarm in the older man's face made him speak quickly, having no actual desire to refer to the sexual content of that observation unless it was absolutely necessary. 'I saw you on the landing. You put on a cloak. I presume that you then went out.'

'I did.'

'But not by either of the main doors.'

'You followed me?'

Markham ignored the shock in his voice, and continued calmly. 'How could I, since your method of entering and leaving the Picard house is a secret?'

'I had business to conduct.'

Markham looked out over the Petite Rade. 'Might I be permitted to ask what kind of business?'

The look in Rossignol's eye, as he opened his mouth to answer, made Markham suspect he was going to be fobbed off with a lie. Which was the last thing he wanted, since if the old man did that, he'd have no choice but to take his suspicions elsewhere.

'Before you answer, monsieur, let me add some of the other things that trouble me. I cannot comprehend how you persuaded the Picards to allow us to billet in their warehouse. What treatments are the doctors you've employed engaged in? Why do you coach young Jean-Baptiste with a book of royal portraits? And just what makes you so important that Colonel Serota feels it necessary to come to the house to tell you personally of the Queen's demise?'

As Markham fired his stream of questions, he could see Rossignol's mind working.

'Colonel Serota does not think me important, Lieutenant.'

'Monsieur Picard?' said Markham, incredulously. The absurdity of that notion had him close to the obvious conclusion just as Rossignol answered.

'No. It is the boy himself.'

'Jean-Baptiste?'

Rossignol dropped his voice to a whisper, indicating with a sharp nod that the others on the top of the tower should not hear what he was about to say. 'Perhaps, Lieutenant, you'd be better to address him by his proper name and title.'

'Title?'

'His Majesty, King Louis the Seventeenth of France. I had better complete my labour for the day,' said Rossignol, waving a soothing hand. 'We can talk on the way back to the Picard house.'

'How much do you know about events in Paris, Lieutenant?'

'What I read in the London newspapers.'

'Then you will perhaps be aware that the whereabouts of the Dauphin, once he'd been separated from his mother, was a secret.'

'Vaguely aware, yes.'

'I wish I knew what they did to that boy,' Rossignol sighed. Seeing the look of inquiry on Markham's face, the Frenchman continued, 'If we had information regarding the cause, we would perhaps have a path to the cure.'

'I have seen men in a similar state after a battle.'

'God knows the battles the poor boy has had to fight. Perhaps they made him witness the death of his father. He was certainly subjected to a very harsh régime.'

'Some recover naturally.'

'And many never do, Lieutenant. Pity him, and France.'

Markham had been thinking about Jean-Baptiste and his bland expressionless face. But Rossignol's melancholy mention of France brought him back to the present. His next question had more than a trace of incredulity in it, evidence despite all Rossignol's assurances that what he was saying was true, and his own sudden deductions, he didn't actually believe him.

'How did he come to be here?'

'We tried to save the King and Queen by helping them flee, and failed when they were apprehended at Varennes.'

'We?'

'All right-thinking Frenchmen, Lieutenant, those who believe that to murder an anointed sovereign is sacrilege. And that is not just the nobility, it is most of the people of France. Those Jacobin madmen who run the Committee of Public Safety are but a small minority.'

'You failed at Varennes,' said Markham, bringing him back to the point.

'We did, though his late Majesty must bear most of the blame. Then, when Louis was murdered, we tried to save the Queen.'

'And failed once more.'

'You have a cruel way of alluding to the truth,' replied

Rossignol softly, with a catch in his throat. He turned away, pulling out a handkerchief to dab at his eyes. 'But it's nothing less than that. We failed them, may their souls rest in peace.'

Suddenly his voice recovered its normal strength, and he began to wave a triumphal fist. 'Yet we succeeded with the son. Against all the odds, when everyone despaired, we managed to seize him from their grasp, to put another in his place.'

'If you did that, why were they pursuing you?'

'They didn't know who was in the coach. If they had, believe me, you and your men would have died at Ollioules. But now we have him here, safe under your guns in Toulon.'

'Safe and mysterious.'

There was a look of desperation in Rossignol's eyes at that point. 'What would you have us do? Proclaim to the nation that a boy lost in a world of his own, who cannot bring himself to speak even a simple sentence, who does not respond to his own name, is the rightful King of France?'

'This, monsieur, is incredible.'

Rossignol carried on as if he hadn't spoken, his tone a mixture of eagerness and frustration. 'We were making progress undoing the cruelties that have made him so. The doctors were sure that with time he would recover his wits. Now, he seems to have gone silent again. They say it is a temporary relapse . . .'

They were outside the house now, with Markham looking up at the hoist above the double doors on the first floor. 'That is why Madame Picard changed her mind about accommodating us.'

Rossignol banged on the door. 'Yes. She can see the rewards that will come to those who are at the side of the King when he takes his rightful place.'

'Hanger and Serota?' asked Markham as it opened.

Rossignol handed the servant his easel and telescope,

then waited till he had departed before replying. 'Are aware of the situation, plus, I am forced to admit, the problems. They agree that with the boy in his present condition, to try and proclaim him would not improve matters. Quite apart from the idea that he might be named an impostor, the increased pressure on young Louis might make a full recovery impossible. His uncles, the late king's brothers, would take over his care, and I wonder whether they would put his welfare above their own claims to the throne.'

'And this is a secret?'

'Certainly! The least hint of the truth could be fatal.'

Markham, as they crossed the courtyard and entered the hallway, was thinking about Nelson and Troubridge. Then there was Lizzie Gordon. She too had referred to the possibility of a Bourbon prince coming to Toulon, which meant that the matter was not as secret as Rossignol supposed. But he was also remembering the way Jean-Baptiste had looked at Celeste, how he'd heard him singing more clearly than he had when being examined by the doctors, and her words to him when he'd found her in his room, laying out his uniform.

'I must admit to being astonished,' he said, temporising.

'That would hardly be surprising, monsieur,' replied Rossignol, with a knowing smile. Then he laid a hand on Markham's arm and squeezed, his voice suddenly rather oily. 'It is the most extraordinary thing. And rest assured, Lieutenant, when matters are brought to a rightful conclusion, you will have a claim, as I have, on the new King's generosity.'

'Colonel Hanger has no doubt received the same guarantee.'

'Of course,' said Rossignol, turning towards the study door. 'Now if you will forgive me, I must appraise Monsieur Picard of these developments.'

Markham watched his back as he disappeared, then

made for the kitchens. Failing to find Celeste, he carried on to Jean-Baptiste's room, and entered without knocking. They sat on the floor, Celeste's hand spread wide, her fingers holding the threads of a cat's cradle. The boy was trying to copy her, but judging by the tangle of wool, was having little success. His sudden entrance made both look up in alarm. Markham asked Celeste to accompany him to his room. Once there, she stood, her head bowed, not wishing to look him in the eye.

'The other day you implied that something was going on in this house.' Her head stayed down. 'Look at me, Celeste.'

She obeyed, though it took her some time to do so, her dark eyes large and sad. 'Who is Jean-Baptiste?'

Rossignol was alone, staring at the papers on Picard's round table, one hand fingering the heavily-bound book of royal portraits. He look up slowly as Markham entered and shut the door behind him.

'You think of me as an English officer, monsieur.'

'Are you about to tell me that you're not?'

'No, I'm Irish. But to you, probably, we are all the same. I come from Wexford, a part of the world where the telling of tall tales is a national pastime. And the trick, my friend, if you're going to concoct a story, is to make the lie so big that most people will believe it just because it's so damned impossible.'

Rossignol was looking at him, without expression. 'I think you'd better tell me the truth. And that truth would include the nature of the relationship you have with Pascalle, whom you claim to be your daughter.'

'Claim?'

'I was outside your door, Rossignol, long before you came out to put on that cloak. And the measure of the affection you showed Pascalle, while deep enough, was not that normally demonstrated by a loving parent.'

The Frenchman threw back his head and laughed,

which surprised Markham. 'You're sharp enough, Lieutenant. Eveline told me that you were getting suspicious. But it's only by being in this house that you could have found the means to doubt me.'

'Jean-Baptiste?'

'King Louis,' Rossignol answered, but with an expression that implied it was done more in hope than expectation. Markham shook his head slowly. Tempted to mention Celeste, but unsure what would happen to her if he wasn't here, he kept silent.

The Frenchman caved in immediately. 'The boy is an orphan I picked up on the way south. He is, you will admit, a handsome lad, who could well be a king.'

'Except he's not.'

'No. But the food and lodging you receive from those prepared to believe it's possible has two distinct advantages. It is excellent, and it is free.'

'Are you a lawyer?'

Rossignol's eyes narrowed. 'Does that make a difference?'

'Only in so far, monsieur, that if I don't have the whole truth, I won't know what to do about you.'

'The truth?' Markham just stared at him, until he started to speak. 'I'm many things, Lieutenant, but not, strictly, a lawyer. I am what you might call a trader, who seeing opportunity, finds it difficult to let it go by.'

'A projector?' asked Markham, wondering if the word had the same connotation in French as it had in English.

He'd met the type, men who always had a scheme to make money in their back pocket, usually a fortune and all for no effort. Gold and silver mines were a favourite, or navigation canals that the investor would pay for, but never see dug out. Clearly it did, since Rossignol nodded. His story, as it emerged, confirmed that description, though he was careful not to be very specific about his previous activities, in fact quite able to talk of himself as if he were an upright and honest man. With everything lost in the Revolution, and a government in power that was inimical to the kind of activity he excelled in, security could only be found away from Paris. But with limited funds transport was hard to come by, as was food and lodging. The lucky coincidence that had turned up Jean-Baptiste, just as speculation became rife about the fate of the Dauphin, was extremely fortuitous, allowing him to progress south in comfort.

'And these people believed you?' asked Markham doubtfully.

'It is not so very surprising Lieutenant, since I did not seek to appeal to their loyalty, but to their greed.'

'Does that include Hanger and Serota?'

'Yes. Especially Colonel Hanger.'

'Has he told his superiors?'

'We agreed that he should not, that is until we had effected a recovery. Lord Hood and Admiral Langara would, we felt, be obliged to communicate his presence to the Bourbon princes.'

Markham smiled slightly. Hanger would keep such information to himself only to secure what he considered a proper reward. His smile broadened as he imagined Rossignol playing on his avarice and vanity to block off the information being passed to Hood.

'You are amused by something, Lieutenant?'

'It's the idea of you duping Hanger, monsieur.'

'He is, I believe, the second son of a Lord. I think he hankers after a title of his own. I think he suspects that Lord Hood has quite enough already.' Markham actually laughed then, which produced a grin of pleasure from the Frenchman. 'You see, Lieutenant, it is, in my business, very necessary to promise people that which they want, while also advising them of the quickest way to forgo it.'

'You're a rogue and no mistake.'

'Do I detect by your tone you no longer disapprove of me?'

'Pascalle?'

Rossignol shrugged. 'She is sometimes my daughter, at other times my sister, or even my wife. It very much depends on what seems most appropriate.'

'Was distracting my attention appropriate for Eveline?'

Rossignol leant forward, his look sincere. 'Let me say. Lieutenant Markham, that your attention was fortuitous. Of the many tasks dear Eveline has been required to perform, that one has given her the most pleasure.'

His manner changed, become suddenly more serious. 'The question I must now pose to you, is what are you going to do about what I have said?'

'Well, if you've got Augustus Hanger salivating, I'm not one to want to interfere.'

'I doubt that he'd accept the truth with understanding.'

'He'd hang you, Rossignol, and God knows what fate he'd dictate for Pascalle and Eveline.'

'That, I must admit, is what troubles me most.'

Markham was quite prepared to take that statement with a pinch of salt. But there was no doubt about the sentiment. Hanger, having found he'd been practised on, would probably go berserk. As to the Picards, they could afford to feed and defer to Rossignol, as well as billet his men in an ease they'd never manage to equal elsewhere. Then there were his own comforts. The siege would go on for months yet. Eveline, who was no more of a daughter than Pascalle, found his company congenial. It would be a pity to let that go, the chance to come from the pressure of war to a welcoming pair of soft, enveloping arms.

'The boy must stay mute,' he said, watching Rossignol closely. When he nodded, Markham knew that the Frenchman had no idea that Celeste could communicate with Jean-Baptiste. Not properly, but enough to establish a bond. Somehow the idea that Rossignol, too, was being fooled added spice to the whole thing.

'I see no purpose in exposing you, monsieur.'

'Thank you, Lieutenant,' said Rossignol, as Markham turned to leave. 'I will be forever in your debt.'

263

# Chapter nineteen

'What are those stupid sods about?' said Tully, the arm emerging from his stolen cloak pointing to the field piece being hauled, by hand, onto the open ground, well to the fore of the other French emplacements. The officer in front, small and slim, was looking towards the British lines, as if defying them to react.

'Perhaps he wants to hawk it,' Halsey replied, indicating the cloak, which Tully had acquired one day after a visit to a whorehouse. 'In which case he's come to the right spot. He must know this ditch we're in is full of villains who'd trade with the devil hisself. Best double back and fetch Rannoch.'

Tully shivered. 'Ain't that a job for a Lobster?'

'Don't fuck me about,' said Halsey wearily, realising that Tully was grinning. 'Just do as you're told, there's a good lad.'

Markham, just returned from the Picard house, came forward with Rannoch. By that time the cannon was set up, the men who had hauled it into place now working furiously to construct defences. Behind him Fort Mulgrave lay atop the Hill of Caire, with his positions in the trench line on the forward slopes. The French were dug in on another incline opposite, the floor of a shallow valley marking no man's land. It was into this exposed position that the gun had been manhandled. Enough fascines had been erected in front to deal with musket balls. Now they were shovelling hard to throw up the kind of revetted earthworks that would provide effective protection against counter-battery fire.

'That's a crazy place for a field gun,' said Markham, his gaze sweeping round to take in the positions to his rear, the deep bays both north and south, including the pontoons with mortars. Those in the north supported both Mulgrave and the Spanish position at La Seyne. Others lay close to the southern bay, to protect that flank, as well as the narrow, fortified bottleneck that led to the St Mandrian peninsula.

General opinion held that whoever was in charge of the guns opposite Mulgrave, already spiked once, had made several odd decisions, sighting emplacements that did little to threaten the garrison. One in particular, the Batterie des Sablettes, halfway between Markham's trench line and the southern peninsula, could hardly be brought to bear effectively on either position. It was therefore useless. But this one was the strangest of the lot.

'They can't avoid being caught in a crossfire.'

Rannoch nodded in agreement. But what bothered him most was the fact that the elevated muzzle was pointed straight at their position. A low charge and a short fuse could produce a shell which would explode right above their heads.

'I think they are getting ready to let fly with a round,' he said. 'It might be shrapnel.'

'Everybody down,' yelled Markham, jumping into the trench. The boom of the cannon followed within a second. But it wasn't case shot. It was a shell, and it came nowhere near them. Every head lifted and turned as it arced over their position. They stood up to follow its path as, clear against the pale blue winter sky, it carried on to land on the main works of Fort Mulgrave. The shell struck one of the casernes near the northern wall, then exploded, sending up a great cloud of dust.

'Reloading,' murmured Halsey, who'd kept his eye on the gun. 'They seem a sharp bunch, even if they're as thick as pig shit.'

'This is all wrong,' said Markham, almost to himself.

Fort Mulgrave was strong enough by itself to warrant caution, but the shape of the land that projected out into the harbour like the head and beak of a bird allowed naval guns to operate, which made what they were about suicidal. Yet the calm behaviour of the French officer engendered a nagging suspicion that, although it might look like stupidity, it was exactly the opposite.

'He'd best be off, sir,' Halsey said, pointing out to the south. One of the bomb ketches, with a pair of mortars aboard, was using its sweeps to get into a firing position. 'They's got about ten minutes before our lot put a ball right down their gullet. Even if they're full of rum they can hardly miss.'

The French field piece, which looked like a twelve-pounder, boomed out again, sending a second shell into the defences. Markham was wondering if he should form up, ignoring the dangers of mounting an impromptu attack. But that might just send the French artillerymen scurrying back to their original emplacement.

'Jesus Christ, they're fetching out another one,' said Yelland, pointing to the left.

It was true. Hunched soldiers, pulling on long, thick ropes lashed to the trunnions, raced forward in a long arc that left the muzzle of another cannon facing the British lines. As soon as they reached their position they slewed to a halt, the gunners following up to detach their ropes. Those who'd hauled now set to work, in a carbon copy of the original, laying defences to protect the guns. Legs straining, the sweating gunners manhandled the second heavy field piece into place alongside the first cannon, which fired its third shell as a greeting.

'On your feet,' called Markham. 'And fix bayonets.'

'Our guns will be at it in a minute, sir,' said Rannoch.

'If we attack now, there are no defences. We'll concentrate on the second gun. Who knows, maybe we can take it before it gets to fire a round.'

'Form yourselves up,' shouted Rannoch, waving his

arms to hurry all eighty men out of the trench. The Frenchmen appeared on the opposite slope as soon as they did, twice their number and equally ready with their bayonets. The diminutive artillery officer, still standing before the newly-dug earthworks, was using a small telescope, ranging it along the line of redcoats.

'Ten paces forward,' Markham said quietly. 'Let's see what they do.'

As soon as Rannoch relayed the order, and the men started to advance, the French did likewise, the sun gleaming off their weaponry. When the British stopped, so did the enemy. The message was plain. If you attack, so will we, but if you stay still then we will do likewise. The boom of the British guns came to their ears just as the first ranging shot swished overhead. They hit a point just between the French defences and the rogue battery, sending a great clod of brown earth high into the sky.

'Yelland, take my watch. Get back to the officer on those guns. Ask for a full salvo just short of the French line in ten minutes. Until then, keep his cannon ranging to fool the enemy. Rannoch, we're going to try and draw the Frogs out, far enough from their own defences to be at the mercy of our artillery.'

'Sir.'

It was like the kind of game a child might play on a table with toy soldiers. The British would move forward a few feet, matched by the enemy infantry, while the first French cannon kept up a steady fire, and the second was trundled into place some twenty metres to the right, men shovelling earth into the empty cane fascines that they'd laid along the front of the position. Meanwhile single shots would come over Markham's head as each gun behind him sought to fix its range. Earth flew up about the French position, though none was close enough to cause real damage. Then the entire artillery section opened up, the great boom sending shockwaves through the air. Markham twirled his sword above his head and, praying that the guns of Fort Mulgrave were accurate, ordered the advance.

The French were running within seconds, desperate to get out of the arc of deadly fire that was beginning to rain down on them. It was almost as if their officer had heard his instructions to Yelland and taken precautions to thwart them. Smoke and dust rose to obscure the churned-up ground in between the two sets of defences. But when it cleared, Markham could see, quite plainly, that the French infantry had retreated unscathed, while the guns were still in place. So was the diminutive officer who'd led them out into their present position.

With no infantry to oppose them, and his own artillery now silent, taking those field pieces looked easy. Yet Markham, shouting to keep the line intact, was troubled. There was no sign of any extra activity around the battery, which were being reloaded without haste. Stranger still, the small officer in command was making no attempt to alter their range or elevation, behaving as if the advancing British infantry posed no threat. And the French soldiers had stayed in their trenches.

'Halt!' he screamed, a yell that was taken up by both Rannoch and Halsey. It seemed to take an age before every man could be brought to obey, during which he examined the horizon through his telescope. The silence was unnatural, the position ridiculous, with his men strung out in two files across a hundred yards of churned-up earth. He wouldn't have seen the other new battery position if it had not been right in the centre of his glass when it fired. The flashes highlighted the position long before he heard the boom, which gave him just enough time to order a retreat. Taking their cue from their officer, the men didn't fall back in a disciplined line, they ran.

That halt, the swift order to fall back and the speed with which it was executed, saved them from the mincer of two well-directed artillery salvoes. They landed right above the terrain they'd have covered had they continued, the case shot bursting open to shower the ground with hundreds of small deadly balls. As an extra sign of determined defiance, both the forward cannon opened up, sending another two shells streaming into Fort Mulgrave.

'Saucy bastard,' said Rannoch, as he dropped back into their trench, his chest heaving. Then he looked at his officer, his flushed face a measure of the slight embarrassment caused by using that word.

'A bastard with a death wish, I think,' Markham replied.

He indicated the bomb ketch now in place, with its anchors out, the ropes used as springs to get the vessel into its final position. The officer commanding the British artillery had seen them fall back. Now every gun the British could muster fired on the French position. The whole area for a hundred yards around was clobbered, and while the last of the dust was high in the sky it was bombarded again. Yet when the earth settled back to a thin haze, Markham could see that nothing had changed. Meanwhile the main French batteries, heavy siege pieces, joined the action, pounding Fort Mulgrave, which of necessity distracted the Allied gunners, forcing them to use some of their own cannon in defence. But the mortars, firing from their floating platform, were now ready to play on the original target.

Yet still the Frenchman didn't withdraw. Then the cannon from the Batterie de Sablettes opened up, and it was only when they hit the calm waters of the bay, their target those very same floating mortars, that the sailors realised the danger they were in. Sablettes, which had looked useless, was now revealed as deadly efficient. The first salvo straddled the ketch, sending up massive founts of water ahead and astern. Through his telescope Markham could see several of the men aboard frantically chopping at the anchor cables while the rest manned the sweeps.

They were too late; the following shots struck the hull

with a resounding crash that echoed across the whole landscape. No shells this time, but red-hot balls of solid iron that embedded themselves in the thick hull, and immediately set light to the timbers. The ketch, now freed, drifted away from the shore, the men aboard frantic as they fought the blaze which threatened to engulf the ship.

But that didn't mean this mad Frenchman was safe. Markham knew it merely reduced the odds from certain, to probable death. 'I don't know whether to admire him, or laugh at him.'

'Pray for him,' Rannoch replied. 'Because he has been lucky until now. But when the guns do get him, there will be not a thing left to bury.'

It seemed as if the Frenchman had a charmed life, and so did his men. Salvo after salvo was fired in their direction, yet not one struck close enough to put them out of action. The rate of their discharge, so rhythmic, made it seem as if they were on a practice range. Although the other batteries had ceased firing, a steady stream of shot was sent into the redoubt, each one resulting in a plume of dust and earth as some part of the defences took a hit. After about half an hour, the officer turned and left the field, stopping by his cannon as they survived one more salvo, before making his way to the rear.

There was a magical quality to what happened next, as if his presence had deflected the Allied fire. He'd no sooner departed than the original cannon took a direct hit. One shattered wheel flew high enough to clear the debris, spinning slowly in the air before crashing back onto the fragmented gun. The screams of the surviving gunners floated across the gap. Markham swung his glass to the second gun, fully expecting to see the French abandoning the piece. Instead, what he saw was another gun being dragged forward. He watched with fascination as the wrecked cannon was removed, several men looping a rope round the barrel so that they could drag it away. Others cleared bits of timber, ignoring the chunks of human flesh. And as soon as they were finished, the new weapon was put in exactly the same spot, with the small officer personally leading forward the men who would man it.

'He is mad,' said Markham quietly. 'Stark, raving mad.'

Whoever he was, he lost men and guns on a regular basis. Counter-battery fire wasn't easy, a field piece representing a small target for another cannon to hit. Charges varied slightly, as did weight of shot. Then there was the ability of the officer doing the aiming, so human frailty was added to what was anyway an inexact science. Naval gunners jeered at their land-based colleagues, quite forgetting the size of their own targets, and the number of times they missed.

But the result of a success was always the same. Another cannon was fetched out, always led by the same small officer, more men came forward, and the guns were in action again within half an hour. Even during the short winter day, the French lost a lot of men, the bodies of those either dead or too wounded to move left where they'd fallen. Finally, an hour before dark, the truce flag came out, with a request from the artillery officer that he should be allowed to clear his casualties. Markham, having agreed, walked out into no man's land to supervise the truce, to be met there by the author of all this mayhem.

He was a small, intense man, a captain, and had a pallid complexion, with that colouring which spoke of a Mediterranean skin carefully kept from the sun. Round of face, he looked well fed and healthy. His eyes, though they were very dark brown, had a piercing quality that made them disconcerting. They exchanged nods and stood back to watch his men clearing away the bodies and the debris.

Normally when officers met in no man's land, it was

considered impolite to discuss anything other than the most general matters. Clearly good manners excluded questions related to the condition of the opposing army. And in a siege, even one so easily supplied from the sea, one could not mention victuals. So small talk was the order of the day, with allusions to previous battles, potential mutual military contacts, and references to family and friends the main topics. Not for this fellow. As soon as Markham mentioned America he was pounced on.

'You fought there?'

'Yes. In the Carolinas under General Cornwallis.'

'So you surrendered at Yorktown?'

'No. I'd departed by then.'

The eyes were on him, as if checking the veracity of that statement. 'Good. It is better to die than surrender. Ancient warriors fell on their swords. We should do the same.'

'Is that what these guns are about?'

Markham knew he shouldn't have asked, and was quite prepared for a sharp response. But instead the captain smiled in a rather engaging way.

'I call it the "Battery for men without fear". It has become a challenge amongst the gunners. They are the best trained men in the Bouche de Rhône army. Few are prepared to admit to being cowards.' Markham was about to ask if they would admit to madness, but he wasn't given the opportunity. 'Tell me about the Carolina campaign.'

'There's not much more to say than that it was murderous.'

'Yes, yes! All war is that. I meant the details.'

Markham obliged, telling him of the deep forests and long straight tracks which passed for roads. Of the difficulty of manoeuvring, because of that and the lack of forage, in anything other than reasonably small numbers.

'The people there, what are they like?'

Markham smiled. 'Like the men holding Toulon, only tougher.'

'Why tougher?'

'The life they lead. Most have upped and left a home to create another in a wilderness. So, outside the few cities, they are inured to a harsh climate, and constant danger. They can shoot, and use the terrain to their advantage.'

'Not all of them sided with the rebellion.'

'No,' Markham replied, unwilling to make the obvious point that the same thing applied to the spot where they were standing.

'You were too soft on them.'

Recalling what had happened, in his experience, it seemed anything but soft. But this small artillery captain was adamant.

'You should have strung up every colonist you captured in '76, men, women and children. Anyone who so much as possessed a gun. Lined those tracks you mentioned, with their bodies, as Crassus did to the slave army of Spartacus. That would have brought them to heel.' He flipped out his watch, hard to see in the sudden gathering darkness. His skin had taken on a luminous quality, which seemed to extend to his eyes. 'After all, the way you describe it, America was worth fighting for.'

'Time?' asked Markham. The Frenchman nodded, and both turned to order their men back to their lines. 'Tell me, Captain. How many men are you prepared to sacrifice on this battery?'

Again, it was precisely the kind of question he shouldn't have asked. But this officer was more than willing to oblige.

'All of them, Lieutenant.' The smile had no warmth. It was a cold, calculated mark of his determination. 'You see, I have studied all my life for just such a moment as this. Everything I learned at the Auxonne artillery school will be distilled into the destruction of your position in Toulon.'

'It won't be that easy, Captain.'

'It will, Lieutenant. Toulon is very much like my home. Ajaccio, in Corsica, has the same kind of double harbour, is also surrounded by hills. I have been planning to reduce a fortress like this since I was a mere boy.'

The eyes seemed to have expanded, till they filled Markham's vision. This fellow was obsessed, and quite likely, slightly deranged. 'Tell me, captain, do you know a man called Fouquert?'

'I do. Why do you ask?'

'You remind me of him in some ways.'

Oddly enough, the small artillery captain looked pleased by the comparison. 'Can I pass on your compliments?'

That idea tickled the Irishman, and he had to force himself not to grin as he responded. 'By all means. Tell him Lieutenant George Markham is looking forward to renewing our acquaintance.'

'George Markham?' he repeated, to ensure he'd got it right.

'Yes. And you, sir, are –?'

'Bonaparte. Captain Napoleon Bonaparte.'

Markham looked up at the quartet of officers sitting on their horses, curious about the identity of the immaculately dressed naval captain. He wore, across his chest, a blue silk sash and a huge jewelled star. So far, he hadn't even looked at him. No one had bothered with an introduction, and from the mood of the group it seemed his presence wasn't welcome. He was of medium height, fair haired, with a steady gaze. Everything about him had a slightly gaudy appearance as though the blue broadcloth and his gold braid came from a different and more expensive supplier than that of the man beside him, Elphinstone. Certainly the wearing of an Order of Chivalry, here in the field, was extraordinary.

Mulgrave and Hanger made up the foursome, all eager

to witness the destruction of the man Markham had identified. From that point, on the forward slopes of the hill of Caire with the morning sun at their backs, they could see the entire French position, and observe that for all their activity with the guns, there was little evidence of any attempt to move forward with the saps and parallels that must presage an assault.

'Corsican by birth,' Markham added, 'but trained in the French Royalist army. Typical gunner.'

That required no explanation, and brought forth a grunt from Mulgrave. Infantrymen disliked gunners for their arrogance, plus the fact that they never seemed to be able to hit that which the soldiers required. They were nearly as unreliable as cavalry.

'What did you say he's called the damned thing?' growled Elphinstone.

'He's named it *"La Batterie des hommes sans peur"*.'

'Never mind what the damn thing's called,' said Mulgrave. 'What are we going to do about it?'

'Ignore him,' said Hanger. 'And keep destroying his guns. And I beg to repeat my earlier observation that we have no need to mount a counter-attack to drive the enemy back. Dugommier had allotted few infantry to this sector, so the idea of an offensive here is pure moonshine. Mont Faron is where his army is massed, and that is the place where matters will be decided.'

'I beg to differ, sir,' said the unnamed captain. His voice, though strong, had a musical quality which entirely suited the rest of his flashy demeanour.

'Do you, by damn?' snapped Hanger.

'Not having any official duties, I've taken the opportunity to move along and observe the whole defensive line.'

'I suppose you think we have stayed indoors, Sir Sydney,' said Hanger, 'scratching our parts?'

'If I may be permitted, gentlemen,' the naval knight replied, dismounting gracefully from his horse. On the ground he pulled out a sword, which was jewelled on the hilt and engraved on the blade. He then began to draw on the ground. Mulgrave and Elphinstone craned forward to look. Hanger merely snorted.

'Have any of you gentlemen come across the written works of a French officer called the Chevalier du Tiel? I refer specifically to a treatise he wrote called, if my memory serves me, *L'Emploi de l'artillerie nouvelle*.'

He paused for a moment, as though waiting to see if the name registered. What greeted him was a wall of incomprehension, with only Markham showing any notion of understanding.

'It was written at the French Artillery School at Auxonne.'

'What has that got to do with Toulon?' asked Mulgrave.

'A great deal, sir.'

Hanger raised his crop and slapped his boot angrily. 'Are we to be treated to a warmed-up lecture from some Crapaud knight?'

Mulgrave answered Hanger without looking at him. 'If I'm prepared to listen to Sir Sydney, Colonel, I don't see that it should trouble an officer who is my junior.'

There was much in those few words about the nature of their relationship to cheer Markham immensely. Sir Sydney continued as though Hanger hadn't spoken. 'Since they reorganised the French artillery their leading thinkers have been striving for two things. Increased mobility and a chance to win a battle without a massed infantry assault. The natural order of things is that artillery supports infantry. The aim is to reverse that.'

'That is complete nonsense,' growled Hanger. Seeing both Elphinstone and Mulgrave begin to frown, Markham cut in quickly.

'This Bonaparte trained at Auxonne.'

Sir Sydney gave him a smile so dazzling that it entirely lacked sincerity. It came and went like the shutter of a lantern. Then the sword was scratching busily in the hard earth, showing a rough plan of the western end of the Petite Rade.

'This fellow opposite has sited more than a dozen batteries in the last few weeks.'

'We are aware of that,' said Elphinstone. 'All of us.'

'If you look at the ordnance, you will see that apart from those opposite Malbousquet and the Batterie de Bregaillon, the guns are field pieces, which makes them mobile. What's more, they are designed to link with, and provide, a defence for each other.'

'And what, pray, does that signify?' demanded Hanger.

'It means that they can advance without being destroyed. That is, unless we are prepared, in trying, to accept casualties, and even lose ships.' He smiled again, but it was the look of an adult indulging children. 'I don't think, as you do, Colonel Hanger, that the key to Toulon is Mont Faron. I think this Bonaparte has spotted that it is Fort l'Eguillette, right behind Fort Mulgrave, which must fall if the defences in front of it crumble.'

'Which is why we have built this redoubt,' Mulgrave replied.

'Assuming I'm right, I need hardly point out to you the effect on the fleet,' said Sir Sydney, looking hard at Elphinstone. 'If the French retake l'Eguillette they put the whole anchorage in jeopardy. And we have already observed, from what happened today, that they have furnaces for heating shot?'

Elphinstone didn't have to reply. Markham, likewise, could appreciate the danger, and see that the siting of those guns was, as he'd earlier suspected, anything but stupidity. The anchorage would become a naval death trap, the ships locked inside as securely as if he had a key. And everyone present knew that possession of the harbour, plus those ships inside, constituted the whole reason for holding Toulon.

'Sir   Sydney   is   right   about   l'Eguillette,'   said

Elphinstone, just in case the army men hadn't seen it for themselves.

'Just as Colonel Hanger is right about Mont Faron,' replied Mulgrave. 'Dugommier has massed his troops there. This is a very pretty idea you paint, Sir Sydney, but I think you're wrong. There's no way that artillery can achieve such a result on its own, and no amount of French theorising will change that. This sector is secure unless Dugommier reinforces it with infantry.'

'Besides, this Bonaparte fellow can't keep it up for ever,' growled Hanger. 'He can't afford the losses.'

'He will,' Markham insisted, breaking, for the second time, the convention that an officer of his rank should remain silent unless specifically asked for an opinion. 'Believe me. In some strange way, it's doing wonders for the mood of the French troops. The more men he gets killed, the better their morale.'

'Have you spoken with them too?' asked Hanger, the crooked smile aimed at the other senior officers, designed to ensure that they saw the absurdity of the notion.

'No. But unlike you, Colonel, I have a brain, and I face them on a daily basis.'

It was worth it for the way it wiped the smile off his face, even if it did anger Elphinstone and Mulgrave.

'You have a loose tongue for such a junior officer, Markham,' snapped Mulgrave, losing control of his emotions for the first time. He probably didn't like Hanger himself, but he could not stand by and allow a mere lieutenant to insult him. The way he took hold of the bronze medal round his neck seemed a deliberate allusion to America.

Elphinstone, brows knitted, was growling in agreement. 'I can see that in being allowed to speak you have been over-indulged. And it is unbecoming to hint at any man being shy, especially in your mouth.'

'Did your conversations extend to finding a solution, Lieutenant Markham?' barked Mulgrave.

'Abandon Toulon,' Hanger sneered.

Markham spoke without thinking, in his eagerness to top Hanger quite ignoring the potential consequences of his words.

'What if we were to capture his forward guns, instead of destroying them? They hauled them into position using manpower today, so we know they can be moved without horses. What if we do the same, pull them into our lines in full view of his infantry? That would destroy their morale. The whole edifice this Bonaparte has built up collapses the minute we succeed.'

'We lack the troops for such an action,' said Mulgrave.

'We most certainly do, sir,' Hanger added. 'It would mean denuding our redoubts on Mont Faron, and that, I beg to suggest, could presage disaster.'

'It need only be a limited affair,' said Sir Sydney. 'And I might add that I think Lieutenant Markham is right.'

Seeing Mulgrave ponder that, as well as the way the general was looking at him, brought home to Markham just what he might have let himself in for. Taking those guns, when they were inferior to the available French infantry, would be difficult. And he had more than a sneaking suspicion that such an assault was exactly what Captain Bonaparte wanted. It was as though the Corsican was issuing an invitation, as a way to gain not only a victory, but as a sure method of reducing the Allied strength.

Hanger lost his temper then, bringing out into the open all the simmering resentment that existed between the Army and the Navy, which plagued every combined operation, not just this one.

'Right! Are we to be dictated to by the ramblings of a popinjay who has no function here, that added to by a mere lieutenant? One, I might add, who can't make up his mind which coat to wear or which way to face. Forget this damned Corsican. I am as inclined to attack as any man alive, but only when the conditions warrant it. That rule does not apply here.'

'You're wrong, Colonel,' said Sir Sydney, in the same calm voice he'd used throughout, though Hanger's deliberate insult allowed him some umbrage. 'If you fail to impede that damned Corsican, as you call him, you may well lose Toulon.'

'While I don't quite agree with Sir Sydney,' said Elphinstone coldly, 'I fear I may be obliged to pay him heed. We cannot just leave this fellow to do as he wishes. Judging by those two new positions he's constructing either side of his present battery, they are nearly ready to be manned. And might I remind you that he has shown us already how dangerous it is for us to engage him with ships? He must be checked, if for no other reason than that the whole French effort must be discouraged. And I am prepared to pass on Sir Sydney's opinions to Admiral Hood.'

That gave Mulgrave a problem. It was obvious that Hood, as one sailor to another, would back Elphinstone. It was a question of agreeing with grace, or being forced to do so by the overall commander-in-chief.

'If you can achieve anything with the means at your disposal, you may attempt to capture the guns. But I stress, Lieutenant Markham, the means at your disposal.'

'If I may say so, sir,' Markham replied, with a confidence he didn't feel, but which further infuriated Hanger, 'I'm convinced that will work out for the best. I favour the idea of a night attack, one that avoids engaging his infantry, the sole object being the capture of the guns. If we don't have to fire a shot, I would count that as a success.'

'Sir,' said Hanger.

Mulgrave, still looking at Markham, held up his hand to stop Hanger speaking. 'How long will you need to prepare?'

'I'd like to leave Bonaparte time to get all his guns into position. We should attack as soon as he does.'

The general then proved that he was not a complete fool, by the adroit way that he placed the responsibility, fairly and squarely where it lay. 'Then I'm sure Captain Elphinstone will be happy to issue you with your orders.'

Augustus Hanger spurred his horse violently, hauling it round with a vicious tug on the bit, and departing in a cloud of dust.

# Chapter twenty

There was plenty to prepare; bayonets to be sharpened, powder and shot to fetch from the arsenal, lengths of rope from the naval stores, food to make a hot meal and rum to stave off the chill night air and settle the nerves of those who feared to fight in the dark. And all the while Bonaparte continued to lob shells into the British positions from his forward battery, every so often losing a cannon and several of its crew to return fire. Rannoch busied himself manufacturing musket balls, detailing Halsey to fetch the things they needed, while their officer studied the terrain in minute detail, committing to memory every hummock and hill, and mapping out a route by which those cannon could be bodily hauled over the rough ground. The luxury of horses was denied to him, since he could not take the creatures close to the enemy lines and at the same time guarantee silence. One of them would be bound to snort or whinny, or crack its hoof on a stone, and alert the defenders.

He was annoyed when Admiral Gravina himself came out from Fort Mulgrave, followed by an entourage of splendidly clad officers, so numerous they wouldn't have disgraced a king. Markham's observation, delivered in a strained tone, that such a party might alert the French to the coming attack, was treated with icy disdain. That was returned when Colonel Serota asked Markham if he'd like help. He wanted nothing less. The Spanish soldiers were a product of their leaders; wretched, dispirited, unkempt and totally lacking in the kind of *esprit de corps* which would be required for success in the action he planned.

He made his way to the Fort de la Malgue to receive his orders, only to be informed that Elphinstone was dining with Colonel Hanger and Miss Gordon, the written instructions being passed to him by Driberg. The boy seemed changed, perhaps sharing some notion of how such an idea annoyed Markham. In fact Driberg seemed eager to engage him in conversation, hopping from foot to foot and uttering a stream of inconsequential chatter, clearly reluctant to let him depart.

'That officer who came to the Fort Mulgrave today, the one with the star. Who was he?'

'Sir Sydney Smith,' replied Driberg, his spotty face screwing up with distaste. 'He was in Smyrna on a mission for the Admiralty. He's nicknamed "the Chevalier". Thinks himself a dazzling sort, but it's all show.'

'Well, thank you for that,' said Markham, turning to leave.

Driberg's next words were blurted at his back. 'They say Sir Sydney is very highly regarded at court. King George knighted him personally, even though the star he wears is a Swedish decoration. There's lots more I can tell you about him – that is, if you have the time.'

Markham turned round slowly. 'Is there something you want of me, Driberg?'

'There is, sir,' the youngster replied eagerly.

'Well, what is it?'

Driberg, now blushing, pulled himself to attention. 'I'd like permission to join you tonight, sir, and take part in the action Captain Elphinstone has ordered.'

'Have you asked him?'

'No, sir.'

'Then I suggest that is your first task, Driberg.'

'And if he agrees, sir?'

Markham smiled. 'Then, provided you promise to cease your gabbling, I will take you with me.'

'Thank you,' he replied breathlessly.

'Then you can tell Miss Lizzie Gordon you've been in a real battle.'

Driberg blushed again. Markham laughed out loud, knowing that he hit the target dead centre.

He found the Chevalier, telescope in hand, standing on the parapet just to the rear of the forward trenches, watching the French putting the last of their cannon in place. The sun, having dropped below the canopy of grey cloud that covered the sky, was sinking in the west, illuminating the whole landscape with a rich golden glow. It was also glinting off his bejewelled star and the polished hilt of his sword, flashing straight at the positions they were about to attack.

'With respect, sir, can I request that you desist?'

The telescope didn't move. 'Why?'

'I wish the enemy to see everything before them as normal.'

'One officer taking a look will make no difference, Markham. They'd expect to be observed.'

'That depends on how he is dressed, sir. With that star on, in this light, you look like half the general staff.'

'Do I indeed,' Smith replied, finally dropping the instrument and turning to face him. Oddly enough, he was smiling. 'One must cut a dash, Lieutenant, or risk being overlooked.'

Markham suddenly realised that he'd been flattered by the remark, not offended. 'It's a handsome bauble, don't you think, the Swedish Grand Military order of the Sword? I got it for saving Gustavus himself in an action against the Russians. Do you know the Baltic, Markham?'

He wasn't sure why he shook his head, but he did.

'I know it intimately. Indeed, I'd go so far as to say that any future service in that sea will depend on the observations I submitted to the Admiralty. The same will apply to the Turkish shore. That's were I was when war broke out. Damned annoying, Markham. I should have one of those ships out in the roadstead, and be advising Hood officially, instead of the fools he's surrounded himself with.'

'Why, that's a great loss to him, I'm sure,' Markham answered, with a degree of irony that Sir Sydney totally missed.

'It's worse than that. Reputations are being made here.'

'I daresay the odd one might be dented.'

'How right you are, Lieutenant. But not tonight, eh! What time do we move forward?'

'We?'

'I suggest that you take command of one section, to destroy one of the two new emplacements, while I lead the main party straight for Bonaparte's guns.'

'My orders say nothing about your participation, sir.'

'Nor would they,' he snorted. 'Elphinstone would see me damned before he'd give me a chance of action. Fortunately, he's not here.'

'But I am, sir, and so is Midshipman Driberg, who is a protégé of the captain.'

Smith had the telescope to his eye again, though the sun had gone, leaving just a thin orange strip that glowed behind the western hills. 'The day has yet to come when either lieutenants, or favoured midshipmen, tell Sir Sydney Smith what to do.'

'With respect, sir, I have already singled out my own Hebes to attack the central gun position. I cannot countenance putting them under another officer.'

'Even if it is a direct order?'

'I would have to query that with a higher authority.'

'You would do well not to make an enemy of me, Markham.'

'Nevertheless, sir I'm prepared to risk that.'

Smith jumped down from the parapet and slapped him on the shoulder. For once the smile was genuine. 'Damnit, Markham you're a man after my own heart.'

'I'm pleased to hear it.'

The Chevalier missed the irony again. 'I do hate supine officers, who only have the wit to do as they're told. I never subscribed to that myself. I even had to remind Admiral Hood today that he didn't have a monopoly on military wisdom.'

'He must have been grateful for your advice, sir.'

'He was. Damned grateful, and those were his very words.'

For all his bombast, the Chevalier listened patiently as Markham outlined the requirements of the operation. Nor did he insist on taking the 'battery for men without fear' himself. He even deferred to him as he gave Driberg equal prominence, allotting him half the Alcides and the task of taking the northern position, while Smith was given an equal number to attack the new emplacement to the south.

'Absolute silence going forward,' said Markham, as he distributed pieces of burnt cork so that his men could blacken their faces. 'Take no equipment that you don't need, belts and shoulder straps to be turned inside out. Remember, the object is to take the guns, failing that to spike them. If we can do that without even killing a Frenchman I'll be happy.'

They'd have to sit it out in no man's land, in the long winter night, till the first grey tinge of dawn, so close to the enemy that a cough could be fatal. At least the cloud cover was thick, with not a single star showing in the night sky. But the French campfires, which they'd use to hold their direction, were numerous, and an unwary movement might just reflect something which would alert the gun crews.

'As soon as you see a hint of dawn, get into the emplacements and deal with the gunners. The men to attach the cables already know what to do. Leave them to their job and take station to the rear, ready to deter any counter-attack.'

He made light of the next part, as though it were a fairground game. That it would be fun to lash their muskets to the guns while under fire from the enemy; to grab the ropes and haul them out from their positions, an act which would, initially, take them closer to the French trenches. Once they were clear, they'd need to turn and run, dragging the heavy cannon over ground cratered by their own barrage, through an arc of crossfire that they'd already experienced that day, their only advantage the fact that the French gunners would be kicked from their slumbers to man their weapons; that they would do here something he had considered ill-advised at Bregaillon, with only the darkness making the difference.

'Speed and silence, those are the key elements. As soon as we're spotted, the batteries from Fort Mulgrave will open up to give us covering fire.' He paused for a moment, looking into eyes that were full of questions. But there was really only one that mattered: who would live and who would die. 'Corporal Halsey, a tot of rum all round.'

Driberg was shivering, even after the tot of rum, something he tried to control as Markham moved close.

'Have you eaten, Driberg?'

'I had some of the food left over from Captain Elphinstone's dinner, sir.'

'I find it hard to believe he entertained Hanger, especially after what transpired this morning.'

'It wasn't him, sir,' Driberg replied, the bitterness very evident in his voice. 'It was his niece.'

'Well, well,' Markham said, feeling the response inadequate.

'She surely can't admire him, sir.'

Markham remembered the day he'd met Lizzie Gordon; Driberg's eagerness, Hanger's rudeness and the lady herself observing that her late travelling companion was 'exceedingly rich'.

'Is she an heiress?'

'Lord no, sir. Her relationship to the ducal Gordons is very tenuous, a cadet branch at best. Were she in line for a fortune, it would be crass indeed to pay her my respects.'

'You admire her that much?' Markham asked, hiding the smile that threatened to crease his face.

'She has responded to me very warmly, sir,' he said, in a voice that conveyed, as it dropped into deep gloom, the exact opposite, 'obliging me in the many small courtesies that lead me to believe my attentions are not entirely unwelcome.'

Markham could imagine her being kind to the blushing, spotty-faced mid, but the idea of forming an attraction towards him was risible to everyone but Driberg himself. He'd been there himself, suffered just as Driberg was suffering now, and knew that to say he'd get over it would achieve nothing.

'She can't marry him, sir, can she?'

'Not when she hears how you have behaved tonight, Driberg.'

'Yes, sir,' he replied breathlessly, all his optimism suddenly restored, which made Markham uncomfortable.

The move forward had gone well, better than Markham could have anticipated. He'd not heard any sort of sound that would carry, and he supposed that his men, like himself, were kept silent by fear rather than ability. The looming bulk of the emplacement, where he'd stood the day before listening to Captain Bonaparte, told him he was close. He stopped, turning and putting up his hand to prevent Rannoch bumping into him.

'Tally off the men,' he whispered.

So close, eyes straining forward in the darkness, he could hear the whispers as the Highlander reminded the Hebes of their orders. 'Halsey, eighteen paces, Yelland sixteen paces, Tully fourteen. Hollick twelve, Dymock ten, Gibbons eight, Quinlan six, Ettrick four.'

The commands were repeated, the eight men following sent in the opposite direction. The last pair, Dornan and Schutte, carrying the thick ropes around their bodies, were set either side of Rannoch and Markham. The earth was cold, and as the night progressed the temperature dropped. Forced to leave their greatcoats behind for the sake of speed, the men shivered in silence. Markham had left it as late as he could, well aware that too long an exposure to the cold night air and his men would be incapable of walking, let alone running. But he'd had to leave enough time to ensure he could get them in place, which, he reckoned, left about another hour. The whoosh of the flares streaking through the black sky completely changed that.

They seemed to explode right above his head, a dozen blue lights that bathed the whole landscape. The grey, crouching lumps of men's bodies were starkly illuminated, as was the mound of earth right before them. The cloud cover, which had given protection, now acted as a reflecting screen to the flares, multiplying their effect to a disastrous degree. The French sentries were suddenly wide awake, the first wild musket shots being fired off to discourage whatever it was the perfidious British had planned.

'Move forward,' he shouted, leaping himself for the dubious shelter of the gun emplacement. Some followed, others didn't, frozen like rabbits. The first heads appeared over the parapet of the gun position, bayonetted muskets thrust forward ready to fire. Those who moved fared best, by increasing the angle at which the muskets were forced to discharge. Those who stayed, now crouched like crows feeding in a newly sown field, took the brunt of the enemy fire. Markham, who'd intended to keep his head down, was forced to scramble up the slope in an attempt to disrupt the enemy. He'd just reached the very edge of the embankment when a hand grabbed his collar and hauled him back.

'We have got to run,' gasped Rannoch, 'or we will be butchered.'

Markham had ended up in a heap, right back where he'd started at the bottom of the mound, with Rannoch now trying to help him up in the last dying flickers of blue lights.

'Hebes, to me,' he yelled, not quite sure if the sergeant was right or wrong. The flares had died away, so they only had his voice to go by, that and the flash of muskets from Smith's party to the south. 'Dorman, Leech, get rid of those ropes. The rest of you, keep the enemy camp fires on your right hand and move.'

'We have got to get back, sir,' shouted Rannoch.

'Not across that strip of land,' he hissed. 'Now do as you're told and follow me.'

A volley of musket fire, which flew over their heads, concentrated everyone's mind. It was no time for a discussion of tactics, more a time to take a chance and hope that their officer had made the right decision. Another set of flares shot skywards, bursting above the broken landscape, throwing every hummock and hole into sharp relief, and highlighting the running, crouching figures of the redcoats. The guns opened up behind the French lines, orange flashes that added to the surreal nature of the surroundings. The pattern was laid from the previous engagement, and the shells landed right on the line of direct retreat from Bonaparte's main battery.

As the blue lights began to fade, Markham, realising they'd reached a halfway point between the central and the southern battery, stood up, waved his sword and yelled for his men to retreat to their own lines. He was praying that a corridor would exist which had yet to be covered by crossfire, one that would be hard to conjure up in the dark. Musket flashes still appeared from the south, though fewer in number. There was nothing at all from the north, where Driberg was supposed to attack.

The next set of flares showed him why. The men

retreating at this distance, looked like ants scurrying back to their nest. Guns were going off all around him, musket balls cracking in his ears and cannon booming out as they fired salvo after salvo. So for him to try to yell orders to Driberg, whom he couldn't distinguish from the others, was a waste of time. The midshipman hadn't been up in the lines today, and hadn't seen the damage wrought by Bonaparte's covering fire. So to the youngster, the oblique angle at which he'd chosen to retire, one which would confuse the French infantry, made absolute sense.

That aura of time suspended returned once more. Even his hoarse and useless shouts seemed to slow in speed. His legs, carrying him towards them, seemed leaden. The guns flashed and boomed. He fancied, though it was impossible, that he saw the shells arc towards the ground in front of the main French position. But he did see them burst, well above head height, the smoke of the explosions, in the ethereal glow, creating great puffballs like clouds as the metal was spewed in all directions. Driberg's men spun and writhed like maddened puppets as the case shot ripped into them. A few, miraculously, survived to stagger on. Others, wounded, dragged themselves upright and tried to follow. The next salvo, explosive shells, ripped into both them and their wounded and dying companions. Great clods of earth flew skywards, seeming to stop for a second to form a murderous and petrified forest in which the branches were mud and the leaves human limbs. Two more followed as the first cascaded back to the ground, tearing up the same bloodstained dirt, with not even a scream from a dying man to break the rhythm of the explosions.

Markham stopped, sure that to continue would mean certain death, and convinced that all he would find were remains, since no creature could live through that barrage. He turned back towards his own lines, praying that the Chevalier had not perished in the same manner, wondering how many of his own party had succumbed. The British guns, right before his eyes, belched forth in such numbers that the glow of the discharge ran like a continuous strip across the skyline. His legs, as he tried to run, were like lead. Curses were mixed with prayers as he ran under the salvo, beseeching the deities to give him the strength to get clear. The blast, a wall of air, hit him in the back like a huge shovel, throwing him forward. His hands went to cover his head automatically as the ground behind him erupted.

They found him an hour later, in full daylight when the guns had fallen silent, half buried under a pile of loose earth. Concussed and confused, the words he uttered sounded like the ramblings of madman. Rannoch took him to the hospital ship personally, along with nearly half the men he'd led into battle. Markham lay semi-delirious as all around him men died, some from their wounds, others from the efforts of the surgeons to cure them. Legs and arms were amputated, the screams of the conscious victims mingling with those that filled his head, the sound of men dying in the dark for a piece of his own vanity, Driberg torn asunder so that he could no longer flatter Lizzie Gordon.

When he did come round, there was silence. Those too badly damaged to survive had expired, taking their noise with them. Those who'd lived lay still, either praying to God, or silently reliving the nightmare they'd passed through. His tongue was as dry as parchment, his lips cracked and sore. Consciousness brought pain, as the multitude of cuts and bruises made themselves known. A croak brought a loblolly boy, a bucket and a ladle, and the welcome relief of clean refreshing water, most of which seemed to spill across his naked chest. The loud bang made him jump with fear, and try to sit up.

'Rest easy, sir,' said the loblolly boy, his face full of concern. 'It's only lightning and thunder you're a'hearin', a December storm. You just lay back while I fetch the surgeon.'

'They feared for your wits, of course,' said the Chevalier, 'what with you raving away about treachery. There was a woman in there somewhere, as well.'

'Driberg?'

Smith shook his head slowly. 'They found his hat, I believe, but like the rest of his party there was precious little left to bury, and not enough clothing on the pieces to identify them.

'Your Captain Bonaparte pounded that particular stretch of ground right up till we asked for a ceasefire.'

'And you?'

'Light casualties, wounds only and not a single man lost. From what Rannoch told me my thoughts were very like your own, that to retreat direct was to invite Johnny Crapaud to shoot us in the back. I made for the southeast shore, got behind the dunes and set up a defence. At first light someone had the sense to stretch the terms of the truce and take us off by boat.'

'I need Rannoch to report to me.'

'Then I shall make it so, Markham. I know that what he will have to tell you will wound you, but I cannot have you thinking that you were foolish.'

'Who said I was foolish?'

'You did, according to the surgeon, in your ravings. Mind, how he would know when he's full to the brim with rum, I cannot tell. The attack on the guns was my idea, and it was a sound one, as I told Admiral Hood. As for the losses, you cannot make war without risk.'

To Markham's recollection, the notion of the danger Bonaparte's dispositions posed had been outlined by Smith. But the actual idea of taking the guns had been his. But even if he'd wanted to say that, he was given no chance, as the Chevalier rattled on.

'And I see it as a fine piece of work, Markham. I was

taken to task for presuming to lead it, of course, with Elphinstone being very sour. He and that Hanger fellow seem to have suddenly become bosom companions. Some of the things he said might have had me calling him out. But I imagine the loss of young Driberg weighs on him, so I let his insults pass. I stuck to my main purpose, which was that I be given the task of writing the despatch. I hazard that when you read it you will be pleased. I have detailed the events of the action most accurately, and rest assured your part in advising me has not gone unmentioned.'

Markham lay back and closed his eyes, which the Chevalier saw as tiredness, not disbelief. 'I make you weary, I see. The surgeon reckons you to be up and about in a day or two, and I have bespoken you a cabin of your own at my expense.'

'I must see Rannoch.'

'Of course, man. And you will need him to fetch you a change of uniform. Yours was sadly tattered when they found you. But another day will make no difference. Better that you see him well, than still swaying from your knock.'

He was on deck at first light, sheltering from the teeming rain under an awning, when the boat brought Rannoch and Frobisher's sea-chest out to the hospital ship. The first flash of lightning streaked across the sky as they exchanged a look that spoke volumes for the tale he was about to hear. He took his dripping sergeant below to the tiny cabin that the Chevalier had bribed the ship's captain to put at his disposal and listened, head bowed, as Rannoch, in his clear, precise Highland lilt, told him what he wanted to know. In the background, the crack of lightning and the rumbling of thunder seemed a fitting accompaniment.

'Twenty-six killed and fourteen wounded.'

The groan was muted, but still audible. 'Forty casualties out of less than eighty, a third dead just to appease my vanity.'

'We have been broken up. The Alcides have been sent back to their ship.'

'Hebes?'

'Six dead and the same number near enough to warrant a ticket home. Yelland took a ball across his backside and Tully lost half of his ear.'

'How many men do we muster now?'

'Twelve, with Leech back on duty.'

'How did Schutte behave?'

'He went forward and came back. That is all I know.'

'Where are the men now?'

'Back aboard the *Hebe*, being rested, they say.' Markham looked up then, his eyes fixed on those of the Sergeant. 'Spotted Dick still finds it hard to accept us soldiers, and since we are without an officer he has seen fit to question my position. Both Schutte and Halsey, however, refused to oblige him by replacing me. That threw him into a rare passion, I can tell you.'

'I don't think there is anything I can do to change that, Rannoch. At least not till I'm back aboard.'

'No, sir. I do not suppose there is.'

'Yet he let you come over from *Hebe* to visit me?'

'Only because that gabbling captain with the gaudy star insisted. I did not overhear it myself, but Halsey was told by the steward that the man threatened to tell the King, in person no less, of Captain de Lisle's behaviour.'

'He's quite a fellow, our Chevalier.'

'A little bit less of the talking would do him no harm, though I will grant you he is a kindly fellow.'

'You might as well ask a stallion to ignore a mare.'

'Speaking of that, Sir Sydney took word to the Picard house, at my request.'

'Thank you for dragging me back from my one-man attempt to end the siege.'

'It was only the kind of folly that comes to a man when he feels betrayed.'

'I wondered if anyone else noticed.'

'I did, sir. But I have had the good sense to keep my mouth shut until I could speak with you.'

'I have sent a letter, requesting an interview with Lord Hood. It is my intention that he shall be the first to hear it.'

'Did you say anything to Sir Sydney?'

'No Rannoch, I did not.'

The muted noise of the storm altered as Markham began to change his clothes, becoming louder, and both knew that the extra level of sound was caused by gunfire. This was interrupted by a cough, which strained to be polite, since it had to be loud to be heard. The canvas screen was pulled back and one of the *Dolphin*'s midshipmen stood there.

'I have a boat standing by, Lieutenant Markham, with orders to ship you over to *Victory*.'

Rannoch stood up, crouching low to avoid the deck-beams. 'I'd best return to the *Hebe*, sir, in case we are required ashore.'

'This kit here, Rannoch,' he said, pointing to the things he'd discarded. 'Take it back with you. I will join you as soon as I've seen the Admiral.'

Gunfire vied with the storm to make the greater noise, as he was rowed across the choppy waters of the Grande Rade under a black winter sky. The sea wasn't blue now, it was grey and forbidding, which perfectly matched his mood. The quarterdeck of the flagship was crowded with officers as he came aboard, Hood very obvious in the middle. They all had telescopes to their eyes, switching them between Mont Faron and Fort Mulgrave. The party on the Grosse Tour was sending a steady stream of signals, each one of which seemed to add to the gloom of the assembled dignitaries. He was met at the entry port by one of Hood's civilian clerks.

'As you will have seen, Lieutenant, Admiral Hood is somewhat engaged at the moment. There are, unfortunately, quite a number of officers waiting to see him.'

'Something is obviously happening.'

The civilian's pinched face screwed up even more. 'The French have launched an assault on Mont Faron, as well as Fort Mulgrave. It seems our guns are outclassed at the latter, while Mont Faron is held by our allies. I need hardly point out what an unsatisfactory situation the Admiral is presented with.'

Markham looked along the gloomy gundeck, at the cannon bowsed tight to the sides, with mess tables in between. All the implements to man the guns, swabs, rammers, wormers and the like, were neatly stowed by the bulkheads. The planking beneath his feet, as in all warships, was painted red, so that the blood would not show in the heat of the battle, to inform those fighting of the carnage in which they were engaged. That colour made him think of the losses he had suffered in front of Fort Mulgrave.

'Would I be permitted to go onto the upper deck?'

'If you do so, you risk forfeiting a place.'

'I'll chance that.'

# Chapter twenty-one

Markham didn't have to be on deck long to discover what was happening, especially with Sir Sydney Smith reeling off 'I told you so's' every two minutes. The rain had eased, lifting the cloud cover. The signal station on the Grosse Tour was in plain view and, just beyond the Tour de Balaguier, some of the action could be observed from aloft. The looks Smith was getting seemed to have no effect on his absolute confidence in his own opinion. Much as his contemporaries were annoyed, they were stymied by the fact that he was being proved right.

Dugommier had finished his sapping and attacked on Mont Faron, driving several wedges into the Allied lines around the highest defensive post, the redoubt Croix de Faron. A major assault, it sucked in every available man in the Allied reserve. As soon as that happened the French opened a secondary attack from la Valette, again investing the Forts of Faron and l'Artigues. Attacking from a much closer trench line, they'd driven in the forward piquets and were now fighting for the main bastions. Finally, with all the defenders committed, including units from the other redoubts, Bonaparte had started to employ his guns against Fort Mulgrave, destroying one position after another before bringing his cannon forward to bombard the remainder. The attack had commenced in the midst of a ferocious storm, which continued throughout, the violence of that exaggerating the drama being played out all round the perimeter.

Reports were coming in of the wavering nature of the battle, as the Allies regained ground lost, only to be taken in the flank and driven back. Markham heard the messenger who delivered even more ominous news, that the French were massing before the forts on the western edge of Toulon, Des Pomets, Rouge, Blanc and Malbousquet, in numbers that indicated an imminent assault. But Fort Mulgrave caused the greatest concern, as Bonaparte, moving his guns independently of infantry, bore out everything the Chevalier had said about the new tactics. The battery names were reeled off with increasing gloom as report after report came in. *Grande Rade* supported *Sans Peur. Jacobins* and *Chasse Coquins* were pushed forward to either side of *Sans Peur*, the latter flanking the Mulgrave defences. Any infantry attack trying to take them was beaten back by two factors: lack of numbers, and the devastating barrage that Bonaparte could lay down on the approaches to his positions.

'I cannot emphasise enough, gentlemen,' boomed the Chevalier, 'the necessity of reading everything published of a military nature, especially the opinions of our enemies.'

'Perhaps if you had a ship to run, Sir Sydney, you would find yourself with less leisure to read and write.'

Markham recognised Troubridge's voice, which had a confident tone, since he knew that he was speaking for every serving sailor on the quarterdeck. The Chevalier turned sharply, quite prepared to put this interloper in his place, especially since the officer was junior to him on the captains' list.

'Might I recommend you an efficient First Lieutenant, Troubridge? Those who gain a place with me have the good sense to leave their captain time to hone the skills of his profession.'

'I dislike the inference, sir,' snapped Troubridge.

'Enough!' Hood spoke without looking at either man, in a voice that had no need to be raised to be obeyed. 'This is no time for squabbling. We have a crisis developing.'

'It is more than a crisis, sir,' Smith insisted. 'It is, potentially, a defeat. I told Mulgrave that the destruction of those guns was essential. But, like all Bullocks, he thought he knew best. That Germantown medal has convinced him that he's a fount of military wisdom. Instead he is a trough of stale ideas. Hanger is worse, so smitten with Elphinstone's niece that he can barely be brought to concentrate on his duty. This Bonaparte, a mere artillery captain, has cooked our goose by doing the unexpected. He'll have l'Eguillette before midnight tomorrow.'

Markham turned every time the pipes blew on the maindeck to welcome a naval captain aboard, the only one to do so. He heard Hood order a boat ashore with one of *Victory*'s lieutenants, given instructions to request that all the senior officers attend a conference as soon as darkness fell, and that they bring with them an honest appreciation of the situation. Messages were sent to the Spanish flagship and the Commodore of the Neapolitan contingent. Listening to all this, Markham didn't notice that Nelson had taken station beside him.

'You too have come to observe the beginning of the final act, Markham.'

'Is it that, sir?' he said, turning to face the small, fair-haired captain.

Nelson pointed towards the Grosse Tour. 'I daresay you can read the signals as well as I.'

'Unfortunately, no.'

'Of course,' Nelson replied quickly. 'Forgive me, I forgot this is all new to you. I have been watching them from *Agememnon*, since we sailed back into the Grande Rade. Hood asked if any troops could be spared from Mont Faron to launch an attack to protect Fort Mulgrave. The reply was a decided no.'

'He's called a conference of senior officers for tonight.'

'I daresay. But he has also called for a conference of captains before that, which is why I came over.' Seeing that Markham was confused he continued. 'We must decide what we are going to do before we tell the soldiers, or the Dons. I just hope the French leave us enough time to reach the right decision.'

'Sir Sydney seems to think we only have until tomorrow.'

They could hear the Chevalier still, praising his own abilities while, by association, he denigrated those of everyone else. The mention of the name made Nelson frown.

'I wonder if he does himself any favours by being quite so forward.' Markham observed that there was more behind those words than their mere content. Nelson didn't like Smith, but he wasn't prepared to say so in front of a junior officer. The frown disappeared as quickly as it came, to be followed by a smile. 'I've not inquired for your health, Markham. Seeing you upright, I assume that you are wholly recovered?'

'An ache or two, sir, when I move. But otherwise, I'm in one piece. I wish I could say the same for others.'

The rain began again, a grey curtain that swept across the deck, blotting out the signal station. No-one could move until Hood did, and he seemed to take a perverse pleasure in ensuring they all suffered a good soaking before he obliged. Markham and Nelson, both still wearing cloaks, fared better than most.

'That seems to have taken the shine off Sir Sydney's star,' said Nelson happily, as the bedraggled Chevalier rushed past them, heading for the companionway and shelter. Both men now followed the clutch of officers, as they followed in the wake of their admiral.

'I know why I am here, Markham,' Nelson said, 'but what brings you to the flagship?'

'I have sought an interview with Admiral Hood regarding the events surrounding my last engagement.'

Nelson indicated the crowd that now stood before the bulkhead that separated Hood's quarters from the maindeck. 'Then you're in for a long wait, I fear, especially with what is happening ashore. Is it important?'

'Yes, sir. Very important.'

'My God, Markham, it cheers me to see you up and about.' Both men turned to meet the Chevalier, who was coming towards them with a beaming smile on his face. That became fixed as he gave the slightest nod and said, 'Nelson.'

'Sir,' Markham replied, pulling himself stiffly to attention. Smith leant between the two men, his voice low and conspiratorial.

'He's a fine officer, Nelson, despite what you may hear to the contrary. I know that I've inspired him by my own example, but that only goes to prove the necessity for leadership.'

'I have always thought it a most commendable quality,' Nelson replied, the only sign of his amusement the ghost of a smile around his lips. Smith opened his mouth to proffer further advice just as a loud voice behind them invited all the captains to enter the great cabin. As the Chevalier spun round, Nelson addressed his next words to Markham.

'I do hope you don't have to wait too long, Lieutenant. It all depends on how long-winded some of my colleagues are.'

'You're right, Nelson,' said Smith. 'Some of these fellows do go on. I wonder sometimes how the Admiral stays awake.'

Military life, by land or sea, inures a man to waiting, patience being an absolutely essential component of martial existence. So Markham, like the others queuing for an interview, sat on a gun, or paced up and down, as a stream of messengers came and went throughout the day, each one bringing further depressing news about events ashore. Croix de Faron had been abandoned, giving the French a perfect point for an artillery bombardment of the other forts. Mulgrave, fearful of casualties, had ordered Des Pomets, Faron, l'Artigues to be given up, likewise the now outflanked Rouge and Blanc, and pulled his troops back to the Camp de St Anne and Fort St Catherine, close to the northern edge of Toulon.

The meeting of naval officers continued all the while, which left those waiting wondering what it was these men could find to talk about. The smell of food wafted through the bulkhead and the admiral's steward, no doubt used to a continuous stream of supplicants, sent a servant out with something to eat. And all the while, Lieutenant George Markham rehearsed, over and over again, what it was he was going to say to Admiral Hood.

Darkness came early in December, the fall of night hastened by the appalling weather. Yet that teeming rain had one good quality. It made night fighting arduous, and imposed some check on the enemy's attacks, which apart from the guns before Fort Mulgrave faltered and died away. The sound of whistles could again be heard, as those in command on shore came aboard. Admiral Langara, the Spanish commander, came first, followed by Serota and Gravina, looking neither left nor right as they strode across the maindeck. Elphinstone acknowledged him with an unfriendly glare. Mulgrave, with Hanger at his heels, was the last to arrive, looking depressed. If either man, in the dim lantern light, saw the look of hate that Markham directed at the Colonel, they ignored it. Not that they had much time to do so, since the Brigadier-General was ushered into Hood's cabin without pause.

Another hour passed, while a steady stream of captains, all with an air of purpose, left through the entry port. Their boats, which had been sitting in the water all this time, were hailed by name. Whatever was in their demeanour had an effect, since the flock of supplicants thinned, until only one was left. Nelson was one of the last to exit, and he at least seemed to have time to spare to tell Markham what was happening.

'We're abandoning Toulon,' he said. 'Mulgrave cannot hold the east and the defences are in tatters everywhere else. That Bonaparte fellow could be in l'Eguillette within forty-eight hours, sooner if Dugommier gives him a few battalions of infantry.'

'When, sir?'

'Beginning tonight, though it could take days.'

Despite his own concerns, Markham couldn't help thinking about those in the Picard house. 'Will we be taking off any civilians?'

'As many as we can, but they cannot have priority over the embarkation of the soldiers. The Spaniards are falling back from La Seyne and Malbousquet and will pull out first, then the Neapolitans will go aboard *Samara*. *Robust*, *Leviathan* and *Courageux* will load our marines from la Malgue as soon as they have destroyed the installations.' Suddenly Nelson snorted, unhappily. 'And guess who has secured for himself the task of destroying those ships we cannot take with us.'

It wasn't difficult, given the look in his eyes, to guess. Markham was just about to say the name when the Chevalier burst out of the cabin doors. 'Markham. Just the fellow I want to see. I need a party of marines to be under my personal command. If you're up to it, I'd like you to lead them. I'll send the orders over to *Hebe*. You get back there yourself and prepare your men.'

He was gone, calling for a boat, before Markham got a chance to reply. Seeing him stamping his foot impatiently by the entry port, he was just about to follow when Mulgrave and Hanger came out. They nodded to Nelson, and Mulgrave spared Markham a quick glance. But Hanger stopped.

'What are you doing here?' he demanded. 'If you're fit for duty you should be ashore where you're needed.'

'I'm waiting to see the Admiral,' Markham replied

calmly. Mulgrave stooped a few feet away, lost in his own thoughts. 'I've something to say to him about the attack on Bonaparte's guns.'

'The only thing you can say about that, Markham, is that you failed again. Thank God I was on hand and could order a barrage to stop the Frogs.'

'I didn't think you'd stayed away.'

'D'you imagine I'd leave the fate of the whole position to you and that dandy, Smith?' Hanger looked at Markham hard, not wishing him to mistake his meaning. 'Damned fool of a gunner wanted to wait, to make sure you all got clear. I had to order him to fire. It pains me that, by all accounts, I hesitated a fraction too long.'

'You also sent up those blue lights, didn't you, Hanger?'

'What blue lights?'

'The ones that illuminated the whole position, and every man under my command, when we were lying out in the open.'

Mulgrave had turned back towards them, the rising sound of Markham's voice impossible to ignore.

'What are you talking about?' demanded Hanger.

'I'm talking about what I want to tell Admiral Hood. Those flares didn't come from the French side of the line, they came from ours. What was the reason? Were you so determined that we should fail that you sabotaged the whole thing?'

Hanger's face had gone bright red, the scar on his cheek a ragged creamy-white, and Mulgrave had moved towards them. 'Damn you, you cowardly bastard.'

Nelson's hand caught Markham's as it was on the way to the hilt of his sword, and the Brigadier-General had interposed himself between him and Hanger.

'Enough of this,' cried Mulgrave. 'We have enough fighting still to do without indulging in private quarrels.'

'Have you heard what he just said?' Hanger shouted,

trying to push Mulgrave aside. 'Damn my rank, sir, you will withdraw that or meet me!'

Markham's voice was just as loud. 'I have been waiting for that opportunity for a whole twelve years.'

The door opened and Admirals Langara and Gravina came out, followed by Serota and the rest of their staffs. Nelson, taking advantage of this, pushed him backwards, till his spine was against the bulkhead. Everyone on the deck, barring the Spaniards, was now looking in their direction as the naval captain spoke to him, softly but insistently.

'What is the matter with you, man?'

'I told you all. Those flares that destroyed our attack came from behind our own lines. Because of that my men were blown to bits so small that they couldn't be identified. Somebody betrayed us to the French.'

'You can't believe for a moment that Colonel Hanger was responsible.'

'He was against the attempt from the beginning, angry at Smith for proposing that something be done, even more at me for agreeing. We have a past, him and I. God knows he hates me enough.'

'Enough to betray his country?'

'Those flares came from behind our lines!'

'Do you know where they were fired from?'

'Close to the La Seyne redoubt,' Markham replied, the first hint of doubt entering his voice, 'which is just north of Mulgrave.'

Nelson was as quick as he was. 'And how long was it between the flares going off and the order that was given to fire off the barrage that flattened you?'

Markham sighed and bent forward.

'A man cannot be in two places at once, regardless of how much he hates.' Nelson paused, waiting for Markham to look at him again, waiting for him to acknowledge openly that he accepted the obvious. 'You must apologise.'

'To him!'

'Lieutenant Markham, I've never referred to your past. I judge a man by what he does today, not yesterday. But neither you nor I can wish it away. You've publicly accused a senior officer of being a traitor. If you don't apologise, you'll be ruined.'

Over Nelson's shoulder, Markham saw that the Spanish officers had engaged Mulgrave and Hanger in conversation, which debarred him, temporarily, from continuing his argument.

'I cannot. Not to his face.'

'In writing, then?'

The pause seemed to last a long time, before Markham nodded. But all the events of his life had passed through his mind in that brief moment, and the thought had formed that to continue would only see him bested by Hanger one more time.

'Come then,' said Nelson, taking his arm. 'I will get my barge crew to take you back to *Hebe* once I'm aboard *Agamemnon*.'

They turned towards the entry port, their way partially blocked by the knot of British and Spanish officers. Skirting round them, Nelson spoke, as Markham kept his eyes fixed firmly in front of him.

'The Lieutenant has not fully recovered from his wounds, gentlemen, which will be obvious to you.'

It didn't matter if it was in the words or the look. Hanger understood, and nodded in triumph.

'What the devil are these?' demanded de Lisle, puffing out his chest as he waved the orders which had arrived no more than an hour after the officer they mentioned.

'It is not a duty I sought, Captain. Sir Sydney asked me to undertake it while I was aboard the flagship.'

'Something you've yet to explain to me. It is not proper for you to seek an interview with the Admiral without my permission.'

'It was a private matter, sir.'

'There's no such thing in the Navy. I am your captain, and you report to me.'

Spotted Dick was piqued. Captain of a frigate, he'd not been invited to the conference. The idea that his marine lieutenant had been aboard *Victory* at the time, and knew more about what was happening than he did, had upset him. It was doubly annoying that he'd returned in Nelson's barge, which hinted at the kind of valuable connections he so assiduously pursued. Now that it seemed Markham was to be involved in the final act of the siege his ire had multiplied even more.

'Damn Sir Sydney Smith,' the captain shouted. Then he added, in a tone that sought to be friendly, 'You can, of course, with my complete backing, decline the honour.'

Translated, that meant that de Lisle couldn't interfere with what looked like a direct order. Angry he might be, but the idea of crossing swords with someone who was said to be close to the King was out of the question. In the short time he'd been aboard, Markham had heard how his men had been treated, put to swabbing the decks and other such duties normally confined to sailors. Even the Lobsters, who should have been happy to be back aboard ship, seemed keen to get off *Hebe*, even if was only for what looked like a day and a night.

'I'm sorry, sir,' Markham replied, with a feeling of pleasure he'd not had since he'd first accused Hanger. 'You will readily appreciate that for me, that is impossible.'

The evacuation had started before he left the ship, the forts that fronted the Grande Rade filling up with Spanish soldiers as they fell back, through British marines who remained to fight a rearguard action from the ancient town walls. The rest of the marines were massed in Fort St Catherine, the only force that stood between the French and total victory. Fort Mulgrave had been overrun, and with all the heights in their hands the French were shelling the town. All around the harbour emplacements, ammunition, guns and stores were being destroyed. This, added to the flickering torches and the continual gunfire, presented what looked like a scene from hell.

Ashore, he was ordered to assist with the Neapolitans, who'd panicked as soon as the order to withdraw had been given, and were now threatening the whole process by their eagerness to get onto their hundred-gun ship, the *Samara*. They crowded the routes that ran through the dockyard buildings on to the quay, their flaring torches throwing giant shadows onto the brickwork and windows, and reflecting in the black water of the harbour.

The line-of-battle ship was slowly warped in, to tower over the ropewalk and sail lofts, the sheds and store-houses, a long gangplank stretching from the entry port to the cobbled quayside. The unfurled but empty sails, and the flag of Bourbon Naples, looked dejected, as if they reflected the feelings of those now desperate to abandon Toulon. Shouted commands from officers of their own nationality had little effect on the Neapolitans who were screaming too loud to hear them. They broke through the cordon of sailors who had been sent ashore to get them in line and herd them aboard. What had been a pretty poor bunch of soldiers turned, very swiftly, into a screeching, dangerous mob.

Markham ordered the Hebes to form a line at the bottom of the gangplank as the evacuees jostled foward. Every insult in the Italian canon was aimed in their direction, and judging by the races of those at the very forefront, faced with a mere dozen redcoats, they definitely thought they had the advantage, and would brush them back into the water.

'Hebes, present,' Markham yelled. They still pressed forward, shouting and gesticulating wildly, using their thumbs to spit imprecations about British manhood. 'Fire!'

The first volley went over their heads, with Rannoch screaming at his men to reload. He needn't have even raised his voice. The entire mob went silent as if they had one, now sealed, throat. The effect on their behaviour was also instantaneous, making another volley superfluous. Each face before them was now full of silent pleading, the odd sob or plea to God adding to the air of unreality. The sailors had got in front of them again, and, with a discipline that would have shamed the Foot Guards, they were arranged in lines, shuffling towards the gangplank of the *Samara*, which was waiting to take them aboard, smiling as they passed the redcoats who'd forced them to behave.

Troubridge appeared, and seeing what they'd achieved ordered them off towards the arsenal, quite oblivious to Markham's objection that they were under the orders of Sir Sydney Smith. His previous antipathy to Markham seemed to have evaporated. In fact, his voice was almost friendly.

'You'll have time for a bit of pyromania before that buffoon needs you, God rot his vainglorious soul.'

The quay was crowded with civilians, thousands of them, all carrying heaped bundles of possessions, each one eager to find a way out of the port before the Terror arrived. The quays, once home to hundreds of fishing boats and small trading ships, was emptying rapidly as the better off, who had their own transport, departed with their furniture and fortunes. No pity was shown to their fellow Frenchmen, and shots were fired to discourage anyone trying to board a ship that wasn't theirs.

'When will the civilians be taken off?' asked Markham, running alongside the naval captain.

'We'll take off what we can when we've got the soldiers away,' he replied, in a voice that, even running, held a note of deep sorrow. 'But it will be nowhere near enough. Mercy is the only thing that will save most of these poor souls.'

The arsenal was still under guard, red-coated marines standing sentry beneath the flaring torches. Troubridge ordered the men outside to stay at their posts and make sure no one entered. Once inside he issued a string of orders, which had the Hebes smashing open barrels, distributing their contents liberally all over the ground-floor area. Markham and Troubridge were cutting lengths of slow-match, which were then tied to the bottom of the ceiling supports, before being entirely covered in black gunpowder. Turpentine from the naval stores was poured across the floor to aid in the spreading of the fire, its pungent odour so overpowering that the men could hardly breathe.

'There'll be quite a display when this lot goes up,' said Troubridge, when he was satisfied. Then he ordered them outside, where they gratefully sucked in mouthfuls of air. All around the arc of the Petite Rade, guns were blazing. Through the drifting smoke, highlighted by leaping flames, Markham saw that the final battle for Fort l'Eguillette was in progress, with boats off the stone bastions, taking the last of the defenders to safety.

'Best get your men back to la Malgue. Your buffoon is there, boasting away as to how he's going to sink every ship in the harbour.'

They fought their way back through the crowds, Markham praying that those in the Picard house had found the sense to depart. The Toulon merchant had several boats of his own, and in Rossignol, a source of information which should have given him ample warning. He could only hope that they'd take off Celeste as well. At that moment the arsenal went up with an enormous blast of sound and fury, which added to the increased screams of the poor people around him, and wiped any thoughts of Rossignol, his family and his charges from his mind.

*

'I would be happier without the Dons, myself,' said the Chevalier. 'But Admiral Langara offered to do the job without us, and Hood had to argue hard that we should share the duty. Langara wasn't pleased, and I thought that Colonel Serota was about to get a sword in his ribs for the way he addressed His Lordship.'

'But we're not actually working together?' said Markham, the only man aboard who'd had that unfortunate experience.

'No, thank God. And if they operate in their usual dilatory manner, we might find we have to take over some of their duties.'

The cabin of the *Swallow* could barely contain the number of officers present. Sixteen in all, including two commanders, there was not one of them over the age of twenty-one, which made Markham feel like an old man. None of the condescension he'd been exposed to in the past was present here. Either they were too young to know or care, too buoyed up with the excitement of what they were being asked to do, or Sir Sydney Smith's introduction, which would not have disgraced the Grand Cham of Tartary himself for fulsomeness, had quelled any doubts they had about him.

The drawing on the table showed every feature of the harbours and the inner basin, with each French ship named. Those containing powder, and due to be sunk by the Dons, were coloured red, and were to be avoided at all costs. Smith was issuing instructions to the sailors about getting the ships they were going to burn into a position that would inflict the most damage on the stationary fleet. Since his job was to stay with the Chevalier, and to provide protection for the entire party against any kind of attack, these details didn't really concern him.

His men sat on the equally crowded deck, checking their equipment over and over again. Going round each one, he issued a quiet encouragement that he realised carried more than a touch of King Harry in the night. But

312

they were names now, not just faces. He wondered if they had come to trust him, but had no way to ask. Not even Rannoch, who'd mellowed to point where he felt free to exercise a degree of irony, would have answered that question.

By the rail, as they sailed past la Malgue, he fingered the parchment in his pocket, the note from a gloating Hanger accepting his apology, and the addendum that announced his forthcoming engagement to Miss Elizabeth Gordon. Ashore, a steady stream of Toulonais were edging up the gangplank onto the British men o' war, bundles too big to be accommodated being unceremoniously thrown aside, to land in the sea with a great splash. The collective misery of these people seemed to waft across the still waters as they played out the last act of their drama. The aims of the revolution they so feared were being applied here. Neither wealth nor position could guarantee security. Places aboard these ships were going to the first person in the long straggling queue.

Markham turned away from that miserable scene, towards the darkened area of the Petite Rade. He could just see the departing warships, their great white sails billowing as they took the wind. They were leaving. But the *Swallow*, with the brig *Union* in company, was heading to perform the coda to the long drama which had been the siege of Toulon.

# Chapter twenty-two

Silence had to be observed as they passed through the gap between Fort l'Eguillette and the Grosse Tour, but with so much light close to the western fortifications, as the French struggled to get their guns into place, they stood in little danger of being seen. The whole waterfront was still crowded, and over the sea came the sound of people singing. It was too early for the Revolution to have taken full control of the city, but no doubt those elements who were either true to its tenets, or determined to appear so, were busy making merry. There would be looting and robbery a'plenty. And that, with people like Fouquert on the way, was just a prelude to a river of blood.

Once they were within the Petite Rade, Smith's little flotilla headed for the dockyard, while the Spaniards working from the shore were responsible for the main concentration of French ships, berthed in the inner basin. Aloft, a sailor was looking at the tops of the three ships of the line waiting to load at la Malgue, their limp sails reflecting the torchlight from the battlements.

Once they completed their assignments, the storehouses would be fired, which would be the signal for the final detachments of the rearguard to embark. Then the men of the *Swallow*, seeing those topsails fill with wind, could complete their mission. It was an eerie feeling, with the noises from the shore muted, and every one of the Hebes felt it. Here they were, in the midst of turmoil, suspended on a calm stretch of water, with only the faint glimmer of reflected light picking out their faces.

'*Robust* signalling, sir,' the lookout called. A flare shot into the sky to seawards, as an added aid to the man's eyesight. The dull boom of explosions, as the underground storerooms of the forts were destroyed, followed immediately. Flames began to lick at the furthermost dockyard buildings as the fires took hold, igniting creosote, turpentine, oils and ropes, barrels of salted meat, canvas for sails, yards, masts and all the myriad other items needed to supply a fleet. Soon the whole area between the Grande and Petite Rades was a mass of flames, with billowing clouds of black and grey smoke rising into the night sky. The outlines of the ships of the French fleet stood stark against this glowing background, providing just the level of light Smith needed to do his work.

The explosion, coming from an entirely different direction, sent a shockwave across the harbour that nearly threw the *Swallow* on its beam ends. The brig *Union*, further inshore and closer to the source, was blown apart, its crew thrown bodily into the water. A great fiery cloud erupted into the night sky like a mushroom of red, yellow and gold. Bits of ship mingled with the flaming holocaust, and the skeleton of the shattered hull was ablaze from end to end. Scraps of burning canvas covered the sky like stars, then dropped like spills of paper, to be extinguished in the waters of the harbour.

'They've blown the bloody *Iris*,' Markham heard Smith shout. Searching his mind, he recalled that she was one of the ships, marked in red on the Chevalier's map, that was laden with gunpowder. He knew the plan had been to sink her, since fired it was more of a danger to the Allies than the French. For obvious reasons, she was moored well away from any other vessels, so those heading for the dockyard were the only ones to suffer. 'Get one of the boats over the side and see if any of the *Union*'s men are alive.'

Smith had taken the wheel himself, and aimed the

*Swallow* for the stern of the nearest French ship of the line, the 120-gun *Dauphin Royal*. Moored as they were, bulwark to bulwark, with the cold, light breeze coming in off the sea, setting just that one ship ablaze would destroy a dozen more. Markham made his way to the bows, followed by his men. He was thus the first to see the muskets on the poop of the *Dauphin Royal*, which were pointing in his direction. His shouts to Smith brought the Chevalier running to join him, his Swedish star flashing as it picked up the glow from the wall of flames dead ahead.

'Who the hell are they?'

'They can't be Frenchmen, sir, not yet. But whoever they are, it looks as though they're waiting for us.'

'Do we know if she has got guns?' asked Rannoch.

'It makes no odds,' Smith replied. 'All the line-of-battle ships were stripped of their powder.'

They opened up with a volley of musket fire, peppering the woodwork and the sea around the *Swallow*. It wasn't deadly by any means, but it promised to be so if they got any closer.

Smith was angry. 'The Dons were supposed to make sure none of those ships were boarded. And they were also instructed to scuttle the *Iris*, not blow her up.'

'We were mighty close to that when it happened,' said Markham. 'Another half minute, and we would have been blown apart like the *Union*.'

'Helmsman!' Smith yelled, as another group of musket balls peppered the side. 'Bring us about and head for the inner basin.'

'Aye, aye sir.'

A last volley of musketry hit them as they spun round. There was too little wind, and with only topsails drawing they crawled across the anchorage. The opening to the basin was narrow, no more than a hundred feet across. French ships were moored along the inner side of the twin moles that protected the dry-docks and slipways of the Toulon yard. These were the hulls refitting, not ready for sea, but no less dangerous as a long-term threat than those moored in the deeper water of the Petite Rade.

Smith was at the side of the ship, a telescope to his eye, using the burning hulk of the *Iris* as an aid to his sight. Her cables had either been blown apart or burnt through, so the flaming hull was drifting out into the middle of the harbour. They heard the hissing sound as she heeled over, the water beginning to enter her hull.

'Thank the Lord. She's not going to collide with the *Montréal*, he said, as Markham aproached his side. 'Which, if there are Spaniards aboard, is a mixed blessing.'

'I don't follow.'

'She's the second powder ship. They're supposed to sink her too.' The burning hull of the *Iris* tilted to one side, throwing a sudden flash of illumination across the harbour, one that lit up the deck of the *Montréal*. 'There are men aboard her, I can see them moving.'

Both Markham and Smith were thrown to the deck as the *Swallow* stopped dead in the water, right between the outer edges of the twin stone walls that formed the entrance to the inner basin. Within seconds the ship was going backwards. Smith leapt to his feet, running to the bows, and was just in time to see the boom that had been placed across the mouth sink back into the blackness beneath.

'What happened?'

When he turned to face Markham, Smith had lost all of his urbanity. His eyes were wild, and he replied with a snarl. 'We've been betrayed, Markham, that's what has happened. The only people who could have put a boom across the harbour mouth without us knowing are the Spanish.'

'Why?'

'I don't know, man. But I do know this. I'm not leaving here with all these ships intact, Dons or no Dons.' He shouted to the helmsman again. 'Lay me alongside the mole.'

Men rushed to man the falls as an officer by the wheel shouted out the requisite orders. The ship found way, then as she swung round the falls were sheeted home again to carry her in on the breeze until her larboard bow scraped the granite. Men leapt from the bowsprit to land heavily on the *pavé* that formed a roadway from the quay. Lines were thrown to haul the *Swallow* in until she touched amidships. A cable was thrown next, wrapped round a bollard to warp in her stern. As soon as he was alongside, Smith yelled his orders, sending his shore party, with their combustibles, towards the nearest two 74-gun ships.

'Markham, get your men into a boat. Row for the *Montréal*.'

'I doubt my men will be much good in a boat, sir.'

'I have no choice, man. You are the only armed party at my disposal. The Dons are on that ship. For all I know they may be trying to scuttle her, and if they are, leave them be. They may, God knows why, be intent on blowing her up as well. What worries me is that they will do nothing, and just leave all that powder for the French to salvage. You must prevent that. Shoot them if necessary. I want that ship at the bottom, and if you all have to go down with her then you'll just have to climb the masts until I can come and get you.'

'Sir?'

'No ifs and buts, Markham. Just move.'

He was gone, over the side, landing on the stones and rolling over onto his feet, almost running before he was upright and heading for the stern of the closest ship.

'Halsey!'

'Sir?'

'Get that damned boat we're towing alongside. Lobsters to give their weapons to the Bullocks and man the oars.'

'All we require now,' said Rannoch, looking at the starlit sky, 'is a bloody fiddler.'

\*

It wasn't pretty, nor was it smooth. But the Lobsters had all rowed in their time, so progress was decent. Markham called for them to be silent as they got close, and the boat, still with some momentum, drifted towards the side of the *Montréal*. Markham tapped Halsey gently on the shoulder.

'Who's the best man aloft?'

'Leech is pretty handy, and his leg is as good as ever.'

'Pass word to him. As soon as we get aboard, he's to get up into the rigging and keep an eye out for the Chevalier.' The side of the ship was deserted, and though he listened he could hear no sound of either voice or movement. That was odd, since Smith had said quite clearly that there were men aboard. He cursed under his breath, knowing that there was a method of doing this, honed by years of boarding practice, which every marine officer would have been trained for. But he wasn't a marine officer.

'Have you ever done this before, Halsey?'

'No, sir. Nor has anyone else, that I'm aware. But generally, the trick is to board forward, using the chains or the catheads.'

'Row for the side,' he called gently. 'Leech, this is going to be untidy. You get aboard on your own as soon as we touch. If you wait for the rest of us it will be dawn.'

'Straight to the cap, sir?'

'If you please.'

They hit the side about half a dozen times before anyone got a hold. Leech was already gone. He'd taken his shoes off and as soon as the boat skirted the side he seemed to run up the planking. It was only when they were past it that Markham saw the rope hanging down from the shrouds. Looking up, he saw the white soles of his feet disappearing up those same knotted ropes, which ran like a ladder from the side of the ship to the tops.

He'd seen men do that whenever they set sail, but it was not something he ever fancied trying himself.

Tully grabbed at another line and missed, falling head-first into the water, only saved from going right overboard by the grip Gibbons took on his belt. Finally Dymock stood up under the cathead, grabbing hold of one of the ropes that hung from the great square block of wood that protruded from the side of the vessel.

'Right, up we go,' Markham called. No-one moved, but many a pale face was turned in his direction. Cursing, he stood up, took off his sword, handed his pistol to Yelland, and jumped. That action, rocking the boat, took all the momentum out of his effort. He did grab one rope and, by a mighty effort, got one foot over the beam. But it was damp from rain and slime, so he could feel himself slipping. Hands pressed into his back and pushed him higher. Looking over his shoulder he just glimpsed the bald head of Schutte.

That help allowed him to get both legs on top, the rest of his body following. Standing up, he staggered along the cathead till he could leap over the side. Looking along the deck, which seemed empty, left him wondering if Sir Sydney had been imagining things. But that thought had to be put aside. He had to get his men aboard and he wasn't quite sure how to do it. Walking along the side of the ship, he finally spied what he was after: the point where the bulwark could be removed to provide a gang-way, and below that the neat line of wooden steps attached to the ship's side.

'Back here,' he called softly. The pegs that held the gangway in place wouldn't budge, which obliged him to use a marlinspike, and that negated any attempt he'd made to maintain silence. Finally they came out, and he was able to open it. The men arrived at the same time and clambered aboard untidily, some with their weapons and some without.

'Make sure to tie that boat up,' he called.

'Please do, Lieutenant.'

Markham spun round and found himself faced with a line of raised muskets, all in the hands of Spanish soldiers. Serota coughed before continuing. 'After all, my men can use it to get ashore in more comfort. Our boat was exceedingly crowded on the way out.'

He had a hope, a faint one, that Hollick, who was still in the boat, would have the sense to stay quiet. But he called up, curious at the sudden stillness, his questions dying in his throat as a pair of guns were aimed over the side at his head.

'Best come aboard, Hollick.'

'Your weapons, please,' said Serota. 'Then I'd be obliged if you'd line up behind the wheel.'

'You're supposed to be on our side, Serota.'

'Am I, Lieutenant?' he coughed. 'Next you'll be telling me that I am, like Colonel Hanger, a traitor.'

'I didn't know you'd heard.'

'I didn't. But I could hardly fail to be informed of the accusation you made against such a fine upstanding officer.'

Markham spotted the deliberate irony in Serota's tone. 'If you see yourself in the same way, I can't fault the sentiment.'

'That is because you are English.'

'Irish, if you don't mind.'

'Please,' he said, waving the pistol in his hand. Markham nodded to his men, who moved backwards slowly, covered by the Spanish muskets. 'You should have stayed where you were, Lieutenant, though with a little luck it will make no difference.'

A sudden whoosh of fire made both men turn. They saw the flames shoot up the side of the warship's rigging like some animal speeding to safety. In the light they provided, they could see Smith's men running around, torching everything they could, while in the background the rows of warehouses burned steadily. Gunfire was coming from the town itself, as the rearguard made a disciplined withdrawal.

'A pity,' said Serota. 'That is a fine seventy-four-gun ship.'

'It's a French seventy-four.'

'Yes.' He started to cough, this time enough to make his body shake, waving his pistol. 'Always the same with smoke.'

Markham was looking at his men, now being tied to the taffrail. A cold sensation, made up of fear and imagination, gripped him. 'Sure, I hope it chokes you.'

Two soldiers grabbed him and tied his hands. Then they dragged him towards the wheel and lashed him to it, so that he was facing the row of Lobsters and Bullocks he'd led aboard. Leech wasn't there, and the temptation to look aloft was almost unbearable. He had to know what was going to happen; prayed that the Spaniard's voice would carry to the only hope they all had of survival.

'Am I allowed to ask why?'

'Let us just say that I am a Spanish patriot.'

'I'm Irish, remember. I'll need more than that.'

'Do you really think we would want the only complete fleet in the Mediterranean to belong to the English? Can you not see where that would leave Spain?'

'As an ally, no.'

'But we are not allies by nature, Lieutenant. And it is a prudent man who looks to the future, who sees a day when we might be enemies once more, glad that there is a French navy big enough to help us defeat you.'

'I'm wondering who the prudent man might be. Langara? Admiral Gravina? Or is it just you?'

'Mention Gibraltar to any Spaniard.'

'So it's all of you?'

'Sentiments vary, as do notions of honour. Some men act, while other merely choose not to see.'

'And what's my fate to be?'

'Come, Lieutenant Markham. No care for the fate of your men? Is that not the first duty of an officer?' He grinned, exposing long, yellow teeth. 'You might die from suffocation, or even burning. But it is my guess that when this ship, which is full of gunpowder, goes up, you will go with it. And if we can time the fuses right, we shall also extinguish the brilliant career of that idiot, Sydney Smith.'

The sound of gunfire had increased. 'As you can hear, the Republican forces are taking over the town. Soon they will be on the quayside, then out on the harbour wall, and that man who brought you here will be forced to flee. As he goes by the *Montréal* . . .' He threw his arm in the air. 'Whoosh. A French fleet with no powder won't be tempted to pursue. But the real bonus will be no more Smith and no more Markham.

He spun round and started giving orders. Men rushed below, while others headed for the boats. Serota had gone to the side, and was listening intently to the gunfire. At the moment he judged it to be close enough, he called out the order to fire the fuses.

'Am I allowed one more question, Colonel?'

He sniffed loudly at the acrid odour of slowmatch coming up the companionway. 'One more, and only if the answer is short.'

'The night we attacked Bonaparte's guns, where were you?'

'To the north of you, Lieutenant. Near the redoubt of La Seyne. Just close enough to ensure a proper outcome.'

'Do you believe in God?'

'That's another question, Markham,' he said, as he made his way back to the side of the ship. The effect he sought was somewhat spoiled by the weakness of his voice. But it was, nevertheless, very like a battle cry. 'But I'll answer it anyway. I am just like God. Both he and I believe in Spain.'

His body disappeared over the side, and just before his

head followed he said, 'Goodbye, Lieutenant Markham. I hope you believe in God.'

'What about Leech?' whispered Rannoch.

'Quiet. Let them get well away from the side.'

'I do not know if you have noticed, but we are a little short of time.'

Markham wasn't listening. He was wondering how many of his men could swim. Not all of them, that was certain, so just untying them would not be enough. They had to find a way of staying afloat in the water. The deck was untidy, littered with barrels, ropes and yardarms, seasoned lengths of timber that normally held the smaller sails. The flash of white made him look up. Leech slid down the blind side shrouds without making a sound. He crouched below the level of the bulwarks and slithered across the deck, his bayonet coming out before he reached Markham.

'God be praised they didn't see you,' whispered Markham as Leech stuck the point of his bayonet in the knot and began to lever it open.

Markham was free, the ropes half sliced and half untied, and he scurried for the companionway immediately. The smoke from the fuses billowed up at him as he tried to go below, stinging his eyes and burning his throat. Four steps down he couldn't breathe and had to retreat. On deck Leech was still silently trying to undo his mates, while Rannoch and Halsey had run to retrieve their own bayonets. Looking over the side, he could see Serota and his men, in both the boats, rowing for the shore.

'Who can swim?' he called, since they were now far enough away not to hear. Three voices answered: Schutte, Ettrick and Dornan. 'Right, that makes four. Rannoch, Schutte, get hold of this yardarm, and heave it over the side. Ettrick, Dornan, into the water and hold it close enough to the side for those jumping to reach it. Schutte, you get in the water too, and make sure you get hold of anyone who goes under.'

A sudden fusillade made him turn to the shore. By the light of the burning ships he could see the *Swallow* casting off, men poling furiously to get her clear of the mole. Others were aloft, letting drop the sails that they hoped would take them out of danger. A sudden brilliant flash highlighted Smith's star. He was by the stern rail, directing musket fire at the party of soldiers trying to make their way towards the ship. As they got clear, Markham realised that *Swallow*'s bowsprit was headed straight at the *Montréal*, with the Chevalier clearly intent on sailing by to pick up him and his men.

'Fire, for Christ's sake, someone start a fire. We've got to make the *Swallow* sheer off.'

There was an oil lamp by the binnacle. Halsey grabbed it and emptied it onto an untidy pile of canvas and frayed ropes. Then he bent down, pulling out his flints. He was rubbing wildly when Rannoch pushed him aside, laid his gun by the oil and pulled the trigger. Halsey jumped back as the ball shot forth, but the Highlander had achieved his intention. The flash from the pan lit the oil, and as the fire took hold it spread rapidly, snaking across the deck. Markham grabbed one end of the tarred rope and pulled it along the deck, looping an end round the square, knotted shrouds.

'Over the side, all of you. This bloody thing is going to go up in about five minutes.'

The yard went first, hitting the water point first and sinking like an arrow, which induced the same emotion in Markham's heart. But it bobbed up quickly about twenty yards away. Ettrick and Dornan had taken off their coats and belts, then kicked off their boots, transferring the few personal possessions they could manage to the crutch of their breeches. They jumped out as far as they could, then swam to the log of floating wood, pulling it in close to the side. By that time Schutte was in the water himself, having thrown in several barrels to help those who needed to float independently.

'Get your coats off. And that goes for belts, cartouches and anything else that's heavy, including boots. They're no good to you now. If you're going to keep anything, make sure it's light.'

The thud of falling kit was not followed by any enthusiastic rush to the side; the men seemed more intent on stuffing pipes, tobacco and what little money they had into their breeches. Rannoch, Halsey and Markham had to push men towards the possibility of salvation. In some cases blows were needed. Behind them the rigging had started to burn, and as the flames touched the first corner of a sail, that went up, illuminating the upperworks. The smoke coming from below was beginning to choke those still by the rail. In the water men went under, then resurfaced. If they were close enough to the yardarm they grabbed it. If not they sank again. Schutte was diving and grabbing, showing scant gentleness as he hauled men to the surface and pushed them towards the wood. Ettrick and Dornan had to yell at them to take a tight hold, one man at a time either side, or risk the whole thing rolling so much that all the non-swimmers would drown.

Markham tossed the last ranker, Leech, overboard, then turned to his two NCOs. 'Over you go, both of you.'

Halsey complied, his fingers holding his broad nose, and his eyes closed as he jumped. But Rannoch spun round and ran towards the entry port, returning with Markham's sword and his own musket.

'It has taken me years to get a proper stock fitted to my Brown Bess, I will not leave it now.'

'You're a damn fool. Hanging on to that could kill you.'

'Don't worry,' he said, handing over the sword. 'I'll let it go if I am drowning. Do you want this?'

'I'd better,' Markham replied. He managed a smile, which in the flickering light made him look slightly deranged. 'Jesus, I haven't paid for the damned thing yet.'

Rannoch laughed out loud as he jumped, landing with a mighty splash right alongside the log. Markham looked over the other side, glad to see that *Swallow* had spotted the danger and sheered off, and was heading away from the *Montréal* as fast as the light breeze would allow. Then, sword in hand, he followed his men.

'Kick with your feet, all of you,' he yelled taking in a mouthful of seawater as he sank slightly. Nothing happpened at first; they seemed stuck to a point ten feet away from the side of the ship. But slowly their strokes had an effect, and the log began to move, The *Montréal* was well alight now, flames licking through the rigging and the smoke from the fuses hanging like a cloud over the deck. They were only halfway to the shore when the first dull boom of an explosion came at them through the water. Contained by the ship's planking, the force went upwards, removing half the deck. The rest followed as the vessel literally blew itself apart. They could feel the shockwaves in the water, pushing into them. Bits of wood rained down from a fire-filled sky. Leech let go and slid under, but Markham managed to grab his shirt and haul him back up.

'Stay afloat, you bastard, or I'll break your other bloody leg.'

# Chapter twenty-three

They emerged from the water like half-drowned rats, onto a strand of beach well to the west of the main quay. There were crowds here too, many carrying flickering torches which added a hellish quality to the miserable scene. Some cried, others wailed. The majority shouted into the blackness of the harbour, as if the means to rescue them lay just out of sight. They'd been driven to the water's edge like lemmings, fearful of what awaited them when the Jacobins came. Stories of what they'd done with the guillotine in Marseilles had grown with every league they'd travelled, and since the cruelty had been enormous, the entire population was in a state of uncontrolled panic. Markham, counting off his men, wasn't panicking, but he was worried.

'We've got to get to the Fort de la Malgue, and hope that some of the rearguard are still there.'

'The French are between them and us,' said Halsey, pointing towards the basin and the line of enemy war-ships, only a few of which were burning. His pepper and salt hair was black now, and streaked across his face, rendering his pallid complexion more startling.

'Rannoch?'

'Present,' replied the Scotsman.

Peering through the tight group of men, Markham saw his sergeant sitting down, water dripping from his long blond hair into his lap, assiduously using a piece of cloth he'd found, trying to dry the firing parts of his musket.

'Come on, or we'll end up in a French dungeon.'

'No spare flints, God be damned,' he cursed, before

turning to look at the soaked, shivering party. 'Did any of you lot think to line your private parts with a set of flints?'

The look in Rannoch's eyes underscored the futility of the question. Whatever these men had saved in the way of personal possessions, it wouldn't include anything to do with soldiering. But just as guilty himself, he could hardly berate them. He jumped to his feet, looking over Markham's head towards la Malgue. 'If you do not mind me saying so, I see no sign of any topsails where our ships once lay.'

'There may be some still berthed there, a sloop perhaps.'

'With respect, if you look at the route we would have to follow, there are thousands of these poor souls in the way. What we require to get away is a boat.'

Goaded by Rannoch's ponderous delivery, Markham made no attempt to disguise the exasperation in his voice. 'If you find the magic potion to conjure one up, don't let me hinder you.'

'I do not think a display of temper will do us much good. Did you see where that Spaniard went with our own cutter?'

Markham tried to match his sarcasm. 'It was difficult, Sergeant. My head was under water.'

Rannoch beamed at him, the flickering light making his green eyes twinkle amongst the creases in his face. 'Not as much as mine, it was not.'

'We have to try,' said Halsey. 'And the longer we wait the worse it will be.'

'Seawater clearly does something to improve the brains of Lobsters,' Rannoch replied. 'Do you think you can do the next bit and walk along the sea-bed?'

'Only if you drink all the water in the harbour. And what with you being a greedy Jock, that should be easy.'

Some of the others had started to chuckle. Then, as the absurdity of doing that in their present state took hold, it turned to general amusement. Without knowing why, Markham found himself laughing too. The people around them, fearful and abandoned, looked upon these sopping wet madmen with pity.

'On your feet.'

They obeyed, but the giggling didn't stop. Looking back at them staggering along, elbowing each other, sharing a very private joke, Markham thought they looked like a bunch of witless fools. When they reached the quay the numbers of refugees thickened considerably. The crush was so great that those by the water's edge were being bundled into the harbour, now completely clear of boats. Any attempt to help them only endangered the Samaritan, so that those who couldn't fend for themselves in the water, men, women and children, were left to drown.

As an organised party, they carved a path through the mob in a way denied to most, and benign fate did not let them see how that barging and shoving impacted in other places. It was Schutte, a fraction taller than Rannoch, who picked up the hint of approaching danger. It was heralded by distant screaming, mingled with the odd crash of a shot; that overborne, closer to them, by loud singing, a rendering of the 'Ça ira' with those right ahead seeking mercy by cloaking themselves in the anthem of the Revolution. Schutte's warning was louder still, and the group used their strength to get off the quay, throwing less fortunate people out of the alleys so that they could escape.

'Have you seen where we are, sir?' said Tully. The bandage he'd worn on his ear had come off, leaving the scabbed wound on his lobe exposed. 'It's the bloody Picard house.'

'Jesus, Mary and Joseph, you're right.'

Markham was tired, and nothing underlined that more than the use of such an avowedly Papist curse. That, and the way he'd missed this familiar building. But then no-one else other than Tully had seen it, which indicated that they were in a similar state. The boom of musket fire reverberated off the high walls, so that they could almost feel it physically. The Jacobin army was between them and the Fort de la Malgue. And even if they could get there, it wasn't certain that they'd find a ship. They needed rest, a place to hide, and they needed it now. Being close to a building they knew so well, it seemed stupid to go on.

'We'll have to go in through the back. There are too many people at the front.'

No-one even grunted an acknowledgement. They fought their way up the side alley in single file, till they found themselves in the street that ran along the rear of Picard's property. The crush was as bad in this, the more open space of the boulevard. But people were trying to move in both directions, seeking security with only the vaguest notion of where it lay. Slowly they made their way till the whole party was pressed against the wide double doors. They were bolted and chained, and it seemed no amount of pushing would budge them.

'Saving your presence, sir,' said Quinlan, bowing his head to shorten even his limited stature. 'I think this is a job for Ettrick and me.'

Markham hesitated. But Rannoch's soft voice, right by his ear, was confident. 'They are a right pair of villains, sir. I do not know an officer's mess that they have not robbed.'

This was new to him. But then, he had nothing to steal. 'As you will.'

Ettrick put his back to the wooden door and held his hands like a cup. Quinlan was on it and up in a move that would have done credit to an acrobat. The gap at the top of the door looked far too small to allow a human being passage, but Quinlan, once he got his head and shoulders through, wriggled like an angry snake till a full three-quarters of his body was hidden. Then, somehow, he managed to turn sideways, so that when he brought his legs through he could use his hands to lower himself to within a few feet of the ground.

'There you are, sir,' whispered Rannoch. 'Those two have drunk more good claret in their time than any officer in Farmer George's army.'

'We calls Quinlan the mouse,' said Ettrick, with some pride.

'He still has to unbolt the door.'

'Never fear for that, your honour,' Ettrick scoffed. 'Locks are no more strangers to him than floorboard cracks. He has his picks snug in his breeches, right by his most precious parts.'

The door creaked as they swung open, with Markham wondering how he hadn't seen more of this sort of thing before, then consoling himself with the thought that part of their expertise would be in avoiding any recognition of their skills. Rossignol's doorless coach still filled the rear courtyard, and he led the way as they skirted round it. The rear doors were open, and he was just about to go through, when he heard the unmistakable voice, accompanied by the slight hacking cough, of Colonel Serota. His hand flew up so quickly that everyone behind him froze.

'It is nothing personal, Rossignol. It is merely that you are a loose end that requires to be tidied. Everyone in this house knows of my association with you. Even the boy could recover one day and tell the world of this little deception.'

When Rossignol replied, Markham could not help but admire him. Clearly he was in mortal danger, but there wasn't even a hint of fear in his voice. 'Naturally, Colonel, I understand your concern. But you must realise that Monsieur Fouquert, having ample evidence of the valuable services I can provide to the cause, will be most unhappy should anything untoward befall me or my family. You may find that it is I who need to intercede on your behalf, since your function, indeed your usefulness to the Revolution in Toulon, ended with the siege.'

'You are such a brilliant talker, Rossignol, that killing you will provide me with no pleasure whatsoever.'

'Then why do it?'

'I cannot have my country branded treacherous.'

'Even if it is true?'

The note of levity in Serota's voice evaporated. 'You are careless with your tongue, Rossignol.'

'I have secreted certain papers, Colonel, that will tell all who wish to know just how much they can trust Spain as an ally.'

Markham knew it was the wrong thing to say long before Rossignol finished speaking. A bluff too far. He burst through the open door just as the shot rang out, sword extended and yelling like a banshee. Rossignol had taken the ball in the chest, the weight of the shot throwing him backwards, so that Markham cannoned into his falling body, holding it upright while he registered the shock in the Spaniard's face. The two men escorting him were in more control of themselves, and had lowered their muskets to shoot, waiting only for this rescuer to come out from behind the already dying Rossignol.

But Serota had no intention of delaying. And the click of Rannoch's musket, misfiring on his soaked flints, was all he needed to convince him that discretion was the better part of valour. He turned, his pistol still smoking, and headed out into the courtyard, ordering his men to cover his retreat.

Markham was stuck, his only protection Rossignol's body. And the old man was failing, his legs beginning to bend so that he had to be supported just to remain a shield. What hit Markham's shoulder was so overwhelming that both he and Rossignol were swept aside. Rannoch, with one of the coach doors held out in front of him, charged at the two Spaniards.

Common sense would have had them holding fire, to let the man pass by so that he could be shot in the back. But that was a hard concept to hold to when faced with a piece of solid wood travelling at ten miles an hour, a door which emitted the stirring yet eerie battle cry of a puissant Scottish clan. Their shots splintered the wood, and slowed the Highlander a fraction. But it was no more than that, and when he was abreast of them he used the door to fell one Spaniard, before turning on the other and grabbing him round the neck with his bare hands. The bone went in what seemed like an instant, and the victim crumpled to the floor with Rannoch's hands still around his limp neck. The man struggling to get out from under the door was dealt with by a vicious back-handed swipe that, with every ounce of the Scotsman's strength in it, smashed the side of his face.

It was Rannoch's turn to be brushed aside, as Markham went after Serota, sword extended once more as he crashed through the courtyard doors. The Colonel should have shut and barred the entrance to the warehouse. But a combination of panic and insecurity, brought on by the sight of a man who should have been dead, had made that obvious precaution seem superfluous. He'd run right through, and was scrabbling at the outer door, his fingers dragging at the bolts. His breath came in great gasps which seemed to sear his hollow chest.

The door swung open, to reveal a solid wall of human flesh, the refugees who filled the quays, which for Serota made escape impossible. The thought of trying to plough his way through that mob clearly terrified him more than the idea of going back. It took all his strength to shut the door again, and had those pressed against it been more alert he would have failed. But he got the bolts home, turned round, and saw the scruffy, barely dry figure of George Markham in the doorway, knees bent, sword extended, inviting him to fight.

'You may give me your sword if you wish, Colonel Serota.'

The Spaniard was on the first rung of the stairs before Markham finished speaking, his boots pounding on the wooden treads as he shot up to the first floor. Markham followed cautiously, well aware that his quarry had even less chance of finding a way out on the upper floors than he did on the ground. He heard the high boots echoing on the bare floorboards above his head; was slightly bewildered when that noise ceased, even more mystified when he exited onto the floor his men had used as a billet. There were more stairs, of course, on the far side of the chamber, which led up the top level, an area he'd never visited.

He was just about to cross to them when he heard Serota's footsteps coming down. Taking station with his back to the double doors that formed the loading bay, he waited, sword by his side, while the Spaniard descended, the lantern he held forming a pool of light around his feet. The long cavalry boots appeared first, then his thighs. It was only when he got down to the level of his waist that Markham realised how much trouble he was in. So much danger that he pressed back against the doors, feeling through his still damp shirt the cold chain that held them closed.

'You're a hard man to kill, Markham. The flares at Mulgrave were meant to destroy your command. But this one is just for you.'

'It can't be done, Serota,' said Markham, his eyes fixed on the point of the flare, which protruded no more than an inch from the end of the firing tube. He was a good thirty feet away from the Spaniard, and in between him and the steps lay several of the makeshift cots of his Bullocks. He knew that it didn't actually have to hit him. If it exploded close enough to his body, he would certainly be maimed, if not killed outright. 'Light that fuse, and you will be in as much danger as I am.'

335

'Do you know, Lieutenant, that at this moment you sound just like that scoundrel Rossignol? Lies come so easily to your lips. Death, I'm afraid, is sure to follow, just as it did to him.'

'Did this warehouse provide the flares when we attacked Bonaparte's guns as well?'

'I have never known a man on the edge of perdition who asked so many questions.'

'It's a bad habit. I'm so fond of it, I'd like to keep it.'

'The Irish have a reputation for being amusing.'

'There are a dozen men downstairs. They won't let you pass.'

Serota waved the open lantern at the truncated trail of fuse which hung from the edge of the rocket, cut so that it would go off in seconds. 'Then you must order them to do so.'

'I'm sorry, Colonel, I can't do that. You are a man who has betrayed more than your allies. You even butchered your own men in that useless attack on the Batterie de Bregaillon. I don't know Spain, which you claim to represent. But there's hardly a doubt in my mind that most of the people who live there would be deeply ashamed of what you've done. I think they'd like to see a garotte round your scrawny yellow neck as much as I would.'

Serota moved to the side of the rocket tube, and shifted the lantern till the candle touched the fuse. He was on his heels, anticipating the moment when Markham would try to rush him. Instead the cold indifferent stare from that quarter induced confusion, forcing him to look at the weapon he'd chosen to assure himself it had no faults. If he saw Markham's hand behind his back it didn't register. He was looking down at the short spluttering fuse, giving it more attention than his intended victim.

There is a point, when setting off a rocket, as the fuse enters the body of the piece, a moment when it seems to go silent. That is the very second at which it fires. It did so now, throwing Serota backwards as the flames shot out of the rear. He lifted his head to look at his victim, and the bang as the rocket smashed into the double doors threw him momentarily. They were blown open, crashing against the outer walls. Within the blink of an eye the flare exploded, lighting up the whole of the quay and the harbour. But then the doors swung back, to reveal his intended victim, whole and unscathed, stretched out on the floor.

Serota didn't know his uniform was alight, smouldering where the flames had scorched it, didn't know as he rushed at Markham that he trailed smoke behind him. His sword was out, intent on impaling the Irishman. He cut hard enough to throw Serota back. The yellow teeth were bared, the eyes maddened and the breath rasping. Serota was beyond any sense, and seemed to run himself on to Markham's sword rather than take avoiding action.

Rannoch's head came level with the top of the stairs as the Spaniard crumpled in a heap at Markham's feet. 'There was a moment there, sir, when I have to admit you had me worried. But you Irishmen, when it comes to danger, have a luck we Scotsmen lack.'

Markham, panting more from relief than effort, pulled his sword from Serota's hollow chest.

'Then why is it, Rannoch, that when the Scots are con-. quered in battle, they end up, within a decade, running the whole bloody British government?'

'Might it be brains, do you think?' the Scotsman replied, as he began to remove Serota's boots.

They'd carried Rossignol into the study and laid him on a chaise. He was breathing heavily, with Pascalle kneeling, weeping, at his feet. Eveline stood by one wall clutching and unclutching her hands, her eyes unfocussed, like someone whose world had fallen apart. Celeste held Jean-Baptiste's hand, he alone unaware of what was happening. Markham had Rannoch lead Pascalle away, then knelt to examine the wound. Then he took the hand that the old man waveringly extended.

'There was no malice, Lieutenant,' Rossignol whispered. 'I hope you know that.'

'Yes. I do.'

'But I did lie to you many times.' His eyes shut suddenly, his chest swelled, and a rasping noise came from this throat. But it didn't stop him talking. 'You thought you'd found me out, but I merely had to use one lie to disguise another.'

'Sure, if I had a coin for every lie I've told, I'd own half of County Wexford.'

Rossignol didn't understand, and the confusion showed on his face. 'Serota never believed in the boy. But neither did you.'

'Hanger?'

His voice gurgled as he replied, almost as if he were trying to laugh. 'Him, yes. I count your Colonel as a success. His vanity was the greatest. That is my supreme asset, the vanity of others. No one flatters a man more than he will flatter himself. Once I have found the key to that, people make themselves my hostage. And they are so happy. The Picards were even delighted that you were not part of our shared secret. It is like conjuring, letting each person know only that which they need.'

'Yet it all ends in tragedy, as it has here. And something tells me, Rossignol, that this isn't the first time.'

'It is the nature of my life. And time is an enemy. Perhaps I spent too long in Toulon. One small untruth must be used to support another. Too many, or one unguarded moment, and the edifice begins to unravel.'

Markham was tempted to ask about lies that could be classed as great whoppers, the category most of the things Rossignol had told him fell into. But to chide a dying man would be heartless.

'Pascalle and Eveline?' Rossignol croaked.

'Celeste and Jean-Baptiste,' Markham replied.

That brought a ghost of a smile to the now bloodless lips. 'You catch me on the thorn once more, monsieur.'

'Where are the Picards and their servants?'

'Gone,' he growled. 'Took ship as soon as they knew that the town would fall.'

'Without telling you?'

'Their money and their lives meant more to them than their loyalty to their King.'

'But he wasn't their King.'

Rossignol tried to raise himself, his voice rasping and angry. 'They thought he was. And these are the kind of people who look down on such as me.'

Markham changed the subject to calm him down, his voice dropping even more so that only Rossignol coud hear him. 'You told me about Pascalle, but who exactly is Eveline? Not your daughter, I'm sure.'

'No. A collaborator, a good one, who enjoys subterfuge as much as I do. Shall I call her an actress, and a consummate one, who has been unlucky in her chosen profession. With me, she had a chance to exercise a wasted talent.' That, no doubt evasive, still imparted a great deal, and had him lifting his head to look at Eveline. The appellation actress covered a great variety of vocations, which, in an overcrowded milieu, ranged from leading lady to common whore. Just where she stood on the rungs of this ladder was something he really didn't want to know. 'But she was fond of you, Lieutenant, truly so. I didn't deceive you about that. It would grieve me if anything happened to either of them.'

'I cannot guarantee anything for my men, let alone the rest of the people in this house. Right now we are all safer here. Perhaps, when the streets have cleared, we will be able to get out of Toulon.'

'But you will try.'

'Yes.'

Rossignol's body was racked by deep pain as Markham

339

nodded, but the words he managed to gasp made him considerably tighten his grip on the old man's hand. 'Fouquert will come here, looking for me.'

'Why?'

'I was his liaison with Serota. They communicated through Guillaume Rossignol. That is why we didn't flee when we saw your troops withdraw. We knew we were safe.'

'How did this come about?'

The head turned away. 'Circumstances.'

'You released him from the coach while I was asleep.'

Rossignol's eyes, when he turned to face Markham again, held not a trace of guilt. 'You left the wounded soldier's bayonet beside me. It was an opportunity. It is unhealthy, in today's troubled world, to make enemies in any quarter. And it was you who told me that the British would not send troops. A man like me must prepare for everything.'

'Did you offer to sell him Jean-Baptiste?'

That produced a fit of coughing, and the first hint of frothy blood around Rossignol's lips. But he didn't answer the question. 'Use the old smuggling tunnels. They lead from an entrance in Picard's study. Eveline and Pascalle will show you.' The pain he was suffering made him screw up his face. 'Are you a Catholic, Lieutenant?'

'If you want a priest,' Markham whispered, 'I don't think I can get you one.'

'No priests!' He clutched Markham's hand a bit tighter. 'If I must confess, let it be to a man who feels he has as many faults as me.'

'And what, pray, are my faults?'

'Vanity, monsieur, like all men. But not so much that you do not know your own weaknesses. Your past troubles you, and sometimes blinds you.'

The light was beginning to go from the eyes. Markham had seen it before, that moment of approaching death, when pain ceases and only the surprise shows in the pupils.

'I can't confess you, Rossignol, since any faith I had died long ago. But there is an English writer called Shakespeare, who said something about every exit being an entrance somewhere else. If there is a supreme being, I'm sure he'll open the door for a scoundrel like you.'

'Sure,' he sighed.

'Even Almighty God needs a laugh.'

Guillaume Rossignol died as the first sounds of the Rape of Toulon penetrated the thick walls of the Picard house.

# Chapter twenty-four

There was no time for sobbing, and little time for sleep. Markham had his men carry Rossignol's body up to the first floor of the warehouse, there to join that of Serota. His boots had been removed too, and now graced the feet of Quinlan. The two Spanish soldiers felled by Rannoch, one dead and the other unconscious, had been stripped, though looking at Dymock and Leech, both with Spanish muskets in their hands, he could see that their footwear was of poor quality. All the while, loud enough to penetrate the thick stone walls, the sounds of death increased outside on the quay.

'They're bayonetting them, sir,' sobbed Yelland, who'd been put to watch, his fair hair flopping over his eyes. 'Men, women and bairns. If they run, they drown.'

He couldn't bring himself to admit that they needed that quay cleared to have any chance of escape. It was just too cruel a thought to contemplate. 'I'd like to stop it, Yelland. But if we show our noses outside that door it will be bayonets for us, if not something much worse. Now get some sleep, and put wadding in your ears if you can't shut out the noise.'

Eveline and Pascalle had gone to their room. He thought about knocking, to say that they should, for safety's sake, be ready to leave, but decided against it, unwilling to undergo another dose of Pascalle's grief, and even less inclined to exchange so much as a look with Eveline, in case, in her eyes, he would see that he'd been the final victim of Rossignol's deceit.

He found Celeste and Jean-Baptiste in the kitchens,

sitting at the table, the young girl wearing an expression that exactly matched that of the boy, as she contemplated a repetition of her previous experiences.

'Do you feel up to preparing some food?'

'Why?' she asked softly.

'My men will need it, and so will you if we are to escape.'

'Escape! To where?'

Markham, weary himself, couldn't quite yet answer that. The French army was still camped all around the city, blocking off the land routes. Only the sea offered safety, and that was precarious to a man who had no idea how to navigate. But they couldn't stay here. Almost any other building would do, as long as it allowed them to hide. But where that might be, he could not bring himself to guess. He needed to shut his eyes, if only for half an hour. Then perhaps he might be able to think straight.

'Food, if you please.' Before turning to leave, he laid his watch on the table. 'I'm going to have a sleep on that chaise in the main hall. Please wake me in half an hour.'

The doors to the Rossignol rooms were shut. He passed by quietly, entering his own. Opening Frobisher's sea-chest, he took out his best shoes and put them on, followed by a fresh shirt and the uniform coat, the pair of pistols and the cartouche containing powder and balls. He laughed inwardly, recalling how he had said that he'd return the valuable items. That was going to be a very difficult promise to keep. Returning to the hall, he lay back and closed his eyes.

Celeste woke him, as requested, laying his watch on his chest without saying a word. Markham pulled himself to his feet, his first conscious thought being that, if he'd dreamed at all, it hadn't provided him with a way out of his predicament. Gathering Frobisher's things, he crossed the courtyard. He'd barely entered the warehouse when the banging started on the heavily studded door that led to the quay.

'Everybody up,' he yelled as he ran for the first floor. He threw Frobisher's possessions into the first available pair of hands, ordered the pistols to be loaded, and struggled out of his coat. Stepping over the bodies of Rossignol and Serota, he inched open one of the loading bay doors. Through the slight crack he saw a multitude of torches, and by their light that the harbour was full of floating corpses. He imagined the quayside being dark brown from their blood, interspersed with deep red pools where the cobbles sagged to form a puddle. The crowd, waving makeshift tricolours, clothing stained to match the red caps of liberty, had turned from their killing and was now milling outside the main entrance. Someone saw the door to the loading bay move, shouted and raised a hand to point, every eye then following the gesture. Markham slammed it shut as the crowd roared. The overall effect was indistinct, but the words 'traitor' and 'guillotine' were clear enough.

'Halsey, get the Rossignol girls out of their room. Dymock, Hollick, I want the means to make a tricolour flag. Tear down the drapes if you have to. Those of you who've not got anything on your feet, search the house for footwear. And take anything you can find to use as a weapon.'

'Which way will we get out?' Rannoch asked softly. Markham, with no conviction at all, nodded towards the rear of the building, a notion which made little impression on the Scotsman. 'If those intent on looting the place are out the front, sir, they will be at the back also.'

'Check that, they might not have thought of it yet.'

Markham heard Rannoch call to Gibbons as he inched the door open again. A group of citizens were pushing their way through the mass of bodies, carrying a heavy ship's spar big enough to batter the door down. Several missiles, accompanied by curses, flew in his direction, bouncing off the thick wood of the door as he slammed it shut.

'The Rossignol girls have gone!' yelled Halsey, his head appearing at the same time. 'Cleared out by the look of it, though they've left most of their clothes.'

'Damn! They must have slipped past me while I was asleep.'

Rannoch pushed past the marine corporal. 'The mob out the back is thicker than the one in front, and they are at the timbers with an axe. We pushed the coach right up to the door to slow them up, and Gibbons is keeping watch.'

Pascalle and Eveline must have used the tunnels. In a city being put to the sack, the girls had only one place they could go to feel safe. That was to Fouquert. And the only thing they could offer him as an excuse for keeping their heads attached to their necks would be information about him and his men. One by one they'd drifted back, armed with knives and cleavers from the kitchens, all with something on their feet. Tully and Yelland looked particularly incongruous in highly polished dancing pumps.

'Ettrick, Quinlan, search Picard's study. There's an escape route somewhere, and I need you to find it. Dornan, my pistols, if you please.' Dornan passed them to him, without any attempt at haste, which earned him a glare. 'Stand here. When I say so, push the door open. As soon as I've fired my pistols shut it again.'

Raising one, he nodded, and Dornan obliged. The men with the spar, the only regular grouping in an otherwise heaving mass, were easy to spot. He'd be lucky to actually hit them, but that didn't matter, since a ball into the surrounding mob would cause enough panic to slow them down. The crash of the pistols, in the low-ceilinged chamber, was deafening, slowing Dornan's reactions just enough to allow those below to aim several pieces of the torn-up *pavé* in his direction. One came right through the gap, forcing Markham to throw himself backwards to avoid serious injury.

He glared into Dornan's bovine face. 'A little swifter next time, if you please. Leech, Dymock, there's a party with a battering ram below. You'll see them as Dornan opens the door. Don't bother to aim, just get as close as you can.'

Ettrick came up behind him as he began to reload the pistols, and tugged at his shirt so that he could whisper in his ear. 'The study door was locked, but Quinlan picked it. One of the bookshelves has a handle at the back, but we was afraid to tug at it without your say-so.'

'Good. Sergeant Rannoch, everyone bar Dymock and Leech into the hallway outside the study. Halsey, get Celeste and the boy, as well as any food they can carry. Schutte, take Yelland and set up something at the bottom of the stairs to start a fire.'

Dornan swung the door too wide, giving Markham a fleeting glimpse of the Grosse Tour, as the two men fired off the unfamiliar Spanish weapons. Even as he was yelling at him to shut the damn thing, he had the ridiculous notion of taking Rossignol's unfinished painting with him. What a pleasure it would be to present it, as a wedding present, to Hanger! But there was no time for such fantasies. He didn't have much hope that they would survive. And if they were to have any chance, they had to leave now.

At the bottom of the stairs Schutte and Yelland had stacked everything loose they could find around a barrel of turpentine, then placed a lantern on top. That last, hastily-fired salvo had gained little in the way of time. The crash, as the battering ram hit the door, reverberated round the chamber. The temptation to light it now was strong. But logic dictated that he wait until he knew they had an escape route themselves.

'Get something across that door to hold them up.'

Rannoch was in the hallway, loading a fowling piece that he'd found. Halsey was taking food from Celeste and Jean-Baptiste, passing it round, stuffing it into mouths where the hands were too occupied to receive it. Hollick had draped himself in the strands of the makeshift tricolour he'd been asked to find. Markham pushed past and joined Quinlan in the booklined study. They hadn't even tried to conceal the handle properly. The dull bronze shone in the candlelight, the ledgers that were normally used to hide it thrown carelessly on the floor.

'Quinlan, take this pistol. Aim it at the door. If there's anyone on the other side, shoot them in the face.'

He turned the handle and pulled, watching Quinlan's screwed-up features and stiff shoulders for the first sign of trouble. As they relaxed, so did he. Stepping round the bookshelves, he looked into the void, his nose twitching at the musty smell that wafted out. There were stairs cut into the rock, and slipping down, lantern in hand, he saw that after a few yards the tunnel split in two.

'They're nearly through the doors at the back, sir,' shouted Ettrick. 'Sergeant sent me to tell you.'

Markham emerged from the tunnel as a shot rang out from behind the house. 'Fetch the rest of the men from the warehouse. Tell Schutte to set light to that turpentine barrel. Get Rannoch and Gibbons in, then bar the back door. Everyone else in here.'

They crowded into the study, knocking over the round table as they filled the room. The heavy book with the embossed cover fell, sending Rossignol's drawings flying. Jean-Baptiste let go of Celeste's hands and scrabbled around picking them up. Halsey tried to stop the boy, since time was precious, but Celeste pushed him back, and got down on her knees to assist. Markham, watching, was vaguely aware that the drawings were numerous, and that some had been added to those he'd already looked at, these being coloured rather than just linear sketches.

By the time they were gathered Rannoch had shepherded the rest into the room to join them. 'The door to the warehouse is bolted,' he said, his speech controlled even in this dire emergency. 'But that will not stop the flames. And I do not think the rear door to the house, a flimsy thing, will stand for long against those axes.'

'We have a way,' Markham replied, addressing them all, as he grasped the handle. 'This leads to an old smuggling tunnel. God knows where it comes out. We can't get out the front or the back without passing through that mob. And we can't stay and hold the place. Even if we succeeded, Fouquert is bound to come here. That's the man we tied to the back of the coach at Ollioules. I'll leave you to guess at the fate you'll have in his hands.'

The question of where they were to go, even if they did get clear of the Picard house, hung in the air. But no-one asked it, since without an opinion such an enquiry was worthless.

'We may come out into a public place. Front and back, the crowd outside are scum. There's not one of them who hasn't committed murder since last night. If they get in your way, kill them. Rannoch, behind me. Halsey, you bring up the rear. Celeste and the boy in the middle. Quinlan, re-lock that study door.' The soldier knelt down and pulled out a set of picks as they filed down the stairs to crowd into a small chamber at the bottom. 'There has to be a way to shut that entrance, Halsey. Wait till Quinlan's through. If there's a bolt of some kind, use it.'

Markham was thinking back to the day he'd gone after Fouquert, and the way he'd disappeared, which meant he knew about these tunnels too. That was worrying, but it was a case of the lesser of two evils. One of these exits must lead to the alley into which he'd been chased, or to a building that backed onto it. But which one? They had little time in which to make a mistake. Looking at the floor, covered in the accumulated dust of ages, he saw the faint traces where something heavy had recently been dragged across it. It could only be Eveline and Pascalle, inadvertently leaving a trail to be followed.

There was a dull thud, that seemed to come at them

through the very walls, which he hoped was the barrel of turpentine exploding. With luck the whole warehouse was now alight. In time, the fire would reach the top floor, and all those combustibles that had so worried Picard. Then, with luck, they would go up, taking the whole of the rampaging mob with them.

'Wait here, while Rannoch and I go forward and look.'

They didn't have to go far. The tunnel ended at a sort of spiral staircase, which rose to a wooden trapdoor. Rannoch, having first put his ear to the timber, and heard no sound, pushed gently. When it didn't move, he tried more force, increasing that till the veins were standing out on his neck. He couldn't even budge it a fraction, which indicated that it was either tightly bolted, or under something so heavy that it was impossible to lift.

'We'll have to try the other way,' said Markham.

'Well, let us hope that leads to somewhere,' Rannoch replied. 'It is for certain that we cannot go backwards.'

This proved a much longer tunnel, which twisted and turned so that they soon lost any sense of direction. If there were exits, they weren't visible in the light from his lantern. Frustrated, Markham called a halt and stood still for a moment, feeling the temperature rise as the heat of . candle, added to human bodies, filled the confined space. He was trying to get his bearings, conjuring up a picture of the study, its position in the house, and the turns they'd taken.

With everyone still and silent, he heard clearly the first high-pitched squeaks. The noise didn't increase slowly, it arrived suddenly, filling the whole of their narrow tunnel till it was difficult to communicate.

'Get the boy off the ground!' he bellowed. 'And Celeste. The rest of you, open your legs as wide as you can.'

Seconds later he felt the first of the rats run over his

shoes, picking up at the same time a faint trace of the smell of smoke. Within seconds, the tunnel was flooded with the creatures, scratching and biting as they sought escape from the threat of the flames behind them. The Picard warehouse would have been home to these vermin. Now that it was ablaze, they were heading for safety. Markham, lantern held high, watched the writhing grey sea of bodies ahead of him. He didn't like rats at all. But in their flight they were certainly heading for a way out.

The frenzy soon passed, a few stragglers disappearing out of the circle of his light. Celeste and Jean-Baptiste were put back on the ground, and with a quick word to ensure that everyone was all right, Markham set off again. His step was certain now, but his thoughts were anything but. For all the distance they were covering, they'd not come across a single exit.

'That looks like a ladder ahead,' said Rannoch.

His hand was pointing over Markham's shoulder to where the worn wooden rungs disappeared into a dark, narrow shaft. The rest of the tunnel was nothing but a black hole beyond the range of his lantern. Opening it, he exposed the flame, which didn't even flicker in the still, fetid air. He walked forward, only to find himself standing in front of solid rock.

'Let's hope this one isn't blocked as well, Rannoch,' he whispered, as he returned to the group. Handing the lantern to his sergeant, he took off his sword and pulled his pistols from his belt. Both, in the narrow shaft above his head, were too bulky to be anything other than an impediment. 'I'll take your bayonet, if you don't mind.'

Grasping the lowest rung, he began to haul himself up. There was barely enough space in the shaft to accommodate him, and no light at all, since his own body blocked what little filtered up from below. And it was hot. Through his shirt he could feel the bricks of the right-hand wall getting hotter, at one point close to causing actual pain. He eased himself up a bit further, every sense alert for the exit that this must surely lead to, aware that the bricks were now merely warm. He could smell nothing but the acrid reek of long-dry dust. No crack of white appeared, the gap at the base of a door that would indicate an escape route, so that he was forced to blink, just to make sure his eyes were actually open. Then, as the bricks grew hot again, the top of his head touched unyielding stone, and he could ascend no further.

Hanging on the ladder, Markham fought the sense of panic induced by his disappointment and dark isolation. There had to be a way out, or the ladder served no purpose. He racked his brains for a solution based on logic. Hot bricks at his side could not hold a way out, since they must be a lot warmer on the other side. Why were they warm? It had to be some kind of fire. And given the construction of his narrow shaft, and the number of rungs he'd climbed, were these bricks part of a chimney?

If there was an exit, it could only be on two of the four sides. One was blocked by the ladder, the other by heat. If it was a chimney then the logical place to conceal an entrance was at the side, not the front. He descended slowly, tapping very gently on the wall to his left. The hollow sound, as the stone changed to wood, made every nerve in his body jump. Scrabbling around for a handle proved fruitless, so, placing his knees and hands against the searing bricks, he used his back to push hard.

The wrenching, tearing sound barely registered, since Markham was too busy trying to grab a rung to stop himself falling. Fine dust filled his nostrils and his mouth, making him gag and sneeze. Something furry landed on his face and, fearing a rat, he screamed and lashed out. The light that suddenly flooded in, as another door crashed open, blinded him, so it was several seconds before he realised that the dust that filled the air was powder, and the creature he was trying to fight off, which seemed to envelope half of his arm, was a full-bottomed wig.

The room he walked into, once a bedroom, lit by the red glow of dying embers from the huge fireplace, had been demolished. Mirrors and pictures had been ripped from their frames, drapes pulled from the windows and trampled underfoot, the four-poster bed smashed, the sheets torn and stained. In between the folds lay the remains of a small chandelier. A buzz of noise, like a swarm of angry bees, puncuated by the odd cry, came through the smashed windows. As he walked towards them the noise increased in volume.

Lights from hundreds of torches lit the scene. The windows, on the second floor of the building, overlooked a large square, which he recognised as the one which stood before the Bishop's palace. Leaning out, he could see that it was packed with people, a tumbril full of dejected souls, all with their hands bound, parked at the foot of the steps that led up to the palace entrance. On the elevated porch under the classical portico lay a long table, with a clear space around it. Before that stood a woman in a ragged dress, her hair in disarray. Five men sat behind the table, lit by flambeaux affixed to the walls. They wore, in their hats, the red, white and blue feathers of the Revolution. One of them, his face in shadow, barked a question, which produced a whimpering response from the woman, followed by a growl from the crowd.

The man in the centre of the group, who held a wine bottle, stood up and shouted, his free hand shooting forward towards the victim before him. A great yell erupted from the throats of the mob, and the woman sank to her knees in supplication. But the finger remained in place, as two soldiers stepped forward to lift her to her feet. This they did, applying some force. The woman screamed, a clear plea for pity, as she was dragged through the crowd.

The guillotine stood in the middle of the square, surrounded by a sea of eager faces. The avenue from the portico to the rough wooden steps was lined with troops, so that the poor victim, still refusing to walk, could be observed easily as she was pulled across the cobbles. They practically had to lift her up the steps on to the square, planked platform, this action accompanied by the raising of the blade. Over the swelling sound of the mob, Markham imagined he could hear the ropes squeaking through the pulleys, the gentle bump as the heavy sliver of steel slotted into the catch that held it in place.

They dragged her forward, pulling her head back and forcing her to confront the mob. A shiver went through Markham's body as he recognised Pascalle. In her torn dress, with hair wild and unkempt, her identity had been hidden. Now her tear-stained face and reddened eyes seemed to be looking straight at him, as if in accusation for this unwarranted fate. They shoved her head onto the block, lashing her body so that she could not squirm. The five men who'd sat at the table came out, their plumes dancing in the wind. When they reached the platform the crowd fell silent, as if some heavenly conductor had waved a wand.

Pascalle's accuser, having handed over his bottle, raised his arm as he spoke, the words indistinct as they floated up, yet clearly a sentence of execution. Then one arm dropped, and the executioner pulled at the rope. It required no imagination now. The whoosh of the blade as it fell, gathering speed between the two wooden channels, was all too plain. The roar of approval from the mob was but a split second behind the thud as it hit the solid oak block under Pascalle's neck, the yells of frenzy full-throated as the blade bounced up, sending a fount of blood shooting forward, to cover the decapitated head as it dropped into the waiting basket.

The man who'd given the order raised his hat, and now his features were no longer in shadow. Reaching for a pistol that wasn't there, his teeth grinding so hard they threatened to break, Markham saw the grinning, drunken, hook-nosed face of Pierre-Michel Fouquert.

# Chapter twenty-five

The whole party was up the ladder and in the room before the next victim was dispatched. Markham sent two of his men to bar any access from the ground floor, then took station by the window to observe the carnage below. The murderous activity continued throughout the night, the guillotine slamming down time and again as those disliked by the Revolution, or denounced by their neighbours, rich, poor and innocent, were butchered like so much red meat. Fouquert had relinquished the task of announcing the sentences to his fellow deputies, and stayed behind the tribunal table, drinking from his bottle.

With each female victim, Markham found it hard to breathe, praying that it would not be Eveline. Whatever her motives, they had been lovers. That attachment could not just be broken by Rossignol. He, knowing he was dying, may well have spoken the truth. Markham was well aware that he didn't love Eveline, but he was indebted to her for the hours of happiness she had given him. Yet he also knew, in his heart, that her death could very easily have preceded Pascalle's; that her beautiful features might adorn one of the spikes which, jammed between the cobbles, surrounded the place of execution.

But she didn't appear. The mob that watched, sustained on a diet of bloodlust and ample drink, grew hoarse with yelling, until it seemed that even the endless stream of decapitated corpses, the severed heads passed around to be spat on and abused, were insufficient to keep them entertained. His men watched alongside him with grim fascination, wondering when, if at all, the supply of victims would dry up. Endlessly, the notorious Committee of Public Safety sat in judgment, applying laws that contained no justice, since not one of those brought before it was granted mercy.

Finally Fouquert staggered back to the execution platform, to see to the dispatch of an elderly, white-haired priest. The sight of him had Markham reaching for a musket, only to find that another, stronger, hand had taken hold of it as well.

'I would like to kill him as well,' said Rannoch.

'Not as much as me.'

'That is as maybe. But to do so now would only see us all with our heads on pikes.'

Fouquert, in the meantime, had raised his hands to speak to the crowd, the slurred words reverberating off the surrounding buildings. 'Citizens! We have only just begun the work that needs to be done. There are thousands of traitors still out there, hiding like the vermin that they are from the bright gaze of revolutionary justice.'

The voice dropped, exactly matching the needs of the audience, who had, apart from the odd drunken yell, gone silent. 'Let them have one more night. Let them sit and ponder the fate that awaits them, an ordeal as cruel as any known to man. They know they are going to die, as surely as the sun rises and sets. Nothing can save them. So, tired, weary and in despair, they will not sleep. They will weep until they are found. Then, fellow citizens of Toulon, we will make them weep some more.'

The crowd responded to that, but in a low-key fashion which demonstrated that they were near exhaustion themselves. 'Reason and truth will triumph, and those who have had their feet on your necks for centuries will pay with their blood for the crimes they have committed. But the hand of vengeance must rest. A curfew must be imposed, so that our enemies cannot use the hours of darkness to effect their escape. Go back to your homes and stay indoors. Anyone seen out after curfew will be shot. Tomorrow, at noon, the work of the Revolutionary Tribunal will resume. And since we are few in numbers, we depend upon our citizens to ensure that Madame Guillotine does not want for the means to apply our rightful vengeance. Sleep, friends. When you wake, tear this town of traitors apart, so that every one of their scrawny necks can be placed where it belongs, on the block of history.'

They watched as the mob began to disperse, the soldiers gently shepherding them out of the square. An officer was detailing men to guard the guillotine, as well as the entrances to the palace. The long table was now empty, and soldiers' boots rang on the cobbles, as those not set as sentries were allowed to go to their billets. They were, if not actually in the lion's jaws, certainly in the jungle. But, for this one night, Markham felt safe in rooms which had already been looted. His only fear, the reason he'd insisted that everyone stay on the alert, was simple: that once the butchery was over, the mob would try to use this place as somewhere to lay their heads, smashing the flimsy barrier he'd erected.

Clearly this was not to be. Indeed, he could see some of the troops steering tired *sans-culottes* away from some of the other buildings. The palace was Fouquert's headquarters, and for all his professed love of the children of the Revolution, he had no desire to share his surroundings with them. The square was soon devoid of people, the empty tumbril long gone, its iron-bound wheels faint in the distance as it headed for the prison within the Fort de la Malgue. A party of men were busy sluicing down the blood-soaked guillotine, and somehow that act, so mundane, made the whole of what he'd witnessed that much more barbaric.

'We're safe here, at least until dawn,' he said, checking the drapes that had been put back over the window so that they could safely use their lantern. The room had been tidied, his men laying the mattress to provide a cot for Celeste and Jean-Baptiste. The girl lay on her back, dark, liquid eyes wide open, with the boy asleep, still clutching his drawings, in the crook of her arm. His men had eaten, and, with Rannoch watching them closely, had sipped sparingly from their canteens. 'What I can't tell you is how long that will last.'

'We could go back to the tunnels,' Rannoch replied, without enthusiasm, 'and hide out there till matters settle a bit.'

Markham shook his head. 'As far as we know they don't go anywhere except back to the Picard house. Besides, Fouquert is aware they exist.'

'There is no certainty that those poor women betrayed us,' Rannoch continued. Markham, just as he wished Eveline alive, would have liked to agree, even if he didn't believe it either. 'I would be right in thinking that we will still require the use of a boat?'

The Scotsman had just as much knowledge as he did about how matters stood. The question was being posed on behalf of the men. They sat on the floor, watching him, eager to hear him say that he knew how to get them to freedom. But he didn't. With anyone but Fouquert, he might have advised surrender. But having watched that drunken butcher at work, little imagination was required to guess what fate would await his men. His own, no doubt, would be that much worse.

'Time for sleep. I will keep watch for the first hour.' Rannoch was looking at him quizzically. 'I speak French. If we're in any danger, I'll hear it first. Later on, when the whole garrison's bedded down, it won't matter quite so much.'

Time passed as they each struggled for comfort on the hard floorboards. Being soldiers, they required less of that commodity than others, and soon the sounds of gentle snoring punctuated the silence. Markham sat staring at the ceiling, his mind going back to that day he had confronted Fouquert at Malbousquet. No doubt now why he'd called him a mercenary. All the time the city had been under siege, he'd had comprehensive information, from Rossignol and Serota, about the entire garrison. What a pity that he couldn't make good the desire to meet him on equal terms. One to one, with sword or pistol, he knew he could take the Frenchman.

Try as he might, he couldn't keep Eveline's face from his thoughts, nor help recalling every word or movement, intimate and conversational, that they'd exchanged. She'd deceived him, of course, though he was a willing victim. But since love didn't enter into their relationship, it was hard to see it as betrayal. They had merely been two people who had enjoyed each other, who in other circumstances would have gone their own way without recrimination. And, while deeply sad about Pascalle, he was tormented by the thought of Eveline's beautiful head adorning some pike. He could imagine Fouquert taunting her, perhaps treating her the way he'd abused Celeste, a thought that had him easing his pistol in his belt. Perhaps, given her beauty, he hadn't guillotined her after all. It could be that she was a prisoner in the palace across the square.

The snoring was regular now. In the faint gleam of the shaded lantern light not one of his men, apart from the odd twitch, showed any signs of being awake. Gently, he eased himself to his feet and crept past them. The door to the landing presented no obstacle, having been torn from its hinges. But the lack of light forced him to stop on the landing to allow his eyes to adjust. Just as he was about to put his foot on the first step of the staircase, the soft, lilting voice made him freeze.

'It is not wise, Lieutenant Markham,' whispered Rannoch, 'to be considering rescuing damsels in distress.'

'I need to know if she's dead.'

'You do not. You need to look after the men you command. That is your duty. And I cannot help but think, that once you are out in the square, you might, on one of those pikes, find a sight that will destroy what little sense you have.'

'You can't talk to me like that, Sergeant.'

'I can and I will. You said earlier that you speak the language. That could be a priceless asset to every one of us.'

'I need to know.'

'With respect, you needed to know at the Battle of Guilford, too, and look where that led you. If fate has it in mind for you to kill that pig Fouquert, then the opportunity will come in time. But this, with the man surrounded by guards, is not it.' Rannoch took Markham's arm, and with very little force pulled him back towards the room. 'You sleep, and I will keep watch.'

The remark about Guilford, no less than the absolute truth, stunned him, and he allowed himself to be shepherded back to the spot he'd chosen by the window. But sleep wouldn't come, and now his thoughts had returned to the problem of making an escape. He lay back and closed his eyes, racking his brain for a solution. They needed a boat, and the only ones that would still be in the harbour were those lashed to the decks of the French warships, which could be the moon for all the good it would do them.

In time, despite the revolutionary fervour, Toulon would return to being a naval port. The quay would then be full of boats. But by then, through either capture, hunger or sheer desperation, this last remnant of the British presence in the city would have been forced to surrender. Part of his mind was accepting the inevitable, while another was screaming 'No!' Just to give up was anathema. Better that they die fighting. He opened his eyes again, to look at what he had at his disposal.

'Sergeant Rannoch, a word if you please,' he said loudly, which woke everyone in the room bar Jean-Baptiste.

'I have no more mind than you to surrender to the likes of Fouquert,' the Scotsman replied, when he'd posed the question.

'And the others?'

'Halsey is a good man, even if he is a Lobster, and will obey orders. And I think the rest of his men will follow. Schutte and Leech owe you their lives, after all.'

'The soldiers?' Markham added, realising as he did so the implicit admission that, even after all this time, and all they'd been through, he didn't really know his own men.

'They could very well agree, and do the exact opposite when the time comes. Quinlan and Ettrick are thieves, as you've seen for yourself. Tully ran for the colours to avoid being strung up for rape. Dornan will be fine, since he's too stupid to think.'

'What a bunch,' sighed Markham. 'The only one who seems to carry an honest streak is Yelland.'

'Not that honest.'

'A bit of poaching hardly makes him much of a criminal.'

'Is that what he told you?' Markham nodded, knowing as he did so that he was about to be exposed as a gullible fool. 'They say the girl he loved wed another. They found blood by the gallon, but no bodies. Rumour has it that he chopped them both to bits, and spread their remains over half of England.'

'Then he should have hung.'

'No bodies, no crime. That is the law. And he is such a sweet-looking youth that older heads, who should know better, are easily taken in.'

Stung, he nearly spat the next question. 'And you, Rannoch? Perhaps you're with us because of that brand on your thumb.'

The whispered reply was much more damning for its utter lack of passion. 'I'm here because one of your kind, a damned pig of an officer, ordered it so. He did it out of malice, not good sense. And hell will freeze over before I tell you anything more, for it is none of your affair.'

Rannoch moved away, watched by the others, all their eyes searching his face to try and discover the nature of that whispered, bitter conversation. Markham felt like a wretch, wondering how much of what he'd asked had been revenge for Rannoch's allusion to his behaviour at the Battle of Guilford.

Still cursing himself, he was thinking that if they were not true soldiers before, with uniform coats and hats, they were even less so now, Lobsters or Bullocks. Their shirts and breeches were torn and filthy, their faces haggard and unwashed. They had an assortment of weapons and footwear, plus a few possessions in makeshift bundles. The only red coat the group possessed was the one he wore. In fact, they were no different from the mob outside. With the addition of a little smeared blood, plus a few curses in French, they could mingle easily. Not even Fouquert would spot them. The notion was in his head before he'd finished looking.

'Did anyone bring needle and thread with them?'

'I did, sir,' Yelland replied, reaching into the tied bundle that lay at his feet. Others had raised their hands to let him know they, too, had the means to sew. He stood up and slipped off his coat, beckoning to Rannoch. 'Cut that up and get the men sewing. I want every one of them wearing a red cap of liberty. We'll trim some of that cloth Hollick's wrapped in to make cockades, though we must leave enough for a flag.'

'Permission to ask what you have in mind, sir?' said Rannoch, in a stiff tone that he'd not used for weeks.

'I intend to disguise us as Frenchmen, and march out of here, escorting Celeste and the boy as though they are our prisoners. And I am also sorry for prying too deeply. Your past, if you choose to keep it to yourself, is none of my business.'

'Sir,' Rannoch replied, with a ghost of a smile.

They were ready at dawn, all in red caps, the flag sewn by Celeste tied on a pole which had previously held curtains. Those drapes had been removed, flooding the room with light, so that they could check their appearance. It was a clear crisp morning, a winter sky in which the low sun cast long shadows. Jean-Baptiste, eyes wide with excitement, if not actual knowledge, skipped around the room getting in the way, seemingly happy until Markham tried to remove from his hand the drawings he had picked up in Picard's study. The squeal of despair, plus the stubborn tug of war that ensued, brought Celeste to his side. She pushed Markham back, looking at him in anger.

'I don't think, if he's supposed to be our prisoner, he should be gaily waving bits of paper around.'

She bent down and began to talk to him softly, one hand prising the drawings out of his tightly clenched fist. The way he looked at Celeste brought a lump to Markham's throat. The trust was absolute, a bond that excluded everyone else present and seemed to lock them in their own world. He couldn't hear what she said to him, and was just about to tell her that it didn't matter, when Jean-Baptiste surrendered the papers. Celeste took them and, smiling at the boy, handed them on.

The flash of colour made him examine them. That, in turn, induced a grim smile. Rossignol, true to his character, had used his time atop the Grosse Tour well. Ever the opportunist, who couldn't be sure what had value and what didn't, he'd copied out a whole sheaf of the signals that had been sent by the midshipmen who shared his perch. How he'd managed to identify them was a mystery, but each coloured drawing, with the bright square flags running top to bottom, was annotated with the appropriate message; *Signale privée, nombre de bâteau, message*. It looked as though he had, in the time available, copied the whole book.

Jean-Baptiste was looking at him, the concern in his huge brown eyes more solicitous than words. Markham grinned, and handed the papers back to him. The expression of appreciation that earned him made him feel good for the first time in an age.

With curfew over, the square had started to fill up again, mostly with people who looked as though they'd spent the night drinking rather than sleeping. The soldiers, though sober, showed no great desire to demonstrate efficiency, probably because their officers were still abed. But even so, care had to be taken to get the men out of the door without being observed. Markham went first, to lean on the surround like a man contemplating being sick. The main body of guards was concentrated in front of the Bishop's palace. But at the bottom of the square, on each side where it joined the roads that led to the quay, a post had been set up to vet those coming and going. The examination was cursory, but it was there and would have to be bypassed.

'Now, Rannoch,' he whispered, as the nearest sentry turned away to look into the faces of some recent arrivals.

The Scotsman had his musket wrapped in the flag, so it looked like an innocent curtain pole. He was out and sauntering away, in deep shadow, before the guard turned round again, stopping some twenty yards from the exit, leaning back against a wall, the hidden gun swinging up to cover the soldier. One by one they came out, hiding whatever weapons they were carrying as best they could, until Rannoch was surrounded by red-hatted revolutionaries.

Markham suddenly realised that they were attracting too much attention, and that some of the locals were wandering in their direction, drawn, as people are, to a crowd. One pipe-smoking individual was no more than five feet from Tully's back, the look on his swarthy face ample evidence of his confusion, as he heard words that to him made no sense.

Markham had to walk towards him, since to run would only alert others. And he was forced to proceed in an arc that kept him out of the man's eyeline. Someone in the huddled group must have used a word that identified them as British, since the fellow straightened, the stem of his pipe shooting forward as though he were about to cry out. But he didn't. He began to spin round towards the sentries just as Markham came up behind him.

'Gaston, you rogue,' he cried, slapping the man on the back so hard that he staggered forward. 'We never thought to find you here this morning, did we lads?'

Those with their backs to him had turned, and as Markham pushed the eavesdropper hard, they opened ranks to receive him. His mouth was open to protest as Markham's fist took him in the kidneys. Suddenly the man was surrounded by hard, unforgiving eyes, his efforts to speak stopped by fear as well as pain. Rannoch spun him round, one hand covering his mouth while the other went round his head to break his neck. Markham was the last to join, putting his arms round Tully and Dornan.

'Don't kill him, for the love of Christ. Just silence the sod, and sit him against the wall.'

Trusting Rannoch to obey, his next task was to fetch Celeste and Jean-Baptiste, still hidden indoors. The commotion under the bishop's classical portico distracted him, as the soldiers there came to attention in a manner which denoted the sudden appearance of a high-ranking superior. The sensation, as Fouquert appeared, was just like an unseen hand clutching his stomach, and it caused him to freeze for a split second. Then the Frenchman began to descend, four soldiers at his heels and an officer running to keep up with him, Fouquert's eyes ranging across the square before him with an assurance born of his certain superiority.

Only distance saved Markham, who was staring at him hard, and had to fight the temptation to spin round, since that would only make his presence more obvious. Instead he moved slowly, covering the last few steps towards the door and leaning against it in his original pose, as though he were in some distress.

'Fouquert is coming. Stay back.'

Celeste's terrified gasp was plainly audible, and so was the crunch of soldiers' boots as Fouquert and his escort came closer. Even in the cold air the grip on Markham's pistol was slippery with sweat. He slipped it from his breeches and held it close to his belly, cocked and ready to fire. Underneath his arm he could see that his men were in the same huddle. There was no way to warn them, to tell them to keep their faces hidden. His only hope was that the sound of marching would alert them, and that Rannoch would do what was required.

Fouquert passed within ten feet of him, talking in a loud, rasping voice that contained the residue of the previous night's drinking. Yet Markham's thoughts were in such a turmoil that they made little sense. There was something about quartering off the town for a proper search, as well as an allusion to the bulk of the army, which would enter the town that day. But the bent figure in the doorway, who didn't merit a glance from such a great man, was fighting his own inclinations to stand upright and shoot from a range at which he could hardly miss. He wanted to shout 'Fouquert!', have the swine turn to face him, see the look of fear in his eye as he pulled the trigger. His imaginings didn't end there; they carried on to the point where the escort raised their muskets and filled him full of holes. Only that stopped him from acting, and by the time his breathing had returned to something approaching normality, Fouquert had passed his men and was accepting the salutes of the sentries at the exit.

'Celeste. Now!' If she was fearful, his sharp command

overbore it. She guided Jean-Baptiste out of the door and followed Markham's pointed finger. He reached the huddled knot before they did, pushing them apart to let the pair enter. 'Get that flag unfurled, muskets on your shoulders, and follow me. And for Christ's sake try to look like killers.'

Fouquert was just out of sight as they set off. The sentries, watching the Citizen Commissioner's back, didn't see those behind them form up, so that when they turned it looked like a party who had marched all the way from the palace. The tricolour, though makeshift, had caught the breeze and was fluttering valiantly. With their red caps and their dirty, unshaven faces, the group must have looked threatening. In any event, the men guarding the exit, after an initial move forward to inquire their business, stepped back and waved them through.

'God almighty,' said Yelland. 'That was close.'

'Quiet,' growled Rannoch. 'And that goes for all of you.'

Markham could see the party still ahead, marching along in a way that made people coming towards them shy off. Fouquert himself, out ahead with the officer by his side, strutted rather than walked. Oblivious to the bloodstained cobbles, and unconcerned about the bodies still floating in the harbour, he held his head back slightly, hands behind his back as he dared any one of the citizens of Toulon to meet his eye. His arm waved at certain buildings, probably alluding to the owners, who, if they hadn't fled, would be his future victims.

Markham saw boats in the harbour, few in number, which had started on the task of clearing away the bodies. This they achieved by stabbing at them with pikes and swords, puncturing the cavities that contained the gases that kept them afloat, then pushing them under the water with bars, not granting any of them so much as a sign of the cross to ease their passage to the afterlife.

Underground, they'd felt the blast as the Picard

warehouse went up, so they'd known it to be serious. But Markham wondered if any of them would have recognised their location if Fouquert hadn't stopped. The whole of the top half of the building was gone, the rest a mere shell of still smoking timbers. The warehouses on either side had lost great chunks of their upper storeys, and the air was filled with the acrid odour of burnt wood soaked with water.

They too had to halt. Markham turning towards the quay, his hand shooting out as if he were identifying one of the hundreds of bodies in the water. Out of the corner of his eye, he knew that the move had attracted Fouquert's attention, since he threw a quick glance in their direction. But it was no more than that, and he went back to telling the officer escorting him whatever it was he wanted to impart. That was the moment when Jean-Baptiste, who'd been silent, decided to speak.

It wasn't coherent, but it was high-pitched and excited, just the sort of thing to arouse curiosity in the other people on the quay. The boy was waving his coloured drawings, pointing out into the harbour and tugging at Celeste's sleeve. Markham grabbed Rannoch and Leech, practically dragging them till their bulk hid the girl. A sharp word to Schutte had the bald Dutchman bending his knees so that he was less prominent. But Jean-Baptiste squealed on, as an increasing number of heads turned to look.

'For Christ's sake shut him up, Celeste.'

Tully showed less concern, if more presence of mind, by stepping forward and clapping his hand over the boy's mouth. Dragging his head back into his stomach made Jean-Baptiste spread his arms. This gave Markham the opportunity to grab the drawings, obviously the spur of the youngster's excitement.

'Gently, Tully. Don't hurt him,' he said, kneeling down so that he could calm the boy.

He looked at the top drawing, on which Rossignol had

sketched the private signal. Jean-Baptiste's eyes, fearful, wide and looking past him, made him glance towards the Grosse Tour. The first thing he saw was a boat pulling for the watergate, the rate of the oars indicating haste. Then he looked up. Flags streamed from the ship's mast on the top of the old tower, and they precisely replicated the flags on the drawing in his hand.

Another set was hauled upon the other side of the mast, the jerk of the man on the halyard bursting them open. Scrabbling through the drawings, Markham eventually came to the one that told him the signal. That did nothing to enlighten him. Quite the opposite. Why should the French be sending Lord Hood's private signal to an approaching ship, and telling that vessel it was safe to enter harbour?

'Holy Mother of God,' he said softly, standing upright. 'It has to be one of ours.'

Standing upright, he threw a nervous glance towards Fouquert, who still hadn't moved. Then he looked down into Jean-Baptiste's eyes, trying to smile and nod to let the boy know that he understood. But that occupied only a fraction of his mind. The rest was taken up with the consequences of what he'd seen. A British ship, definitely a warship, was approaching Toulon. Less than twenty-four hours since the end of the siege, and having missed any patrolling frigates, whoever it was didn't know that the French had taken the port. So they were coming on, enticed by the very signals they had in their own book.

A warship, probably with several hundred men on board, was going to glide straight into a trap, which was something he and his men could not allow to happen.

# Chapter twenty-six

Time for explanations didn't exist. That ship wouldn't need actually to enter the Petite Rade. Brought within range of the crossfire from Forts St Louis and l'Eguillette, and with its own guns housed, it would be reduced to matchwood within minutes. So all his men got was a staccato few words before Markham, pistol out, was heading straight for Fouquert.

The Frenchman's turn was slow; his face, when they saw it, puffy. The bloodshot black eyes nearly popped out of his head when he recognised his assailant. A flick to the side showed him Celeste standing by the water's edge. And if he doubted the danger he was in from Markham, he only had to look at her to guess his fate. The soldiers, with the exception of the officer, had stayed facing forward, and their commander, still examining the damage to the building, had no chance to intervene. Markham put his pistol under Fouquert's chin, an action which made him shut his eyes. The whole party was surrounded before anyone could utter a word. Quickly, his men took the soldiers' weapons, Rannoch relieving the officer of his sword and pistol.

'What is the meaning . . .?'

'Shut up,' hissed Fouquert, the words difficult because of the metal pressed against his windpipe.

'I hope you do open your mouth,' said Markham, pushing so hard that Fouquert's head was forced back. The Frenchman gagged. 'Open your eyes, and look at the Grosse Tour. There are signals on those masts. British signals to an approaching warship. We are going to go out there and get them cut down.'

Fouquert couldn't nod, but several blinks indicated agreement. Markham eased the pressure just enough for him to order the officer of his escort, a heavily moustachioed major of chasseurs, to comply. That produced from him an explosive response, which pushed his chest out several inches.

'Never!'

Seeing the slight commotion, some people had stopped. That induced curiosity in others, and a crowd was beginning to form.

'A clever trick, citizens,' Markham called, careful to keep Fouquert from talking, 'to disguise yourselves as soldiers in a bid to try and escape.'

'Lies!' shouted the major.

That earned him a punch from Rannoch that first knocked him to his knees, then had him falling forward onto his hands. The four soldiers were ordered to take an arm and a leg each. Weaponless and confused, they could do little but obey. Markham was facing the crowd again as he called out: 'To the Fort de la Malgue. Let Citizen Fouquert decide what to do with these vermin.'

Halsey and Leech detached themselves, pushing through the stationary Toulonais to fetch Celeste and Jean-Baptiste.

'That is Citizen Fouquert,' said one of them. 'I saw him in the square last night.'

Markham pulled at Fouquert's hair, first to drive him to his knees, then to show his face to the crowd. In evident pain, he didn't look quite so superior as he had the night before. 'If you want to escape Madame Guillotine, what better way can there be than do yourself up to look like the Citizen Commissioner?'

'But ...'

The interloper got no further. 'Look at the clothes, man. They're false. Anyone saying otherwise we'll take along with us.'

That halved the crowd in the space of two seconds. Even if they hadn't witnessed the tribunal, they knew it to be capricious, more interested in the quantity than the quality of its victims. But the man who'd been talking wouldn't be cowed.

'Well, they look like soldiers to me.'

Markham grinned at him, then half turned, speaking under his breath to Dornan and Gibbons, standing behind him. 'Fetch him a clout and throw him in the harbour.'

He must have guessed what was coming when they started to move, and he was nimble. Dornan reached for his shirt, but failed to get a grip, and the man slipped out of his grasp and began to run. Dornan lowered the musket he was carrying, and uttered the fatal words, in clear, plain English.

'Halt or I'll fire.'

The stunned silence that followed affected everyone, French and British alike. Markham had a moment when his heart sank. Fouquert one where his nostrils flared and his eyes lost their look of stark terror. Then they all moved at once. Halsey and Leech ducked under Dornan's weapon, to bring their charges into the circle of safety. Some of the braver souls in the crowd moved forward, only to backtrack when they were faced with lowered weapons. The French soldiers dropped their officer on the cobbles and tried to grab the nearest enemy. They had their back to them and were taken slightly by surprise, so this quickly became a brawl.

Markham, still holding Fouquert's hair, fired his pistol over the heads of those closest to him, passing the empty weapon to Celeste, pulling the second one from his belt. The crowd had broken up, but no-one seemed sure of which way to head for safety. The discharge of the second pistol seemed to untangle their wits, and they ran off in both directions. Fouquert, trying to take advantage of the mêlée, squirmed in an attempt to get free. Celeste, who'd hardly taken her eyes off him, hit him with barrel of the gun she was holding. Not enough to knock him out, it certainly changed the Frenchman's mind, and Markham found that he was supporting him by the hair, rather than restraining him.

'On your feet, you shit,' he yelled, tugging hard. Behind him the French soldiers had been clubbed to ground, and were lying with their hands over their head as the Lobsters and Bullocks, with Schutte to the fore, piled into them with the butts of their muskets. The moustachioed major, who'd obviously tried to take part, was in a heap by the warehouse wall, with blood streaming from his head.

'Leave them!' Markham shouted, an order he had to repeat, with his men intent on taking revenge for what they'd been forced to witness the previous night. 'Follow me.'

The fellow who'd recognised Fouquert had run back to the sentries at the exit to the square. Not that he needed to raise the alarm; Markham's gunfire had done that. But those soldiers, too few in number, were disinclined to move. They would want to send back for an officer, someone to take responsibility, before they set off in pursuit. That hesitation was his only chance to gain some distance. Even then, he wasn't sure that he'd achieve what was required. It was half a mile to the Grosse Tour. The remaining ships of the French fleet, those not burned by Sydney Smith, lay in the inner basin, dominating the right of the quay halfway to his goal.

Running was made harder by Fouquert, who stumbled repeatedly on the cobbles. Only the fact that he might be needed stopped Markham from killing him on the spot. Not that they were much threatened. The citizenry of Toulon, good or bad, had a well-developed sense of self preservation. Seeing a party of armed men running towards them, they quickly got out of the way.

But that still left the crews of the ships that lined the

inner basin. Above the heads of those in front he could see a group gathering at the top of one steeply angled gangplank. This ran up to the entry port of one of the 100-gun ships, where an officer was busy distributing weapons and powder. Slowing slightly, he let Rannoch catch up, the question he asked delivered with barely enough breath to be understood.

'We've all got guns now,' Rannoch gasped, as they came abreast of the ship's stern. Men were leaning over the taffrail, yelling insults at them and throwing anything they could find, marlinspikes, blocks, pulleys and small kegs. 'But they are a right mixture, two Spanish, four French and the rest from God knows. And we've got no way of reloading half of them.'

'One volley,' he shouted, pointing to the arched entrance that led to the maindeck of the ship, twenty feet above them. 'Aim right into that entry port. If we don't scare off those sailors we'll have a mob to deal with.'

His men stopped, chests heaving with exertion. Fouquert was on his knees again, sobbing. A chunk of hair had separated from his scalp, which was bleeding profusely. Markham grabbed a bayonet from the nearest soldier and handed it to Celeste.

'Hold this hard on his neck. Hebes, form line and take aim on the ship. Sergeant Rannoch will give the order to fire.'

A capstan bar, thrown like a spear from the upper deck, missed Rannoch by a fraction of an inch as he stepped forward to give Markham the French major's sword. It bounced on the cobbles, and whacked Halsey right across the side of the face. The corporal collapsed in a heap, red cap flying. Rannoch yelled for them to ignore him and the rest of the flying objects, waited several seconds till he felt their breath had settled, then shouted for them to fire. The men had vacated the gangplank, taking refuge in the entry port. Half the balls peppered the side of the ship. But judging by the yells that echoed from between the narrow decks, some of those fired had found flesh.

'Move,' Markham shouted, pleased to see that Schutte had thrown his musket to Leech, grabbed hold of Halsey, picking the older man up like a doll, and slinging him over one shoulder, while with his other hand he picked up the capstan bar that had felled him. They were running again, skirting round the point where the inner basin joined the dockyard, moving through the destruction caused by the retreating Allies; smashed and burnt-out buildings, some still smoking, filling the lungs of the worn out Hebes with an acrid taste.

Markham cursed as he threw a swift glance backwards. Sailors were pouring down the gangplank now, like bees from a threatened hive, several officers at their head, harrying them to make more speed. They were fresh, and unencumbered. He couldn't hope to stay ahead of them, and given their numbers, even a volley from muskets, always assuming they could load them, might do little to deter them.

Another nervous backwards glance showed them spewing onto the quay. More enthusiastic than sensible, they ran right amongst a more disciplined party of soldiers from the Bishop's palace, throwing their ranks into disorder. The Army officer in command was lashing about with his blade, berating the crewmen and ordering them back, while his naval counterparts were doing the precise opposite, the subsequent mêlée opening the gap between the groups to something over a hundred yards. But with five times that still to cover, it was a narrow margin still.

Fouquert was in a bad way, his distress caused as much by despair as exhaustion. He kept falling to the ground, to be hauled back to his feet with little compassion, by a man whose eyes showed just how much he cared for the Frenchman's well-being. 'Fall once more and I'll skewer you where you lie.'

'I can't go on.'

Markham swung the sword he was carrying, using the flat of the blade. In doing so he relaxed his grip on Fouquert's oiled and bloodsoaked hair. Not much, it was just enough to let the Frenchman slip from his grasp. The sword whistled past Fouquert's ear as he dropped to the ground. That coincided with the first volley of musket fire from their pursuers. The air was suddenly full of whistling lead balls, one of which cut a groove across Markham's extended forearm.

The pain made him recoil. Fouquert scrabbled out of reach; driven by terror, he opened enough distance to get to his feet. Everyone else had turned to face the gunfire, those with the means trying desperately to reload, with only Rannoch's Brown Bess presented and ready.

Fouquert was now upright, running for his life, screaming and yelling to the men on the top of the Grosse Tour to help him. They were too far away to hear, standing on the battlements under their streaming signal flags. But the gunfire had alerted them. Behind, order had been imposed, with the soldiers out front reloading while their officers restrained the more eager sailors. Guns loaded, the whole mass set off in pursuit, the front line setting a good pace that kept their formation intact.

Markham was screaming too, yelling frantically to get his men moving. Even if they'd had their own muskets, they didn't have the firepower to check the pursuit. Their only hope was to get to the Grosse Tour and use it as a place of defence. Even if that didn't last, they would, at least, chop those signal flags down and alert the men on that warship.

He was running out in front, with only the sound of pounding feet evidence that his command was being obeyed, his eyes fixed on Fouquert's back, and the flapping green coat that he was still wearing. He kept shouting, trying to wave his arms in a way that wouldn't slow his speed. Markham saw some of the signallers move back from the battlements, but with he and his quarry matched for pace he had to concentrate on running rather than speculation. Sweating, his breath coming in great gulps, he had the consolation that Fouquert was certainly in a worse state.

Another volley of gunfire swished past, the crack making him duck involuntarily. One ball seemed to pluck at the shoulder of the dark green coat. The irony that the sod had nearly fallen to his own side forced a smile from Markham. That faded as he saw the result. The threat had given Fouquert an extra bit of speed, and he was now opening up the gap.

At that moment, at about a hundred yards distance, they both caught sight of the same thing: the very edge of the old wooden drawbridge as it began to rise. Markham remembered the well-oiled mechanism, which lay just inside the left-hand side of the gateway. If the men who manned the tower succeeded in raising it, he would be left standing in the open, there to face a foe who would overwhelm him in seconds.

The drawbridge inched up, too slow to be in the good working order that he'd supposed. Suddenly he stopped and turned, reeling as first Dornan, who was pulling Celeste, and then Dymock, carrying Jean-Baptiste, ran into him. Rannoch was at the rear, chivvying everyone along, his face showing the strain of his exertions.

'Rannoch, your musket,' shouted Markham, when the Highlander skidded to a halt. 'Take aim on that gateway to the tower, to the left, about six feet inside. There are men there trying to haul up that drawbridge.'

No further explanation was necessary, especially as the leading edge moved up another fraction. 'The rest of you, face the rear and load. Let's slow the bastards up.'

Schutte dropped the capstan bar and rolled Halsey off his shoulder. The corporal had regained some measure of consciousness; he was able to stand, unsteadily, on his feet. Then the Dutchman took his musket, which hadn't been discharged, and aimed it at the French soldiers, waiting for the rest of those with cartouches to complete their task. Seven or eight muskets was a pitiful number against such odds. But the aim wasn't to kill, merely to slow them a little.

'Aim for the cobblestones in front of them,' yelled Markham, looking anxiously at Rannoch, who was taking an age to steady himself, then at the drawbridge, creeping inexorably up. He was hoping that the shot would send up some stone fragments. And perhaps a lucky ricochet would do damage. 'Schutte, you give the command.'

The huge, bald-headed Hollander, halfway through reloading, turned a fraction, and Markham was sure he saw him grin. The French were now less than seventy-five yards away. Turning, he hissed at Rannoch. 'Now, for Christ's sake. Now!'

Rannoch's weapon went off with a crash. Fouquert, with the crack of that shot in his ear, fell flat on his face. The Scotsman didn't look and see what effect, if any, he'd achieved. The rammer was out by the time the butt crashed to the ground, into the barrel with the swabber on the end. Out it came, to be replaced by a cartridge and a ball, then it was back in, pressing them down. He threw the heavy gun up, as if it was feather-light, so that it landed flat in his left hand, while his right brought the powder flask up to his lips. The stopper was out, the pan primed almost before the musket had stopped moving. Rannoch let the vessel drop, raised his gun, and within twenty seconds put another ball in exactly the same place as he'd aimed the first. Fouquert, who seemed winded, had just got to his feet. He threw himself sideways this time, rolling over and over on the rough cobbles, no more than fifty yards from the now still drawbridge.

'I was tempted to take him,' said Rannoch.

'He's mine,' Markham croaked, rushing forward with Rannoch at his heels. Schutte's command rang out simultaneously, and the muskets behind exploded. The roadway in front of the advancing French soldiers threw up spurts of stone and dust, and one ball clipped the officer in charge, causing him to spin away. But he pulled himself round again, standing upright, calling on his men to prepare to return fire.

Fouquert was on his knees, trying to get to his feet, when Markham's foot took him in the stomach. He fell to one side as the next blow, delivered with the point of Frobisher's best right shoe, took the Frenchman in the groin. Markham hauled him to his feet and began to drag him on. Rannoch, standing above the hunched Frenchman, was reloading as he moved. Schutte and his party were retiring steadily, their guns facing the French, too slowly for their own ultimate safety.

'Come on, men, let's get to that bloody tower.'

Markham, aware of Rannoch reloading beside him, cursed when he saw the drawbridge move again. The French were gaining, the officer more determined than ever to catch up, which left no time to reload and impose any more delay.

'Hold him,' Markham barked, as he raced for the rising platform. He didn't see Rannoch club Fouquert hard with the butt of his Brown Bess, but was vaguely aware of the sound of boots behind him, and the shout that was aimed at those following to bring the Frenchman on. The gap between the quay and the drawbridge opened at increased speed, getting to about waist height as Markham reached it. He leapt onto the top, rolling over to retrieve his footing, then rushing down the sloping platform, his curses echoing off the narrow stone archway.

Of the four men working the mechanism, only two stood their ground, the other pair rushing for the watergate. And only one of his opponents had a weapon ready, a musket which he was raising to aim at Markham. It was momentum which saved him, carrying him too far forwards to stay upright on the gradient. He fell as the musket fired, the sword flying out of his hand as he rolled over and over, to cannon into the man's legs before he had the wit to lower his bayonet. But with his first enemy falling over him and trapping his arms, he was at the mercy of the second, who had a club raised, ready to batter his head.

Rannoch didn't try to climb onto the drawbridge. Instead he used it as a rest, the long muzzle steady as he fired. At no more than twelve yards, the man with the club had little chance. The ball took him right in the chest, throwing him back against the wheel that operated the drawbridge. His body dislodged the pawl that acted as a brake, his weight holding it away from the gears so that the bridge slammed down. Markham, meanwhile, had managed to get one of his empty pistols out, and was trying to brain the Frenchman lying across him. Success at that did little for his mobility, the man's dead weight pinning him to the stone floor, until Rannoch arrived to pull his victim off.

'Fouquert?' Markham gasped, looking out at the men streaming towards the tower. Celeste ran alongside Dymock, who was still carrying Jean-Baptiste. Ettrick and Quinlan had Halsey between them, the other seven men strung out behind, with Schutte bringing up the rear. The line of French soldiers, now fifty yards behind him, stopped, muskets raised, preparing to fire.

'Tully's got him, and Hollick.'

The hint of the green, dust-smeared coat between the two men reassured Markham. His voice was nearly drowned out by the French salvo, mingled with the thunder of boots on the wooden platform. Dornan shrieked and spun round as a ball took him in the arm. Luckily his good arm hooked round the lifting chain, which prevented him from falling into the moat. Yelland and Hollick grabbed him and hustled him under the arch, where Markham was issuing a stream of shouted orders; to secure one of the watergate boats; two men should guard the circular staircase, four by the wheel to begin raising the drawbridge; anyone spare to load muskets. Fouquert, as soon as he was inside the arch, was dropped on to the flagstones, with Tully standing on him instead of stepping over.

The enemy commander, bleeding from a wound in his right shoulder, must have realised that he risked losing contact. He ordered his men to rush the archway. Schutte, at the last salvo, had thrown himself flat, and was now struggling to his feet. Encumbered by his musket and the capstan bar that had felled Halsey, he still had twenty yards to cover.

'Drop that damned wood,' Markham yelled, as the edge of the drawbridge creaked, and began to rise. The advancing French were now so close Markham could see the expression of determination on the officer's face, as he harried his men to get them to the drawbridge before these British soldiers could raise it. Given the distance they had to cover, and the speed at which they were doing it, they looked very likely to succeed.

Schutte stopped and looked both ways, so must have come to the same conclusion. He dropped his musket and began to run back towards the enemy, oblivious to the men under the arch who were screaming at him. The capstan bar came up, and spreading it flat, the Dutchman rushed at the enemy. Their bayonets were presented, but he made no attempt to avoid them. The wounded officer, in front, couldn't raise his sword, so was forced back by Schutte on to the blades of his own men. But the Hollander took them too, the grey, bloodstained steel shafts emerging from his back. But he kept going forward, the strength of the dying man, added to his bull-like roar, stopped the French advance in its tracks, bundling half their pursuers into the waters of the harbour.

'Pull,' yelled Markham to the men on the wheel. Nothing could be done for Schutte now. The only reward he could give the Dutchman was to ensure that his sacrifice was not in vain. The gears moved with agonising slowness, a fraction at a time, each inch registered by the smack of a pawl locking home. But the effect on the actual drawbridge was greater, and soon the angle increased. It was at waist level again before the remaining Frenchmen, stepping over Schutte's mangled body, recommenced their advance. By the time they made the edge it was above chest height. Two men, braver or more foolish than their fellows, jumped up and swung themselves onto the tilted platform.

Markham felt the warm wood of a bayonet handle pressed into his hand, and turned to look into the frightened dark eyes of Celeste. He pushed her behind him and turned to face the two soldiers, who were trying, without much success, to keep their footing. The point came where the weight of the structure began to aid, rather than thwart those trying to raise it. One attacker slipped, spinning over the edge. The other ran forward, using the slope to gain speed. Rannoch, Hollick and Yelland stepped past Markham, bayonets fixed. The Frenchman knew he was going to die two or three seconds before he impaled himself on their blades.

Markham called on them to follow and ran for the circular staircase, noticing that at least one boat was still wallowing in the watergate, with Halsey bent over beside it. The signal party were poorly equipped to withstand an assault, armed only with the most rudimentary weapons. As soon as their attackers appeared on the roof they began to surrender, one club dropping to the ground, swiftly followed by knives and the odd sword.

'Chuck them into the moat,' he shouted, turning to look at the ship in the outer roads. A frigate, it was probably already within range of the shore-based guns. He ran to the mast, the bayonet already swinging to cut the halyards. But he stopped just in time, reached forward, and untied the knots instead, stepping back as the flags fell about his ears.

The guns of Forts St Louis and L'Eguillette, loaded and ready, fired the second the ship put up her helm. The water around the hull boiled furiously as the heated iron balls dropped short. Then the ship was round, heading away from danger, the deck full of frantic sailors clearing for action.

'What do we do now?' asked Rannoch.

'Get Jean-Baptiste up here with his drawings. I have a signal I want to send.' A glance around the harbour showed any number of boats putting off, all heading for the Grosse Tour. And the quay was filling with soldiers. Worse than that, Markham knew they were well within the range of the guns of Fort l'Eguillette, manned by an artillery officer who would happily blow the ancient tower to pieces. 'And bring Fouquert up here as well.'

The Citizen Commissioner was in a terrible state, barely able to stand, his clothing ripped, his face scratched and swollen, with blood congealing at the base of his hooked nose. He watched, with unfocussed eyes, as Markham, using Jean-Baptiste's drawings, sent up a series of flag-borne messages. Hardly proper in the naval sense, they kept the frigate away from shore, while also ensuring it didn't disappear altogether. If Fouquert knew how many people were coming to rescue him, it didn't register until the first warning shot hit the water just inshore of the Grosse Tour.

'Is there a white flag in that locker?' Markham asked Yelland. When the fair haired youngster nodded, he ordered it raised. 'We need to buy ourselves some time.'

As soon as it was aloft, fluttering in the breeze, he walked over to Fouquert. 'We need you to get us out of here.'

Fouquert shook his head slowly. Markham, as scratched and filthy as the man he was addressing, smiled.

'We're not about to surrender, and that white flag won't silence Bonaparte's guns for ever. He's too eager to use them. So you have a choice. You can either die with us, or accept my word that if you get us clear, I'll spare your miserable life.'

Fouquert's head lifted at the word surrender, and he seemed to recover some expression in his eyes. By the time Markham had finished speaking they held that same look as when he'd interrogated him at Ollioules; cunning mixed with superiority, the air of a man who thinks he has gained the upper hand. It was that which made Markham walk away, and determined the question he put to the knot of men watching the forces gathering in the harbour.

'Where is Celeste?'

'She's downstairs, sir,' said Gibbons, 'with Sergeant Rannoch. They're tending to Halsey and Dornan.'

'Ask her to come up here, would you? Tully, Leech, tie that specimen to the mast. I want him facing Toulon.'

He started gabbling as soon as they came for him, a spate of words telling the men that if they were prepared to surrender their officer they had nothing to fear from him. Leech slapped him hard, adding yet another red weal to those that covered his face. Markham went to the top of the circular staircase and waited for Celeste. As she emerged from the gloom he was struck by her eyes as well. They'd lost the hunted look she'd had these last months, and now seemed more luminous. He led her to the mast, behind Fouquert.

'Will you guarantee a safe conduct?'

'Not for you,' he replied, then he raised his voice. 'Your men, yes. I have no quarrel with them, and neither does the Revolution. They are as oppressed as any Frenchman.'

'Then you leave me no choice but to force you.' The sound Fouquert responded with was very close to a laugh. Markham took Celeste's hand. 'You think I lack the will to force you.'

'You are a coward, Markham. Even I know that. Would you men give up your lives to save a coward's neck? If you stay here you will die. Come ashore with me, you will want for nothing.'

The note of triumph died as Markham led Celeste into view. Stark terror took over when he saw Markham hand her a bayonet. He had to look away from her face, not soft now, but cruel, the dark brown eyes full of hate.

'Do you remember this girl, what you did to her, and to her father? I have promised her one part of you, Fouquert. And I think even you might be able to guess which that is likely to be.'

The cannon boomed out on Fort l'Eguillette. This time the shot landed on the seaward side of the peninsula, away from the boats now crowding the landward approach. 'If you don't get us out of here, I'll give you over to her completely.'

He was nodding before Markham finished, too frightened to look Celeste in the eye lest by doing so he provoke her. Markham half turned to order Fouquert released, which slowed his reaction when Celeste jabbed forward with the blade. It sliced into Fouquert's groin, deflected downwards by one of his breech buttons, and slid through the cloth just below his scrotum. The girl drew the blade back for another stab, but Markham had hold of her wrists, forced to use all his strength to restrain her.

'Untie him, quick,' he yelled, as he saw the first hint of blood seep through the cloth between his legs. 'And get him up on the battlements.'

He had Celeste by both arms now, holding her out of the way as his men complied. 'I would like to kill him as much as you. But it is better to live.'

'For you, perhaps,' she said, as her shoulders slumped. All the strength had gone out of her arms, and she fell forward onto his chest, sobbing. Jean-Baptiste ran towards her and threw his arms round her hips.

'He needs you,' said Markham softly, as he spun her round so that she was embracing the boy.

Fouquert, sobbing and trying to look at his wound, was lifted up to where he could be seen. He started screaming as soon as he saw the men in the boats, ordering messages to be sent to the forts to cease firing; giving instructions for the boats to be withdrawn; commanding that the soldiers fall back; that these British soldiers had his personal safe conduct to go aboard the frigate in the roads. It was a telling comment of the fear in which he was held that those below complied without hesitation.

There was a mast in the boat, which they lashed him to, still bleeding, his pleas for assistance taking second place to the urgent need to get away before someone countermanded his orders. As they pulled out from the watergate a pair of French boats fetched their wake, close enough to see Fouquert, if not the blood that covered the front of his breeches. The white flag had gone from the mast on the Grosse Tour, to be replaced by another, defiantly flapping, naval signal.

Markham sat beside Fouquert, a pistol aimed at his head, in case he should suddenly change his mind. Looking back at the landscape where he and his men had spent the last four months, everything that had occurred ran through his mind. The battles, both triumphs and disasters. The pleasures, as well.

'Eveline Rossignol,' he said suddenly, pushing the pistol up towards Fouquert. 'Did you murder her, too'

'No,' he pleaded, 'she is still alive.'

'Pity,' said Markham, after a slight pause, his voice bitter. 'The bitch helped the old man betray me.'

It was hard to know if it had worked, but he prayed that what he had just said would make sure that if Fouquert was telling the truth, and she was alive, being known as someone he abominated would keep her that way.

*

They had the guns run out on the frigate, so when they were within range Markham called the two French boats to come alongside. Fouquert, cut down from the mast, had to be helped to transfer to the waiting cutter. But he raised his head when he was aboard, to fix Markham with a malevolent stare.

'It is my fond wish, Fouquert, that I never see you again. If I do, I shall most certainly kill you.'

The Frenchman didn't have the strength to reply, but the look on that Moorish face, particularly in the black eyes, was enough to tell Markham that if he didn't take the first opportunity, he certainly wouldn't be allowed a second.

As they came alongside, every man on the frigate fetched them a spontaneous cheer. The captain had put a proper ladder out, with red silk-covered side ropes, and ship's boys standing by to help them aboard. Markham went first and found himself, dirty of face and apparel, on a spotless deck, lined with officers in their very best uniforms. Pipes squealed and hats were raised, before the captain, a stocky individual, stepped forward.

'Who, in the name of God be damned, are you, sir?'

'George Markham, sir. Lieutenant, either of the Sixty-fifth Foot or the Marines, I know not which.'

'And you sent that signal?'

'I did.'

'That is a damned cheek, sir.'

'I accept the reprimand, captain, but having saved your ship from certain destruction, I claim the privilege.'

'And you shall damn well have it,' the captain replied, stepping forward with a broad smile, hand outstretched. 'Allow me to introduce myself, and thank you heartily. I am Captain Samuel Hood, and this is the frigate *Juno*.'

'Hood?'

'My father is Lord Bridport, but I am named after my uncle.'

'Admiral Lord Hood?'

'That's him.'

'The signal,' Markham stuttered. 'If it caused offence?'

'It caused mayhem, sir,' Hood replied with an even wider grin. 'How dare you send my ship's number, and follow it with the signal "Prepare to receive Flag"?'

'I don't run to army clothing, Markham,' said Hood, passing a bowl of nuts. 'But I'll stake you as many Lobster uniforms as you like. And I'm sure my marine officer will oblige you with a loan of some of his kit.'

'Would that I had the right to wear it, sir.'

'What's this nonsense?'

The explanation that followed was brief but accurate. 'And I have been informed many times, Captain, that it takes a degree of patronage to be granted a marine officer's commission. That, I fear, is something I lack.'

'You may have lacked it, Markham. But that is the past, this is the present. If my Uncle Sam won't grant you a commission, he'll have to deal with my father, who is not someone he cares to trifle with. Consider it as good as done.' He saw the slight look of doubt on Markham's face, which made him frown. 'That is, if you want the damned thing.'

'Could I be excused a moment, sir?'

Hood looked at him oddly. 'Of course.'

Below decks, it smelled as bad as he remembered. They'd put his men in a mess of their own, and every tar aboard had brought them food and drink. Halsey, bandaged, wasn't white-faced now; he was bright red with too much rum and warm air. Even Rannoch was affected. But over it all there was a sadness, a combination of weariness and a sense of comrades lost. They'd started out thirty-four strong, and now they numbered less than a dozen. He struggled to remember some of the names of the dead, but they wouldn't come.

The survivors all began to stand as he came close, and

he had to insist that they sat while he was present. Dornan, with his one good arm, passed him a tot of rum.

'God bless all here,' he said, raising his tankard, pleased, though he tried to hide it, by the murmured replies. Suddenly, the image of the huge blond Dutchman dying on those French bayonets filled his mind. Without that sacrifice, and the precious seconds it had bought, they might not be here. 'And raise your drinks once more, lads, to the bravest of us all.'

'Schutte,' said Rannoch, unbidden.

There was no murmuring now. Every man spoke that name loud and clear, and drained his cup to show he meant it.

'I have a question to ask,' said Markham, talking as the men refilled their cups.

'So what you are saying, sir,' Rannoch said, when he'd finished, 'is that we can all be fitted out as marines.'

'Including me, it seems.'

There was an exchange of looks, some pulling of faces, but many smiles, and all ended up as nods. He held out his tankard for his own refill, then raised it again, laying on the Irish with a trowel.

'Well, my brave boyos,' he toasted. 'It seems we're all bloody Lobsters now.'

# Historical note

While the characters in this book are fictional, the action described is real. Since the siege of Toulon lasted four months, certain events have been somewhat telescoped for the sake of the narrative. Also, students of naval history will note that, as a piece of dramatic licence, I have kept Captain Horatio Nelson and his ship, *Agamemnon*, engaged in the action, when they were in fact detached for service under Commodore Linzee, and sent to North Africa to threaten and cajole the Bay of Tunis. They rejoined Hood at Leghorn, prior to the assault on Corsica, which will provide the setting for the second in the *Lobsters* series.

All Orion/Phoenix titles are available at your local bookshop or from the following address:

Littlehampton Book Services
Cash Sales Department L
14 Eldon Way, Lineside Industrial Estate
Littlehampton
West Sussex BN17 7HE
*telephone* 01903 721596, *facsimile* 01903 730914

Payment can either be made by credit card (Visa and Mastercard accepted) or by sending a cheque or postal order made payable to *Littlehampton Book Services*.
DO NOT SEND CASH OR CURRENCY.

**Please add the following to cover postage and packing**

*UK and BFPO:*
£1.50 for the first book, and 50p for each additional book to a maximum of £3.50

*Overseas and Eire:*
£2.50 for the first book plus £1.00 for the second book and 50p for each additional book ordered

---

BLOCK CAPITALS PLEASE

*name of cardholder* ...............................

...............................

*address of cardholder* ...............................

*delivery address*
*(if different from cardholder)*

...............................

...............................

...............................

...............................

...............................

...............................

*postcode* ...............................

*postcode* ...............................

☐ I enclose my remittance for £...............................

☐ please debit my Mastercard/Visa (delete as appropriate)

card number ☐☐☐☐☐☐☐☐☐☐☐☐☐☐☐☐

expiry date ☐☐☐☐

signature ...............................

*prices and availability are subject to change without notice*